MIDNIGHT CAPTURE

Irony turned to study the man sleeping on the blanket, barely a foot away. She found herself dredging up every disreputable thing she'd ever heard about Indians, but to no avail. She thought Hawk was handsome and fascinating.

She tried to imagine what it would feel like to kiss him. Should she dare? She sidled closer to him and barely touched her lips to his when she heard a low growl.

In a flash, Hawk was grasping her shoulders and flipping her onto her back. In one fluid movement, he settled his strong, sinewy body astride her, his hands gripping her wrists.

"So — you chose not to heed my warning?"

Irony blinked twice. Then she screamed.

Hawk swiftly cut off the scream with his mouth, and used his body to subdue her thrashing.

Irony struggled, but deep inside felt compelling yearnings she'd never before experienced. Soon she stopped seeking escape from his hold and started longing for release of another kind . . .

HEARTFIRE ROMANCES

SWEET TEXAS NIGHTS   (2610, $3.75)
by Vivian Vaughan

Meg Britton grew up on the railroads, working proudly at her father's side. Nothing was going to stop them from setting the rails clear to Silver Creek, Texas—certainly not some crazy prospector. As Meg set out to confront the old coot, she planned her strategy with cool precision. But soon she was speechless with shock. For instead of a harmless geezer, she found a boldly handsome stranger whose determination matched her own.

CAPTIVE DESIRE   (2612, $3.75)
by Jane Archer

Victoria Malone fancied herself a great adventuress, but being kidnapped was too much excitement for even Victoria! Especially when her arrogant kidnapper thought she was part of Red Duke's outlaw gang. Trying to convince the overbearing, handsome stranger that she had been an innocent bystander when the stagecoach was robbed, proved futile. But when he thought he could maker her confess by crushing her to his warm, broad chest, by caressing her with his strong, capable hands, Victoria was willing to admit to anything. . . .

LAWLESS ECSTASY   (2613, $3.75)
by Susan Sackett

Abra Beaumont could spot a thief a mile away. After all, her father was once one of the best. But he'd been on the right side of the law for years now, and she wasn't about to let a man like Dash Thorne lead him astray with some wild plan for stealing the Tear of Allah, the world's most fabulous ruby. Dash was just the sort of man she most distrusted—sophisticated, handsome, and altogether too sure of his considerable charm. Abra shivered at the devilish gleam in his blue eyes and swore he would need more than smooth kisses and skilled caresses to rob her of her virtue . . . and much more than sweet promises to steal her heart!

Available wherever paperbacks are sold, or order direct from the Publisher. Send cover price plus 50¢ per copy for mailing and handling to Zebra Books, Dept. 3459, 475 Park Avenue South, New York, N.Y. 10016. Residents of New York, New Jersey and Pennsylvania must include sales tax. DO NOT SEND CASH.

SCOTNEY ST. JAMES
WARRIOR'S ECSTASY

ZEBRA BOOKS
KENSINGTON PUBLISHING CORP.

This book is dedicated to my good friend and agent, Beverly Wadsworth—in appreciation of all she does for me and with sincere thanks for her energy, encouragement and enthusiasm.

ZEBRA BOOKS

are published by

Kensington Publishing Corp.
475 Park Avenue South
New York, NY 10016

First printing: July, 1991

Printed in the United States of America

Calling One's Own

(Ojibway)

Awake! flower of the forest, sky-treading bird of the
  prairie.
Awake! awake! wonderful fawn-eyed One.
When you look upon me I am satisfied; as flowers that
  drink dew.
The breath of your mouth is the fragrance of flowers in
  the morning,
Your breath is their fragrance at evening in the moon-
  of-fading-leaf.
Do not the red streams of my veins run toward you
As forest-streams to the sun in the moon of bright
  nights?
When you are beside me my heart sings; a branch it is,
  dancing,
Dancing before the Wind Spirit in the moon of straw-
  berries.
When you frown upon me, beloved, my heart grows
  dark —
A shining river the shadows of clouds darken,
Then with your smile comes the sun and makes to look
  like gold
Furrows the cold wind drew in the water's face.
Myself! behold me! blood of my beating heart.
Earth smiles — the waters smile — even the sky-of-clouds
  smiles but I,
I lose the way of smiling when you are not near,
Awake! awake! my beloved.

— Translated by Charles Fenno Hoffman (1806-1884)

Chapter One

JUNE 1896

Methodist School for Indian Boys
Sweetwater Lake, Minnesota . . .

"Perhaps you could help me—I need a man."

As soon as the words were out of her mouth, Irony McBride realized she probably should have phrased her request in a more ladylike fashion, if the startled expression on the headmaster's face was any indication. And it might have been better had she not burst into his office, flinging the door wide in her haste.

She cleared her throat and tried again. "What I mean is, I have to get someplace in a hurry, and I need a guide."

The man sitting at the desk frowned. "Why would you come to me with such a problem?"

"One of the teachers told me you were in charge of the school," Irony explained, crossing the carpeted floor to stand directly in front of him. "He thought you might be able to suggest someone to aid me. It's very important."

"Since you've spoken to a member of my staff, you realize we are facing a serious situation of our own."

"Yes, I heard about the murder of Mrs. Sparks, and the unfortunate kidnapping of Reverend Josiah Goodman. But, you see, that is exactly why I need to speak with you."

The man leaned back in his chair and rubbed a plump hand over his tired eyes. "You have information about this heinous crime?"

"No, not really. It's just that—"

Impatiently, the man interrupted. "Who are you?"

"My name is Irony McBride."

"Miss McBride, if you have nothing to contribute to the solution of the matter, then I'm very much afraid I don't have time to squander. I regret being abrupt but I really must ask you to leave."

"You don't understand. I came all the way from Thief River Falls," she protested, indicating the worn carpetbag she still carried, "and I simply cannot abandon my mission now. As a matter of fact, the crime committed here this morning makes it imperative that I carry on."

"Why is that?"

"The man I'm searching for is the Reverend Goodman. He has . . . certain papers and documents that belong to my family. I intend to retrieve them."

"But, Miss McBride," the headmaster argued, "the fellow has been abducted—carried away by a gang of thieves and murderers."

"All the more reason to track him down," Irony declared. "I understand that Goodman was about to set off on a journey, and that his kidnappers apparently took his luggage, too. That must mean they have the papers with them." She leaned forward. "It would never do for those documents to fall into the hands of people even more unscrupulous than Reverend Goodman."

"Unscrupulous?" gasped the man behind the desk. "What are you saying? He's a man of God." The headmaster rose to his feet, his face flushed with indignation. "And he must have been utterly distraught at the death of his fiancée, the widow Sparks."

Irony's mouth dropped open. "Did you say . . . *his fiancée?*"

"I did."

"Then that settles it. I'm going to find that man if it takes the rest of my natural life."

"I can't pretend to understand . . ."

"It really isn't necessary that you do. Tell me, sir, do you know of anyone familiar with the country along the Canadian border? Someone who would be willing to act as my guide to the Lake of the Woods?"

At her words, she heard quiet movement behind her and turned to find a second man in the room. One who had stopped leafing through the book he held to observe her with steady intensity.

"Oh, Hawkes," the headmaster murmured, "I'd almost forgotten you were here." His eyes narrowed. "Say . . . you're from that part of the country, aren't you? And weren't you asking about a leave of absence to go home?" With an inspired smile, he slid his gaze to Irony. "Miss McBride, I'd like to introduce you to Raphael Hawkes, one of our instructors here. I believe Raphael has done some guiding."

"How do you do?" Hawkes asked politely, closing the book and placing it back on the shelf.

Irony inclined her head, her mind busy with its assessment of the man. He looked harmless enough, she decided—maybe too harmless. How could she be sure he'd make an adequate guide? It seemed he'd be more at home with math equations than with forest trails, and yet . . . he was an Indian, and they were all supposed to possess some special knack for scouting. She had good reason for the distaste she felt for Indians, and ordinarily she would never have considered entrusting her safety to one, but now it seemed her only choice.

Anyway, the man wasn't a pureblood. He was most likely a mixture of French-Canadian and Indian, and a striking example of the best of both heritages, she admitted. The short, stocky build of the French-Canadians had been transformed into a tall, lithe gracefulness that might have had an athletic quality had it not been for the black suit in which it was clothed.

His facial features were arresting—spare, angular, and hard-planed. His pleasantly bronzed skin was smooth, an indication of his good fortune in avoiding smallpox, which had once swept through the tribes of the north with devastating regularity. His hair was an unrelenting black, worn just long enough to pull back and tie with a narrow leather thong. Somehow that small detail disturbed Irony, because it hinted at an in-born savagery not entirely eradicated by education and training.

Hawkes removed the gold-rimmed spectacles he wore and with an air that suggested it was a habitual gesture, began to polish them with a handkerchief he took from his breast pocket. He silently returned Irony's gaze, and when she received her first glimpse of his eyes, a sensation of fear and fascination coiled along her backbone. His eyes were fierce; in no way had they been tamed, and the look he gave her seemed to strip away the layers of her own refinement, touching some wellspring of primitive emotion deep inside.

Irony blinked, and suddenly the man's gaze was as civilized as the rest of him. She felt embarrassed for having thought otherwise. Taking a closer look, she saw that his eyes were a soft black, gentle and even a bit dreamy, the eyes of a scholar. How could she have ever thought his limpid, heavily-lashed regard was threatening?

"Now, if you'll excuse me," the headmaster was saying as he walked toward the door, "I have a meeting with the authorities at the . . . er, scene of the crime. I'll leave the two of you to discuss your own arrangements." He flashed a hearty smile before closing the door behind him. "By the way, Raphael, I grant that leave of absence. Our summer schedule is light, so take all the

10

time you need—as long as you're back by September."

The young schoolteacher was carefully folding his eye-glasses and slipping them into his pocket, but Irony couldn't fail to see his frown. Obviously, he wasn't happy about the prospect of guiding her. Well, she wasn't exactly overjoyed at the thought of days in his company, either . . . but it seemed they might be stuck with each other.

"All right, Mr. Hawkes," she said in a businesslike voice. "I need a guide, and I'm prepared to pay you well. What is your usual fee?"

"I'm sorry, Miss McBride, but I'm not interested in employment. However, thank you for your kind offer."

"It wasn't meant to be kind," she stated. "It's a matter of great urgency."

"To you, perhaps. But to me? No." He shrugged. "Again, I'm sorry."

"I need your help, Mr. Hawkes. Believe me, if there were any other alternative, I'd be only too delighted to take it. But since there is not . . ."

"I cannot act as your guide," he said abruptly. "I have business of my own to attend to."

Irony heaved a loud sigh. "I regret the necessity of this, I assure you—but perhaps you'd care to reconsider?"

One dark eyebrow lifted in surprise, but that was the only move Raphael Hawkes made as Irony raised her right hand from the folds of her skirt and pointed an Army-issue Remington revolver straight at his chest.

Once they were inside Hawkes' bedroom, Irony set down her carpetbag and held the pistol with both hands. As the man efficiently packed a valise, she let her gaze drift around the small room. It was somewhat stark, with white walls, a narrow cot and one straight-backed chair. To her notion, it would have been monkish had it not been for the low bookcase and a jar of

11

wildflowers on the windowsill.

Hawkes had made no further effort to dissuade her, once she'd drawn the gun. She had halfway expected him to attempt to disarm her, and in some far corner of her mind, she was a little disappointed he hadn't. He might not have the dangerous appearance of an outdoorsman, but neither did he look like a coward. Still, since bravery on his part would undoubtedly have prompted her to shoot him, it was probably best he'd been prudent.

Hawkes surreptitiously watched the girl as he folded two extra shirts and tucked them into the open case. Did she really think she was intimidating him with that antique weapon? He knew the Remington .44 had been popular during the War between the States, and damned if the one she was holding didn't look every bit that old. It wouldn't matter much if she could hit a target or not, because the thing would probably explode in her hands if she tried to fire it.

Not that that was the reason he hadn't simply reached out and taken it away from her. No, from the instant she'd pointed the gun at him, something about the determination in her extraordinary eyes had intrigued him. Who was this woman? What on earth was she doing at Sweetwater alone, preparing to go off into the wilderness with a total stranger?

He snapped the valise shut and allowed himself a slow, deliberate survey of his captor. She was average in height, but appeared smaller because of a delicate bone structure. Her hair, thick and black, was pinned atop her head. He had the definite impression that those tresses had started the day severely anchored into place, but had escaped the combs and pins bit by bit. Now there were wisps at her temples, with longer curls covering her ears and the nape of her slender neck.

In contrast to the dark hair, her skin was pale — a soft peach, glowing and smooth, and most attractively freckled across a straight nose. The jaw was defined, hinting at a touch of willfulness, the chin raised just enough to suggest defiance of the world in general.

Beyond the shadow of a doubt, her most alluring features were her eyes and mouth. The eyes looked huge in her small face, framed as they were by curling black lashes and finely arched brows. They were a gloriously clear green—the same color as the emerald ring she wore—with flecks of russet that gave them unending depth. But it was her mouth that made Raphael Hawkes suddenly remember how long it had been since he had enjoyed the company of a pretty woman. A warm rose hue, her lips were soft and full, and slightly smudged-looking, as though she had recently been kissed, and kissed quite thoroughly.

As he studied her, those lips thinned in irritation, and Irony spoke. "I do hope you're not contemplating some act of stupidity, Mr. Hawkes. I can and will fire this gun."

"Who taught you to shoot?" he asked, unexpectedly.

"What?"

"Shoot," he repeated. "Who taught you to shoot?"

She blinked, twice. "My . . . uh . . . my father, of course. Why do you ask?"

"No reason," he said blandly, satisfied with the reaction his query had gotten. She was obviously lying, which must mean she had never shot the gun at all. It was valuable knowledge to be stored away for the time when he might choose to end the farce, and end it he would, but not, he promised himself, before he found out exactly what the daring Miss McBride was involved in.

"You don't believe I know how to use this weapon, do you?" she asked, the heavy gun wavering slightly in her grip.

Hawkes held up a placating hand. "Lady, you know which end to point, and that's enough for me."

He cast one last look about the room, then swiftly bent to select a book from the shelf. Irony stiffened, expecting him to hurl it in her direction. Instead, he un-snapped the valise and slipped the book inside.

"Poetry," he explained, seeing her perplexed expression. "I do love to read while on the trail." Her amazement was so complete that the barrel of her gun lowered a full six inches, without her even noticing. Hawkes nearly chuckled as he took a blue harebell from the jar on the sill and, gently snapping its stem, tucked it into the buttonhole in his lapel. "Shall we go, Miss McBride?" he asked. "We still have to barter for supplies and a couple of horses."

Irony watched as he left the room.

Great God Almighty, she thought, using an expression that would have caused her aunts to swoon, *what in the world have I gotten myself into? A wilderness guide who reads poetry and wears flowers? Damn!*

She hurried after the schoolteacher, with a rather belated warning. "I'm hiding this gun in my skirt now—but if you try to ask for help, I swear I'll pull it out and shoot you in the . . . the . . ."

He turned to face her. "Ass? Is that the word you're searching for?"

Irony's face grew pink. "I guess it's as good a word as any."

He nodded. "I'll keep the warning in mind."

Hawkes informed her that the best way to continue the journey north from the Methodist School was by horseback. While she stood by, he used her money to secure two horses and a pack mule from the local stables, and camping gear and food from the trading post.

Sweetwater Lake was in the northwestern corner of the state of Minnesota, on the edge of a prairie which gradually gave way to the forests of the Far North. In the beginning, the settlement was a huddle of trappers' shacks, and it hadn't been until after the founding of the Indian school that the town had grown to any size at all. Following the close of the War between the States, many churches began to address themselves to the Indian issue, and one of the resulting institutions was the Sweetwater mission. Small, poor, and isolated, the settlement rarely experienced such drama and excitement as it had known since the discovery of the morning's murder and kidnapping.

As the shopkeeper scooped dried beans into a sack, he couldn't resist commenting on the situation. "Reckon that poor reverend's soon gonna be food for the crows. Them fellers that took him was nuthin' but savages." He glanced up from beneath shaggy brows. "Pardon, Raphael—I know they was Ojibway."

"No offense taken." Hawkes stood at the counter, Irony close behind him, the gun she held nudging his hip uncomfortably. "Any man who would commit murder is a savage, no matter what his race."

"The murderers were Indian?" Irony asked. Strange, no one had told her that. When she'd stepped off the train, the first thing she'd heard had been news of the crime, but concern had been for the unfortunate victims, not the men responsible. "Then there must have been a witness to the murder?"

The old man tied up the sack of beans and tossed it onto the pile of supplies. "Nope, not exactly. One of the other teachers walked into the room jist after they'd killed poor Miz Sparks. She was layin' on the floor, her throat cut, and an Indian feller standin' over her, a bloody knife in his hand. The teacher screamed and fainted dead away—by the time help came, they wuz gone, takin' the reverend with 'em."

"How dreadful," Irony murmured, but her mind was reeling. Indians? That put a whole different slant on things. She had expected to be trailing an inept gang of dissolute freebooters, ignorant men who would make no effort to hide signs of their progress through the woods. Her plan had been to simply wait until the thieves drank themselves into a stupor, then steal back

15

what they had stolen from her. How foolish that now seemed. If they chose, the Indians could disappear into the forest like silent shadows, and tracking them would be nearly impossible. Especially with a guide like the one fate had sent her. . . .

"At least they got a good description of the killer," the storekeeper went on, slicing strips of meat from a side of pork. "He was young—'bout yer age, Raph—and had a tatoo on the back of his shoulder. Some kind of a circle with a bird flying across it. That'll mark him, fer sure."

Though Hawkes didn't say a word, Irony was aware that he had grown very still as he listened. Intuition told her that the words meant something to him, and she wondered if he'd recognized the description of the tatoo.

"What will happen to the killer if he's caught?" she asked.

"They'll hang him," Hawkes curtly replied, seizing the wooden crate of supplies and starting for the door.

Irony quickly hid the revolver behind the folds of her skirt. With her free hand, she tossed enough money on the counter to pay the bill, then hurried after her companion. She had been afraid he would abscond with the food and horses while she was detained, but she needn't have worried. With a distracted air, he was lashing the gear into place across the mule's broad back. When he swung up onto his horse, Irony hastened to do likewise.

"Several people saw the culprits leave town by the north road," he said grimly. "I would imagine they'll follow the river into more wooded country."

"We'd best get started if we hope to catch up with them." Irony's hand tightened around the smooth wooden handle of the gun to reassure herself. Hawkes' reluctance to guide her had inexplicably turned into a strange eagerness, and she intended to keep the weapon handy in case he planned on tricking her with an ambush of some sort.

No, she did not propose to let him lead her into the woods and abandon her. She might not have a great deal of practical knowledge about the wilderness, but she'd wager her new lace-trimmed petticoat she couldn't be outwitted by a poetry reading school-teacher.

"Have you seen any sign of them?" Irony asked, when they had been riding for more than an hour.

"No."

"No? But I thought you Indian guides were supposed to be so proficient," she muttered skeptically.

"Using logic, it should be a relatively simple matter to find them."

"Oh?" Skepticism became unadulterated doubt.

"It's my belief the men we're looking for are planning to disappear into the lake country just over the border. All we have to do is head in that general direction."

"That is not very reassuring, Mr. Hawkes. Do you mind telling me the basis for your theory? It seems a somewhat . . . casual method of operation for a sea-soned guide." She brushed back a wisp of hair and favored him with an irritated glare. "You are a seasoned guide, are you not?"

"The best Sweetwater has to offer," he replied solemnly.

Oh, well, she thought, *that explains it! Sweetwater Lake, Minnesota, probably hasn't spawned many Kit Carsons.*

"Actually, this map seems to uphold my assumption." He drew a crumpled piece of paper from his pocket.

"May I see it?" she asked.

It was difficult to read the fine writing as the horse jounced along, but eventually, Irony discovered she was looking at a map of the Lake of the Woods. There were six hand-drawn X's marking various locations around the lake. With an indrawn breath, Irony studied the map more closely.

"Where did you get this?"

"From Reverend Goodman's room," Hawkes answered.

Her eyes lifted to his. "What were you doing in Goodman's room?"

"That's not important. Tell me, what is there about the map that interests you so?"

"These X's. I think I know what they are . . ."

"What?" he asked quietly.

"If I'm not mistaken, they pinpoint certain properties—properties owned by my father. Goodman must have marked them on the map, which means he is well aware of their significance." Stiff from riding sidesaddle, Irony rubbed the small of her back. "You see, the deeds to those pieces of land were stolen from my family by Goodman, and now I fear they have fallen into the hands of his kidnappers."

"And that's why you were following the reverend in the first place?"

"One of the reasons."

"What do you think he intended to do with the deeds? They're not in his name."

"That wouldn't stop someone like Goodman. He'd simply represent himself as my father, sell the property and forge the name wherever necessary. Some of the land is very valuable, and he could stand to make quite a profit."

"He—or whoever now has the deeds."

"Exactly." Irony gave him a severe look. "So you see why I question your methods? Perhaps proprietary responsibility isn't something your people place in high regard, but . . ."

Hawkes reined in his horse, causing Irony to do the same. He narrowed his eyes slightly. "Miss McBride, are you aware of the way your charming lips curl every time you make reference to my heritage?"

"W-what?" Instinctively, Irony's hand crept to the revolver which was now holstered at her hip. "I don't know what you mean."

"Oh, I think you do," he said in a mild tone. "You've made it more than obvious that you have a distinct contempt for my people, as you call them."

"All right, let's be frank, Mr. Hawkes. I do have a less than agreeable opinion of Indians, but that shouldn't have any bearing on our association. I am paying you to do a job for which you are supposed to be qualified. As long as you meet my demands as an employer, your ancestry is of no importance."

"Very well." He gently slapped the reins against the horse's neck, and it began ambling on down the trail. "But that brings to mind yet another question — why are you here and not your father? *Civilized* young women rarely travel unchaperoned."

"My father is dead," she replied evenly. "Killed by Indians."

With that, she raised her chin and rode past him, momentarily forgetting that he was her hostage.

They made slow, but steady progress for the rest of the afternoon, stopping beside a noisy stream to cook supper. Irony had no intention of allowing her guide a gun to hunt game, but she had hoped he might provide a few fresh fish for the meal. Instead, he squatted by the fire — an incongruous sight in his black suit and string tie — to cook beans and fry slices of pork. Even that simple fare began to smell delectable, and Irony eagerly dug two tin plates and forks from the canvas pack.

"You'd better take that meat off the fire," she pointed out after a time, "or it's going to burn."

Hawkes had been lost in thought, regretting his casual question about her father. At her words, he quickly reached for the iron skillet, singeing his fingers on the handle and spilling their supper into the ashes.

"Oh, damn!" Irony cried, going down onto her knees. "You've ruined it!"

Hawkes seemed more interested in her unexpected profanity than in the destruction of their meal. Even in the twilight, she thought she could see his lips twitch.

"Pick it up," she ordered through clenched teeth.

"It'll taste like ashes," he warned.

Irony pulled the Remington from its holster and used it to gesture at the smoking meat. "I said, pick it up. I'm starving, and this looks like the only possibility of supper."

Shrugging, the man speared the meat with a fork. "Perhaps I could wash it off in the stream." He gave her a look that dared her to comment. "I've had to do that before."

Irony wasn't surprised. She watched as he swished the meat in the clear water and then dumped it onto the plates. When he handed one to Irony, she took it with her free hand, then pointed the gun toward the coffee-pot. "Pour me some of that, too."

Laying the revolver on her lap, Irony picked up the meat and shook off the excess water before taking a bite. Despite its washing, it had a definitely sooty flavor that she tried to drown with a cautious swig of hot coffee which, in turn, tasted as though it had been dipped from the bottom of the river. She choked.

"You're not much of a cook, are you?"

"I'm the best—"

"I know," she interrupted. "You're the best Sweet-water has to offer."

She caught sight of his face and again, sensed he found her annoyance quite entertaining. Turning back to her supper, she determinedly ate every bite. When Hawkes had also finished, he scrubbed the plates with sand and rinsed them in the stream.

The moon had not yet risen, so the evening was dark. Hawkes broke up a few dead branches and dropped them onto the fire, causing a sudden flare of light and heat.

"It's going to get cold tonight," Irony announced.

"I think I'll change into warmer clothes."

"And I'd like to get out of my suit."

"We'll dress here in this shrubbery," she decided. "You stand over there . . . and keep your back turned. Don't forget I'll have the gun handy."

Without a word, Hawkes took his valise and walked into the edge of the shadowy bushes. Satisfied that he was not going to cut and run, Irony laid the revolver on a small boulder beside her, and quickly unfastened her traveling skirt and petticoats, stepping out of them. The corduroy trousers she pulled on belonged to the neighbor boy back home in Thief River Falls, as did the shirt and jacket that followed the removal of her own shirtwaist. It had been as necessary to sneak the clothes past her aunts as it had been the gun.

With a quick glance, Irony saw that Hawkes had taken off his jacket and shirt. As she realized a gleam of white meant he was wearing nothing but a pair of underdrawers, the whiteness disappeared, and she was seeing Raphael Hawkes completely unclothed. Her cheeks grew hot as she thanked the Lord for the duskiness of the night. The man was pulling on a pair of trousers as she turned away.

When Irony emerged from the bushes, Hawkes was spreading the bedrolls on either side of the fire. He looked up, and this time his somber face actually broke into a slow smile.

"Don't you dare say a word," she warned. "Men's clothes are much more practical for riding than women's. Besides, they're warmer." She dropped onto her bed. "Anyway, I'll only wear this garb while we're in the woods."

Hawkes sat cross-legged on his own bed, reaching into his case for his spectacles and the book he'd brought along. But instead of opening the volume, he asked, "Tell me, Miss McBride, have you no brothers to see to this matter?"

"No, nor sisters."

"So it's just you and your mother?"

Irony shook her head. "Had it not been for my aunts, I would have been an orphan. My mother died when I was born, my father when I was twelve. I was raised by my Aunt Alyce and my Aunt Valentine in Thief River."

"And your aunts were the victims of the theft?"

"It goes far beyond a mere theft, Mr. Hawkes." Irony sighed, remembering the strange circumstances that had led her to this bravely flickering campfire. "My aunts were well-respected before Josiah Goodman came to town, but now their integrity is being questioned by everyone in the community.

"You see, Goodman is a traveling evangelist who came to Thief River a few months ago. My Aunt Alyce is a spinster and really quite immune to men, but Aunt Tiny . . . well, she's a widow and lonely. Unfortunately, she fell under the Reverend's charming spell, and they began to keep company. Before we knew what had happened, they were engaged." Irony settled back against the trunk of an aspen. "Two weeks later, the villain disappeared with every dollar Aunt Tiny owned, as well as her jewelry and the property deeds. To make matters even worse, she's the church treasurer, and Goodman took that money, too. The congregation is threatening a lawsuit because they're not completely convinced my aunt wasn't a party to his scheme."

"So you set out to vindicate her?" he asked quietly.

"I set out to get back what belongs to my family and the First Congregational Church of Thief River Falls. There wasn't anyone else to do it."

"No sheriff?"

"He was too busy and too shorthanded to take on the job, even though he'd telegraphed around the state and found that Goodman was wanted in several cities. Swindling women out of their lives' savings was the way he earned a living." Irony gave him a wry smile. "And it seems he has at least three wives scattered around the territory."

"Well, well," Hawkes commented. "Quite a background for a man of God—a civilized man, I'm sure you'd say."

She sniffed. "I do not miss the point you are making, but not all civilized men are so unscrupulous."

"Neither are all Indians savage."

"Mr. Hawkes . . ."

"Tell me," he interrupted, "are you, like your Aunt Alyce, immune to men?"

Irony felt herself blushing. "That is really none of your business—but, yes, I can say with assurance that I am indeed." Turning away, she slipped between the blankets of her bedroll. She shifted onto her side, careful to keep the gun close at hand. With what could only be called a chuckle, Hawkes rose and tossed more wood on the fire. He was dressed in a plaid wool shirt and a pair of Levis, and Irony couldn't help but recall that he wore nothing beneath the close-fitting pants. The thought caused her to squeeze her eyes shut in an agony of self-loathing, and she momentarily wished for a larger measure of her aunt's immunity. She had never succumbed to lecherous notions before, and she certainly wasn't going to do so now. Opening her eyes, she spied a pine cone on the ground near her bed and, picking it up, pretended to study it intently.

"Would you mind if I ask one more question?" Hawkes, having found his own tree to lean against, opened his book.

"What kind of question?"

"How do you come to have such an odd first name?"

"It's simple," she said, but something in the tone of her voice told Hawkes it wasn't as uncomplicated as she'd like him to believe. For one thing, her silence went on a moment too long as she toyed with the pine cone, and when she looked up at him, there were shadows in her eyes.

"My father had taken a job in the wilderness, but when my mother discovered she was to have a child, he insisted she return to Thief River until I was born. They were separated for six months, and at the appointed time, he came for her, only to find she had . . . died in childbirth."

"That must have been a shock for him," Hawkes murmured.

"Yes, it was. For my aunts, as well." She gave the pine cone a casual toss, following its ascent into the darkness with an unseeing gaze. "He took one look at me, so I'm told, and said, 'You should name the child Irony.' Then he left and didn't come back to visit until I was two years old. That, Mr. Hawkes, is why my aunts named me as they did."

"A painful story," he acknowledged. "I hope it did not upset you to tell it."

"Not at all," she said briskly. "I have grown used to telling it. As you can imagine, my name never fails to arouse curiosity in those I meet."

"It is, in my opinion, quite a nice name. There is a certain dignity about it." Or, he wondered, was the dignity simply an innate part of the small, determined woman relating the story? "And it's a refreshing change from all the Marys, Anns and Charitys in the world today."

"There have been many times, however," Irony said quietly, "when I wished my name was Mary or Ann . . . or that my father had seen fit to look at me and envision Hope or Faith . . . or Joy." She gave a slight, self-mocking laugh.

"Irony, you are what you are, no matter your name. And you can't blame your father for the grief that caused his negligence of you. . . ."

"It was grief that caused it then—later, there was always something else." As if suddenly realizing she was revealing too much, she turned the conversation away from herself, her tone becoming brusque again. "But what of your own name? Raphael seems a strange choice."

"It's not my real name, of course—that's Ojibway and difficult to pronounce, though it translates into Moonhawk. When I was sent to the Methodist school, the teachers chose an English name for me. Even as a lad I had served as a guide, so they gave me the name of the archangel from the Apocrypha who was sent to guide a young boy named Tobias. He was on a journey to recover debts owed to his blind father, you see."

"The Apocrypha? Aren't those the books that were removed from the Scriptures because they weren't written in Hebrew?"

"Indeed. Undoubtedly the teachers didn't want to waste a truly Biblical name on a heathen."

"Undoubtedly," she agreed, annoyed that he kept prodding the subject like a sore tooth and that, subtly, the rare moment of closeness between them had been destroyed.

"But, one word of caution, if you please," Hawkes went on. "I may be a guide like my namesake, but I warn you, I am most definitely *not* an angel."

Seeing his angular faced highlighted by the fire, Irony was absolutely convinced. There was a subtle wickedness about him, barely kept under control. As his dark eyes gazed into hers, she could almost imagine that she was falling victim to the excitingly evil spell of Lucifer himself.

And then Raphael Hawkes put on his spectacles and turned back to his book, and Irony chided herself for such a flight of fancy. How could she ever, even for one moment, have thought of that meek-mannered schoolteacher as . . . threatening?

Chapter Two

On the trail . . .

The campfire had burned low.

Irony rested fitfully, falling asleep only to be disturbed by sounds in the night. It was painful to drag herself from the depths of slumber back to a hazy awareness, and yet she did not dare become too vulnerable.

Opening a sleepy eye, she could see Raphael Hawkes just a few yards away, sitting against a tree, reading his book of poetry. He looked perfectly harmless, as usual, but she couldn't trust him. Somewhere behind that stoic exterior, there had to be at least a small measure of anger at her for forcing him to accompany her at gunpoint. No man would relish being told what to do by a female — and surely not a man with even a drop of Indian blood. He might be biding his time, waiting until she fell asleep. Then he could snatch the weapon from her, or simply disappear into the night, leaving her alone to face the wilderness.

No. . . .

Drowsily, she reached for the gun, feeling the cold metal under her fingers. Gripping it firmly, she struggled into a sitting position, propping herself against the trunk of the aspen. She saw Hawkes glance up, and she tucked the blankets around her defiantly, keeping the revolver within the line of his vision. She did not want him to have the slightest doubt as to who was in charge of their situation.

As the dying firelight flickered over the angles of his face, Irony thought she saw his mouth curve upward in amusement, but knew it was probably her imagination. No male would find anything funny in being bested by a woman — although there had been moments when she'd definitely felt he was only humoring her. She shook her head fiercely, trying to dispel the cobwebs exhaustion was spinning within her mind. Her fingers tightened on the butt of the Remington, renewing her assurance that she was maintaining control.

Her head nodded . . .

The fire flared with a last display of energy, and Hawkes gazed through a shower of sparks at the woman across from him. She was obviously asleep, her head lolled to one side, the hand holding the gun draped loosely over her bent knees.

He laid his book aside and, removing his spectacles, put them in a case and dropped them back into his valise. Stealthily, he got to his feet and edged his way around the fire toward her.

The low, haunting cry of an owl came from somewhere in the darkness behind him, and Hawkes froze as Irony stirred, jerking the pistol upward wildly. He only relaxed when her eyes remained closed, and her breathing continued in the measured rhythm of slumber. Slowly, the barrel of the gun lowered.

After a few seconds, he smiled and softly quoted the poet Longfellow.

> "Stars of the summer night!
> Far in yon azure deeps,
> Hide, hide your golden light,
> She sleeps!
> My lady sleeps!"

Gently, he removed the gun from her fingers and laid it on the ground beside her. He had no real desire to be shot, accidentally or otherwise, and he knew instinctively that Irony McBride would never hesitate to shoot him if he gave her cause.

He studied her face, young and soft in repose, and wondered again at her courage. She was so fragile to be on her own, so naive in assuming she could tame the wilderness. But he had to admit she possessed a great undaunted spirit. He had never known a woman like her . . . except, perhaps, his mother.

Hawkes straightened the woolen blanket around Irony's shoulders and turned away to rebuild the fire. It had been a long time since he had thought of his mother—really thought of her.

Of course, the memory of who she was stayed with him all the time, but the moments when he allowed himself to truly recall the way her life had been were rare. Thoughts like that brought back too much unhappiness, too much angry pain. But now, in this place and with this woman, it was impossible to keep those memories at bay.

Hawkes sank onto his blankets again and stared into the darkness beyond the newly-bright flames. Her name had been Heron Woman, and for ceremonial occasions, she had worn the feathers of the blue heron in her straight, black hair. She had been beautiful, with a gentle, spiritual quality that set her apart from the other Ojibway women with their ribald talk and boisterous humor. How often, even as a child, he had thought she should live among the creatures of the forest instead of being such an insignificant part of tribal life. Insignificant because she had no father or husband to protect her—unimportant and socially outcast because she had once been a white man's whore.

Hawkes had never known his father's name or anything about him, other than the fact that he was a trapper who had taken Heron Woman as his mistress, then callously left her and their infant son behind when he chose to return to civilization. Hawkes had never wanted to know more about him, for it would only have inflamed his hatred, and perhaps goaded him into a vengeful search for the man.

Indian women who were taken by the traders and trappers to be country wives, the old term for concubine, were looked upon with envy by the other women in the tribe. At least for a short time, those select few might live in an actual wooden house, eat the strange foods of the white man, wear clothes that were nothing like their usual buckskin or shapeless calico dresses. If a country wife was very fortunate, her man might legalize their union and accept full responsibility for the children she bore him. Some few of them had even left the forest to live in a town or city somewhere; a few more were lucky enough to have their husbands choose to settle in the lake country.

Heron Woman had not been fortunate in any of those respects. Her man had walked away without a backward glance, leaving her with no money or worldly possessions. Had she not had the responsibility of a baby, Hawkes knew she would simply have faded into the forest, to either live with the animals or die alone, whichever fate had decreed. Instead, she stifled her pride and returned to her people, reduced to begging for a lodge to live in and food to eat.

Those who had once been jealous of Heron's good fortune took great delight in her humiliation, reminding her at every turn that she was a woman scorned and unwanted — a woman who, only through their mercy, was allowed to live among them. Naturally, their ridicule extended to her child, though the ostracism had never bothered Raphael for himself. Looking back now, he realized it was the reason he and his mother had been so close, so united in spirit and purpose. They had lived at the edge of the village, and Heron had earned her keep by helping the sick and elderly, doing cooking or laundry, or caring for children. Two other women in the same situation had become tribal whores, but Heron refused to even consider such an alternative. She had entrusted herself to one man — she would never have dealings with any other.

Hawkes often recalled the times his mother had taken him into the woods to try to teach him to hunt and track. He had never learned much from those outings, but they had been the best times of his childhood. No Indian woman was trained in the use of spear or bow and arrow, but for the sake of her fatherless son, Heron had tried. That unflagging perseverance was what had driven her, and what he suspected drove Irony as well. In that way the haunted woman who had been his mother and the black-haired thunder-spirit disguised as a proper young lady from Thief River Falls were very much alike.

He grinned in the darkness. Very much, indeed.

When Irony awoke the next morning, her first emotion was panic. Where was the gun? Had Hawkes taken it and fled? Furious with herself, she sat upright, relieved to see the man still sleeping on the other side of the campfire, and the revolver laying on the grass near her. She seized it, thankful Hawkes need never know how unguarded he had been.

She took a closer look at him, drawn by the innocence of his face, relaxed in sleep. There was a harsh beauty about his features, which looked as though they might have been carved from sandstone. But as austere and uncompromising as they were, the sweep of long, black lashes over his high cheekbones and the unexpected tenderness of his mouth added an undeniable note of purity and sensitivity. Strangely, Irony felt a distinct twinge of sympathy for the man. It must be difficult to be born a poet instead of a warrior.

Though he remained still, Irony suddenly knew Hawkes was no longer asleep. Behind the closed eyelids, she sensed that he was alert and waiting . . . for what? Did he think she would shoot him as he slept? Smothering the sardonic laugh that thought prompted, she quickly moved to throw more wood on the fire. She did not want him to know she had been staring at him, as if transfixed by his heathen attractiveness.

And he is a heathen, she reminded herself sternly, *despite the thin veneer of sophistication and schooling.*

Irony was searching through the supplies for something for breakfast when Hawkes tossed aside his blankets and arose.

"Good morning, Miss McBride," he said casually, stretching and yawning.

"Good morning." Irony kept her gaze averted from the surprising display of musculature beneath his plaid shirt, but when he didn't say anything further, she forced herself to look up. Hawkes was striding off into the underbrush with rapid deliberation. "Wh-where are you going?" Irony exclaimed, half-afraid he was about to call her bluff as far as the gun was concerned.

Her guide stopped short, then whirled to face her, a devilish look shining in his eyes. "Don't be alarmed, Miss McBride. I'm merely setting off to . . . well, I'm not certain what terminology you ladies use, but I need to . . ."

Irony's face flamed. "Never mind—I understand." She tossed her head, succeeding only in adding to her embarrassment as the untidy knot of hair worked free of the last pins and fell about her shoulders in a tangled mess. "Just don't wander too far or stay too long. I still have my—"

"Gun," he finished for her. "Yes, I know."

When Hawkes emerged from the woods, he paused at the edge of the stream to splash cold water over his face. Irony, watching with interest, was intrigued by the way the droplets sparkled as they caught in his eye-

31

lashes and beaded upon his faintly coppered skin. As he adjusted the leather thong at the nape of his neck, she envied the thick smoothness of his hair, knowing her own must look like a pack rat's winter home. She raised a hand and felt the wild, unbridled curls and, with a sigh of disgust, reached for the hairbrush in the bottom of her carpetbag.

"Am I mistaken or were you about to cook breakfast?" Hawkes asked, eyeing the muslin-wrapped pork Irony had taken out of the pack.

"You're the cook," she retorted. "I was simply trying to help by putting out the food."

With a grimace, he reached for the frying pan. "Tell me, why don't you like to cook? Most women seem to."

"For one thing," Irony said around the hairpins in her mouth, "I am not most women. And for another, it's not that I don't like to cook. I never learned how." She began braiding her hair with swift, severe motion.

The man stared at her in amazement. "A woman who doesn't know how to cook?"

Irony dropped the pins into her lap. "You forget, I was brought up in a household of ladies, and even though my aunts are both excellent cooks, they hire the kitchen work done. So I've just never learned how."

"What about when you marry? Won't your husband expect you to fix his meals?"

"I assure you, Mr. Hawkes, culinary skills will have nothing to do with the reason a man marries me."

His black eyes were intent. "No . . . I imagine not."

Blushing, she coiled the braid at the nape of her neck, jabbing it with hairpins to anchor it into place. "What I meant to say . . . hey, would you mind watching that side meat a little more carefully? I don't want to eat another burned meal."

It was obvious she didn't care to discuss marriage at any length, and Hawkes wondered why as he filled the coffeepot with water from the stream and set it on the fire. He was amused as he remembered her statement that both she and her Aunt Alyce were immune to men. But he'd seen the way she'd watched him with curious absorption and knew she wasn't as unaffected as she might like to believe.

Of course, she would never openly confess to any interest in him because of his heritage, and that was a damned shame. She was the first woman who had caught his attention in longer than he cared to admit. It seemed a cruel twist of fate that she would have such an aversion to Indians.

Not, he thought as he turned the strips of meat, *that I can blame her. The destiny of a father seems to have a great deal of influence on the child.*

He knew that bitter fact well from his own experiences.

As they plodded on through the marshy, thinly-forested country, Irony strained her eyes for any sign of the men they were following. Once or twice they saw the blackened remains of campfires, but Irony had no way of telling how old they were. When she asked Hawkes, he only shrugged, leaving her feeling more hopelessly frustrated than ever.

By mid-afternoon, she was convinced they would never catch up with the kidnappers and Reverend Goodman. They had seen nothing to even give her any hope they were going in the right direction. She was stiff and tired, and thoroughly ill-tempered, and to make matters worse, the sky had gradually darkened to the purplish-black color of the eggplants growing in Aunt Valentine's garden back in Thief River, and an ominous wind had sprung up.

"It's going to rain," Hawkes called back over his shoulder, causing Irony to roll her eyes heavenward in disgust.

"So—you do know *something* about nature," she remarked with sarcasm. "Even I can see that it's about to rain. The question is, what are we going to do about it?"

"Take the only shelter we can," he said evenly, apparently unmoved by her childish spate of temper.

"And what, pray tell, is that?"

"That square of tarpaulin we bought at the trading post." Hawkes' teeth gleamed whitely in the gathering gloom. "I trust you're speaking in jest."

"I'm afraid not. Unless you like cold drizzle down the back of your neck, we'd better make camp right away. I can already smell the rain."

Hawkes chose to put the tarpaulin beneath a huge pine tree, using a rope to secure two corners to the bottom branches.

"Is it safe to be under a tree in a storm?" Irony questioned.

"As long as there's no lightning. Besides, it provides some shelter for the animals."

He piled their gear under the canvas, leaving a small space at the front for them and their bedrolls. He had barely finished when the rain started falling, like a gray curtain thrown over the forest. The makeshift shelter faced away from the wind and all in all, Irony decided as she ducked inside, it was a fairly snug arrangement.

Just how snug she hadn't realized until she was seated on the blankets with Hawkes squeezed in beside her. Their shoulders bumped together every time either of them moved, and unless she sat ramrod straight, Irony's thigh brushed against his. But however constrained the situation was, Irony was positive its merits outweighed its drawbacks. The rain was cold and silent, the kind that soaked through one's clothes, seeping right into the marrow of the bones. Irony shivered.

"Are you cold?" Hawkes asked. His polite, inquiring gaze was so unnervingly close to her that Irony shook her head, then burst into stilted conversation.

"Tell me about yourself, Mr. Hawkes. How did you happen to become a schoolteacher?"

34

He shrugged. "It has become fashionable to educate the natives, you know."

Instantly on the defensive, Irony bristled. "No, I didn't know. As a matter of fact, I was under the impression the . . . natives were all extremely *uneducated.*"

"Touché," Hawkes murmured.

"Oh, good heavens," Irony exclaimed, "I'm sorry. I shouldn't have said that. I just thought we might talk — to help pass the time. I didn't mean to be so nasty. I'm not, usually . . ."

"I goaded you," he admitted. "Shall we start over?"

Irony sensed his amusement, but realized he seldom smiled. What passed for a smile was ordinarily little more than a twitch of his firm lips. She felt her eyes drift unerringly to those very lips, and with an effort, dragged her gaze away and said, "Yes, that would be best. Uh, how did you become a schoolteacher?"

"I enjoyed my years at Sweetwater and thought perhaps I could help other young boys better their lives."

"What do you mean?"

"I mean that the old ways are gone forever. There is no room in today's world for tribal customs or traditions. Everything the Indian once knew must be replaced by new knowledge. We must learn to adapt to the changing times."

"Then you believe the Indian must live as . . . as . . ."

"As the white man does," Hawkes said. "Or die."

"But what about the areas the government set aside as Indian land?"

"The reservations?" He said the word with a sneer that caused his finely chiseled mouth to twist sarcastically. "Their purpose is not to preserve the ways of the red man. They're only conveniences for the whites, a means of keeping the Indian out of the way. As long as civilization has access to the Indians, it will impose its sicknesses and sins — and the boundaries of the reservations will grow smaller and smaller."

"So what solution do you suggest?"

Hawkes' expression was bleak. "There is no solution. The only thing the Indian can hope for is to be allowed to live among the whites, as a white. To do that, many things will have to change . . . and I don't think they will. Unfortunately, I believe the tribes are doomed to extinction—but then, it would just be one more noble race to fall from glory. A not uncommon happening in the history of the world."

"A rather gloomy outlook, don't you think?"

"An educated man is often forced to maintain a gloomy outlook. Human nature forces mankind to keep making the same mistakes over and over."

"You may think this is an impertinent observation . . ."

"Impertinent?" Hawkes said in a droll tone. "You? Surely not, Miss McBride."

Her eyes sparked, but she continued calmly. "I am assuming that you are not a full-blooded Ojibway. Therefore, you already have one foot in the white man's world . . ."

"I don't have a foot in either world."

Irony was somewhat startled by his flat statement. "And yet, you champion the Indian. Why is that?"

"A man must associate himself with something." He turned to look at her. "If a star does not attach itself to the galaxy, it will wander in empty space for eternity."

Irony nodded. "I see. And you feel closer to your Indian roots?"

"Yes—my mother's people."

"And your father?"

"I never knew him. He deserted my mother when I was just a few months old."

"How terrible for you. But I . . . I didn't really mean to pry, Mr. Hawkes."

"I know. Anyway, it would only have been terrible had I gotten to know the man before he left. As it is, he means nothing to me."

"Is your mother still living?"

"No, she died when I was seventeen."

"Again, I'm sorry. When a parent is the only one you've ever known, and then you lose her . . . well, it must be very difficult."

"My mother was an extraordinary woman," Hawkes commented suddenly, as though the words were drawn from him against his will. He could not remember the last time he had discussed her with anyone. "She's the one who taught me to hunt and track."

Unexpectedly, Irony's throat closed, congested by sympathy for the man. No wonder he was such an inept guide—no wonder he didn't have even a rudimentary understanding of woodland skills. Poor child, growing up without a father's influence. How could he have turned out other than the way he had?

She placed a hand on his forearm, feeling the muscles turn to granite beneath her touch. "I don't think you have had an easy life, Mr. Hawkes."

Her eyes were soft and melting, filled with a potent mixture of pity and admiration. Hawkes had never seen eyes so green. They reminded him of pine forests, of secret, verdant glades. . . .

The lack of a reply on his part made Irony uneasy. She tried to let her gaze fall, but somehow it snagged on his full, sensuous mouth and she could not seem to summon the strength to tear it away. She caressed the curve of his bottom lip with her eyes, and felt its smooth warmth as surely as if she'd used her fingertips.

Outside the rain fell with a faint, silvery whisper of sound, and the smells of wet grass and canvas rose in her nostrils. The air within the shelter had become close, almost humid.

"Don't look at me that way," Hawkes suddenly said, his voice ragged.

Irony blinked, twice. "What way?"

"As though you were wondering how it would feel to kiss me."

Her cheeks burned hotly. "You have a great deal of nerve," she stormed, her anger inspired only a little by guilt. "The last thing on earth I would ever consider is how it would feel to kiss a man like you!"

"Then you are wise." His face remained completely solemn. "As I once warned you, I may be a gentleman, but there is nothing of the angel about me. If a woman chose to make herself available to me, I could not promise to be scrupulous enough to refuse her."

Irony's enraged gasp filled the small space. "You— you just go to hell!"

He laughed then, a low rumble of pleasant sound. "Yes, I expect I will. In the meantime, shall we find a new topic of conversation?"

"I have no desire to converse with you, Mr. Hawkes. In fact, I think I shall cease talking and take a nap."

"Very well—you do seem tense. I'll read some poetry to help you relax, shall I?"

Irony sniffed. "Don't think I'll fall so deeply asleep that you can slip away."

"In this rain? I wouldn't dream of it."

As he reached into his valise for his book and glasses, Irony was forced to believe him. She couldn't imagine Raphael Hawkes discommoding himself in any way. Still, as she inched away from him and curled up on her blankets, one hand fell to the handle of the gun she wore at her side. Her head butted his leg and she sighed in exasperation.

"Sorry—it's just so crowded in here."

Hawkes shifted as far to one side as he could. "There, does that give you any more room?"

"I'm fine," she stiffly replied. Besides, if she bumped him every time she moved, it would prove his continued presence, and the last thing she needed at this point was to have her guide take advantage of her inattention and steal away.

She closed her eyes and after a moment or two, heard

the rustle of book pages followed by Hawkes' somber, mellow voice.

"Should you ask me, whence these stories?
Whence these legends and traditions,
With the odors of the forest,
With the dew and damp of meadows,
With the curling smoke of wigwams,
With the rushing of great rivers,
With their frequent repetitions,
And their wild reverberations,
As of thunder in the mountains?
    I should answer, I should tell you,
From the forests and the prairies,
From the great lakes of the Northland,
From the land of the Ojibways,
From the land of the Dacotahs,
From the mountains, moors, and fen-lands,
Where the heron, the Shuh-shuh-gah,
Feeds among the reeds and rushes.
I repeat them as I heard them
From the lips of Nawadaha,
The musician, the sweet-singer.' "

Irony felt like a child, wrapped in the warmth of Hawkes' voice and rocked by the gentle, droning cadence of the poem. Slowly, easily, she slipped into a peaceful sleep.

Looking down at her, Hawkes felt something akin to indulgent protectiveness, a new emotion for him. Laying the book aside, he reached for Irony, settling her more comfortably against him. Then he took up the book and continued reading Longfellow's epic of Hiawatha.

Irony had no idea how much time had passed since she'd fallen asleep, but she was horrified to awaken and find her face pressed against the hard curve of Raphael Hawkes' thigh. She sat bolt upright, ignoring the fact that his mouth quirked with its usual acknowledgment of his amusement.

He took in her irritation and confusion, thinking she looked utterly delightful with her hair curling about her face in deliberate defiance of the braid she had imposed upon it. He coughed lightly. "It has stopped raining," he said.

"Has it?" she asked crisply. "Then I suggest we travel on a little further before making camp for the night." She got to her feet, stiff from the cramped position in which she had been lying. "At the rate we're going, we'll never catch up with Reverend Goodman."

Hawkes watched her stalk out of the would-be tent and sighed with relief. The last hour had taken its toll. Even the usually soothing poetry had failed to reduce his unexpected and unwanted reaction to the feel of her soft lips resting so close to his . . . leg.

God, it would feel good to get back onto that horse and ride until he was too tired to speculate any further on the emotions created by a rainy afternoon . . . and the disturbing nearness of Miss Irony McBride.

Chapter Three

In the woods . . .

The next morning they left the boggy, tree-lined edges of the prairie behind as they entered the deep woods. After just a few hours of slow progress through feathery spruce and pine groves, Irony knew there was something wrong. Hawkes seemed tense and uneasy, and he kept casting quick, sharp glances over his shoulder or into the dark shadows along either side of the narrow path they followed. With a sinking heart, she began to suspect they were lost. Not long after they'd made a brief stop for lunch, her fears were confirmed.

The morning had started out cold and foggy, so she'd put on her jacket until the sun burned away the chill. While taking the coat off after lunch, she caught the sleeve on a tree limb and tore it. Over an hour later, plodding along on her horse, that same scrap of dark blue had taken her eye. They were traveling in circles!

Before she could make any of the biting comments that came to mind, Hawkes reined in his horse and said, "You look tired. I think we should stop and rest."

"What?"

"You tossed and turned so much last night that I know you couldn't have slept well," he said patiently. "And falling asleep on your horse isn't advisable."

Irony was chagrined to realize he was aware of how restless she had been the night before and wondered if that meant he, too, had not slept well. She'd blamed

41

her own sleepless state on the nap she had taken, but the truth of the matter was that she couldn't seem to get the thought of waking with her head on Hawkes' thigh out of her mind. She had never had such intimate contact with a man before, and she hadn't been prepared for the strange, fluttery feelings it had fostered within her virginal soul. Inwardly, she snorted with self disgust and wondered again just what had kept Hawkes awake.

"If we don't push on, we're going to lose the men we're following," she protested, albeit weakly.

"There are only so many places to go along the border," he assured her. "When we get there, we'll find them easily enough."

"Yes—unless they didn't even travel this direction." At his cool look, Irony immediately regretted her sarcastic tone. After all, he was doing his best to guide her.

"They came this way," he said.

"How do you know?"

"Intuition."

Oh, thought Irony, *I should have guessed.*

"Look," Hawkes went on, "you toss a blanket down on those pine needles over there and have a rest while I do some scouting around."

"But . . ." Suddenly Irony's natural compassion took hold and silenced her tongue. Hawkes knew they were lost and was obviously trying to save face. Well, for once she would play his game, ignore his inadequacies and permit him a bit of time to try and rectify the mistake he had made. With any luck at all, he might wander around a bit and get his bearings. And, Lord knew, she could stand a short nap.

"Very well."

"You're not going to question my motives?" he asked. "Aren't you worried that I'll sneak away?"

Strangely enough, for once she wasn't. They needed to get to the same place, and something told her he was just as glad for company as she was.

"There comes a time, Mr. Hawkes, when we must

trust each other. If you choose to disappear, then you are not the gentleman you have portrayed yourself to be."

"You trust me?" he repeated, as though astonished.

"I've decided to, yes."

"So we're to be friends?"

She hesitated. Friendship was not something she had considered, but . . .

"Friends, it is."

"Then for heaven's sake, please stop calling me Mr. Hawkes. My friends call me Hawk."

"Then so shall I."

"And I'll call you Irony—if I may."

The sound of her name on his lips was another of those things that had an odd effect on her, but she strove to ignore it. "You may. Now, I think I'll get on with my nap. We can't afford to waste too much time."

He tied the horses and pack mule behind a screen of trees, then saw Irony settled on her unrolled bedding before starting off on foot. She watched him go, making up her mind that if he had not returned within the hour, she would fire the gun to apprise him of her whereabouts. Even their new status as friends didn't preclude her notion that he would probably only become more lost than before.

Irony dreamed she was back in Thief River, taking afternoon tea with her aunts in the front parlor. Vividly she saw Aunt Valentine, wearing a lavender gown with a crocheted lace collar, sitting on the velvet loveseat. She was pouring tea into delicate china cups hand-painted with violets, and with her upswept white hair, childlike blue eyes and pink cheeks, she looked like a charming picture rendered in soft watercolors.

Just entering the room was Aunt Alyce, a tall, willowy woman with handsome features and neatly styled ash blonde hair. Wearing a white sailor blouse and dark

43

blue skirt, she gracefully crossed the room to place a plate of sliced pound cake on the tea table.

Irony herself was seated in a wing-backed chair, the toes of her best black slippers barely peeping out from beneath the full skirts of her favorite satin damask day dress. Her arms still ached from the brushing she had given her hair, but at least she was satisfied its usual wildness had been properly disciplined for the occasion. It felt full and heavy coiled into a crown atop her head, and she knew the style was most advantageous for showing off the emerald earbobs Aunt Tiny had given her that morning for her birthday. Suspended from the chain around her neck was the pendant watch that had been Alyce's gift.

Irony realized she was frowning and wondered why. The answer stunned her with its simplicity. There she was, twenty years old, still feeling like a little girl because she sensed Aunt Tiny's eyes upon her and knew she had been caught using her napkin to try and hide the fact she had clumsily sloshed tea in her lap — again.

Damn, would she never learn to behave like a lady?

Kindly, Tiny murmured, "Did you see what a certain young man brought you, my dear?" A third gift, a small box with lovely green ribbons lay on the tea table, awaiting her attention. It was from the man in the fawn-colored suit, sitting across from her. Irony tilted her head and gave him her most captivating smile.

"Why, Nathan, how thoughtful of you . . ."

Suddenly, the dream began to fade and, even as she drifted into wakefulness, Irony was stricken by the sense of loss she felt. She missed her aunts, missed the times they spent together in the tidy, somewhat stuffy parlor back home. She knew they must be worried about her and wondered how long it would be before she could send a message to assure them of her well-being.

She sighed softly, opening her eyes to gaze upward through the tree branches to the sapphire sky beyond.

44

Naturally, she and Hawkes . . . Hawk . . . would have to discover exactly where they were first! And determine just how far the nearest settlement of any size was.

Thinking of Hawk, she turned her head and saw him lying on his own blanket, barely a foot away. She hadn't expected him to have returned, and she certainly hadn't imagined that he'd be indulging in a peaceful sleep practically right beside her. She rolled over on her side and, propping her head on one bent elbow, studied him. He was an enigma, in the mildest sense of the word.

Irony found herself dredging up every disgusting and disreputable thing she'd ever been told about Indians, but to no avail. She thought Raphael Hawkes was beautifully handsome, and for some irritating reason, she was becoming fascinated by him.

It's only because he's so different from . . . from the men back home, she thought. *He's an oddity, that's all.*

But despite her efforts to explain away his appeal, her traitorous eyes traced every line of his face and body, returning again and again to the tempting curve of his mouth. Hating herself for thinking such a thing, she tried to imagine what it would feel like to kiss him. His lips looked hard, unyielding . . . and yet, she had seen them soften from time to time in one of his almost-smiles. Would they be cool or warm? Warm, she guessed . . . maybe even as heated as the look that sometimes flared in his usually guarded eyes.

Irony drew a deep breath, and felt her palms grow clammy. Would she dare? Hawk was deeply asleep, his chest rising and falling in a smooth, unbroken rhythm. Surely he would never know if she was cautious.

No, she silently reprimanded herself. *Why, the aunts would disown you if they knew you'd even considered such a thing. No well-bred lady would ever entertain a scandalous notion of that nature — let alone act upon it.*

But then, no well-bred lady would ordinarily set out

to chase down a villain like Goodman, traveling either alone or in the company of a half-wild stranger. And the aunts had given that particular venture their reluctant blessing.

Only because there was no one else to go, Irony admitted. *And only because they didn't know I would be alone . . .*

On the other hand, how many times had she heard Aunt Alyce expounding on the merits of practical experience? "Waste no time in learning all you can about any subject that interests you," she had said at least two hundred times in the last year. Well, Irony was in the mood for a little knowledge and, whether for good or ill, the man beside her seemed to be a subject in which she was increasingly interested.

Who knows? she continued her internal debate. *Perhaps I could steal one tiny kiss and satisfy my curiosity about him. What better way to quell a disquieting urge?*

Even Valentine was one to advocate broadening one's horizons. In her younger days, she had gone as far south as Minneapolis to attend a finishing school . . . and that made her one of the more well-traveled citizens of Thief River.

All things considered, Irony would no doubt be better off if she simply gave in to her secret desire to kiss Hawk. Once accomplished, she could forget about it, the air would be cleared.

She sidled closer to him, hoping he might wake and put an end to her nonsensical scheme, but also praying that he wouldn't. Hawk didn't move.

The first touch of her lips to his was so tentative that Irony felt nothing more than a brief, unfulfilling warmth. She leaned closer and slowly lowered her mouth, allowing her lips to shape to his for the briefest instant. She had barely formed the impression of sweet, yielding firmness when, with a low growl, Hawk grasped her shoulders and flipped her onto her back. His lithe body followed in one fluid movement, and he settled himself astride her hips, his hands gripping her

46

wrists to hold her arms straight out to the side.

"So—you chose not to heed my warning?"

Irony blinked—twice. Then she screamed.

Hawk moved swiftly, cutting off the scream with his mouth. Unable to breathe, Irony tried to thrash her head from side to side, but to no avail. He used his body and the pressure of his kiss to subdue her. It wasn't until she lay quietly beneath him that he loosened his hold somewhat, although he did not discipline his marauding mouth.

Irony was stunned by the so-much-more-than-pleasant taste and texture of his lips. When he twisted his head to slant his mouth in a slightly different angle, the rub of his flesh against hers sent showers of heat through her body. Filled with strange, compelling yearnings she had never before experienced, she stopped seeking escape from his hold and started longing for release of another kind. She arched against him, and when a small, strangled groan sounded in the silence, she could not be certain if it came from her throat or his. She felt the tip of his tongue gently stroke the inner softness of her lips and shuddered uncontrollably.

Hawk's lean fingers loosened their grip, his thumbs massaging the tender skin of her wrists. Then, slowly, he slid his palms along her arms, curling his hands around her shoulders, then slipping them beneath her. Holding her closer, he rolled over, taking her with him, and unexpectedly, Irony found herself lying atop his chest, her legs entangled with his. He moved one hand to the back of her head to hold her lips in place against his.

Again, he teased her with his tongue and in an impulsive response, she parted her lips and allowed him entrance. To her utter amazement, ripples of excited pleasure started at the point of contact and coursed down her spine, concentrating somewhere in the area of her hips. She shifted against him, and Hawk moved

47

the arm he had around her waist lower, pulling her tightly to him.

Irony might have been virginal, but she was not a complete innocent. At the feel of the rock-hard body straining beneath her, every warning instinct within her began to clamor. Something told her that, unless she put an immediate stop to matters, Raphael Hawkes was going to take her right there on the ground, treating her like the experienced bawdy-woman that . . . that she was acting like! He'd only reacted to her initial advances, after all, and God save all virtuous maidens, she'd reacted right back with too much curiosity for her own good. But it couldn't go on—she had to regain control and in a way he couldn't resist.

When he ground his hips against her, she was suddenly filled with righteous, rejuvenating anger, and her mind cleared. She curled the fingers of one hand around the butt of the gun she still wore strapped to her side, and with a swiftness born of desperation, yanked the gun free and jammed the barrel into the vulnerable flesh just beneath his jaw. Hawk's mouth slackened and went still, and his hands dropped to his sides.

Indignant green eyes met inscrutable brown-black ones for a long moment, and then Irony clumsily rolled away from him, scrambling to her feet. She kept the gun leveled at him.

"How dare you?" she gasped, panting with fury.

One thick eyebrow quirked upward. "How dare . . . I?"

"Yes! How dare you touch me in such a manner?"

"I was under the impression that you touched me first, lady wildcat."

"Don't call me that! And I did not . . . touch you."

Hawk lazily hoisted himself onto one knee, and Irony backed away a few steps, holding the gun stiffly in front of her.

"Was I dreaming then?"

"I was only looking to see if you were asleep," Irony

lied, and went on lying. "Before I knew what was happening, you had grabbed me and . . . and were attacking me."

"You're a liar and you know it."

Irony's mouth turned down in a guilty scowl.

"Why should I lie about something like that?"

"Because you've wondered about me for two days and aren't honest enough to admit it." He surged to his feet, but stood his ground. Nevertheless, Irony retreated another step. "But now you know, don't you?"

"Oh, yes, now I know what sort of unscrupulous rogue you really are, Mr. Hawkes."

"Oh, so now it's back to Mr. Hawkes, is it?"

"I think it's time that we re-establish which of us has the upper hand in our relationship."

"That has never been in doubt."

"You seemed very uncertain of it only moments ago."

"Moments ago I was very certain indeed."

Irony could feel the heat creeping into her cheeks, but she tossed her head and waved the gun threateningly. "Whatever you thought then, I am in control now."

"Because you have that gun?"

"Can you think of a better reason?"

"I'm not worried by that rusty piece of junk," he declared, starting to advance on her.

"You should be," she warned. "I'll shoot you if you come any closer. I swear I will!"

With a seemingly effortless movement, Hawk reached out, snatched the Remington from her shaking hands, and hurled it into the underbrush.

"You go get that right now," she stormed, unable to completely repress the fear that sprang into her eyes. "I demand it!"

"You demand?"

"Yes—have you forgotten who is paying whom?"

"I've told you, Irony, I don't want your money. I never intended to be your hired man."

"Considering your extreme ineptitude, you are right in not wanting to charge people for your services," she snapped, "but the fact remains, I hired you and I am the boss."

"Not likely."

"What do you mean?"

"I mean, if you had any illusion that you were in charge of our situation, it's because I allowed it."

"You allowed?" Irony shouted. "You? You—who couldn't find a clue as to which way our quarry had gone? You who couldn't keep from getting lost on the only trail that goes through this forest? Ha!"

"Lost?" His dark eyes narrowed. "You thought we were lost?"

"We've traveled in circles all day, and I pitied you too much to mention it."

For the first time, Hawk laughed aloud. "We are not now, nor have we ever been, *lost*."

"But why have we been going in circles?"

"We're being followed, Irony, and I wanted to give whomever it was a chance to get closer to us."

"We're being followed?"

"Yes. Do you have any idea who might have a reason to trail us?"

"N-no." She shook her head vehemently. "Not at all."

Hawk merely studied her, making her so uneasy she continued speaking in a distracted way. "Did you get a look at him?"

"How do you know it's a man?"

"I don't. But it's unlikely to be a woman, isn't it?"

"There was a time I would have thought so," he replied. "But after meeting you . . . who knows?"

She ignored his jibe. "What are we going to do?"

"Make camp and watch for him."

"We can't do that. I mean, if we keep wasting time, we'll lose Reverend Goodman for certain."

"We'll find Goodman, don't worry. But for now, we'll make camp."

"No! We're going on."

"I say we stay."

"But I'm the boss."

"Prove it."

Irony glared at him, enraged by his cool challenge, but unable to think of a single way to force him to do her bidding. Finally, she came to the realization that he had undoubtedly been telling the truth—he had been in command all the time, only letting her think she was. And she had been so smug, so proud of her determined ability. Dejected, she turned away.

"It seems that you will have your way, Mr. Hawkes," she muttered ungraciously. "Do whatever you want."

"Whatever?" came his low, insinuating remark.

Irony whirled to look at him. "Whatever. So long as you keep away from me."

She stooped to gather up her bedding, then stalked away into the trees. Twenty or thirty yards from the trail, she found a small pool formed by a spring and, deciding to stay there, tossed down the blankets.

"This will make a good place to spend the night," Hawk observed, close behind her.

Though he had startled her, Irony didn't say anything further. She busied herself spreading out the blanket, studiously ignoring him. But later, as she sat in affronted silence, pretending to watch the pair of ground squirrels that had invaded their camp, she could not help but be impressed by his swift efficiency as he tethered the horses, unpacked the gear, built a fire and set about cooking supper.

He had obviously been amusing himself by posing as an unskilled, uncertain woodsman. The thought of how he must have laughed at her made her blood boil—she could almost hear its hiss in her ears. Irony had felt like a fool too many times in her life to overlook this latest incident. She was nearly overcome with embarrassment as she recalled the occasions she had waved that damned gun around, thinking Hawk too much a sissy not to follow her orders. Why had he permitted her to go on? What perverse pleasure had he gotten from watching her humiliate herself?

When he handed her a plate of beans and side meat, she accepted it without raising her eyes to his, sure that she could not bear to see the amusement she knew she'd find in his glance. After eating the best meal she'd had since leaving Sweetwater Lake, she rinsed her plate in the spring, dried it and put it back into the supply pack, not even peeking in his direction. Then she lay back down on her bed, turned her face away and pretended to be asleep. She needed time to decide what she was going to do next.

By the time night had fallen, casting the woods into inky darkness and turning the campfire into a bright golden glow, Irony's mind was weary from the thoughts churning inside it. She had tried to assess her situation and analyze her choices, but somehow, in the middle of all her problem solving, her mind would wander back to the shamefully intimate kisses she had shared with Raphael Hawkes. Her lips still felt swollen and . . . and violated, she tried to tell herself. *Unsatisfied,* her inner self insisted.

In trying to be utterly objective about her reaction to him, Irony decided that it had to be the result of the strange adventure in which she was engaging. She had been kissed by men before. No . . . not men, boys. With some kind of intuitive conviction, she knew that Hawk was the first person to ever kiss her as a man kisses a woman. She had never experienced such wild sensations prior to that afternoon, and certainly not with . . .

She heard a slight rustling noise and whirled about. There, standing beside the fire, was an Indian, so frightening and fierce-looking that Irony could only draw in a shocked breath and hold it.

The man was tall and lean, his magnificently muscular body naked except for the brief leather breechclout hung casually about his narrow hips and the fringed moccasins on his feet. Two jagged streaks of carmine red bisected his wide, smooth chest, its warlike look enhanced by the wooden club he carried in one hand.

"I didn't mean to frighten you," the man said, stepping closer, and for the first time, Irony realized it was Hawk. She released her pent-up breath.

Biting her lower lip to keep her mouth from dropping open in astonishment, she stared up at his shadowed face. His eyes were underlined with dramatic slashes of charcoal, his forehead streaked with carmine. The mild schoolteacher had completely disappeared — in his place stood a savage. Even though she had just spent most of the evening silently cursing Raphael Hawkes, Irony wished he was back. The man facing her was a stranger, one who could as easily kill her as look at her, or so it seemed. His black eyes glittered as the firelight washed over the bronzed expanse of his chest, and he seemed the embodiment of evil.

Despite her suddenly dry mouth, Irony managed to find her voice, though it sounded small and infuriatingly weak. "What on earth are you doing?"

"I'm going to lie in wait for our friend," he explained.

"But why are you dressed like that?"

"Because I want to scare the hell out of him," Hawk replied. "It may loosen his tongue if he thinks he's dealing with a heathen warrior."

"Yes, I should think it would." Irony was pleased that her own tongue had regained a bit of its usual tartness. "But are you sure there's only one person following us?"

"I am. And he's riding a shod horse, so he's one of your people." He paused just long enough to let the subtle sarcasm register, then went on. "He's determined, because he keeps pushing on despite the fact that his horse is tired and weakening. I suspect Jeb Uriah at the livery stable pawned some old nag off onto him."

"How can you tell such things?"

"By the tracks he's leaving. One of every four hoof-prints is deeper than the others, so the horse is favoring his right front leg."

"So you really are a guide? I mean, you really do know something about the wilderness?"

"Yes, I do know a little something," he answered without false modesty.

"But tell me, if you doubled back behind whoever is following us, why didn't you simply stop and confront him then?"

"I wanted to give him a chance to show me what he's up to. I want to know what he'll do if he thinks he's caught us sleeping."

Irony's eyes widened. "You . . . you aren't going to hurt him, are you?"

"Only if it becomes necessary. Why? Do you know who he is?"

"No! I've already told you."

"Very well. I'll believe you until events prove otherwise."

Irony bristled. "You think I'm lying?"

"It wouldn't be the first time."

"Oh, you're a fine one to talk. Look at the way you deceived me . . . right from the beginning."

"That doesn't absolve you—it only means we're both reprehensible," he said calmly.

"If I've told any falsehoods, I've only done so because it was for the best."

"Ah, for the best," Hawk commented. "Well, I happen to agree with the poet James Stephen, who said:

> "Of sentences that stir my bile,
>   Of phrases I detest,
> There's one beyond all others vile:
>   'He did it for the best.' "

"Don't quote poetry to me," she hissed. "It's so . . . so

demeaning. So patronizing." *Especially,* her mind piped up silently, *when you are very nearly naked and so threatening in a multitude of ways.*

"Your pardon," Hawk said, with what might have been the beginning of a smile. "At any rate, it's getting late, so I am going to begin my vigil."

"Where will you be?"

"Just down the trail a short distance. If you become frightened, call out and I will hear you."

"What makes you think I'd call out to you?"

"Who else is there to come to your aid?"

"I'd come to my own aid," she said staunchly. "I have discovered I can no longer trust you."

His patience was clearly at an end. He towered over her, jabbing one long finger in the air between them to emphasize his words. "I know your nose is out of joint, Irony, and I'm sorry. But I don't have time to worry over your childishness now. Take my advice and behave yourself for a change."

Her mouth opened in protest, but he didn't allow her time to speak. "Get into that bed and stay there until I tell you otherwise. It will behoove you to remember that play time is over—that I'm in charge now."

"You—you unprincipled cad. You fiendish rapscallion!"

"One of your Aunt Valentine's verbal condemnations, I'll wager. Stay here—I'll be back."

Irony almost had to laugh at how easily he had detected her aunt's maidenly influence in that stilted bit of speech—Lord, she had lived with them so long she was actually beginning to sound like them.

And then her momentary good humor faded abruptly as she caught sight of Hawk's retreating back. The firelight flickered over a tatoo high on one shoulder—the tatoo of a circle with a bird flying across it.

Chapter Four

The shack on Hangman's Creek. . . .

Irony couldn't believe it—didn't want to believe it. Marking his otherwise flawless back was the strange tatoo that could only mean one thing. Raphael Hawkes was a murderer.

And not just a murderer, she grimly reminded herself, *but one who had killed a helpless woman, an elderly schoolteacher who'd probably never harmed a soul.*

But what of her own circumstances? Why had he allowed her to live? Irony bit her lip, trying to corral her scattered thoughts. He must have some diabolical plan.

She shook her head in disbelief. How could a murderer be someone who quoted poetry every time he turned around—someone who picked wildflowers, for heaven's sake! She had thought Hawkes a simple, peaceable man. A gentle man.

An image of the heathenish tatoo surfaced in her mind once again, and she knew that the truth was something altogether different.

She had to get away, that's all there was to it. Without her gun, she was entirely at his mercy, and she was afraid that it would take no more than one look into her stricken eyes for him to realize she had guessed his secret. No, there was nothing for it but to sneak away as soon as possible and try to find her way to help.

She rolled up one of her blankets and stuffed it beneath the other, attempting to make it look like a sleeping body. Hopefully, it might buy her a little time. She worked frantically, constantly expecting the silent shadow of the savage killer to fall over her. When it did not, her rapid breathing calmed somewhat, but she was still panting in her desperate haste.

With Hawk watching the trail only a short distance away, it would make too much noise for her to take a horse, so she must leave on foot, without supplies. She eyed her carpetbag, weighing its bulkiness against the idea of leaving her belongings behind. Finally she decided to take it, since it contained the only clothing she had with her, as well as her money and the letters the bank and sheriff back home had written to the Canadian authorities. If the bag got too heavy, she would have to abandon it later.

She cast one last look at the small camp site, at the warm haven of the fire and the canvas pack of food. With sudden inspiration, she seized the sack and slung it over her shoulder. There wasn't much left — enough side meat for one more meal, a handful of beans, and a bit of coffee. But there was a quantity of dried beef jerky, and that should keep her going. Besides, if Hawkes was short of food, he might not be able to make such a vigorous search for her. She imagined him following her, growing weak from exhaustion and hunger, and then scolded herself for the pity she was wasting on a man who had wasted none on his last innocent victim.

Irony was afraid, afraid of the darkness and the unfamiliar forest. But she was also afraid of Hawkes, and of what he might do to her if he suspected she had figured out his involvement in the crime at Sweetwater. With a short, silent prayer for her safety, she edged away from the firelight and into the brooding shadows of the night.

Hawk peered through the darkness, ears straining for any sound that might indicate the approach of the stranger he knew was out there. The man should have caught up with them by this time, and he wondered if something had alerted him. Was he more skilled than Hawk had previously thought? Had the careless trail he left been a trick? He might have known all along that Hawk, aware of his presence, was setting a trap. Perhaps he planned to throw Hawk off his guard and circle around behind him . . .

Feeling a strange unease, Hawk glanced over his shoulder. He could just make out the eerie glow of the campfire through the trees.

Damn, what if the man following them was shrewder than he'd given him credit for? Even now he could be bending over Irony as she slept. The notion made Hawk's stomach knot. She no longer had her gun, thanks to him. How was she supposed to defend herself? Before she could even scream, the stranger could attack or kill her.

The jarring screech of a nightbird sent a frisson of shock down his spine. God, he'd thought for an instant it had been a woman's cry. He stared at the darkness that shrouded the path ahead — still no sign of anything moving. Again, he glanced over his shoulder, and in that moment, made the decision to give up the ambush and go back to camp. He could keep watch from there, and he would know that Irony was protected.

Stealthily, he crept toward the fire, making no discernible sound. Heron Woman might not have taught him much, but she had shown him how to make his way through the woods as silently as the shadows of the Grandfathers' spirits that hovered, watching over his people.

If she hurried too fast, Irony tripped over roots or rocks, so she tried to content herself with a slower, more consistent pace. There was barely enough moonlight to see by, and she had the horrible sensation of being half-blind. She groped her way, keeping one hand stretched out before her, but the weight of the carpetbag and canvas pack was heavy enough that she had to stop often to switch it to the other arm and shoulder.

Branches snagged at her hair or slapped her face, and she vented her spleen by muttering every forbidden curse word she had ever heard her aunts' hired man use. When she ran out of those and was occupying her mind by making up her own, she banged her shins on a fallen log and fell headfirst over it. The rough bark scraped her knees and ankles, and she twisted one shoulder. Breathless from her hard contact with the floor of the forest, Irony simply lay there. She considered bawling out loud, but only briefly. After all, she had made good progress up to that point, and she couldn't afford to let a momentary setback defeat her.

A full five minutes passed before she got to her feet, brushed the dirt, leaves and pine needles from her hair and clothing, and picked up her carpetbag. Stiffly, and more cautiously than before, she started off again.

She estimated that she had walked another hour at least before she came to the banks of a narrow, rushing stream. Gratefully, she got down on her knees and, after a long drink, splashed the cool water on her face. She rested for a while before deciding to travel upstream, following the winding river. With any luck at all, it would eventually lead her to something.

Irony allowed herself a fleeting thought of Hawkes, wondering if he had discovered her absence yet. The star-glittered night overhead gave her no clue as to what time it was — she could only guess that it was well after midnight. Surely by this time he had returned to their camp. Perhaps, if he'd taken the man who'd been following them hostage, he might not think it worth while to go after her. He couldn't very well drag one prisoner through the dark forest in search of another. At the very least, he'd be forced to wait until daylight. Cheered by the thought, Irony pushed on, stifling the yawns that suddenly began forming in her throat.

By the end of another hour, she started seriously considering the possibility of stopping to sleep a while. If she had any kind of head start, and if she located some sheltered spot to hide, hopefully, she could avoid being found.

She had walked around two more bends of the river before she saw a place to conceal herself. A huge, rotting log lay at the edge of the woods, disguised by ink-colored shadows. Had she not been peering so desperately into the darkness, she would have missed it. Upon closer inspection, she discovered that one end was hollow, and best of all, screened by a thicket of young maple saplings.

Sighing with relief, Irony inched inside the log, feet first. She was only partially hidden, but it was the best she could do. Wishing for her blankets, she settled down to sleep. Her last coherent thoughts were that bears favored logs like the one she was now inhabiting, and that all sorts of nasty bugs were apt to crawl on her and get into her hair. But something that would ordinarily upset her didn't seem to hold much threat at that moment. With one more hearty yawn, she drifted into an exhausted slumber.

* * *

Damn Irony McBride! Hawk expounded silently. *Where in the blazing hell has she gone?*

The camp site showed absolutely no signs of a struggle, so as much as he hated to admit it, she had clearly left of her own accord. It infuriated him that she had tried to trick him with the fake body in the bedroll. It infuriated him even more to discover she had taken all the food, the coffee pot and the frying pan. Not that there was anything too vital concerned — it just seemed to show her total lack of interest in his well-being. Did she really regard him with so little charity?

Hands on hips, Hawk stared down at his moccasins, trying to formulate a plan. It went without saying that he would go after her. He couldn't let her wander alone through the unfamiliar forest, which could be dangerous enough under ordinary circumstances, and certainly so with a gang of thieves and killers somewhere close by. Curse her for starting out at night! She could fall and break her fool neck, or at the very least, twist an ankle. She'd be an easy victim for wild animals . . . or the renegades they'd been following from the Indian school. He might be able to track her in the darkness, but it increased the possibility of making a mistake so much he wasn't willing to take that chance. When he started after her, he intended to overtake her as swiftly and unerringly as he could. He wanted her safe from Goodman and the others, and when he'd made sure she was . . . well, then he'd give her a dressing down that would fairly blister her tender hide.

He judged the time by the night sky and determined it was only an hour or two before daylight. It would be wisest to get what sleep he could, then go after Irony. And since he'd move faster on foot, some-

61

thing had to be done with the horses and pack mule anyway. Before he left, he'd tether them close to the stream and find some sweet grass to feed them. They would be all right until he and Irony could get back to them.

He wrapped up in his blankets and lay down to rest. Because he had trained himself to do so, he fell asleep almost immediately. Though he did have time for one final, satisfying thought of unleashing his oft-times wild temper on that impertinent little snippet who had complicated his life beyond belief since the first time he'd laid eyes on her.

Irony awoke reluctantly. She was cold and her clothes damp. Her knees ached from being drawn up so tightly, but when she straightened them, they felt worse — stiff and bruised from her fall earlier. She might have been older than her aunts' combined ages as she crept slowly out of the log and lurched to her feet.

Dawn was a pink stain across the eastern sky, bringing enough light for her to see her surroundings fairly well for the first time. Her mouth went dry as she saw the deep scarring on the log where she had spent the last two hours or so. The marks could only have been made by bear claws, and she suddenly realized how careless her fatigue had made her.

Well, there was no reason to linger, so she would be on her way. As much as she'd have liked to try building a fire to cook a meal, she knew the inadvisability of that idea. Not only might Hawk catch up with her, but the bear that frequented the insect-riddled log could come lumbering into view at any moment.

The thought of eventually finding a few minutes to attempt to cook breakfast made Irony shoulder the canvas pack again. Besides, if she left it, she'd have to hide it well enough to escape Hawk's notice, and she knew she didn't have the time to spare.

She continued on in the direction she'd been heading during the night, following the churning little river upstream. She was entertaining the notion of crossing the river at some point, then wading back downstream for a while before slipping away into the woods on the other side. She'd heard about outdoorsmen doing such things to throw the enemy off the trail. It would be worth a chance, she supposed, since she really had no other ideas. She'd mostly need to be cautious that she didn't proceed too far downstream and run into Hawk. Grimly, she theorized that that would be just her luck.

She rounded another bend in the river and was startled to come face to face with a big buck deer drinking at the water's edge. She gasped in fright, one hand covering her thumping heart, and the animal, equally frightened, leaped into the brush and fled with loud crashing noises. Irony's breathing remained erratic for what seemed a long time, but she finally got herself under control again. With a mirthless laugh, she decided she was grateful she hadn't run into the creature last night in the dark. Come morning light, Hawk would have found her stiff and cold, eyes staring glassily. It would take a stronger heart than hers to withstand something so unexpectedly scary.

Her nose twitched. There was a faint tang of smoke on the heavy morning air — she was sure of it. Relief washed over her. A campfire. It had to be. She was close to rescue, at last. She began to walk faster, glad the thickness of the pines overhead accounted for the lack of entangling underbrush beneath her feet.

Wait a minute, she cautioned herself, slowing her steps. *Even if it is a campfire, it could belong to the men who kidnapped Goodman. Or, heaven forbid, maybe I've been walking in circles and it's Hawkes' fire.*

No, she couldn't have gotten turned around, she'd been following the river. Nevertheless, she would advance with wariness in case there was any possible danger.

After fifteen minutes she was certain she was getting closer to the smoke; in another few minutes she saw it, hovering over the treetops in a flat cloud. Ears straining for any sound, she moved forward, a step at a time.

Through the trees, Irony could see a tumbledown shack, with smoke issuing from the crooked stone chimney at one end. No one was in sight, so she edged closer.

She was approaching the shack from behind, and because there were no windows in the back wall, she felt relatively secure in dashing across the narrow clearing and flattening herself against the rough logs. She could hear nothing but the sound of muffled snores . . . and those too loud to be from inside the cabin.

Holding her breath, Irony eased her way to the corner, carefully peeking around the side of the structure. There was nothing there, which led her along the shorter wall to the front corner of the cabin. Peering around that corner, she saw the snorer. He was an Indian, sitting cross-legged on the ground, his back against a barred door as he slept.

A guard! That must mean there was something or someone inside that shack who wasn't meant to escape. Irony surmised she had finally crossed the path of the kidnappers, and that the missing Reverend Josiah Goodman was being held captive within those very walls. She bit her lower lip. Hadn't that storekeeper told them there were four abductors? Were the rest of them inside?

Just to one side of the door was a narrow window,

and Irony had a sudden, compelling urge to look through it. The only obstacle between her and that particular goal was the snoring Indian blocking the entrance to the shack. Surely she could deal with one solitary and apparently defenseless man.

Irony's eyes widened as a daring thought occurred to her. She swung the pack off her shoulder, pulling it open as quietly as she could. Her fingers closed around the handle of the iron skillet and she lifted it out, testing it for weight. It would have to do.

She set her carpetbag and the canvas sack aside, then stealthily crept forward, praying the Indian wouldn't awaken. When she was about six feet from him, he shifted his position, and Irony froze in terror. He emitted several rumbling snores, but to her relief, never raised his eyelids. Not willing to take another such chance, Irony firmed up her grip on the frying pan and nearly ran the next few steps, giving herself no time to reconsider. She swung the skillet with all her strength, wincing at the dull thud it made as it struck the side of his head.

"Oooph!" The Indian sagged and fell sideways, unconscious. Irony's shaking fingers released the skillet, which dropped to the grass beside him. She covered her mouth with both hands, trying not to dwell on the fact that that was the first time she had ever done bodily harm to another human being. Even knowing he was a sworn foe was no consolation.

Gradually, she recalled her vulnerable circumstances. She couldn't stand over the fallen enemy forever. He might regain his senses, or someone else might arrive on the scene. Perhaps this was a pre-arranged meeting place, and the culprits were biding their time waiting for Hawk.

Irony had to stand on tiptoe and shade her eyes with her hands to see into the shack. She knew the risk she was taking and hoped anyone inside would be asleep. It took a while for her vision to adjust to the dim interior, but when it did, she discovered there was only one person in the cabin—the Reverend Goodman, sprawled on a rickety cot in the corner, sleeping like a baby.

Irony gritted her teeth at the sight of the man. She wouldn't mind swinging the frying pan at him, even though the ease with which she had adopted such bloodthirsty ideas did amaze and distress her.

If only she had her gun! She could walk into the shack, demand her property back and waltz away, leaving the unscrupulous evangelist to his fate. He deserved that and more for the way he'd treated so many innocent women. Why didn't she have her Remington, damn it!

Her eye fell to the buckskin clad Indian crumpled at her feet. Perhaps he had a weapon. Kneeling, she shoved his body over onto his back, and smiled with satisfaction. There, strapped to his side was an evil-looking hunting knife, and Irony, never one to question providence, seized it. The sight of the wide, gleaming blade just might make Reverend Goodman a religious man, after all.

She lifted the bar on the door and pushed her way into the gloomy interior.

"Reverend Goodman," she called softly. "Psst, Reverend. Wake up!"

Mumbling, the elusive man of God turned over and sat up in bed. "Goddamn it, Three-Fingers, what the hell's going on?"

Irony stepped closer to the bed and brandished the knife. "Hello, Reverend," she said in as menacing a voice as she could muster.

"What th . . . ?" The man rubbed his face and sat up straighter. "Well, well, well. Do my eyes deceive me, or is it little Irony McBride from Thief River Falls?"

66

"Surprised to see me, Goodman?"

He grinned. "I should say. I wonder, though, what your aunties would think if they could see the way you're dressed."

"They sent me after you—why should they care how I dress?" she snarled. "Now, look, I don't have much time. I want the money you stole from us. And the jewelry . . . and most especially, the property deeds. If you hand them over without a fuss, I'll think about setting you free."

"Setting me free?"

"From your kidnappers. I've already dealt with the guard outside."

"You . . . dealt with him?" Goodman looked astonished. "What did you do?"

"I hit him over the head with an iron skillet. The temptation to do the same to you is nearly irresistible, I warn you, so start gathering up what belongs to me."

"If . . . if I've been kidnapped, why would you think I still have your property? Perhaps my captors took everything."

Her gaze narrowed. "Did they?"

"Unfortunately, yes."

"I don't believe you." Her gaze darted around the room, coming to rest on a leather satchel in one corner. "What's in that case?"

"My clothing, nothing more." Goodman eased his rotund body out of the bed, and Irony was embarrassed to see that he was wearing only a pair of long red flannel underwear. "That's why my . . . er, guard and I were here alone. The others rode off to put the money and jewels in a safe place. At least, that's what they told me."

"If they took your ill-gotten gains, why didn't they simply murder you? What purpose could it serve to leave you alive, a witness to their crime?"

"Their crime?" He paused in the middle of stepping

into his trousers. "Do you mean . . . ?"

"I mean the brutal slaying of an innocent woman."

"Oh, yes, my beloved Bessie," the man said, with a belatedly bereaved look. "I suspect the only reason I have escaped the same terrible fate is because I'm a man of the cloth. Since the coming of the missionaries to these parts, the savages have a healthy respect for us and our God."

"You have no God, Mr. Goodman. The only thing you worship is yourself. You are a greedy, despicable parasite! Preying on the weak and trusting."

"Like your silly aunt, I suppose?"

Irony clamped down tightly on her temper. She didn't have time to stand there exchanging insults with the man. "You shall pay for your crimes sooner or later, rest assured. But for right now, all I'm concerned with is getting back the things you stole."

She knelt beside the satchel and when Goodman would have stopped her, she thrust the knife at him. "Stand back, Reverend, or I won't hesitate to start hacking. I may not know much about using a knife, but I'll wager I could relieve you of some items you hold pretty dear."

"No need to be crude, Irony," he chided. She noticed, however, that he came to an abrupt halt.

"Great God Almighty," she muttered, rummaging through the valise. "You thieving scoundrel! Look at all this — why, here's Aunt Valentine's diamond hair clip. She wore that at her wedding, you snake. These are her pearls . . . and her ruby pendant." Irony snatched up the various pieces of jewelry and stuffed them into her jacket pockets. "Do you know how she cried over this?" she asked, shaking an amethyst necklace at him. "It belonged to her mother . . . and her grandmother before her. How could you be so lowdown?"

"Miss McBride . . ."

The sound of horses' hoofs suddenly filled the room, and Irony jerked to her feet. "They're back! Quick, we've got to get out of here!"

She dashed to the door, but the clearing outside was already astir with two men on horseback, both of them Indian, and both of them gaping at her. "Oh-oh . . . too late," she whispered. "We'll have to make a stand." She tossed the preacher a look over her shoulder. "Don't keep staring at me — find a weapon, for heaven's sake."

One of the braves slid off his horse and stalked toward the cabin. "You kill Three-Fingers?" he asked Irony as he bent over the still body of the guard.

"No, unfortunately," she replied, her fingers clammy on the handle of the knife.

"Who is this squaw?" the Indian asked, looking past Irony to the man behind her.

"That doesn't matter," Irony exclaimed, raising the knife. "If you don't let us go, I'll . . . I'll stab you. Get back out of our way."

The Indian grunted, his round black eyes amused. Irony squared her shoulders and started toward him, but with a chopping motion of his hand, Goodman hit her wrist, causing the knife to fly out of her grasp and land at the Indian's feet. Stunned by pain, Irony watched helplessly as the brave stooped to pick it up. She paled as he handed it to Goodman.

"Perhaps now you will behave yourself, Irony," Goodman chortled, running his forefinger gingerly along the edge of the blade.

"I don't understand," Irony began, then shook her head. "No, I think I do understand, after all. You were never kidnapped, were you? You're the leader of this bunch of cutthroats . . ."

Her own words caused her to fall silent as she realized their significance. Cutthroats, indeed. That had been exactly what had happened to Bessie Sparks . . .

and what could easily happen to her, as well, especially after Hawk caught up with them.

"What we do with her?" the Indian asked, and his companion offered suggestions that, even in a language Irony couldn't hope to understand, sounded dire. Somehow, she was just as glad she didn't know what he was saying.

"That all depends," said Goodman, "on how she conducts herself. And how truthfully she answers the questions I'm going to ask her."

The Indians nodded solemnly.

"Running Dog, you go on out and see if you can drag Three-Fingers down to the stream and revive him. Bar the door when you go, in case Miss McBride tries anything heroic." Goodman gestured to the other man. "Broken Knife, you sit over there and keep your eyes on the squaw while I finish dressing. Understand?"

Again the man nodded, moving to a spot in the corner where he sat down, cross-legged. Irony shifted uneasily, nervously rubbing her injured wrist.

"Now, Miss McBride," Goodman said, struggling to pull on his boots. "I want to know if you are alone."

Her chin rose defiantly. "Why? Were you expecting someone?"

"I have a lot of enemies," he observed. "Why else would I sleep with my door barred? I repeat, are you alone?"

"Yes."

"Don't lie to me," he growled. "Young women like you don't travel unescorted, even dressed like that. Besides, a lady wouldn't know anything about surviving in the woods. So—who is with you?" He picked up the knife again and, stepping closer, waved it in front of her face. "Where are your fellow travelers?"

Irony considered telling him she was accompanied by an entire regiment of U.S. soldiers, but somehow, flippancy didn't seem worth the risk.

"I'm alone."

He tapped her cheek with the tip of the knife. "Come now, don't be stubborn. It will go easier for you if you tell me what I want to know."

Irony refused to mention Raphael Hawkes. There was no need for the outlaws to know he was close behind her. He'd keep the planned rendezvous soon enough. "I'm alone, I tell you. Of course, there's no way I can prove it, so you'll have to take my word for it."

"Have you followed us from Sweetwater?"

No harm in admitting that, she reasoned. "Yes."

"Who knew where you were going?"

"Only my aunts."

"No, you ninny! I mean who in Sweetwater?"

"I discussed my plans with no one."

Goodman heaved a windy sigh. "Irony, this is getting us nowhere." He coughed, covering his mouth politely with a puffy white hand. "Don't make me ask the same question again." Again, he coughed.

Irony's eyes began to sting, and she blinked furiously. "Ask as many damned times as you please," she snapped, "but the answer is going to be the same every time. No one knows where I am."

A billow of gray smoke wafted into the room from the fireplace, and the Indian leaped to his feet.

"What's wrong?" Goodman croaked, coughing more persistently. His eyes, too, had begun to smart.

"Cabin on fire," Broken Knife cried and immediately ran to the door. It was barred, and he began pounding frantically, calling out in his own language.

"Damn it, Running Dog, open the door!" Goodman added his angry shouts to the noise.

Another cloud of thick smoke belched out into the room, and Irony pulled her shirttail up to cover her nose and mouth. Goodman used the hilt of the knife to break out the window, but even then there wasn't enough fresh air admitted to alleviate the smoke screen inside the shack.

Irony added her cries to those of the others, and her throat quickly grew raw. Good God, was she going to burn to death in this miserable, abandoned trappers' hut?

Poor Aunt Alyce . . . poor Tiny, she thought, struggling to draw her breath. *They'll never forgive themselves for allowing me to follow Goodman.*

Suddenly, there was a grating noise as the bar was lifted and the door flung open. Choking, Irony started forward. Goodman shoved her out of his way, pushing through the door and falling to his knees, gasping painfully for breath. The Indian followed, but a huge shadow seemed to loom up from nowhere and the next thing Irony knew, something crashed into his head and he crumpled to the ground like a felled tree.

She wasted no time worrying about it — she stepped over his prostrate body, drawn to the fresh air and sunshine that filled the clearing. Ahead of her, Goodman, still on his knees, coughed and retched.

The shadow loomed up again, but this time Irony heard the slap of a decidedly human hand against a horse's rump, followed by the pounding of hoofs. One of the Indian ponies streaked past and, startled, she turned to watch it go. Unexpectedly, a band of steel snaked around her waist, and she was pulled roughly against a broad chest. She found herself looking into the glinting black eyes of Raphael Hawkes, and when she opened her mouth to scream, he closed a huge hand over the lower half of her face. Irony kicked and struggled as she felt herself being dragged away, around the corner of the building.

"Ouch! Stop kicking, damn it," Hawk rasped in her ear. "I won't let you go until you promise to keep quiet."

His assumption that she would calmly deliver herself into the hands of a killer incensed her, and she doubled her efforts to get free.

"I'm trying to save you, Irony," he muttered.

"I . . . don't . . . want . . . to be . . . saved!" she said, her words muffled by his hand.

"That's too damned bad."

He dropped to his knees and, his hold on her tightening, rolled his body into the small, dusty, smoke-hazed space beneath the shack. They came to rest against a barrier of packed earth, Hawk lying full length on top of Irony. He removed his hand from her mouth, but when he felt her gathering air to scream, pushed her face into his chest. The feel of his smooth skin and the sun-warmed scent of his body effectively silenced her.

"Don't worry," he whispered. "There's no fire — I only stopped up the chimney to smoke them out."

She wasn't all that relieved by his words. Her lungs felt as though they had been deprived of air too long, and she wondered if she was going to swoon. If she didn't suffocate, Hawk would surely crush her. But she was growing too weak to even care . . .

"Goddamn it, Running Dog, where the hell have you been?" Reverend Goodman's irate voice sounded close.

"Man sneak up on me," came the reply. "Hit me with tree branch. I will kill bastard if I catch him."

Irony could hear Goodman's cold laugh. "That's exactly what I had in mind. Him and that snot-nosed girl. Here, take this rifle and let's find them. Three-Fingers, you lazy son-of-a-bitch, get your no-account friend on his feet. This isn't some Sunday School picnic."

As she listened to sounds of a confused departure, Irony's chagrin grew by leaps and bounds. She didn't know what on earth was happening. If Hawk was a part of the gang, why was he hiding? He must be double-crossing them, she realized. He was trying to send the others off on a wild goose chase so he wouldn't have to split up the proceeds from the robbery.

"Damn. . . ." she began, but his hand clamped down over her mouth again. That didn't stop her from expressing her anger.

"Yoosummbit!" she echoed Goodman's most recent profanity.

There. She felt better. She'd always wanted to use that word in a fit of temper, and now she had managed it. And under the circumstances, surely not even her aunts would chastise her for it.

"Looks like they took a horse," Goodman yelled. "Three-Fingers, you ride double with Running Dog. It's your damned fault this happened. Let's go—they can't have gotten far."

As soon as the noise had died away, Irony renewed her struggle, certain that Hawk would now release her. Instead, he remained where he was.

"Shhh," he cautioned, his lips close to her ear. One hand came up to brush a strand of hair from her dirt-smeared forehead and Irony realized the tender gesture was supposed to reassure her that he meant her no harm.

They lay quietly for another ten minutes before Hawk moved away from her and poked his head through the opening near the crumbling stone foundation.

"It looks safe," he announced, crawling out, then reaching down a hand to assist Irony.

Once she was on solid ground again, she gave him a scathing look, then tramped around the side of the cabin and through the door.

"It's gone," she wailed. "That miserable thief took his suitcase with him." She whirled on Hawk, too angry to be afraid. "If you hadn't messed things up, I'd have had all my aunts' belongings back by now."

"He had everything with him?"

"I saw the jewelry and some of the money. I'm almost positive he has the deeds in that case, too. Why on earth couldn't you have left well enough alone?"

"You were in the hands of killers," he calmly reminded her. "What was I supposed to do?"

"I could have taken care of myself. I didn't need your interference."

"I expected a little gratitude," he pointed out.

"You shouldn't. I know everything, Hawk," she said.

"I can see that you think you do. But what the hell are you talking about?"

"The tatoo on your shoulder. It's . . . the storekeeper said the murderer had one like it."

"I'm not a murderer."

"How do you explain it, then?"

"You told me yesterday that you were going to trust me," he reminded her. "If you'll do so a while longer— until we can regroup and meet Goodman on our own terms—I'll tell you everything." Picking up the food sack, he spun on his heel and left her to follow. "Now grab your carpetbag and let's get out of here."

Irony threw him a perplexed glance. Was she wrong about him? Or was he simply a consummate actor? Suddenly, she felt too tired, too dirty and too generally depleted to argue the point. She turned to pick up her bag where she'd left it in a clump of bushes and uttered a horrified cry. The contents were scattered haphazardly across the grass.

She snatched up the oilskin packet that contained her letters from home. "Who did this?" she asked, tucking it into the case. "Oh, my God, where's my traveling suit?" Accusing green eyes met those of the astonished man watching her.

"I had to have something to stuff in the chimney," Hawk said defensively. "It was heavy and. . . ."

"It was one hundred per cent Scottish tweed," she declared, tears springing into her eyes. "I had to order it from St. Paul, and it took two months to arrive. How could you be so . . . so careless?"

"I wasn't careless. I thought I was rescuing you. One dress didn't seem all that important at the time."

"Well, it was important to me."

"Oh, hell, Irony, I'll buy you another damned dress."

Hawk couldn't believe that the same woman who had kidnapped him at gun point, who had started through the forest alone at night, who had faced a gang of thieves unarmed, was now shedding silly tears over a stupid dress. Lord save him from genteel ladies! Who could ever hope to understand them?

He strode away, and after shoving the remainder of her clothing into the bag, Irony trailed him out of the clearing and away from the cabin that still reeked with smoke. From time to time, she sniffed loudly . . . but she didn't have a word to spare for Raphael Hawkes.

Chapter Five

War Road, Minnesota . . .

Returning through the woods to the place Hawk had left the horses was a slow, tedious process. He took every precaution to avoid meeting up with Goodman or any of his cohorts. Once, hearing the approach of a horseman, he had thrust Irony face down in a thicket of spruce, using his body to shield hers. She considered trying to scream for help, but quickly decided she would rather be in the company of Raphael Hawkes than Three-Fingers or any of those other stone-faced Indians.

Something about Hawk puzzled her. If he was, indeed, the murderer his tatoo claimed him to be, why had he rescued her from Goodman? Her theory that he wanted the stolen property for himself just didn't hold up under close scrutiny, and she had to admit it. He would never have concerned himself with her safety; his first priority would have been to seize Goodman's satchel and hightail it out of there.

Maybe he was thinking of holding her for ransom. She'd talked about her life back in Thief River enough for him to have surmised her aunts were well-to-do. Maybe he was entertaining the idea of demanding money for her return. Of course, Goodman's nasty scheme had pretty well depleted their finances, but

Hawk couldn't know that. She frowned as a new thought came to her. God forbid that he ever learn about the valuable jewelry she had stuffed in her pockets. Even if she never recovered any of the rest of the property, she'd still have the pleasure of returning that to Aunt Tiny. But at the moment, knowing how close she had come to getting it all back, it seemed a hollow victory. If only Raphael Hawkes had not interfered!

"You could be dead by now if I hadn't interfered," he said suddenly. "I don't think you realize how much danger you were in."

"Do you think I feel any safer with you?"

"I think you know I'm not going to cut your throat."

"How would I know that?" she queried impatiently.

"Because I'd have already done it," he informed her. "Any number of times."

She stopped and tilted her head back to look up into his face. He returned her look with grave sincerity. Irony had no choice but to admit to herself that she believed him.

"Well, be that as it may . . ." She shrugged with elaborate disdain. "I still can't forgive what you did to my traveling suit."

Carefully hiding any trace of the incongruous lightness of heart she felt at deciding Hawk was no murderer, Irony trudged on, leaving him staring after her, a curious mixture of frustration and admiration playing over his austere features.

They located the horses and pack mule without further encounters with Goodman or his men, so Hawk built a small fire and cooked a hasty breakfast from the food salvaged at the shack. After they had eaten, Irony knelt to wash the plates in the spring and caught sight of her reflection.

"My Lord," she muttered, "would you look at me! My hair is a mess—oh, what's this?" Her hands were busily sifting through the thick curls that were springing forth from the remnants of her braid.

"Leaves . . . moss. A few pine needles," Hawk answered, reaching down to pluck a twig from her hair. "And your face is dirty, too."

"It is?"

"Dirt and soot smeared all over it," he replied.

She thought his tone a bit superior. "Well, you don't look so marvelous yourself, you know."

Even as she said it, she recognized the lie for what it was. He looked quite wonderful, in fact, wearing the leather breechclout that left his dirt-streaked chest and legs bare. His war paint was faded and smudged, lessening its frightening effect and heightening its barbaric appeal. Again Irony struggled against her attraction to him, and again she sensed that it stemmed in part from his extreme difference to any man she'd ever known.

"I'll strike a bargain with you," Hawk said. "If you promise to behave and follow my lead for the rest of the day . . . without question . . . I'll give you time to bathe in the river before we go into War Road this evening."

"War Road?"

"It's a village where we can sell the horses and take a train to Rainy River. From there we'll go on to Lake of the Woods by canoe. Within a very few days we should run into Reverend Goodman again . . . and this time, we'll be ready for him."

"We'll stay in War Road tonight?"

Hawk almost smiled. "There's a rooming house there."

Irony hadn't detected the wistful note in her own voice, but she couldn't deny the elation she felt at the thought of lying down to sleep in a soft, clean bed.

"Lead on," she commanded, gaily. "I'll be as obedient as a child at Sunday School."

She gave him an unabashed smile, filling Hawk with the urge to reach out and caress her cheek. Dressed in the filthy, disreputable-looking jacket and pants, her hair straggling about her dirty face, she had the endearing look of a cheerful urchin. But, cheerful or not, he was fairly certain that if she thought he was taking untoward liberties, she'd fend him off with all the ferocity of a cornered wolverine.

He controlled his urge and started packing up the gear. It was time to get on the trail again.

They seemed to have lost Goodman completely, and throughout the day Irony was, by turns, relieved and irritated by that fact. She worried aloud that he'd slipped out of their grasp, but Hawk assured her their paths would cross again and when that happened, the two of them would be rested and prepared. Once they got to War Road, he told her, they'd spend time devising a plan for luring the preacher out into the open.

When they were within a half-mile of the town, Hawk found a shallow, sheltered place on the War Road river for them to bathe. As much as she wished to be clean, Irony was embarrassed by his presence and stalled for time by taking her one remaining dress from the carpetbag, shaking it out and hanging it over a tree limb.

Sensing her hesitation, Hawk said, "I'll go upstream to bathe."

"That's a good idea," she murmured. "Thank you."

As soon as he had disappeared from sight, Irony emptied her pockets of the jewelry, concealing it at the bottom of her bag. Then, taking the soap and soft cloth she had brought with her, she slipped down to the water's edge.

Never having bathed in the open before, she felt uneasy and kept glancing about as though she momentarily expected someone to appear. She divested herself of her clothing with a sharp sense of urgency, and even then, waited until she was shoulder-deep in the river before taking off her chemise and pantalettes. As she rinsed out the undergarments in the clear, cool water, she calmed herself with thoughts of her aunts and their reaction if they could have seen her at that moment. It was almost a certainty that neither of them had ever worn men's clothing or bathed in a river. And, without a single doubt, she knew instinctively they would never have washed an undergarment where there was the slightest risk that a man might see it.

Irony wrung out the scraps of white cotton and tossed them onto the grassy shore. In her case, it simply couldn't be helped. She had one clean set of underwear in the carpetbag, so it was necessary to launder these. She'd roll them up in her towel and hang them out to dry in her room that night. If Raphael Hawkes happened to catch a glimpse of it . . . well, no doubt he'd survive the shock.

As she became accustomed to the brisk chill of the water, she began to relax and enjoy herself. The scented soap smelled heavenly, and she thoroughly appreciated the soothing effect it had on her dusty skin. How nice it was to be clean again!

She tilted her head back to let her hair float out into the water, using her fingers to comb the worst of the sticks and grass from its tangled length. She had just lathered it thoroughly with the bar of soap when she heard the loud snap of a twig and, startled, turned to scan the banks of the river. Arms poised above her head, she searched for signs of an intruder. Unable to see anything amiss, she chided herself for being a silly goose and continued washing her hair.

* * *

Concealed by a moss-grown boulder in the shadows of the forest, Hawk heaved a ragged sigh. He'd almost created a situation that Miss Irony McBride couldn't have forgiven. He should have realized a lady would linger over her bath . . . especially if it was the first one she'd had in several days. He hadn't been thinking when he'd taken his own with swift efficiency, then dressed and hurried back toward their temporary camp. He'd made no particular effort to be silent, and just before he emerged from the woods, the cracking of a limb underfoot sounded as loud as a gunshot. At the same instant, his eyes had fallen upon Irony, still immersed in the river, and fortunately, he'd been able to step behind the boulder to avoid being seen. Instinct told him she would never believe he hadn't sneaked up purposely.

As he pondered the best way to handle his delicate predicament, he couldn't resist another quick glance at the girl. Irony, at ease again, was lathering her hair, making a cascade of bubbles over her naked shoulders. Hawk was fascinated by the grace of her slender arms, and the tantalizing swell of her breasts just barely covered by the water.

Guiltily, he watched, knowing he should tear his gaze away, but somehow unable to do so. He enjoyed the pleasant sight Irony made as she slipped lower into the water to rinse the soapsuds from her hair. Then, smiling faintly to herself as she twisted her hair over her left shoulder to wring out the excess water, she began singing in a light, sweet voice.

Hawk's jaw clenched at the sound, and a line from Shakespeare's Comedy of Errors, appropriately enough, flitted through his mind: "But, lest myself be guilty to self-wrong, I'll stop mine ears against the mermaid's song."

What the hell was the matter with him? Irony McBride was a nuisance — a carping, complaining thorn in his side. She'd caused him nothing but trouble since he'd met her . . . why was he spying on her now as though he was a randy sixteen-year-old and she was the first enticing woman he'd ever seen?

His mental tongue-lashing died an abrupt death as he saw her start toward the bank. She cast a quick look in both directions, then waded out of the water. Hawk found himself gazing with distinct pleasure at a straight, slim back and nicely rounded buttocks. He'd never have guessed at the shapeliness of the legs that had thus far been concealed by long skirts or baggy trousers, and he was immobilized by sudden, erotic visions of those limbs warmly entwined with his own.

"Jesus," he breathed softly, his mouth parched by the unexpected emotion that streaked through him.

Irony knelt gracefully and began rummaging through the open carpetbag. Drawing forth a fresh undergarment, she straightened and stepped into it, then reached for a petticoat.

Hawk rested his chin on his chest for a long moment, striving to master the excited racing of his heart. Wonder at his unrestrained response to Irony and disgust at his own lack of character struggled for the upper hand. Finally, happily, the need for control asserted itself and Hawk resolutely turned his shadowed eyes away from the sight of Irony wriggling into the calico dress she had thrown over the tree branch earlier. Silently, he stole back into the forest in the direction from which he'd come.

Several minutes later, a loud whistling tune announcing his arrival, Hawk strode into the clearing, relieved to find Irony fully dressed and combing out her damp hair.

She looked up and smiled. "That was the most soothing bath I've ever had," she remarked contentedly, not noticing the tiny strained lines at the corners of his eyes.

Soothing? Hawk thought, grimly. *I found it rather more arousing than anything else.*

Aloud he said, "Are you about ready to go? I find myself feeling very hungry . . . for a good, home-cooked meal."

War Road turned out to be little more than a couple of streets of houses and stores, but after the last few days on the trail, it looked wonderful to Irony. Originally, it had been an Indian village located at the northern end of the war path over which the Sioux and Ojibway had traveled to raid each other. Now it was what was known as a White Man's town, settled by fur traders and loggers.

Looking northwest from the main street, Irony got her first glimpse of the open expanse of water which Hawk informed her was Lake of the Woods.

"It looks huge," she cried. "Like an ocean. I've never seen so much water."

"This is only one small portion of the lake," he replied. "The lake itself is over seventy miles long, and some of its bays are more than two hundred miles in length."

She gave him a curious glance. "How do you expect to find Goodman in such a large area?"

"We're going to study that map and head straight for the places marked on it. Sooner or later, he'll show up to have a look at his new holdings."

"That wouldn't be very smart of him, would it? I mean, why wouldn't he simply sell the land and disappear with the money?"

"Goodman isn't an overly intelligent sort, Irony—he enjoys gloating over his victories too much. But this time he won't be dealing with some lonely, defenseless widow."

"You want him, too, don't you?" Her gaze was

84

frankly appraising. "What has he done to you?"

"There'll be time for explanations later," Hawk said. "Right now we've got more important things to do."

"Yes, I want to send a telegraph to my aunts and secure a room for the night."

"Try Flannagan's rooming house," he suggested, pointing out the two-storied building at one end of the street. "The telegraph office is in Laughlin's trading post. Meanwhile, I'll be at the livery stable selling the horses. Meet me there and we'll go to supper."

"You aren't planning on taking the money and leaving town?" Her tone was so gentle, her smile so quizzical, that Hawk took no offense at the question.

"No. We've come this far together, haven't we? Besides, I'm of a mind to prove to you that I'm no murderer."

"I've already said I believe you. I'm not frightened of you anymore."

"But the fact remains that last night you were so convinced of my guilt that you ran off into the woods alone."

"It was the tatoo," Irony stated. "Seeing it so unexpectedly startled me."

"I will tell you about that when the time is right. If you're willing to listen, that is."

"I'm willing. It's the least I can do after you brought me all this way."

"Then go rent a room and send your message."

Irony watched him walk away, leading the horses and pack mule. He was dressed in the levis and plaid shirt again, looking very much like any other ordinary man she might meet on the street, except for the slightly long hair tied with the leather thong. It seemed Raphael Hawkes was one man when attired in his black suit, another when wearing levis, and yet another when clad in the brief, primitive Indian costume. Irony wondered if she would ever learn

85

which was the real Hawkes, or if, indeed, he was some puzzling mixture of all three.

The first thing she saw upon entering Flannagan's was a neatly lettered sign that read: NO ROOMS RENTED TO INDIANS. Surprised by the stark sentiment, Irony debated about what to do. She had intended to secure one room for herself and another for Hawk, but that now appeared to be out of the question.

A scrawny, gray-haired woman came out of a back room, wiping her hands on a dish towel. "Howdy," she said in a brisk, mannish fashion. "Call me Ma Flannagan. What can I do fer ya?"

"I need a room for the night," Irony said. "But I had also hoped to find accommodations for my guide." She gestured toward the sign.

"He an Injun?"

"Mr. Hawkes is part Indian, yes."

"Then he'll have to bed down at the livery. The owner rents out one of his spare stalls for a dollar a night."

"But . . ."

"Sorry, it's the best I can do." The woman's wrinkled face broke into a not unkind smile. "Too many of them fellers off the reservation git lickered up and wanna tear up everythin' in their way. My husband made the rules, and I jist abide by 'em."

"Of course, I understand. Well, I'll take the one room then, and see about settling my guide elsewhere."

Irony paid in advance, and after inquiring about departure time for the train to Rainy River, left an order for breakfast to be brought to her room at seven o'clock the next morning. She climbed the flight of stairs to what Ma Flannagan called the Green Room and deposited her carpetbag and Hawk's valise on the highboy dresser. The furnishings were sparse, but the room was clean and the bed soft and inviting.

After spreading the undergarments she'd washed in the river out to dry, Irony freshened her appearance. She straightened her hair, regretting the fact she had no hat to put on. She took a shawl from her bag, as well as a reticule into which she stuffed enough money to pay for dinner and a telegraph to Thief River Falls.

The telegraph was the first order of business. She made her way to Laughlin's trading post, and there the clerk took the message she wanted to send her aunts. She made it short and purposely vague, merely stressing the fact that she was fine and making progress in locating her quarry. No need to go into specifics—Aunt Valentine's vivid imagination would supply enough details as it was.

Turning away from the counter, Irony's eyes fell upon a display of guns, making her think of her grandfather's Remington that Hawk had so highhandedly thrown into the underbrush. The memory of how helpless she'd felt without it when she'd faced Goodman made her pause, then examine the weapons with more serious interest. She was certain to be in more than a little danger from time to time in her pursuit of the unscrupulous clergyman—why not have some basic protection, at least? She supposed Hawk would disapprove, but she was paying him, wasn't she? He'd just have to go along with her decision in the matter.

When she left the trading post, she carried a brand new Colt .45 and ammunition, wrapped in brown paper. She assured the storekeeper that she was buying the gun as a gift for her brother, then ignored his dubious look when she insisted he show her how to load and fire the weapon. Goodman was not going to catch her unprepared the next time.

There were only a few people on the street as she hastened down the boardwalk toward the livery stable.

Most of them spoke in friendly fashion, but several turned to stare after her with frankly curious appraisal. It wasn't often a young and unchaperoned lady was seen on the streets of a rough sawmill town that virtually hugged the Canadian border.

But, Irony reminded herself, *this is 1896 — not the rowdy days of the Old West. If I care to travel alone, it's certainly my prerogative.*

And yet, from time to time, she shifted the bulky package she carried, just to hear the reassuring rattle of the paper — and her eyes darted here and there, searching for Hawk's tall, distinctive figure. Apparently, he was still inside the stables. Taking a determined breath, Irony made the decision to storm one more male stronghold.

She pushed open a small side door and stepped into the building, pausing to let her eyes adjust to the gloom. Just as she saw Hawk come out of the office, counting a roll of bills, she heard a deep voice grate out an ominous greeting.

"Hey! You there, Indian."

Irony watched as Hawk came to a halt, quickly tucking the money into his back pocket. The figures of three men emerged from the darkness and positioned themselves around him. "How may I help you gentlemen?" Hawk asked calmly, but his eyes were warily assessing the situation.

"Where'd you git them horses you jist sold to Jake? No Injun around here owns horses . . ." The man who spoke looked like a blacksmith, and though Hawk was large, the stranger was half again as big.

"I'm not from around here," Hawk informed him, his voice still calm.

"Don't git smart with us," spoke up a second man, a tall, stringy-looking fellow with a bewhiskered jaw. "Where'd you git them animals?"

"That, my good man, is none of your concern."

Hawk took a step forward, and the men closed ranks, allowing him no further passage.

"I say you probably stole 'em," the third man challenged. He was stocky, with the beefy build of a professional pugilist. Irony swallowed deeply—Hawk was in trouble, and she didn't know what to do to assist him. Briefly she considered going for help, but the one thing she had not seen along the streets of War Road was a sheriff's office. She couldn't afford to waste valuable time seeking aid that might be non-existent in the first place.

"Is that right, Injun? Did you steal them horses?"

Hawk remained silent, his face settling into cold, stern lines as he anticipated the next move his assailants would make.

"Let's see how much money ole Jake paid ya," the first man said, holding out a grubby hand.

"Yeah—we're takin' up a collection." The tall man snickered, looking from one of his companions to the other. "Fer us. Right, boys?"

"Right. But, what the hell, Injun, we're not selfish. We'll leave ya enough to buy a couple of bottles of firewater. You redskins don't need much of anythin' else. Ain't that so?"

"Right now I need for you to get out of my way and let me pass," Hawk said with quiet deliberation.

"No Injun is gonna talk to me that way," the brawny man snarled.

The owner of the livery stable poked his head through the open doorway of his office. "What's goin' on out here? You fellows leave the man alone, why don't you? I ain't needin' no trouble. . . ."

"Shut up, Jake. You know we don't let thieves run loose in our town. Soon as this brave hands over the money you paid him, we'll let him go on his way."

Jake withdrew into his office and was promptly forgotten.

"Yeah—how about it, Redskin?"

"If you want the money, you'll have to take it," Hawk stated flatly.

Great God Almighty, Irony thought, her nervous hands already tearing at the paper covering the gun she carried. *Hawk, you're a madman!*

Fortunately, none of the men were aware of Irony's presence near the doorway. She sank to her knees behind a pile of straw and ripped at the paper in earnest. When the ivory-handled revolver was freed from its wrappings, she tried feverishly to recall the storekeeper's instructions about loading it. She had to lay the gun aside to open the box of ammunition, and then she jammed the shells into the cylinder with shaking fingers. The new mechanism was stiff, and it took considerable strength to pull back the hammer, but finally, Irony scrambled to her feet, the revolver held in both hands, the barrel wavering noticeably. This was no mock, dramatic display meant to frighten—this was a real and deadly dangerous moment. She had to save Hawk from these men who obviously meant him great harm.

She heard the thud of a fist on flesh, followed by a muffled groan, and her horrified eyes flew to Hawk. Was she too late? But no, he stood there, breathing heavily, both fists clenched and ready. At his feet was the crumpled body of the first man who had spoken, the one who looked like a blacksmith. His mouth bleeding, he raised himself on his elbow.

"Kill the son-of-a-bitch," he ordered harshly, and his companions began moving closer to the intended victim. Warily, Hawk watched both of them, trying to determine which would make the initial attack.

The beefy man made a sudden lunge, and when Hawk sidestepped to avoid his flying fists, the second man flung himself on Hawk's back. Winding his arms through Hawk's, he hampered him sufficiently for the other fellow to land a crippling blow to the Indian's midsection.

As Hawk doubled over in pain, Irony gave a small, distressed cry and leveled her gun. "Stop it!" she ordered in a surprisingly firm voice. "Step away from that man and put your hands into the air."

Startled, both did as they were told, but after a quick study of the slight, trembling woman who held the Colt revolver, the first man began to chuckle. "Well, well. Will you lookee here? The pretty lady has a big, bad gun."

"Yeah," sneered his cohort. "Ain't that scary?"

Even Irony had to admit that the Colt was an incongruous sight gripped by her small hand with its birthstone ring and neatly manicured nails.

The big man heaved himself up off the floor of the barn and took a step toward Irony. "Now we ain't about to let no little girl hold a gun on us, honey," he warned.

"Irony, for God's sake," exclaimed Hawk. "Will you get the hell out of here?"

"And let them kill you?" she blazed, waving the gun at the huge man who was still slowly advancing on her. "You — get back! I'll shoot if you come one step closer."

"I don't think you will." He laughed, showing broken and yellowed teeth. "I reckon I can walk sight up to you and take that shiny new toy outa yer hands . . ."

That had happened to her once, and Irony wasn't about to let it happen a second time. "Then think again," she said and pulled the trigger. The shot went wild, barely grazing the man's temple.

"Lord God, she shot me!" he screamed, falling to his knees. His friends dived for cover, leaving Hawk standing alone, looking incredulous. The impact from firing the shot was strong enough to toss Irony backward, causing her to land on her derriere so jarringly that she raised a cloud of dust. She blinked twice, her eyes as round as saucers.

"Grab her gun," yelled the injured man, blood running down the side of his face. He staggered toward her, and Irony scrambled to her feet. Before she could raise her weapon a second time, Hawk threw himself at the man, seizing him around the knees to trip him.

The man came up fighting, snorting like an enraged bull. "Run, Irony," Hawk panted, dodging a blow.

"No!" she replied stubbornly, swinging the Colt back and forth as she tried to find the right target. "Hawk, will you hold still?"

"And let him pulverize me?"

The figure of the tall, thin man came hurtling out of the shadows to join the fray, and Irony chewed her bottom lip in consternation. How could she ever hope to aid Hawk? If she fired now, she'd most likely kill him!

"All right, that's enough!" The new voice rang through the building with authority. Jake, the owner of the stable, stepped out of his office with a double-barreled shotgun in his hands. "I told you I don't want no trouble, and I meant it. Now, let the Indian up."

The men gauged their chances of defying Jake, but finally decided he and his shotgun had the upper hand. Reluctantly, they got to their feet and moved away from Hawk. He sat up and favored the stableman with a crooked grin. "Much obliged."

"Yer welcome. Jist take the lady and git the blazes outa here. I'll send these buzzards packing in about ten minutes . . ."

"That'll give us plenty of time to leave town," Hawk assured him. He reached out and took Irony's arm. "Come on, let's go."

"Wait, let me get my package." She scooped up the

brown paper which still contained the ammunition and a gun belt, then hastily followed Hawk.

Once they were outside the door, he turned to her with a furious glare. "Irony, don't you ever try to save me again."

"Why not?"

"I had that situation under control. I didn't need to be rescued — I didn't want to be rescued."

She glared back. "Now you know how I felt this morning!"

"That was entirely different. You needed help, I didn't."

"Is that why you were facedown in the dust with two vicious animals pummeling you?"

"I was not facedown in the dust . . ." He shook his head. "Oh, damnation, what difference does it make? We don't have time to stand here arguing."

"And that's another thing," she cried. "Why are you letting those . . . those bullies run us out of town? I wanted to sleep in a real bed tonight."

"Give me that." Hawk took the gunbelt and buckled it around his hips. Then, taking the gun, he shoved it into the holster and tore open the box of shells. He stuffed what he could into his pockets and instructed her to put the rest in the dusty reticule which dangled from her wrist. "We're not leaving town. Come on."

"Where are we going?"

"To supper."

"To supper? Now?"

"I told you, I'm looking forward to a good, home-cooked meal."

"But those men . . ."

"Will probably go on about their business. Anyway, they can't do much to us in a crowded dining hall, and we'll sit in the rear with our backs to the wall."

"The one I shot — will he be okay?"

"Madder than hell, but otherwise okay."

Irony allowed Hawk to propel her toward the Northwoods dining hall, and the closer they got to it, the more the delicious aromas convinced her his plan of having a meal was a sound one. Only a few curious glances followed them as they made their way past the front tables to one in a shadowy corner.

Thirty minutes later, when their meal was served, the men from the stable had not made an appearance, so Irony gladly forgot about them and turned her attention to the ironstone plate heaped with food. Moose steaks, fried potatoes and onions, and green beans cooked with chunks of ham were served with light biscuits and maple syrup. Just as Irony thought she couldn't eat another bite, the waitress brought them slices of dried apple pie, and remembering their meals on the trail, she wielded her fork with renewed enthusiasm.

The dim light of a kerosene lantern cast shadows over the red-checked tablecloth and created an intimate, cozy atmosphere. Irony's irritation with Hawk had faded and now she glanced up, prepared to make a lively comment about the next day's journey by train. She was startled to find him watching her, his obsidian eyes unreadable over the rim of his coffee mug. Suddenly, she felt awkward and shy, ashamed of her voracious appetite and completely convinced she had, once again, overstepped the boundaries of delicate womanhood.

"I . . . I was hungrier than I thought," she half-whispered, her tone apologetic.

"Don't feel you need to make amends to me, Irony," Hawk said. He put down his cup, but his eyes never left hers. "I like to see a female with a healthy . . . appetite."

She couldn't help it, she blushed. Every iota of irritation came flooding back. The man was impossible! He could take an ordinary statement and turn it into something lascivious.

Irony's fork clanked against the empty dish. "Would you mind walking me to the rooming house? I'm very tired."

"It will be my pleasure."

"Oh . . . Ma Flannagan doesn't rent to . . . to . . ."

"Indians. I know."

"You can't go back to the stables."

"Don't worry," he assured her. "I'll find somewhere to sleep."

The streets were quiet, with the only light and noise emanating from the saloon at one end of town. To her relief, Irony saw that the men who had attacked Hawk were nowhere to be seen. He escorted her to the front door of Flannagan's and, with the faintest suggestion of a smile, disappeared into the darkness.

Irony had just finished putting on her long white nightgown and was unbraiding her hair when she heard a sharp tap at the window. Her hands froze in mid-air and she whirled to stare at the black glass. Had the men from the stable found her after all? Had they come to settle the score? She frowned as she recalled that her new gun was strapped quite securely to Hawk's narrow hip. Perhaps he didn't mean to, but the man caused her no end of trouble—and always at the worst possible time.

The rapping came again, along with an impatient whisper. "Irony—let me in."

"Hawk?"

She crossed the room on bare feet and leaned close to the glass, peering out. Hawk's strong-featured face was looking back at her.

"Will you open this damned thing?"

Irony undid the latch and pushed the window upward. "What do you want?" she demanded.

Hawk was crouching on the roof, shielded from

view by the high false front of the rooming house. He cast a quick glance over his shoulder, then climbed through the window into her bedroom. He shut the window, locked it and drew the drapes.

"Is someone after you?" Irony questioned.

"Not just yet. But I happened to catch sight of our friends hanging around by the stable and decided it might be safer to avoid them."

"But what do you intend to do?"

Hawk turned his intense black gaze on her, and suddenly Irony was all too aware of her thin nightgown, her loosened hair. She swallowed audibly and took a tentative step backward. Inwardly she cursed him for the amusement that glimmered deep within his eyes.

"It can't be helped," he said quietly. "I'm going to have to sleep with you tonight."

Chapter Six

Ma Flannagan's rooming house . . .

"You are not sleeping in my bed," Irony exclaimed. "I won't allow it, do you hear?"

"I hear. But, as usual, you wrong me. I brought my bedroll. . . ."

"Oh." Irony had the grace to look abashed. "Well, in that case—I mean, of course there's no difficulty, then."

Hawk tossed the blankets into one corner and crossed to the door to check the lock. Satisfied, he turned back to Irony, who was hastily stuffing her clean underwear into her carpetbag. Aware he was watching her, her hands stilled.

The room suddenly seemed too small, too quiet. The only sounds were their breathing and the low hiss of the kerosene lamp on the dresser. No wind rattled the window panes, no street noises drifted up to disturb the absolute intimacy of the moment.

Something dark and dangerous sprang into Hawk's eyes as he studied her, and though she couldn't know it, he was remembering the anguish he'd felt watching her bathe in the river. It wasn't the first time he'd been alone with a woman in her bedroom—it was just the first time he'd been alone with a lady. His inherent respect for Irony warred with his desire to reach out for her. Hawk stood quietly, waiting to see what she would do.

Life with her aunts had certainly never prepared her for this situation. Irony crossed her arms over her bosom and tried to look at ease, even though Hawk's steady gaze was thoroughly unnerving her. She had endured many scrutinies in her lifetime—as a child, she'd had to undergo Aunt Alyce's stringent inspections every morning before school to make sure she'd washed behind her ears or that her shoes weren't scuffed; later, she'd been under Aunt Tiny's watchful eye as she made a concentrated effort to learn even a portion of the knowledge Valentine had gained at finishing school. She'd alternately cowered and blossomed beneath the admiring glances of several young men in Thief River Falls, but never—absolutely never—had she been subjected to anything like the searing appraisal in Raphael Hawkes' eyes. She felt as though the black flames stirring within those eyes were slowly, steadily burning away the layer of thin cotton that covered her, leaving her naked and vulnerable . . . and very, very confused.

She hated Indians, didn't she? And besides that, wasn't Hawk the most troublesome man she'd ever met? Why then did she keep wondering how it would feel if he touched her? She cleared her throat and tried to think of something mundane and normal to say, but the imagined heat of his fingers against her neck rose in her mind and choked the words back. Nervously she moistened her lips, and for the first time, saw Hawk shift slightly, as though something had made him impatient . . . or restless.

The lamplight cast slanted shadows across his face, but Irony could see the faint tightening of his jaw. She ordinarily would have assumed she'd irritated him somehow, but the look in his eyes was not one of annoyance. It was, rather, an unmistakably heated caress.

Hawk unbuckled the gun belt, never taking his eyes from hers, and dropped it onto the only chair in the room.

"Irony," he murmured and took a step toward her.

She briefly considered running, but there was no place to go. She loosened her arms, putting up her hands as if to ward him off. Hawk came closer.

Just as her fingers made contact with the softness of his shirt, which barely masked the hardness of his chest beneath, Hawk reached out a hand and took hold of the high, lace collar of her nightgown. Irony flattened her palms against his chest, thinking to protest his action—but becoming intrigued by the rapid hammering of his heart, instead.

Hawk undid the collar, laying it open to expose her neck and the beginning curve of one shoulder. He deliberately stroked his thumb across the thrumming pulse at the base of her throat, increasing its tempo and filling Irony with a delicious unsteadiness. Swiftly, he bent and laid his lips over the spot where his thumb had been. His kiss was moist and burning, jolting her right to the soles of her bare feet. He drew back and looked at her, his expression somewhat dismayed.

Just then the intense mood was shattered by a sharp knock at the door, and Hawk and Irony leaped apart to stare guiltily at each other.

"Miss McBride?" came a female voice. "It's Ma Flannagan. I'm needin' to talk to you fer a minute."

"Damn," Hawk swore.

"Oh, good Lord," Irony gasped. "She can't find you here. Quick, hide under the bed."

Hawk gave her a disdainful look. "I'd prefer to step into the closet, if you don't mind."

"Just hurry," she hissed, before speaking in a louder tone. "I'm coming, Mrs. Flannagan."

As soon as Hawk had disappeared from sight, she

unlocked the door and opened it. "You'll have to excuse my night clothes . . ."

The door was pushed open to admit four men — Reverend Josiah Goodman and the Indians who had traveled with him from Sweetwater. Ma Flannagan stood in the hallway, her narrow face reflecting her unhappiness.

"I'm sorry, Miss — but yer brother insisted he had to speak with ya."

"My . . . brother?" Irony exclaimed.

"Yes, sister dear," Goodman growled, gripping her arm painfully. "I have a message from our loving parents." With a barely disguised smirk, Goodman turned to Three-Fingers. "Escort Mrs. Flannagan downstairs and keep her company until I'm through here."

Ma Flannagan looked as though she would like to protest, but didn't dare. "Go on, good lady," the reverend prompted. "This business with my sister won't take long, and as soon as we've had our little talk, I'll take my men and be gone. I know how you feel about having savages in your establishment."

The landlady, clearly upset, gathered the remnants of her courage. "Are ya . . . is everythin' all right, Miss McBride?"

Irony contemplated telling the truth — that everything was far from satisfactory. She considered screaming at the woman to run for help, and then she realized the futility of such an action. Mrs. Flannagan could never escape the Indian, and there was no real reason to involve her in the situation. Perhaps it would be best if she left, taking Three-Fingers with her. At least that way she and Hawk would only have three men to battle.

"Everything is fine, don't worry. I'll see you in the morning."

"Very well."

Reluctantly, the thin woman started down the hall, accompanied by the Indian. At the top of the stairs she looked back over her shoulder, and Irony gave her a reassuring smile. When the landlady had gone, Reverend Goodman closed the door and stepped in front of it.

"Well, Irony, my dear, I know you must be delighted to see me again."

"Hardly," she snapped, jerking her arm free. "What do you want?"

"I believe you have something that belongs to me." Suddenly the man's gaze fell upon the gunbelt laying on the chair and, setting down the valise he carried, he picked up the weapon. His small, pale eyes assessed the room, and he nodded at Running Dog, who moved into position by the closet door, knife in hand.

"That's my gun," Irony bluffed. "Put it down."

Goodman raised a gingery eyebrow. "Yours? Now, what would a well-bred young lady like yourself be doing with a gun?"

"A woman traveling alone has to have some sort of protection."

He smiled nastily. "I'm shocked at how easily you've taken to lying, Irony."

"Lying?" she faltered.

"Tell me, why would a woman traveling alone have need of two suitcases and a bedroll? No, I'm very much afraid your aunts would be utterly devastated to learn that you'd locked yourself into a hotel room with a man."

"There's no man here . . ."

Goodman seized her arm, twisting it behind her back with such force that she cried out. Cursing, Hawk burst forth from the closet, only to find himself facing the knife-wielding Indian. His fists clenched as he gathered himself for an attack, but

Goodman's next words stopped him cold.

"Make one move, and I'll kill Miss McBride."

The click of the Colt's hammer was loud in the ensuing silence, and Irony tensed as she felt the chilly metal of the barrel against her temple. Hawk sighed in frustration, but didn't make any further move.

Goodman's gaze narrowed as he sized up his adversary. "You're not who I expected . . . say, you look familiar. Who are you?"

"Raphael Hawkes. I'm a teacher at Sweetwater."

"Hell, yes. That's where I've seen you. But what are you doing in the company of Miss McBride?"

"It seemed we had a mutual objective," Hawk replied easily. "To find you."

"For what purpose?"

"I think you know Irony's reasons. Mine have to do with Bessie Sparks' murder."

"Oh?" Brief surprise showed in Goodman's eyes.

"Where are the rest of your men? There were four with you at Sweetwater, weren't there?"

"That's none of your concern, Hawkes." Goodman lightly tapped the gun barrel against Irony's temple. "So you're the one who helped Irony escape? It seems I have a real score to settle with you then. I don't like being smoked out like a common criminal."

"I see your point," Hawk remarked. "After all, you're not just a common criminal, are you? In fact, I'd say a man who hides behind the Bible and perpetrates his acts of villainy in the guise of a man of God is quite an *uncommon* criminal."

"I don't have to listen to your insults," warned Goodman. "One more word from you and your charming companion here will be splattered all over this room."

Irony caught Hawk's gaze and willed him to feel her apprehension. Something about the cold prod of steel convinced her the reverend wasn't making idle talk. Hawk inclined his head in acquiescence and fell silent.

"Good—you mean to cooperate. A wise decision, I assure you. Now, Irony, let's see if you plan to be as biddable."

Goodman gave her a shove, sending her stumbling against the bed. Hawk took a step, then halted as Running Dog jabbed the knife at his face.

"What do you want?" Irony mumbled, already knowing the answer.

"I want what you stole from me," Goodman answered.

Irony drew herself up. "That jewelry belongs to my aunt! How could you dare insinuate I stole it from you?"

"Jewelry?" Hawk sputtered. "You took jewelry from him?"

Irony's stubborn chin rose several inches. "It belonged to me and my family. Taking it back wasn't stealing."

"But for God's sake, why didn't you tell me you had it?" he raged.

"Was it any of your business?"

"It was. My God, woman, had I known you'd done such a stupid thing, I could have been prepared for this. You should have realized Goodman wouldn't waste any time trying to get it back."

"You assured me he would go directly to the lake," she reminded him.

"Yes, but that was before I knew you had the damned jewelry."

"Enough!" broke in Goodman. "I want the jewels . . . now!" He gestured with the gun and, a mutinous look on her face, Irony picked up her carpetbag. Opening it, she started taking out Aunt Valentine's jewelry and laying it on the bed.

"Good Jesus Christ," Hawk swore. "Irony, you're the

craziest woman I've ever met."

"Quiet," growled Goodman. "Dump this stuff in my valise," he instructed Running Dog, "so we can get out of here."

"What about them?" the Indian asked, ignoring Irony's gasp as he carelessly tossed the antique jewelry into Goodman's case. "We kill them?"

"Hardly, you fool. If we kill them, we'd have to kill the landlady, too. Or are you too stupid to realize she could identify us? As could any number of people who saw us arrive in town." He took a long, considering look at Irony. "No, we can't kill them. We can only inconvenience them for a time."

"You're not being very smart, Goodman," Hawk declared. "Maybe you should kill us . . ."

"Hawk!" Irony cried. "What are you saying?"

"Don't tempt me, man," Goodman said. "And don't suppose that just because I don't kill you tonight that I won't someday. We'll meet again, rest assured . . . and when we do, circumstances may be such that I can dispose of you both."

"With no one to see," Broken Knife added, a huge grin splitting his homely face.

"Then what do you intend to do with us now?" Irony ventured.

"Don't look so worried, my dear." Goodman laughed. "This should hardly be painful at all."

Hawk and Irony exchanged wary glances.

"Tie them up," the reverend suddenly ordered. "You first, Hawkes."

Running Dog grunted and took a rope from the reverend's valise, careful not to turn his back on Hawk.

"But why would you tie us up?" Irony whispered.

"To prevent you from going to the authorities, of course. I need a little time to make certain I'm well clear of War Road."

"But what's to prevent us from shouting for help?" she asked. At the disgusted look Hawk flung her, Irony immediately realized the foolishness of her question.

"I had planned on gags," Goodman replied, clearly enjoying himself. "But since you mentioned it . . . perhaps I should do something a bit more original."

"Gags will do fine," Irony assured him.

"Oh, no. No, no, no . . . we must do better than that, mustn't we, boys? Let me see . . ."

"Look, why don't you bind and gag us, then get the hell out of here?" asked Hawk.

"Too simple." Goodman's fleshy face broke into a cherubic smile. "I've got it! Take off your clothes, Mr. Hawkes."

"Now, just a damned minute . . ." Hawk began.

Running Dog laid the knife against Hawk's neck and Irony cried out as she saw blood begin to well along the blade.

"For heavens' sake," she gasped. "Do what he says!"

"What's the purpose of this?" Hawk demanded, though his fingers had already moved to unbutton his shirt. "Are you merely trying to humiliate us?"

Goodman threw back his leonine head and laughed again, merrily. For the first time, Irony saw something of the engaging demeanor that had attracted so many unsuspecting women. Josiah Goodman was not an imposing figure of a man, to be sure, but there was a presence about him, an air of calm authority. He was only average in height and tending toward stoutness, but his full head of ginger hair, liberally laced with silver, and his burning gray eyes gave him an aura of power. An almost fanatic gleam filled those eyes, giving them a mesmerizing effect, and she realized that he knew how to use it to his own benefit. Entrapped by his magnetism, any lonely woman could easily fall victim to his spell.

"Humiliation seems a worthwhile goal," Goodman agreed, "considering the inconvenience to which you've put me. It amuses me to think of the two of you spending the night bound together . . . naked."

"Naked?" Irony all but shrieked. "Both of us?"

"Can you think of a better way to discourage you from yelling for help?" Goodman's entire body shook with mirth. "Imagine the sour-faced Mrs. Flannagan charging in here to discover the two of you — as bare as the day you were born — in one of her very respectable beds! Why, the scandal would follow you clear back to Thief River, my dear."

Hawk's shirt dropped to the floor, and his hands paused at his belt buckle. "Leave her out of this, Goodman. There's no need to subject her to your perverted humor."

Running Dog twisted the knife blade and fresh blood began to flow. "No talk," he warned. "Unless you want to die."

"Or want your pretty companion to die," Goodman added, brandishing the Colt revolver once again. "It wouldn't suit my plans to kill her now, but never doubt that I'll do it if it becomes necessary. So — shuck those pants and get on the bed."

"Damn your eyes," Hawk muttered, but after kicking off his boots, he undid the metal buttons on his Levis and dropped them onto the carpet. Irony snapped her eyes shut, but the brief glimpse she had of his nudity was burned into her brain forever.

Releasing Irony but still brandishing the gun, Goodman moved to the bed and stripped back the covers.

"Right here, Mr. Hawkes. Stretch out and be comfortable. Running Dog, tie him to the bed railing."

Irony refused to watch, but even with her eyes tightly closed, she could envision the scene. She heard Hawk's muffled footsteps, the creak of the bedsprings, the rasp of the rope and a mumbled curse.

"Oh, too tight?" purred Goodman, laughter in his voice. "How unfortunate. But you see, Mr. Hawkes, it's entirely necessary to keep you from being able to undo those knots the moment we're gone."

"Not get loose from these knots," Running Dog announced with satisfaction, giving the rope at Hawk's ankles a vicious tug.

"Good. Very well, Irony, it's your turn."

Her eyes flew open, though she avoided looking at the man on the bed. "Wh-what do you mean? Surely you can't . . . ?"

"Oh, but I do. Off with the nightgown, my dear, so you can join your friend in bed."

"I won't do it," she said quietly.

"You will."

"For God's sake," fumed Hawk. "Leave her a little dignity, can't you? It will be scandalous enough for her to be found with me. There's no need for her to be unclothed, too."

"Do you want to spoil my fun, Mr. Hawkes?"

"What kind of fiend are you?" Irony blazed, knowing her question was unwise, but unable to stop her mouth from saying the words.

"Don't rile me," Goodman calmly suggested. "Just get undressed."

Irony glared at him. "Then your courtship of my aunt was a complete hoax?" she asked quietly. "You had no kind feelings toward her at all?"

"I don't see what it has to do with anything, but Valentine was a fetching twit. One of my more successful engagements, to be sure."

"If you have any fondness for her at all, think how she would receive the news that I had been found naked . . . with . . ." Irony drew a deep breath. "With a strange man. It would appall her."

The reverend chuckled. "Ah, yes, poor Valentine

would have palpitations for a week." His smile faded and his gray eyes narrowed. "But you're a meddler, Irony, and you deserve this kind of treatment."

He stepped closer to her. "Now, the nightgown . . ." Moving with a swiftness that took her by surprise, Goodman hooked one hand into the neck of her gown and gave it a vicious yank. The soft cotton tore easily, leaving a gaping rend halfway to the hem.

Irony opened her mouth to scream, but Goodman lifted a hand to strike her. "Silence!" he commanded. "Or I'll tear it completely off."

Running Dog guffawed loudly, obviously delighted with the scene. A certain insanity seemed to lurk in his deep-set black eyes, and when he put his hand on Irony's sleeve, she made no protest. She had come to the conclusion that it would be best if Goodman and his men accomplished their mission and left.

As the Indian shoved her toward the bed, Irony once again closed her eyes, hoping to give Hawk, lying naked and trussed, some measure of dignity and preserve what was left of her own. However, when Running Dog pushed her down onto the mattress, one hand instinctively reached out to break her fall and her fingers encountered warm skin. She sprawled across Hawk's chest, her horrified green eyes staring into his emotionless black ones.

"I-I'm sorry," she stammered, snatching away the hand that had fallen onto his bare hip.

Roughly, Running Dog seized her arm and dragged her onto her back, though he left only inches of space between her body and Hawks'. As he circled her wrists with tight loops of rope, she bit her lip to keep from crying out. Like Hawk's, her arms were pulled over her head and lashed to the slats of the headboard, although he did not secure her feet.

"That will hold the squaw," Running Dog said proudly. "No get away tonight."

Irony could feel the anger humming through Hawk's body, and she prayed that he would say nothing to further infuriate the villainous Goodman, but she knew it was taking a huge effort for him to remain silent.

Goodman eyed them speculatively. "I don't know," he said slowly, "it just seems to me that you're getting off too lightly. Perhaps I should . . ."

There was a furtive tapping at the door, then Three-Fingers pushed it open and stepped into the room. "Men come now."

"What men?" Goodman questioned.

"Not know — maybe live here."

"Well, I suppose there's no sense in taking any more risks," the reverend muttered. He pointed a finger at Hawk and Irony. "Be glad I don't have time to linger. But know that, if you continue your ill-advised pursuit of me, I will quickly lose any tendency toward charity. Next time we meet, you may find yourselves stripped naked and tied to anthills. Running Dog and Three-Fingers remember the old ways of torture quite well."

Three-Fingers' smile broadened as he caught a glimpse of Irony's nearly naked breasts, and chuckling, he advanced toward the bed, a hand outstretched.

"There's no time for that." Goodman jerked his head toward the door. "Let's get out of here." Though they grumbled, Three Fingers and his companions reluctantly obeyed. The preacher paused on the threshold long enough to add a final word. "Enjoy your night together . . . and remember, the next time we meet, there'll be no mercy — no matter how much you whine about your Aunt Tiny's sensitivities." With that he shut the door securely, and they could hear his footsteps echo along the hallway and down the stairs.

"I did not whine," Irony snapped, her eyes fixed on

the stained ceiling overhead.

It was silent for a moment, and then Hawk laughed. "What an enigma you are, Irony McBride. Tied to a bed with a naked man, and all you can worry about is that someone accused you of whining. How did you manage to come by such pride?"

She sniffed, still refusing to look at him. "It wasn't something I sought, believe me. My . . . pride, as you call it, was forced upon me by circumstances."

"I see." He heaved a weary sigh. "Well, it looks as if it may stand you in good stead before this night is done."

"What do you mean? Are you saying that we're . . . we're not going to be able to free ourselves?"

"That's precisely what I'm saying. Every time we move, these bonds are only going to cut more deeply, and the rope won't slacken at all."

"That . . . that devil Indian!" she muttered. Then quickly, "I'm sorry. I promised myself that I would make no more disparaging remarks about your people."

"Make all the disparaging remarks you wish about those three," Hawk said with amusement. "I do not number them among my people."

"Calling them names isn't going to help our cause. Are you sure we can't work free?" She gave an experimental tug of her arms and winced at the bite of the rope.

"I'll try, Irony, but it doesn't look promising. At least they didn't gag us."

"If only Running Dog had been as inefficient with his knots," she said dryly.

For the next five minutes, Hawk did his best to loosen his bonds. Irony tried to ignore the soft bumping of his body against hers as he struggled and twisted. She concentrated on shutting her ears to his occasional grunts of pain, telling herself he was

110

strong, he could withstand it . . . that it would be worth a bit of suffering if only he could set them free.

"It's no use," he said at last, despair in his voice. "We're going to have to shout for help."

"No."

"I know it will be degrading for you, Irony . . . but there's no other way. Besides, if we can get loose right away, maybe I can track Goodman down before he gets too far out of town."

"Very well," she whispered, before she could have second thoughts, "Let's get it over with." Being found like this would be the most shameful moment of her life. How did she keep getting into these impossible situations?

On cue, both Hawk and Irony began yelling for Ma Flannagan and, when she didn't answer, for anyone within earshot. Irony screamed until her throat was raw and her voice hoarse.

"No one heard us," she moaned. "What are we going to do?"

"Let's rest awhile, then try again. Surely there are boarders—maybe the men Three-Fingers mentioned will hear us."

Although Hawk did not reveal his fear that Goodman had, in some way, incapacitated Mrs. Flannagan, he couldn't imagine why else the woman would not have heard their frantic calls.

They fell silent for a time, and Irony tried to think about anything except the fact that Raphael Hawkes was lying beside her as bare as the day he was born. Each time he moved, the mattress dipped alarmingly, and she steeled herself to keep from rolling against him. She watched the shadows that danced across the ceiling, staring until her eyes ached, refusing to add to Hawk's discomfiture by indicating one iota of awareness. After all, matters couldn't be any less mortifying for him.

111

"Irony," Hawk eventually said, "do you think you could manage to pull the sheet over us? It might afford us a bit more . . . modesty if and when we're discovered."

"I'll try." She hooked one foot into the roll of sheeting wadded at the end of the bed and gave a hearty kick. The worn linen material fell limply into place around her ankle. Sliding as far down in the bed as her bonds would allow, Irony made a second attempt, again to no avail.

"Try to kick your foot a bit higher," Hawk instructed.

Irony bit back a sarcastic reply — even if she pointed out that it was difficult to concentrate on the task at hand and keep her eyes averted from his nudity, he would no doubt condemn her as a prude. Gathering her strength, she tried again, her body bucking with the effort she made to kick the sheet higher.

Hawk cursed himself for the foolhardy suggestion the instant he saw the length of slender thigh revealed when Irony's nightgown slid upward along her leg. Lord, they had been in enough of a predicament as it was. Any constructive thinking he might have done had already been disrupted by the sight of her in the thin batiste nightgown — now he was sorely tempted to forget calling for help and simply enjoy the pleasure of lying beside her.

Irony, horrified to realize that her legs were exposed, ordered tersely, "Close your eyes, Hawk — I'm going to try again."

He obeyed, albeit reluctantly, and she kicked out with renewed vigor. On the third try, she managed to flip a corner of the sheet high enough to settle over their hips. Exhausted, she muttered, "There, that's the best I can do. If that's not decorous enough for you, I'm sorry."

"It's fine, Irony," he soothed. "You may have just

saved Ma Flannagan from apoplexy when she takes the time to come looking for us."

They lay side by side for ten long minutes, each agonizingly conscious of the other. With every breath that Irony drew, she caught Hawk's scent. He still carried the smell of straw from the stable — an earthy, sun-warmed odor — but he also smelled of leather and soap and something more . . . some vaguely disturbing, masculine aroma that spoke of all the things she was trying to keep out of her mind. She made an attempt to control her thoughts by reviewing the events of the day and admitting that she really couldn't blame Hawk for their latest dilemma.

"I'm sorry about all this," she said suddenly. "I should have told you about the jewelry, only . . ."

"You weren't sure you could trust me," he finished. "I understand. Besides, you're not entirely to blame. I should have expected the reverend to follow us here. I let myself become . . . uh, distracted. By that incident at the stables, I mean."

"Yes, of course. And I was so enthralled at the thought of a real bed . . ." Irony broke off as she realized what she was saying. Somehow, the very word conjured up all manner of improper thoughts. Flustered, she asked, "Should we try yelling for help again?"

"Might as well." Hawk was glad for any distraction. The sweet, floral scent of her lying beside him was pure torture. He kept having thoughts of what it might be like to really share a bed with her — and those thoughts were generating physical changes he'd rather not have Irony notice. She'd had enough shocks for one night, and he was fairly certain a girl raised by matronly aunts would not have had much experience with the more carnal side of a man's nature.

As before, no one responded to their cries and eventually, they abandoned the effort. Irony turned to

113

Hawk to express her opinion that they might as well wait until morning, when her gaze fell to the edge of the sheet and the area of tanned skin it covered. A feathering of black hair swirled around his navel and disappeared into thicker, darker, curlier hair just skimmed by the linen. Surprised because she had always heard Indians did not have body hair, Irony took another quick look. Suddenly realizing exactly what the sheet hid from her, she blushed furiously and looked away.

It was both alarming and stimulating to think that her nearness to Hawk had affected him in . . . that way. The very thought filled her with curiosity, but she doggedly pushed it aside, dredging up an obligatory feeling of shame. What was there about this man that brought out such reprehensible behavior in her, she wondered. Was it the primitive savagery inherent in his ancestry that somehow called out to a corresponding instinct in her? Did every human alive have similar impulses when faced with a situation like this? Would any woman forced into such intimate company find herself wondering what it would be like to . . . ? Irony felt another scalding blush wash over her face and swiftly moved her eyes upward. This time they fixed on an ugly bruise along his ribcage.

"Oh, Hawk, that bruise! It must be so painful." She recalled that he had been attacked twice that evening, and with the memory, came a deeper remorse. "No doubt your life was simpler before you encountered me."

His smile was crooked. "Simpler, but not nearly so adventurous," he murmured. His soft, dark eyes met and held hers and the smile slowly faded. Hawk knew she must have seen the rather obvious signs of his arousal, but he couldn't seem to discipline that response anymore than he could discipline his gaze, which persisted on following the enticing line of Irony's bosom. The position of her arms seemed to thrust her breasts forward in bold invitation, leaving their rounded inner sides bared to his sight, the darker crests making provocative shadows beneath the thin cloth. He could imagine smoothing his fingers over her softness, could imagine the sensation of her nipples thrusting against his palms. The very thought sent a spasm of desire twisting through him. Would that his hands were free . . .

Irony swallowed hard, sensing Hawk's agitation. How on earth were they ever going to get through the night?

"Do you . . . ?" She thought rapidly. "That poem you were reciting yesterday . . . the one about the Indian, Hiawatha. I'd like to hear more . . . if you don't mind passing the time that way."

He seemed relieved. "No, I don't mind."

Irony pulled her gaze from his and concentrated on the ceiling again. After a short pause, Hawk's deep, rich voice filled the room.

"Ye whose hearts are fresh and simple.
Who have faith in God and Nature,
Who believe, that in all ages
Every human heart is human,
That in even savage bosoms
There are longings, yearnings, strivings
For the good they comprehend not,
That the feeble hands and helpless,
Groping blindly in the darkness,
Touch God's right hand in that darkness
And are lifted up and strengthened,
Listen to this simple story,
To this song of Hiawatha!"

Long after his voice had stilled, they lay awake thinking. Hawk pondered the longings and yearnings of his savage bosom, and Irony contemplated the absolutely essential need to pray for strength to deny the temptation presented by the darkly beautiful man beside her.

Chapter Seven

On the train to Rainy River . . .

A shout from the street below awakened Hawk the next morning and, for a few moments, he lay quietly, savoring the strange feeling of peace that seemed to fill his soul. Then, quite suddenly, the events of the night before flashed into his mind, and he knew he shouldn't be feeling peaceful at all. Angry and frustrated, maybe. Or possibly even vengeful. But peaceful? It was a sobering thought.

He turned his head to look at Irony. Despite the uncomfortable angle of her arms, she was sleeping soundly, her head resting on the pillow so that her mass of curling black hair brushed over his shoulder. She must have gotten chilled in the night, for she had moved close to him, and now one of her legs rested across his. The sheet had slipped somewhat lower, and he wondered how he might restore it to its former position. At that instant, he heard footsteps on the stairs.

"Irony," he whispered. "Irony—wake up. I think Mrs. Flannagan is coming."

"Mmmm?" Irony stirred, then tried to roll over. The tight pull of the ropes binding her wrists caused her eyes to fly open in pained confusion. "What . . . ?"

"It seems we are about to be discovered," Hawk warned.

"Oh, no," Irony moaned, and Hawk was dismayed to see the full extent of her dread reflected in her gaze.

A knock sounded at the door and Irony stared helplessly at Hawk.

"Miss McBride?" came Mrs. Flannagan's voice. "Are ya all right?"

Irony took a deep breath. "I'm . . . I'm fine, Mrs. Flannagan. However . . ." Hawk nodded encouragingly and she went on. "I'm . . . going to need your help. Would you come in, please?"

The door opened. "What seems to be the trou—?" A shrill scream abruptly ended the sentence. There was an echoing scream from a skinny, blonde-haired girl who followed the landlady into the room.

"A man!" shrieked Ma Flannagan. "Saints preserve us, you've got a man in yer bed!"

Had the situation been different, Hawk could almost have laughed. The look of incredulity on the woman's face was priceless.

"Mrs. Flannagan, I can explain," Irony began.

"And he's an Injun, Ma," the girl said.

"I can see that, Hortense." The proprietress turned back to Irony. "Now, young lady, would ya care to tell me what in the world is . . . ?"

"And he's nekkid, Ma," Hortense added, her pale blue eyes wide. "I ain't never seen a nekkid Injun before."

Mrs. Flannagan whirled on her daughter. "Hush yer gabblin', Hortense. And quit staring at that man." She shoved the girl toward the door. "Run down to the kitchen and bring me a butcher knife."

Hortense's eyes grew even bigger. "A knife?"

"To cut those ropes. Now, go on." When the sulking Hortense had left the room, Mrs. Flannagan turned

118

back to the pair on the bed. "I'll swan, I didn't understand what was happenin' last night—why yer brother would force his way in here. But now I see. He knew what ya were up to and was hopin' to shame some sense into ya!"

"He wasn't my brother . . ."

"Him bein' a man of God, no wonder he was so upset. I only hope he didn't spread the word about the two of ya. People here know I don't allow Injuns or loose women in my place. I'd be a laughin' stock . . ."

Irony's mouth thinned in anger, but she made an attempt to explain. "You don't understand. Some men were after my guide, and there was no place else for him to go." She cast a quick, guilty look at Hawk. "And there was absolutely nothing between us."

"Not even a sheet, as I can see fer myself!" Mrs. Flannagan fumed. "And to think I doubted yer brother's word when he said you was a wild one."

"I'm not . . ."

"Of course, he didn't have to take his anger out on me, but the Lord knows he had good reason to be hoppin' mad. I suppose he tied me up, gagged me and left me in the pantry so's I couldn't interfere with yer punishment. And I would have, mind you—no doubt the likes of you spendin' the night here has damaged the reputation of this boardin' house beyond all repair. I'm just grateful Hortense came to work early and found me when she did."

"Now, Mrs. Flannagan, your reputation can hardly be damaged by something that no one but the four of us ever needs to know," Hawk spoke up. "We're sorry about Goodman's treatment of you—he's an unprincipled rogue, wanted by the law. We've been tracking him for days, and as soon as you release us, we'll be back on his trail. It's our goal to see him brought to justice."

The woman drew herself up and sniffed haughtily.

"If that's the case, I'm of the opinion that you'd be better off if'n ya paid more attention to your trackin' and less to your lollygaggin'!"

"Mrs. Flannagan," Irony said, exasperated, "this is not what it looks like. Goodman simply tied us to this bed to shame and degrade us. He has a truly evil mind."

Hortense burst back into the room, waving the knife. "Here you are, Ma. Oh, yeah, Mr. Fletcher and old man Wills are downstairs wantin' breakfast."

"They'll have to hold their horses," Ma said, seizing the knife. "First things first." She began sawing at the rope binding Irony's arms to the head of the bed.

"So there are other boarders," commented Hawk. "Why didn't they hear us calling for help during the night?"

"Probably because Mr. Fletcher is deaf as a post, and old man Wills drinks himself into a stupor every night. I could barely hear ya myself . . . and you can be sure I didn't realize there was two of ya!"

Irony gasped in agony as she lowered her arms and experienced the fresh flow of blood to her hands and fingertips. She bit her lip so hard that tears started into her eyes.

"Here, Missy," Ma Flannagan said, thrusting the knife at her. "You can cut yer man loose . . . and then the two of ya had best be on yer way."

"But—won't you please give us the chance to explain what happened?" Irony protested.

The woman, her eagerly staring daughter behind her, paused in the doorway. "There's no need. Believe me, I've seen yer kind before. And I have no use fer a common hussy . . ."

Irony's breath whistled out from between clenched teeth. "Now look here, Mrs.—"

"Irony," Hawk said quietly, "it doesn't matter. Let's just get out of here."

"I . . . oh, very well," she conceded. "Thank you for your kind help, Mrs. Flannagan," she added sarcastically.

"I'll expect more money now," the landlady snapped, pushing her curious daughter toward the door. "You'll be payin' double for him."

Irony opened her mouth to protest, but a shake of Hawk's head and the slamming of the bedroom door saved her the trouble. With a grimace of anger, she proceeded to cut Hawk's bonds.

"Hand me my satchel, will you?" Hawk asked when he was free. "And, if you don't mind, turn your back while I dress."

"Why?" Irony said with asperity. "My reputation for modesty is already in ruins."

"As you wish." Hawk's brown fingers curled around the hem of the sheet, but before he could toss it aside, Irony turned and, with a muffled exclamation, went to stand by the window.

But she fell silent and remained that way, even after Hawk was dressed. She stood clutching the curtains, her head bowed.

"Irony?"

"Hmm?"

"What are you thinking?"

Slowly, she turned to face him. "Mrs. Flannagan thinks I'm a loose woman . . . I've never had anyone look at me like she did."

Hawk stepped closer to her, surprised at the trace of tears on her face. "Are you crying over what that harridan thinks?"

"I'm not crying," Irony declared. "Well, not really crying. I'm only mad, and I always cry when I'm mad. Anyway, I suppose I truly don't care about her—it's my aunts I'm worried about."

"They'll never find out about last night, if that's what's bothering you."

"Perhaps not—but I can't be certain."

Hawk grasped her shoulders and gave her a small shake. "Irony, what happened last night was not your fault. You did nothing to provoke it, and you know it. You cannot be held accountable for the fact that Goodman's mind is twisted."

"Still, it seems my mission in life is to shame my aunts. And myself."

"That's ridiculous."

"No, Hawk, it's true. You don't know! Every time I think I'm beginning to grasp the intricacies of becoming a lady, something like this happens."

"This has happened to you before?" His smile was teasing as he raised his hands to the side of her face and used his thumbs to brush away the remains of her tears.

"Of course not." She pulled away from him and backed up a few steps. "But I'm the one who spills my tea or trips over my petticoats . . . or who forgets and uses swear words in front of the minister."

"Those things are embarrassments, Irony. They're completely different from what happened to you last night. I'll admit, it was the kind of event that could haunt you forever, if you let it, but it was not something you brought on yourself."

"Somehow I put myself in a position to let it happen." Irony's green eyes darkened with self-anger. "What's wrong with me? How do I get into these predicaments?"

"Mayhap you meet life head on," he suggested calmly.

"I'm obstinate and undisciplined . . . and very apt to drive my poor aunts to distraction."

"They want you to be different?"

"They want me to be a lady," she said bleakly, as though that were the last possibility in the world.

"Is it so important, then, to be a lady?"

Her head snapped up. "It is to me."

Genuinely puzzled, Hawk asked, "Why?"

"If we don't seek to better ourselves . . . if we don't strive to rise above the common and mundane, why, we're no better than . . ."

She broke off, her green eyes stricken as they raised to his.

"Savages?" he said quietly.

"Hawk, I didn't mean to imply . . . oh, damn! I'm sorry." One hand went to her mouth. "There! I did it again."

"It may not mean much to you, Irony, but I think it's a refreshing change to hear a female speak her mind, without false sentiment or pretense. You're only human, you know — and there's a big difference between that and being a savage."

"I'm not certain my Aunt Tiny would agree with you."

"But then, she isn't here, is she? And the way I see it, you've only been doing your best to contend with circumstances well beyond your command."

"That's a charitable observation."

His smile was kind, tilting up at one end in a wry manner. "After last night, perhaps you deserve a little charity. Now, while you get dressed, I'll go pay Mrs. Flannagan and purchase our train tickets. Thank heavens, Goodman didn't think to take our money."

When Hawk returned, Irony was still in her nightgown, going through her carpetbag in search of something presentable to wear. Hawk had donned his suit again, but her wardrobe had been seriously depleted. There was one wrinkled cotton gown, or the disreputable-looking shirt and trousers she'd worn in the woods.

"I don't have anything to wear," she wailed when

Hawk tapped on the door, then entered the bedroom.

"I thought that might be a problem," he said, with a smile. "So I got the tickets . . . and this." He handed her a bundle wrapped in brown paper. "It's for you."

"What is it?"

"Just open it and see."

Quickly, she ripped away the paper, then caught her breath. "It's a traveling suit," she cried. "And a hat!"

"The suit's not nearly as fine as the one I ruined, I'm afraid. But it's all the mercantile had on hand. Do you think it will fit?"

Irony held it up to herself, her eyes dancing.

"Give me five minutes and we'll see," she said.

Hawk stepped into the hall while she slipped into the green worsted skirt and matching jacket. When she called him back into the room, he had to smile at the pleased look on her face as she surveyed her own appearance in the bureau mirror.

"It fits rather well," she announced. "It's only a little loose in the waist. And I haven't worn a hat in weeks!"

The hat was at least two years out of style, but it delighted Irony, nonetheless. It was straw, with dark green ribbons above the brim and a wisp of a veil. She tilted her head and admired it from every angle.

"You look lovely, Irony," Hawk said solemnly. "I would recite a line of poetry, but for once . . . nothing that comes to mind seems appropriate."

"Not even something from your beloved *Hiawatha?*" she teased.

"Well, there is one part . . .

"He beheld a maiden standing,
Saw a tall and slender maiden
All alone upon a prairie;
Brightest green were all her garments
And her hair was like the sunshine."

"Only, you're not tall and your hair isn't gold."

"But my clothes are green," she stated. "So maybe it's appropriate enough."

His smile was mischievous. "I don't know — shall I continue? The next lines go like this:

Day by day he gazed upon her,
Day by day he sighed with passion,
Day by day his heart within him
Grew more hot with love and longing
For the maid with yellow tresses."

Irony felt heat creeping into her cheeks, but she merely tossed her head and said, "No, I'm afraid it won't do after all. My hair is quite the opposite of yellow."

"But what of the rest?" he asked with genuine interest. "Has no man ever looked upon you with longing? Or love?"

"Hawk," she protested, "stop teasing me. We don't have time for such nonsense." Then she made a small face. "Of course no one has."

"And why do you suppose that is?" he asked softly.

"Most likely because I am, as my aunts have told me many times, a hoyden — not the graceful, ladylike sort a man admires."

With that, she picked up her reticule from the bureau and her carpetbag from the floor, and started out of the room. Hawk watched her go, a quizzical look playing over his strong features.

"Oh, Irony," he murmured, "what a great deal you have to learn about men . . ."

Keeping an eye out for the ruffians from the stables, Irony and Hawk made their way to the rickety building that served as a train station. A fist fight had broken out between two loggers who'd started their drinking early, so the attention of the townspeople was generally diverted. Just as they heard the distant whistling of the train, Irony stopped and clapped a hand to her mouth.

"Oh, dam—er, that is, I forgot something at the boarding house. I have to go back."

"What did you forget? You've got your satchel."

"Yes, but I forgot to pack my nightgown." She gave him a look that dared him to laugh. "I threw it over the chair while I was dressing. Anyway, it's the only one I brought with me—I've got to go after it."

"Are you absolutely sure this is necessary? I mean . . . well, your nightgown was badly torn."

"I can probably mend it. And I hardly think there will be any ladies' wear shops in the wilderness," she said tartly. "Besides, Aunt Alyce had this nightgown made for my last birthday."

Hawk sighed. The aunts again.

"You wait here," he said, "and I'll go for it."

"No, I can do it. How would it look if you asked Mrs. Flannagan for my nightgown after last night?"

"After last night, what difference could it make?"

"We'll both go," Irony said with decision. "I hear the train—we don't have time to waste quibbling about it."

They hurried back in the direction from which they'd come, dodging the others on the boardwalk who all seemed to be moving toward the depot to meet the incoming train. They turned a corner and Flannagan's boarding house loomed ahead.

Irony came to a full stop as she saw a lanky man with sandy hair standing at the front door, hat in hand, chatting with Mrs. Flannagan's daughter, Hortense. Irony swallowed the horrified gasp that rose in her throat.

Her thoughts were chaotic. *Nate! Oh, my Lord, Nathan Ferguson has caught up with us! I've got to get out of here before he sees me . . .*

Nathan Ferguson was the sheriff's deputy back in Thief River Falls, and the only officer the sheriff could spare to track down Reverend Josiah Goodman. Furthermore, he was a special favorite of Irony's aunts — so special, in fact, they had decided he was the man they wanted Irony to marry. The only reason they had finally consented to Irony making the trip into the wilderness was because they believed she would be accompanied by Ferguson. Had they known she would deliberately give him the slip at the Thief River depot and go off on her own, they'd have succumbed to violent apoplexy. As it was, she knew they probably assumed she was safe in his keeping and had been occupying their time planning the wedding which would be inevitable upon the couple's return.

"Hawk," Irony said suddenly, "I've changed my mind — let's go back to the train."

"What?" His look was slightly mocking. "And leave a perfectly good nightgown with Ma Flannagan? A nightgown that your aunt gave you?"

"Don't poke fun at me," she snapped, resolutely turning her back on the boarding house. "We don't want to miss the train — it's the only one today you said."

"It's just arriving now," he said calmly. "We've got enough time."

"No, it's not necessary. Let's go, please."

"Irony, are you afraid that old witch will insult you again? Look, you wait here and I'll go get the damned nightgown."

"No!" Irony blinked rapidly, annoyed that it was becoming harder and harder for her to summon a nice, ordinary, innocent look. "It's not important, I tell you. I can manage without it."

She started off down the boardwalk and, after a few pleasant seconds of observing the purposeful sway of her new skirts, Hawk followed her. He found himself wondering whether all women were as inconsistent and unpredictable as Irony McBride.

Irony suggested they board the train at once and, not bothering to wait for Hawk, she went up the steps and into the first passenger car she came to. She found two seats in the rear and dropped into one, sliding across to the window. As Hawk stowed their luggage in an overhead rack, she watched for the sandy-haired man she'd seen at the Flannagans'.

"How long before the train leaves?" she asked nervously.

"Another ten minutes or so, I expect. They've got to take on mail and supplies for the settlements along Rainy River."

Irony tried to remember whether or not she had said anything to Mrs. Flannagan about the train, and with a sinking feeling, thought she had. Hadn't she mentioned needing an early breakfast because they had a train to catch? And now, not only had she missed breakfast, she was likely to come face to face with the very man she'd been trying to avoid since leaving home.

She cast a quick look at Hawk's stern profile, relieved that he seemed not to notice her anxiety. Once again she was stricken by the vast differences between him and Nate Ferguson. Even now, dressed in his suit for their short journey, his eyeglasses visible in the breast pocket, he looked untamed and somehow dangerous. Oddly enough, instead of dwelling on the incongruousness of the book of poetry he held, her attention was drawn to the masculinity of the hand resting upon it. It was tanned and strong-looking, and Irony knew from experience that those long fingers could enforce a grip of steel. There was an awe-inspiring power in this man, and she shuddered to think what he might do if he discovered Nate Ferguson was the one who had been trailing them from the Sweetwater school. She might not want to marry Ferguson, but neither did she want him killed or injured. If that happened, she could forget about ever returning to Thief River Falls!

Slowly, with a great deal of hissing and clanking, the train began to roll forward, gradually gathering speed. At last they were on their way. Daring to breathe more freely, Irony flung one final glance out the window . . . and nearly choked. Nate Ferguson dashed across the wooden platform of the depot and, seizing a handrail, leaped onto the train, no more than two cars behind them. Irony's hand went to her heart and she closed her eyes, trying desperately to think.

Nathan seemed so determined, there was no doubt but that he would make his way through each and every car in the train looking for her. There were no private cars, no diner car where she could hide. It was too late to get off, and besides, Hawk's considerable bulk was situated between her and the aisle. Hawk's bulk? That thought gave her an idea—not the most inventive idea of her lifetime, but perhaps a workable one.

She forced a noisy yawn and stretched her arms. "Oh! I'm so sleepy," she murmured. "Guess I didn't rest very well last night."

Hawk gave her a considering look, as if he knew she was up to something, but uncertain as to what that something could be. "Yes, it was a rather long night," he said with a complete lack of expression on his face. "Why don't you take a nap? It'll help pass the time at least."

"That's a wonderful idea," she enthused. "Are you certain you don't mind?"

"Not at all. I'll be reading . . . unless I happen to fall asleep as well."

What a piece of luck that would be. If Hawk were dozing, he wouldn't notice a strange man wandering up and down the aisles, searching the face of every female he passed.

"Oh . . . you wouldn't mind if I rested my head against your shoulder, would you?" Irony questioned guilelessly.

"Be my guest." Hawk's mouth twitched, and Irony had to bite her tongue to keep from making a sarcastic remark. It would be best to let him think what he wanted. She could deal with his mistaken conclusions about her boldness later. Right now she needed a shield to put in place between herself and Nate Ferguson.

Sliding down in her seat, Irony angled her body toward Hawk, resting her head against the bulwark of his shoulder, the stylish brim of her straw hat shadowing her face. Stealthily, she twisted her birthstone ring around until only the plain gold band showed. She hoped that Nate would see the ring, think her a married woman traveling with her husband, and pass on by.

Silently, she counted to five hundred, concentrating on breathing evenly, and then, in almost imperceptible movements, she began to nod, as though relaxing in slumber. With each nod, her head moved lower until finally, it was tucked into the curve of Hawk's body. Her hand slipped downward until it fell across his thigh, the ring displayed prominently.

At her touch, Hawk jumped and quickly looked down at her. What in hell's name was the little minx up to now? She'd been acting strange all morning, and he had to think it was more than lightheadedness brought on by hunger. There was something up her sleeve besides her pretty arm . . .

Irony was actually rather comfortable nestled against Hawk, especially when he shifted positions

130

and draped one arm across her shoulder. She might have protested, had she not decided their posture did, indeed, suggest a happily married couple. She was thankful that her hair was both black and braided—most people who could not see her face would simply assume she was Indian, like the man she pretended was her husband.

She was reading the open book on Hawk's lap through squinted eyes when suddenly, she heard the rush of air that meant someone had opened the door at the end of the car.

Footsteps sounded on the wooden floor, and Irony held her breath as they approached, slowing. She lowered her head, burying her face even deeper into Hawk's jacket. As she moved closer, Hawk began a soothing, almost caressing, motion with the hand resting on her shoulder. Irony was reflecting upon how nice it felt when she heard Hawk's deep voice.

"Are you looking for something?" he challenged.

"Yes . . . a lady friend of mine." Irony stiffened. It was Nathan Ferguson, all right. She'd recognize that slow, drawling voice anywhere.

"Well, this lady isn't your friend. She's with me."

"Sorry."

Irony realized the footsteps were continuing on down the aisle. She raised her chin an inch or two and dared a look. Nathan Ferguson was giving each and every woman his full attention. Thank God, Hawk's possessive manner had convinced the deputy that she couldn't possibly be the woman he sought. At the front of the car, Nathan dropped into an empty seat, his shoulders slumped in defeat. Irony prayed he would surmise she had remained in War Road, and that he would go back on the next train.

Suddenly, she became aware of Hawk's suspicious eyes upon her and knew her actions were close to giving her away. She managed a somewhat feeble smile,

131

then snuggled closer again, missing the flare of pleased surprise that flashed in his dark gaze.

It wasn't much later that the train steamed into the small depot at the village on Rainy River. Irony was careful to make certain Nathan had disembarked before she stirred, pretending to awaken from a sound sleep.

"Why didn't you wake me?" she asked, feigning dismay that they were the last ones in the car.

"There was plenty of time. I figured you needed your rest . . . as soundly as you were sleeping."

Irony studied him. Was there a note of cynicism in his tone? She couldn't be certain, so she chose to ignore it. "Shall we go?"

Hawk pulled their bags down and followed her along the aisle. She had descended two steps before she caught sight of Ferguson, leaning against the depot wall watching the other passengers alight. Without conscious thought, she whirled about and found herself face to face with Hawk.

"What the . . . ?" he growled, staggering backward from the impact.

"Oh, Hawk," she cried, "where are my manners? I just remembered that I haven't thanked you for everything you've done!"

"What?"

One of her small hands fluttered upward, coming to rest on the front of his white shirt. He looked down at it, surprised.

"Irony, what's going on?" he demanded.

She ascended a step, putting herself even nearer to him. "I haven't thanked you properly for this beautiful suit . . . or for your guidance through the woods . . . or for any of the other things you've done to help me."

"And just how do you propose to thank me now?"

he asked, one black eyebrow tilting in question.

She leaned closer. "Perhaps you could think of something . . . ?"

God damn! The deceitful baggage was flirting with him! At that moment, he decided he'd give up half his library to know what was taking place within her devious mind.

Hawk let his gaze linger on her slightly parted lips, and though he knew the invitation was false, he was tempted, nevertheless. He ought to teach her a lesson in honesty. . . .

"Here now, folks," boomed the uniformed conductor. "You'll have to get off the train. We're due to pull out in ten minutes, and unless you have a ticket, you can't travel on."

"Let's go, Irony," Hawk said with such authority that she had no choice but to obey. Reluctantly, she turned and, to her immense relief, saw that Nathan was gone.

But she knew he was somewhere in this tiny settlement that was little more than a handful of shacks and tepees strung along a mud street, and it was imperative that, after all her subterfuge, she not encounter him unexpectedly.

"Where are we going now?" she asked casually.

"There's only one boarding house in town, so I thought we'd better speak for rooms first. Then I'll go in search of a canoe and supplies so that we can be on our way early tomorrow morning."

"Why not go on tonight?" Irony asked. "It's early yet."

"Go on—now? Without a meal or a decent night's sleep?"

"We can cook our own meal on the trail," she pointed out. "And a soft pine bough bed under the stars will be infinitely better than a bug-infested mattress in a cheap rooming house."

133

"But, Irony—"

"Besides," she hurried on, "now that we've come this far, I'm more anxious than ever to get to Lake of the Woods. Please, let's go on." She looked at him with a wide green gaze. "You won't be sorry, I promise."

Hawk felt the need to loosen the suddenly too-tight collar of his dress shirt. What game was she playing? She knew damned good and well exactly what any man would think she was promising . . . he had half a mind to take her up on her implied offer.

"Look," she said, pointing. "There's a building with a sign that says CANOES FOR SALE. Let's go see, shall we?" She started off, then paused to look back at him. "Come along, Hawk. The sooner we purchase our canoe, the sooner we can get back into the woods."

He stared after her, a plan forming in his mind. It would serve Miss Irony McBride right if he called her bluff.

A slow smile curved his mouth. She might be heading into the wilderness with the very civilized Raphael Hawkes, but tonight when they camped, she was going to find the savage named Moonhawk sitting across the campfire from her!

Chapter Eight

On Rainy River . . .

Irony was almost sorry she had chosen to wait at the canoe shed while Hawk purchased supplies. She had thought that sitting on a bench in the shade would be preferable to risking a face to face meeting with Nathan Ferguson, but now she wasn't sure. The proprietor of the shop and his two Indian helpers seemed inordinately interested in her, and she was growing uneasy beneath their frank appraisal.

After Hawk had paid for a canoe and left, she made yet another in a long sequence of hasty decisions. Having seen a small, cluttered desk in one corner of the shop, she had asked the owner if she might leave a message. If Nathan intended to keep following her, sooner or later he would have to acquire a canoe. So she had left a letter for him, assuring him that she was fine and there was no need for him to continue his search. She'd reminded him of the fearful rumors associated with Lake of the Woods, and told him she had no desire for him to be hopelessly lost or at the mercy of the unfriendly Indians who were said to live there.

"Please go home, Nathan," she had finished the note. "Tell my aunts I am well, and that I will contact them as soon as I have retrieved our property from Goodman."

Folding the note and scribbling Ferguson's name across it, she slipped it inside the desk, asking that the proprietor deliver it to the young deputy should he appear in the canoe shop. Then, with a cool demeanor meant to establish her lack of interest in further conversation, Irony had stepped through the door and settled herself on the bench at the rear of the shop.

Two Indians, dressed in greasy buckskins, stood over the frame of a half-constructed canoe. They looked up as Irony came out onto the riverbank and continued to stare at her. One of them slid his glance away from her each time she raised her eyes, but the other gaped brazenly, his bold black eyes and knowing grin an unmistakable statement as to what kind of woman he thought her. Although the stocky French Canadian boat builder watched her just as openly, he did not disturb Irony in the same way the Indians did.

For the first time, she was beginning to have a clearer image of what traveling into the wilderness was going to mean. Even War Road, primitive as it had seemed, had been civilized compared to this place. Here Indians pitched their tepees and walked the streets amongst the ordinary townsfolk, some wearing beaded and fringed buckskins, some attired in *citizen dress*, the suits of clothing allotted to the Indians each year by the government, in observance of the stipulations made in various treaties the natives had signed. In the time she had spent with Raphael Hawkes, her natural fear and dislike of Indians had abated somewhat. Now it came creeping back, strengthened by the disrespectful glances of these men. She bit her lip, suddenly wondering whether she was being foolish by so determinedly dodging Nathan Ferguson. He was the one person in this untamed country that she knew and could trust.

Irony angled her body so the men couldn't see her

face anymore and pretended to gaze out across the river. On the other bank, which Hawk had told her was Canadian territory, she could see another cluster of shacks and tepees, as well as a number of boats tied to a sagging dock.

"Would the little mademoiselle like a drink?" The growling voice of the shop owner startled Irony so much that she gripped the edge of the rough-hewn bench, feeling the splintery wood cut into her palms. The French Canadian held out a tin cup, from which emanated the strong odor of rum.

Irony shook her head. "N-no, thank you."

The proprietor merely smiled and, tipping up the cup, drank the liquor himself. He swiped his mouth with one dirty shirt sleeve as he considered her.

"Is the half-breed your man?" he asked unexpectedly. An avid curiosity shone in his narrowed eyes.

"I beg your pardon!" Even to her own ears, Irony sounded exactly like a shocked Aunt Valentine. The very impertinence of the question seemed cause for alarm. What would he say—or do—next?

"The half-breed—he is a handsome fellow, no?"

Irony squared her shoulders. "I really hadn't noticed. I am paying him to be my guide, and good looks are not a requirement."

"Her guide—ha!" The French Canadian flung the sneering words over his shoulder to the watching Indians. "Something tells me the guide no longer explores virgin territory . . ."

The Indians chuckled and made ribald comments in their own strange, unfathomable language.

"Tell me, Mademoiselle, does the breed earn his money well?"

Slowly, Irony got to her feet, trying to remain calm.

"I suggest you go back to your canoe making," she said firmly. "I have no wish to continue this conversation."

"I myself have no wish to talk," the man agreed.

"But I am bored with the canoe making." He came closer, and Irony caught the unpleasant smell of rum on his stale breath. She wished she had not underestimated the threat he represented, and supposed it served her right for considering only the Indians dangerous. "We could occupy our time with other, more pleasant matters, Mademoiselle."

"I have no idea what you—"

"Perhaps you could show me some of the things the half-breed has taught you," he suggested with a lewd smile. "And then perhaps I could show you some things he may not have."

"Yes, a splendid idea." Hawk's smooth voice fell upon the suddenly still air, and both Irony and the French Canadian whirled to face the newcomer. Hawk was leaning against the door of the shed, a casual stance that belied the tight set of his jaw. "Mayhap you would like to start by showing the lady how a coward dies . . ."

With one graceful movement, Hawk bent, then straightened—the deadly blade of a newly purchased knife he had drawn from his boot gleaming wickedly. In two steps, he had the French Canadian shoved up against the rough wall of the shed, the blade pressed against his fleshy neck. And one warning look from Hawk was all it took to keep the man's employees from coming to his aid.

"Monsieur . . . please . . . ," gasped the stocky fellow.

"Hawk, no!" Irony cried. "Let him go—he meant no harm."

"He insulted you," Hawk reasoned.

"Yes, but so did Mrs. Flannagan. You didn't seem to think it necessary to carve her into bits."

"She is a woman, and I don't kill women. But this—this slab of pork belly seems made for my blade."

"Let's just go," Irony insisted, even though she real-

138

ized that if Hawk truly meant to kill the man, he probably would have already done so.

"Only after our friend here apologizes."

"*Sacré bleu*," the Canadian swore. "You misunderstood my intention—I was only making conversation. I did not touch her. . . ."

"A good thing," Hawk affirmed. "It would be difficult to build canoes with no fingers."

The man paled, his small eyes round with fright. "I knew she was your woman . . . *mon Dieu*, I was only offering her a drink."

"I heard what you were offering. Now, the apology, if you don't mind."

Beads of sweat had gathered on the man's unshaven upper lip, and he wiped them away nervously. "Mademoiselle, I am most humbly regretful for my actions. I meant no disrespect to you or your man."

"He is not my man," Irony snapped. "Hawk, tell him."

Hawk released the canoe builder and stepped away, slipping the knife back into his boot. "Now, which is my canoe?"

"That one on the bank there," the man said, breathing easier.

Hawk strode back into the shed, emerging with two canvas sacks of supplies. These he tossed into the waiting canoe, returning for the bedrolls and baggage that had been piled at the end of the bench where Irony had waited.

As he passed by her, Irony hissed, "I want you to tell him that . . . that I am not your woman!"

"Are you ready to leave?" Hawk asked blandly, as though he hadn't heard her request.

"Tell him you're only my guide," she said, hands knotting on her hips.

Hawk shrugged. "If you're going with me, Irony, you had better get into the canoe." He walked away and began sliding the lightly laden canoe across the grass toward the water.

Irony nearly stamped her foot in frustration. The last thing she needed was for the French Canadian to confirm the Flannagans' tale of her illicit relationship with the half-breed schoolteacher when he talked to Nathan. Then Nathan would carry the tale back to Aunt Tiny and Aunt Alyce, and God knew, they would be furious enough when they learned she had eluded Nathan himself—the man they believed was safely escorting her on the mission to reclaim their stolen goods. But there seemed nothing she could do about Hawk's lack of cooperation.

"Remember to give the letter to Mr. Ferguson," she finally whispered to the newly chastened shop owner, then turned and ran to the water's edge. "Wait for me, Hawk—have you forgotten whose money is paying for this expedition?"

Hawk said nothing, but his eyes approved as she gathered her skirts and clambered into the canoe, settling herself in one end as though she had spent half her life in one of the flimsy vessels.

Irony was dismayed at the seeming frailty of the birchbark canoe, but she was so irritated with Hawk that she refused to show any sign of trepidation. She had never been in a canoe before, even though she had watched them with great longing as they skimmed up and down the Thief River at home. Aunt Tiny thought they were too dangerous, and now Irony could understand why. When the craft was launched and Hawk leaped into it, it sank into the river until the lapping water was less than a foot from the gunwale. Irony kept reminding herself that during the fur trade years, the *voyageurs* had traveled thousands of miles in just such boats—surely it would withstand a few days' trip up the river and across the Lake of the Woods.

Paddling easily, Hawk maneuvered the canoe out into the current, which caught the lightweight boat and sent it sailing along at a quick pace. Soon the river made a lazy turn and the handful of buildings along the docks on either bank had disappeared from sight, causing Irony to reflect that it was probably to be her last view of civilization for a long while.

That was a sobering thought, and suddenly, she wanted to re-establish her authority, fragile though it had always been.

"Why did you let that man think I was your . . . your . . . well, you know what I mean!"

Hawk's face didn't change, but she could see the irritation in his eyes. "It seems somewhat pointless to worry about your reputation now, doesn't it? I mean, the moment you left Thief River unescorted, you made yourself prey for any and all scandalous assumptions."

"Perhaps."

"And it occurs to me that you should be worrying more about what the people back home will be thinking, rather than get so riled over the opinion of a troublemaking boat builder you'll most likely never see again."

Hawk realized he was saying the very things he'd denied earlier in the day, but somehow, the situation wasn't the same. He'd felt protective when Mrs. Flannagan had demeaned Irony, but seeing the French Canadian's lust made him angry, ready to lash out at anyone who might be convenient.

"Are you saying that I shall have to accustom myself to such treatment in the north country?"

"I'm saying that you should expect a certain amount of speculation on the part of people you meet here. After all, not many young women leave home to strike out into the wilderness on their own."

"I had good cause."

"But they don't know that. All they know is what they see — a pretty young lady in the sole company of a man of dubious heritage. They suspect the worst, naturally."

"Well, it's not like that and you know it."

"Do I?"

Hawk's quiet, enigmatic words and the steady gaze of his dark eyes sent a strange sensation spiraling down her spine. She wasn't sure whether it was fear, excitement . . . or something of both. And she knew she didn't want to pursue the topic.

"Um . . . when will we stop for the night?" she asked. -

"Stop? We just got started. And you were the one so anxious to get into the forest again, remember?"

Irony recalled that bit of theatrical nonsense she had indulged in at the train depot. She had been shockingly coquettish, but she had hoped Hawk had forgotten her rashness. Something now told her he hadn't. -

"I-I'm hungry," she said with a trace of defiance. "Don't forget—we haven't eaten all day!"

"I haven't forgotten. Indeed, it seems to me that I mentioned that fact several times myself." He almost smiled at the scowl he saw forming on her face. "Very well, Irony, we'll find a place to camp before much longer. We have a few matters to clear up anyway."

Irony dipped her hand into the clear, cold water of the river, pretending to be entranced by the beauty of the scenery around her. But her mind was racing— *what* matters?

Dear Lord, what was he up to now?

About an hour later, Hawk guided the canoe into one of the streams that occasionally flowed into the broad, placid waters of Rainy River. Several hundred feet up the stream, he pointed to the bank.

"We'll stop here for the night," he said. "Where we won't be seen by other travelers on the river."

"Then you think Goodman is in the area?" Irony

gathered her skirts and prepared to leap to shore and help drag in the canoe.

"He could be." Hawk gave a final push with the paddle, then watched with interest as Irony jumped onto the grassy bank, revealing a flash of trim ankles and ruffled petticoat.

Irony fixed him with a stern look. "This canoe would be considerably lighter if you'd jump out, too."

"Yes, ma'am," he mocked, unfolding his rangy length and stepping out. He helped pull the canoe ashore, then began unloading the supplies.

Supper was bacon and fried potatoes, and slices of white bread Hawk had bought in the settlement. Irony couldn't help but recall the chicken and noodle dinners she'd had with the aunts each Sunday, and though the thought of fresh yeast rolls and gooseberry pie brought a smile to her lips, she realized those highly civilized meals couldn't compare to the veritable feast she and Hawk were sharing. She found that the delicious taste of crisp bacon and smoky potatoes was only enhanced by the loveliness of the evening around them. Tall pine trees reared feathery heads against a sky painted with a dozen different shades of rose, gold and mauve, and threw long shadows on the water. As they ate, Hawk pointed out a beaver gliding silently downstream, dragging a leafy limb in his mouth, and Irony watched in delight.

She had left Thief River Falls with a sense of urgency — time was running out, she'd thought, for any sort of excitement and adventure in her life. She had reached an age where her aunts were expecting her to marry and settle down, and each time they had invited Nathan for tea or a meal, she had felt the bonds of responsibility tighten around her. She acknowledged that, at twenty, she was teetering on the brink of spinsterhood, but Lord help her, she wasn't ready to give up her youth and freedom! When Reverend Goodman had deceived Aunt Tiny, it had provided

143

the perfect opportunity for one last exploit. Irony had tricked Nathan and disappeared into the lake country with an eagerness that surprised even her. But far more astonishing than her enjoyment of the venture was the feeling of contentment that repeatedly stole over her during certain unguarded moments. Until now, contentment had meant an orderly life in the big white house in Thief River, raising a family, and being an active member in the Ladies' Auxiliary. Irony had planned to become a valued and respected citizen, like her aunts. But somehow, sitting on the riverbank and listening to the restless stirrings of a northern stream, she began to doubt the rewards of such an existence. How could it be more exhilarating than this?

Irony sighed. But a life in the wilderness simply wasn't feasible for someone like her. And besides, she knew what such a life had done to her father—and she didn't want that for herself. Best just to enjoy this one, final adventure and then turn firmly away from the haunting beauty of the forest and return to the kind of future for which she was best suited.

"I purchased a small tent for you," Hawk suddenly said, shattering her musing. "I'll set it up before it gets any darker."

She watched him walk away in the gloom and almost chuckled. Raphael Hawkes might like to imply he was a savage at heart, but his actions gave him away. A tent was a fairly civilized item, and the fact that he had elected to buy one for her clearly demonstrated his proper respect for her authority. He might cause her occasional doubt or fear, but in the final tally, he knew which of them was in charge. She supposed the upbringing her aunts had given her had instilled an air of command she hadn't even recognized in herself.

Irony dispensed with the supper dishes before following Hawk through a copse of young birch trees to the place where he had erected the small canvas structure. As she walked, she drew off her hat and took the pins from her hair, shaking out the tight braid. The night wind caught the loosened strands and lifted them, caressing her neck with a soothing coolness. Irony unbuttoned the high neck of her new traveling suit, and raised her face to the breeze. Overhead, a falling star tumbled through the heavens, a streak of fire quickly lost to sight.

"Nice evening, isn't it?" Hawk asked, startling her.

"Oh . . . yes, it is." Irony stared at him, taken aback by his changed appearance. He had removed his suit jacket earlier, but now the white shirt he wore was completely unbuttoned and hanging free of his trousers, revealing a broad, bare chest. As she watched with growing apprehension, he stripped off the shirt and flung it over a low-hanging tree branch.

"What are you doing?" she asked quietly, hoping he wouldn't notice the slight quake in her voice. All her new-found confidence in her ability to command the situation was slowly but surely trickling away.

"I'm wondering, Irony," Hawk said, "if you recall any of the things you said to me back at the train depot."

"Yes, of course," she replied, laying her hat on top of the carpetbag. She didn't add that she had hoped he would not remember them. "I — I merely stated that I was anxious to get back into the woods."

He stepped nearer and, before she realized what he intended, reached out and seized one of her hands. "And do you remember doing this?" Relentlessly, he pulled her close to him, pressing her hand into the hard warmth of his chest. Irony's fingers curled against the urge to stroke the smooth skin. "Do you recall how you pressed against me and looked into my eyes with such . . . promise?"

She gasped. "I did no such thing!" But she had, and she knew it. Unfortunately, there was no way she could explain to him that she'd been trying to distract him from the sight of Nathan Ferguson watching for her. "You misunderstood my gesture," she finally managed to get out.

"Misunderstood?" he murmured, again flattening her hand so that his steady heart beat throbbed intimately against her palm. "Tell me, how does a man misunderstand something as blatant as the looks you were giving me? As openly encouraging as the words you said to me?"

Irony pulled back, but Hawk's free hand caught her waist, holding her in place. "Do you happen to remember what you said to me, Irony?"

"No."

"Liar," he breathed, lowering his head to look directly into her eyes. "You told me that if we hurried back into the woods—"

"There's no need to repeat it," she blurted.

"Oh, so you do remember?"

"No, but surely it's of little importance."

"I happen to think it's very important." His hand closed over her smaller one, bringing it to his lips. As his mouth moved against the tender skin of her palm, Irony's knees weakened and for an instant, she was glad of his hold at her waist. "You told me," he continued, his heated breath teasing her palm, "that if I agreed to leave the settlement and hurry off into the woods, I wouldn't be sorry."

Irony returned his steady gaze, but she felt a hearty pang of guilt and blinked twice in rapid succession. "I only meant that we would be that much closer to finding Goodman."

"Perhaps that's what you meant, but you *implied* I'd be that much closer . . . to you." His hand tugged at her and unexpectedly, she found herself molded against his granite frame. Before she could struggle free, he dropped her hand and snaked both arms around her waist. "Naturally, I assumed you meant to reward me . . . in some way."

"If you don't let me go," she said, trying to keep the breathlessness of fear out of her voice, "I'll . . . I'll . . ."

"What?" he whispered. "Scream?" His short laugh rustled the wispy hairs at her temple. "Scream away, Irony—there's no one to hear."

"You cad," she snapped. "Why do you insist upon interpreting my words in a way I never intended?"

"Oh, come now, sweetheart. I think I took them exactly as you meant. I just don't think you believed I would take you up on your most generous offer."

"I never offered anything!" she cried, pushing against his chest with the heels of her hands.

"You did, and you know it. And I've warned you repeatedly—I'm no angel. When something I want is offered to me, I take it."

Swiftly, he bent his head and placed a kiss at the base of her throat.

"Stop it!" As Hawk's mouth lifted toward hers, Irony whipped her head from side to side, her long hair stinging his face. He was forced to release her with one hand and attempt to capture her chin with his fingers. With his hold on her thus weakened, Irony was able to give him a shove that sent him staggering back a step. She took advantage of the opportunity and kicked out, the toe of her hard leather shoe catching him in the kneecap.

"Damn!" he groaned, sinking to the ground.

Irony turned and fled, blindly. In only seconds, she could hear him thrashing through the brush after her. She skittered past the campfire, nearly stumbling over a pile of supplies stacked nearby. As her foot hit the canvas bag, potatoes, a cooking pot, and eating utensils went flying in all directions. She leaped over the coffee pot and nimbly avoided stepping into a tin plate. Her frantic haste slowed as she caught sight of the canoe. If only she could get into it and push off from the bank, she could be adrift before Hawk could get to her.

"Don't even consider it," Hawk said from close behind her.

Irony whirled, judging the distance between herself and his grasping reach. She'd have to hurry. . . .

Her fingers closed over the smooth birchbark just as Hawk stepped on a potato that rolled under his foot and sent him sailing across the small clearing. He careened into Irony from the back, going down with a thud and taking her with him.

She felt crushed beneath his weight and struggled to free herself. One large hand closed over her shoulder. "Hold still," he panted into her ear, rolling aside to free her.

"And let you . . . ?" Irony struggled to her knees and crawled forward. His hold on her skirt and the sandiness of the soil hampered her progress, but she kept going, not bothering to consider what she would do once she reached the water. With a loud pop, the button on her skirt flew off and the skirt itself began sliding over her hips. Irony uttered a sharp cry, and, yanking at her skirt, redoubled her efforts to get away from him.

Hawk, despite the throbbing pain in his knee, had to laugh as her skirt came off in his hand. With a grin, he tossed it aside and went after her. His teeth gleamed as whitely in the gloom as did her petticoat.

"Raphael Hawkes," she warned, finding herself poised on the brink of the stream, "get away from me right now! What on earth do you think you're doing?"

He had to admire her defiant stand—backed clear to the water, on her hands and knees and very nearly at his mercy, she had not yet given up the fight. Hawk wondered how long she would keep battling were he to continue his pursuit.

To the death, mocked a small voice in the back of his mind. But, of course, he had no intention of carrying things that far. After all, the idea had been only to frighten her a little, to make her pay for her brazenness earlier in the day. She had to realize this was a wilderness where young white women were as scarce as three-legged grizzlies, and that she couldn't issue an invitation to a man and not expect him to accept — with enthusiasm.

"Irony, you made me a promise." His hand curled around her forearm and though she had no place to go but into the water, she pulled back with every ounce of her remaining strength. Hawk rose to his knees and jerked her tight against him, his thighs opening to wedge her hips between them. "And I mean for you to keep it . . ."

His other arm went around her, that hand capturing the back of her head and holding her immobile. Her eyes were enormous as she watched his stern face come closer and closer.

Irony's heart fluttered wildly as his mouth covered hers with demanding firmness. She couldn't move away from his touch, and the sudden confusion within her mind made her forget her initial desire to escape him. The faintest of groans issued from Hawk's throat as he leaned away to look into her eyes, and then he was kissing her again, his mouth both brutal and tender as it slanted across hers.

It was not until she felt the gritty sand beneath her back that Irony realized he had lowered her into a prone position, following and covering her with his own body. She placed her palms against his shoulders, meaning to push him away but succeeding only in gripping his arms tightly.

"Irony . . . ," he murmured. "Irony . . ."

She opened her mouth to speak, but he sealed it with a kiss that stole her breath . . . and the last of her will to fight. His lips roamed over hers, hot and moist, and in spite of her wish to be indifferent, she felt an eager response blossoming within her. She twisted her shoulders, needing and wanting to be closer to him, and he shuddered against her. One hand cupped her jaw, turning her face for a softer kiss, a slow exploration of her mouth that set her aflame in a way she had never before known.

Hawk's hand trembled along the side of her neck, then Irony felt the warmth of his fingers as they slid inside the collar of her jacket and began unfastening the remaining buttons. Cool night air brushed over her skin, but she welcomed the relief from the intense heat that overwhelmed her. Hawk caressed her mouth, her eyes, her temples with sweet, tender kisses as he continued unbuttoning her suit.

Hawk had never meant to proceed so far—but the sight of the acquiescent Irony lying beneath him, her green eyes fired with passion, drove him beyond all reason. Nothing in the world could have deterred him from his purpose now. His desire to see her, to touch her intimately burned like a fever in his brain—and in a brief, fleeting thought, he wondered if he wasn't truly as savage as she thought him.

Drawing a deep breath, Hawk slipped a hand beneath the worsted jacket and cupped one round breast through the soft cotton of her chemise. At his touch, Irony tensed, but did not pull away. Emboldened, he pressed his thumb against the rigid nipple and she cried out, whether in pleasure or alarm he couldn't tell. He rotated the thumb slightly, gently, and she arched against him, telling him plainly that she was enjoying his fondling. A sudden impatience overtook Hawk and before he even realized what he was going to do, he bent his dark head and placed his mouth where his hand had been.

"Oh, my God," Irony barely breathed, one hand moving restlessly to stroke the back of his head, careful not to distract him from his erotic ministrations. Thin, silver wires of delight pulled taut throughout her body and she imagined herself as a marionette, dancing frantically to the seductive music humming through her mind. She was rapidly progressing beyond rational thought — even the image of Aunt Valentine's shocked visage was banished from her consciousness.

Shamelessly, Irony wanted this interlude to continue, to whatever its natural conclusion might be. The fierce joy she felt at Hawk's arrogant touch was perhaps the most exhilarating adventure upon which she'd yet embarked. His sensual invasion of her senses was thrilling beyond anything she'd ever known.

Hawk buried his face against her sweet-scented skin, trying desperately to get himself under control. What had happened to his calm intent, his self-command? He had planned to frighten her, not seduce her. But, as God was his witness, if he didn't back away soon, he wasn't going to be able to.

Something about this woman reached out and touched him in places he hadn't been touched in years — places in his heart, his soul . . . vulnerable places he'd thought safely shut away long ago. He wanted to make love to her, but not for any sort of momentary gratification. He knew without a doubt that one time, twenty times — a thousand times — would never slake his thirst for her sweetness. He wanted more, much more, from her than that. And for that reason, he had to call a halt to a situation that was well out of hand already.

He steeled himself to push away from her — trying desperately to summon his usual will of iron. He supported his upper body with his arms, drawing back to look at her, but as his hips pressed more firmly against hers, she wriggled into snug contact, her arms looping around his waist. She had only reacted to his move with innocent curiosity, yet it was nearly his undoing.

"For God's sake," he rasped. "Stop wiggling, Irony — please!"

Her face reflected her puzzled concern, and he knew she thought she had angered him.

"No . . . it's all right," he managed, silently calling himself fifty kinds of fool for ending what had been one of the most pleasurable moments of his lifetime. "We just need to . . . to stop . . . before anything serious happens." He moved further away, resting his weight on one arm so that he could wipe the sweat from his brow with the other.

Irony's eyes widened in disbelief. "Don't you dare," she exclaimed. "Don't you dare stop!"

"What?"

"You started this," she pointed out, her eyes sparking furiously. "And I want you to finish it, do you hear?"

It was Hawk's turn to be shocked. "You don't know what you're saying, Irony . . ."

She seized his face between her hands and brought it back to her own, crushing her mouth against his in a searing kiss that made his senses reel. The feel of her lips parted in eager passion, the restless surging of her newly aroused body beneath him, and the agitated grasping of her fingers through his hair almost swayed him to her purpose. It would be easy enough to change his mind, take advantage of what she was practically pleading with him to take.

Take advantage. That phrase was what stopped him cold. Despite the way he'd been acting, Irony was in his charge. She was alone with him in unfamiliar territory, and she trusted him. He was all that stood between her and harm. There was an honor within him that would not allow him to violate her trust . . . as much as he would hate himself for it during the long night to come.

"No, Irony," he said, gently disengaging himself from her embrace. "We're not going to do this—I was wrong to start it."

She raised up onto her elbows, frowning.

"I only meant to teach you a lesson," he went on. "I wanted to show you how foolhardy it is to flirt with a man who might be inclined to forget he is a gentleman. Or to forget that you are a lady."

A lady? Irony's frown deepened. She hadn't been acting much like a lady, granted, but wasn't it up to her to put a stop to this kind of situation? How dare he humiliate her by being stronger and more sensible than she?

Without thinking, she snatched up one of the cooking pots that had been scattered from the supply sack and, dipping it into the stream, lifted it and poured the cold water over his head.

Though he coughed and sputtered, Hawk kept his clenched fists tight at his sides.

"There," Irony spat. "Since you want to cool matters down, perhaps that will help."

She flung the pan aside and scrambled to her feet. Wasting not another word on him, she thrust her nose into the air and stalked off toward her tent.

Hawk brushed wet hair from his eyes and stared after her. Dear Lord, what had happened? He'd started out to teach her a lesson, and had ended up learning one himself. A lesson he should have grasped years ago: the man who carelessly plays with fire will surely end up with singed fingers.

He stood and stripped off his trousers. Since he was already wet, he might as well cool down completely in the stream. Irony McBride had singed more than his fingers, he realized. She had left his entire body and soul burning—in flames so high they lapped at the starlit heavens.

Chapter Nine

On Pine Island . . .

Irony was still smarting with shame when she awoke the next morning. She had found the skirt of her traveling suit neatly folded and placed outside the tent, and instead of taking it as a peace offering, she chose to regard it as Hawk's not-so-subtle reminder of her wanton behavior the night before.

She packed the suit away and dressed in her boy's clothing, then tightly braided her hair into two long plaits, wishing she had a cap to put over it. She was in the mood to conceal each and every sign of femininity. As far as she was concerned, her conduct from this point on was going to be so circumspect that even Hawk would have a difficult time remembering her indiscretions.

As it turned out, Hawk paid very little attention to her for the first part of the day. Once they were back in the mainstream of Rainy River, his gaze swept from bank to bank and down the river ahead, almost as if he was searching for someone. Irony's curiosity finally overcame her reluctance to speak.

"What are you looking for?" she asked.

"Who."

"What?"

Hawk grinned. "No, *who*. I'm looking for a person. Goodman, to be exact."

"You . . . you think he came this way?"

"I'm sure of it. There's one thing I hadn't given much thought to before yesterday," Hawk said, plying the canoe paddle with a forward shift of his shoulders that sent the strong muscles of his arms rippling.

Irony forced her eyes away from the sight, keeping them on the sparse line of fir trees along the broad banks. "And what is that?"

"I should have realized it would be to Goodman's advantage to have a buyer in mind before he gets to your father's properties. That way, he can simply point out the land and make the sale, without running the risk of meeting up with anyone who actually knew your father. He can pocket the money and disappear long before the unsuspecting fellow catches on."

"So what, exactly, are you saying?"

"That we need to pick up Goodman's trail and pick it up fast. Once the idea occurred to me, I asked around back at the settlement. It seems Goodman did, indeed, meet up with a gentleman who came in on the train from points east. Goodman's party bought two canoes and left only hours ahead of us."

"So you think he's somewhere nearby?"

"It's possible. We got an earlier start than I intended . . ." He paused briefly and though Irony could feel his intent stare upon her face, she kept her gaze turned resolutely away. "And several men in two canoes are going to be moving more slowly than we are. So, in all likelihood, we could catch them at any bend of the river."

"What do you intend to do if that happens?"

His elusive smile tilted upward at one corner. "I was planning to leave that up to you. After all, you must have had something in mind when you left

155

Thief River hell bent for revenge." With a perfectly straight face, he said, "What were you intending to do? Shoot him? String him up? Take him back for prosecuting?"

Irony was silent. As usual, she hadn't really thought that far ahead. The idea of revenge had been in her mind, certainly, but how quickly it had been overshadowed by the thrill of being on her own, being in charge of herself and her actions for the first time in her life. And even the aunts had not discussed the actual apprehension of the profligate Goodman. No doubt they had merely imagined that Nathan would track the man down, clamp iron manacles on his hands and feet, and as easily as that, good would triumph over evil.

"Irony?" Hawk's voice came softly.

"I'm thinking," she snapped.

"You know, legally, you don't have many rights in the Canadian territory, don't you?"

Her green eyes flashed. "I wasn't concerned with legalities," she stormed. "Goodman certainly wasn't. I guess I just wanted to . . . to find him and somehow take him back to Thief River Falls to stand trial. It would be the only way to really clear Aunt Tiny's name. And don't forget, he needs to answer for his part in Bessie Sparks' death."

"True enough. But tell me, were you going to do this alone?"

Irony looked down at her hands, clasped tightly in her lap. She wondered if he would notice how white her knuckles were. "I could have managed it," she said quietly. "You may recall that I did have a gun in my possession."

"Oh, my, yes," he said, his words all the more biting for the apparent lack of scorn in his voice. "That excellent weapon would have made all things possible. Fortunately, I was able to purchase another gun at that last settlement."

"Well, then, everything will be fine."

"Irony, you amaze me. I swear, sometimes you'd make the damnedest poker player."

"Wh-what do you mean?"

"That bland look on your face." He rested the paddle on the edge of the canoe, and her eyes followed the clear droplets of water that fell from it. "I know something is going on in that devious mind of yours, but I haven't got a clue as to what it might be."

"I'm only mulling over the possibilities—as far as bringing Goodman to justice. We . . . I could think of something, surely."

"Yes, I'm certain *we'll* think of something."

"Then, you'll help me?"

"Have you forgotten that I have a stake in this, too? I want to know who murdered that schoolteacher, and it seems to me that Reverend Goodman must be the man with the answers."

"What was Bessie Sparks to you?" Irony couldn't keep herself from asking the question.

"A friend, as well as an innocent victim."

"And that's all . . . ?"

Hawk lowered the paddle into the water again and propelled the canoe forward. "Irony, you've neatly changed the subject, as usual, but you aren't going to deter me this time. I'll tell you all about Bessie Sparks and my interest in her death later. Right now I want you to explain to me why your aunts permitted you to go off on this journey alone. The more I hear about them, the more I doubt they would ever have done such a thing."

Irony turned her gaze to the far bank and shrugged. "I've already told you, there was no one else to go."

"From what you've said, I can't believe they would

157

have cared more for material possessions than for your welfare. Are you sure you've told me everything?"

Startled by his mild accusation, Irony's eyes darted back to his and were held by his dark, steady observation. She struggled against the sudden urge to tell him everything—to confess that she had given her companion the slip, that he had followed them relentlessly. That she knew he would be madder than Hades if and when he ever caught up with them. But no, there was no sense in borrowing trouble. Irony hoped the letter she'd left with the canoe maker had reassured Nathan enough that he had turned back. Deciding to bluff her way with a little righteous indignation at his prying, she raised her chin noticeably. Before she could scold him, Hawk tossed another query her way.

"What can you tell me about your father?" he asked. Irony lowered her chin and stared at him. "Who was he? How did he come to acquire property in Lake of the Woods?"

At least it was a less worrisome line of questioning. "Well, his name was Samuel McBride. He was raised in northern Minnesota and as a young man, joined a surveying team that was working along the Canadian border. My aunts tell me he loved the country so much he decided to stay on and live there."

"How did he meet your mother?"

"His family owned a number of sawmills back home, so occasionally he traveled south to see to them. On one of his trips, he met my mother. They were married almost immediately, and she came back to the lake with him. Not quite two years later, she returned to Thief River to have me—and you know the rest."

"How did he accumulate property in Canada?"

"He bought up some land for prospecting, discovered quite a quantity of gold—eventually bought more land. At one point, my father became friendly with the Indians in the area and turned over much of his property to them. They were a group of people who had been unhappy with their life on the government reservation . . ."

"You say he turned over his property? What do you mean?"

"He let them live there, use it as their own. And when he . . . died, he left a will instructing that they be allowed to remain there for as long as they wanted. He asked that I never sell the property or cause the natives to be removed from it."

"And you honor that?"

"I do. I certainly have no love for those people, but I believe I must respect my father's dying wish."

"Why is it you have such low regard for the Indians?" Hawk asked quietly. "It seems your father must have held them in high esteem."

Her laugh was short, bitter. "Oh, yes, very high esteem, indeed. In fact, he made it evident that he cared more for unwashed and uneducated savages than he did for his own . . . family."

"His own daughter, don't you mean?" Hawk meant to provoke her into finally revealing something of the truth about herself and her mission, but he regretted his words as he saw pain stir in her eyes.

"Yes, I suppose that is what I mean. It was, after all, somewhat difficult to grow up without either a mother or a father."

"I realize that."

"And I never understood why my father . . . didn't want to see me."

"Perhaps it wasn't that he didn't want to see you. Perhaps he had obligations out here that you didn't know about."

"He wrote a few letters to my aunts—letters filled with his plans for clearing farm ground for the Indians, or creating an efficient water system or bettering their housing. Those were the things he was involved with." Irony trailed her hand in the water, trying idly to catch a drifting feather.

"There was a white man who lived with my tribe for a time when I was growing up," Hawk said. "He always said the whites had taken enough from the Indians—that he wanted, in some small way, to make retribution for that. Perhaps your father felt the same way."

"But it shouldn't have been his first concern," Irony pointed out.

"No, probably not," he conceded.

"As a child, I couldn't understand why my father wasn't at least as interested in me as he was in his Indians. I had a hard time accepting the fact that he wasn't ever going to come home, or send for me."

Irony glanced up, making no effort to hide the self-mockery in her eyes. "For a time," she admitted, "I had a dream of going out to the wilderness to live with him, but as I got older, I gave that up. On my birthdays, if he remembered, he sometimes sent a gift with any traveler who happened to be passing through on his way south."

She scooped the feather out of the water and slowly twirled it between her thumb and first finger. "My friends got toys or books or ponies for their birthdays—I got buckskin dresses or feathered warbonnets or medicine clubs. They thought I was lucky, but I knew they were the fortunate ones. If they needed someone to repair their ice skates or frighten away bullies . . . or take them on picnics, they had fathers. I only had Aunt Tiny and Aunt Alyce . . ."

With those words, Irony looked stricken. "Oh, not

that they weren't wonderful to me! But it's not the same."

"I, too, grew up without a father," Hawk commented. "I know the feeling of being different. But at least I had a mother."

"Children are truly at the mercy of their parents, aren't they?"

"At the mercy of the fates, is more like it. After all, Irony, your father may have had compelling reasons to live his life as he did."

"I suppose that is one of the things that made this journey so important to me," Irony admitted. "I wanted to recover the stolen jewelry and money, and I wanted to stop the sale of my father's land. But it was almost as important to me to see Lake of the Woods for myself—to try and understand why it held such fascination for him."

Hawk nodded, aware that she had just revealed more of herself than she ever had previously. He hoped, for her sake, that she could find the answers she sought, and that they would soothe her anguish.

"He must be buried out here somewhere," Irony went on in a low voice. "No one ever brought his body home."

"I will help you find his grave, if that is what you wish."

"Thank you, Hawk . . . I appreciate that." Irony smiled for the first time. "It's strange that I have come to rely on you so much."

"Why?"

"I . . . I have to confess that, the closer we get to our destination, the more . . . afraid I've become. I've always hated and feared the savages responsible for my father's death, and now I will be going out among them. I wake up at night sometimes and feel cold all over at the thought of it. But I think no, it'll be fine because Hawk will be there." She made a wry face. "And then I remember that you're an Indian, too."

"In the time we've spent together, you've learned I have my virtues and my faults, as any man has, regardless of the color of his skin. When you meet the Ojibways on the lake, you'll quickly find they are no different. There are good and bad people in the world, Irony, and I think you realize their goodness or badness has little to do with their heritage."

"I hope you are right. But I have spent a lifetime blaming the red man for . . . for my own unhappiness. And most especially, for my father's death."

"How did he die?"

"He contracted an illness from the tribe with whom he was living. My aunts told me that many of the Indians became ill with smallpox and my father, thinking himself immune to the disease, tried to help care for the sick and dying. He ended up dying himself."

"That was not the Indians' fault," Hawk said. "Smallpox is a white man's disease—one he brought to the Indians when he came to plunder the wilderness."

Irony opened her mouth to make a stinging retort, then shut it abruptly. After a few seconds, she shook her head and sighed. "You are right, of course. Maybe I have even more to learn about my father's life here than I thought."

"There are many years of loneliness and hurt on your shoulders, but I believe you will work your way through it all in time. You have the look of a warrior in your eyes sometimes, Irony. You're not a weak person."

"I'll take that as a compliment," she murmured, a tinge of rose coloring her face.

"It was meant as such."

"Thank you." Irony smoothed the blue-gray feather

she held and cleared her throat. "What kind of bird does this belong to?"

"A blue heron," he replied. "My mother's totem."

He paddled on, a smile lingering on his wide, firm mouth as he reflected how fitting it was that such a feather had come to Irony—the only person he'd ever met who reminded him of the indomitable Heron Woman.

A short time later, Hawk broke the silence that had fallen. "We're coming to the mouth of the river," he said, "and it's my guess that Goodman may be camping there. At least, someone is . . ."

"How do you know?"

"I smell the smoke of a campfire."

Irony tried sniffing the air, but detected nothing. She looked back at him with new respect. "What if it is Goodman? What will we do?"

"Try to get past without him noticing us. There's an island not far from here where we can camp and wait."

"Wait?"

"For Goodman to embark upon the lake. There's a possibility he's still waiting for someone else to join him. That's the person I'm interested in seeing. Once they start across the lake, it will be an easy matter for us to follow at a distance and discover exactly what they have planned."

"So how do we get to the island?"

"I'm going to go ashore and do a bit of scouting around. If it's not Goodman, we won't have to worry. If it is, I'll come up with something." He nosed the canoe toward the bank. "Will you be afraid to wait here alone?"

"No . . . but what shall I do if you don't come back?"

"I'll be back, don't worry."

"Be careful."

"I won't take any chances on Goodman seeing me, I promise." His tone grew more serious. "By now, he'll be through with playing games."

Hawk helped Irony ashore, then hid the canoe in some rushes. Irony watched him disappear into the forest, then began strolling along the riverbank, grateful for the chance to stretch her cramped legs. Hawk had admonished her to be watchful and hide in the shelter of the trees if she heard or saw any other canoes on the river. She knew he was being cautious in the event they had somehow overtaken and passed Goodman, but she was thinking of Nathan Ferguson, wondering if he had turned back or if he still pursued them.

Hawk was gone less than half an hour. When he returned, Irony was sitting on a sun-warmed boulder watching a tiny blue and green hummingbird dive industriously into clusters of red flowers that hung from a vine. Relieved that he had returned so promptly, she welcomed him with a smile.

"Well?"

"As I thought, it was Goodman and his men." Hawk dropped to his haunches beside her. "There's an older fellow with them now. I assume he's the buyer. But, as I suspected, they appear to be waiting for someone else."

"Do we go on then?"

"Yes. Right now Goodman and his companions are exceedingly interested in corn liquor and a poker game. We should be able to sail under their noses without them seeing us. But, just in case, when we pass by their camp, I want you to lie down on the bottom of the canoe and keep out of sight."

She nodded, not especially enthralled with the possibility of meeting up with the Reverend Goodman again so soon.

Hawk got to his feet and began unbuttoning the red and black plaid shirt he wore. "This is pretty recognizable," he said, stripping off the garment and tossing it into the canoe. "Without it, I might look like any other Indian out fishing, provided Goodman even bothers to look up from his card game."

Hawk helped Irony back into the birchbark craft, then stepped in himself. Before bending to the paddle, he reached up and untied the leather thong that held his hair in place. Then, as she watched, mesmerized, he ran lean fingers through its thickness, shaking his head until the coal black locks fell in disarray across the strong ridge of his shoulders.

"There, do I look more untamed?" he asked, a wry twist to his mouth.

More untamed, indeed, Irony thought. *And wildly, incredibly beautiful.*

"Yes, you look very fierce," she finally said. "I doubt that Goodman would ever suspect you of being Raphael Hawkes."

The remains of an old fur trade post stood about two miles inland from the mouth of the river, and it was here, Hawk told her, that the renegades were camped. Irony, lying in the bottom of the canoe, held her breath as they passed the derelict buildings, but there were no challenging shouts—indeed, no indication they'd been seen at all. Slowly, she released her pent up breath.

"Are we past?" she whispered.

"Stay down a bit longer," Hawk replied. "Just to be safe."

Irony lay where she was, staring up at the half-naked man who silently and skillfully maneuvered the canoe downriver from the camp site. She was fascinated by the way the well-defined muscles beneath his bronzed skin bunched and rolled with each

165

sweep of the paddle. The very movement seemed to invite a woman's hand, and she pondered how it might feel to stroke her fingers along the hard edge of his shoulders, down the smoothness of his chest and into that swirl of coarser black hair on his taut abdomen.

Hawk turned his head to survey the shore with one last, long look, and Irony caught her lower lip between her teeth, awed by the perfection of his profile. Etched against the azure sky, it was flawless and appealingly forbidding. The wind, stronger now that they were approaching the mouth of the river, lifted his hair and flung it carelessly about his powerful neck. Again, Irony's fingers itched with the longing to explore—both the thick, soft strands of hair and the warm, solid flesh beneath.

"We're safely by," Hawk said. "You can sit upright again."

She saw a slightly quizzical expression in his eyes and knew he had been aware of her careful study of him. She reminded herself of her resolve to be circumspect and above reproach, and vowed to do better.

They made camp on a long, sandy island just beyond the choppy waters of the mouth of the river. Hawk explained that here they would wait for Goodman to make his move, because he wouldn't be able to enter Lake of the Woods without them seeing him.

They unloaded the canoe, then hid it among the trees in the marshy, forested center of the island. Their camp, concealed along the edge of those same trees, faced southeast, back toward the entrance to the huge lake. Irony was fascinated by the island and set off to explore it as soon as they had eaten a

166

cold meal.

She soon found that the south side was relatively calm compared to the north, which braved the open waters of the widest part of the lake. There the wind blew fiercely, lashing the water into furious waves that crashed against the sandy beach.

Like a child, Irony had dropped to her knees in the deep sand and was sifting through it, exclaiming over minute shells and bits of colored rock. Hawk stood a few feet away, gazing intently out over the expanse of blue-gray water.

"This must be what the ocean looks like," Irony exclaimed, raising her face to the bracing wind. "I've always wanted to see the ocean."

"This is what they call the Big Traverse," Hawk told her. "It's the largest area of open water in the lake."

"It must be dangerous to cross."

"It can be deadly for the inexperienced, but the *voyageurs* have traveled here for two centuries in nothing more substantial than the light canoe."

Irony noted the rapt look on his face, again admiring the carved elegance of his profile. "What are you thinking?"

"That it is good to be home," he said, dropping down onto the sand. "It has been a long time."

"Then you lived near here?"

He gestured with a casual hand. "Not here, no. I lived in the islands off to the northeast. But the same sky stretches over all the lake, and no doubt these very waters washed upon the shores of the island I called home."

"You're sentimental!" Irony softly accused, her eyes twinkling.

"My Indian heritage."

"But, at times," she murmured, "you can be so cynical."

167

He gave her an unreadable look. "My white heritage."

"Tell me about your childhood. I'd like to hear it."

"There's not much to tell. You already know my father was a trapper who abandoned my mother and me."

"Yes, but I know nothing of your mother. What was she like?"

"Her name was Heron Woman." At his words, Irony's hand went to the heron feather she had tucked into one braid, just above her ear. "And yes," Hawk went on with a smile, "she wore blue feathers in her hair."

"I'm sorry—I didn't mean to remind you of unhappiness."

Hawk's big hand stayed Irony's smaller one. "No, don't take it out. It doesn't make me unhappy. It makes me recall the good times I shared with my mother."

Irony enjoyed the feel of his hand on hers, but the rising specter of impropriety caused her to gently tug her hand free, letting it drop back to the fine, cool sand. Hawk appeared not to notice, and his own hand began smoothing the sand beside his knee first one way, then the other.

"And they were good times, despite my mother's lack of standing in the tribal community. We had a comfortable lodge at the edge of the village, we fished and hunted."

"Did you have other children to play with?"

"All the children in the tribe played together when we were very young. Then, as we grew older, more difference was made between the respectable children of the village and those like myself . . . the half breeds."

"But none of that was your fault," Irony said, surprised at the anger she felt on behalf of the little boy he had once been.

"No, but as the Old Testament tells us, the sins of the fathers are visited upon the children."

"Still, it's not fair." Irony busied herself scooping damp sand, heaping it into a pile which she began to mold with gritty hands.

"Perhaps not, but I didn't mind. That was about the time my friends and I formed the Nighthawks."

Irony looked up, her sand castle forgotten. "The Nighthawks? A club?"

"So to speak. There were five of us — boys about the same age, all fathered and abandoned by white men. We were different from the other children in the tribe, so we decided to band together and create a secret society. Actually, it was nothing more than a means of self protection. We could stand up for one another when there was trouble . . ."

"What kind of trouble?"

"You know, the usual things one encounters growing up."

"Like being teased because you don't have a father?"

"That, and having no one older and wiser to defend you when the need arises. One of our chief's sons organized a campaign to oust us from the community. We had only ourselves to rely upon."

"What happened?"

Hawk's face was devoid of any emotion as he answered. "One of the Nighthawks happened to save the boy's life. After that, his father put an end to the discrimination."

"It was you, wasn't it? You saved that boy's life."

"It doesn't make any difference. The point is, the Nighthawks became my friends and my family. And after we had been to the Place of Dreams, we pledged our loyalty for life."

"The Place of Dreams?"

"An island where the boys in my tribe were taken to search for the vision that would reveal their destiny. It's an Ojibway ritual," Hawk explained. "When a boy is close to sixteen, he is taken to the sacred Place of Dreams and left until he has the vision that will tell him what he was meant to do with his life." Hawk turned his intent gaze toward her, but Irony sensed he was lost in the past. "Afterward, he is given a three-cornered blanket by his mother. That is a symbol of his newly won independence and serves as his pillow, his bed or his coat. It's three-cornered, or unfinished, to indicate continuing maternal love. If the boy wishes, he can live alone from that time on—but his mother is still there if he should need her."

"Did you live alone when you came back from the Place of Dreams?"

"No. I intended to stay by my mother's fireside for the rest of my life. It was she who left me."

"But not from choice."

"No, never from choice." Hawk turned to look out across the water again.

Irony's gaze fell upon Hawk's bare shoulder and the strange tatoo that marked it. "The tatoo you wear—it has something to do with the Nighthawks, doesn't it?"

"Yes. The circle is the moon, the bird flying across it is a hawk. All five of us had the same tatoo . . ."

"Of course!" Irony's green eyes widened with the import of what he had just said. "So when you heard that Bessie Sparks' murderer had a tatoo like yours, you knew he had to be one of the Nighthawks—am I right?"

He sighed. "Unfortunately, yes. And that is what interests me so in the good reverend and his gang of renegade Indians. I want to see what friend betrayed the ideals he grew up with."

"You don't know which of the four he could be?"

"No, I have no idea." Hawk brushed the sand from his hands. "But there are only three others now. One of the Nighthawks died in the smallpox epidemic."

"What will you do when you find the one who was with Goodman?"

"I don't know, Irony. And to be honest, I have my doubts that there is such a man. So far, the only Indians we've seen with Goodman have been Running Dog, Broken Knife and Three-Fingers. The story about the man with the tatoo may have been just that—a story."

A large, foam-edged wave rolled onto the beach and lapped at the sand castle Irony had built. Hurriedly, she reshaped it, packing more sand around the bottom to fortify it against the next onslaught of water.

"Hawk, did you see your vision?" she asked idly. "About how you would spend your life?"

"I did—the spirits told me I would be dragged around the wilderness by a stubborn, wild-haired female who was half-woman, half-child."

She heard the quiet laughter in his voice and looked up from her play in the sand. "Oh, you!" she retorted, making a face at him, but abandoning the crumbling castle. "Seriously, now. Did you?"

He nodded. "In my vision, a huge white owl was flying over the river, gliding through the dark sky, back and forth from one bank to the other. It was as if I was on his back, seeing the treetops and the water far below just as he must have been seeing them. And when he swooped to catch a fish, I could feel the cold air rushing past my face, and the moon glittering on the river shone in my eyes as though we were flying through a multitude of stars."

171

"What did your vision mean?"

"The elders of the tribe spent many hours interpreting it," Hawk replied. "It was finally decided that the owl symbolized one of great learning . . . "

"A teacher," Irony said firmly.

"And the flight back and forth across the river indicated to them that I would always be torn between two countries in the search for wisdom."

"What did it mean when the owl caught the fish?"

His smile flashed momentarily. "One of the weaker aspects of the interpretation, I believe. The elders vowed it meant that, despite my learning, I would retain the heart of a warrior."

Irony was bemused. "The soul of a poet . . . the heart of a warrior." She tilted her head and looked at him consideringly. "I think it's an apt description of you, Hawk. I think you're really like that, though I've never known another man who was . . ."

Without warning, their gazes locked and the lightheartedness of the moment was lost. Irony could see her own reflection in the infathomable darkness of his eyes and felt as helpless as a rabbit in a snare.

A low, frustrated groan bursting from his throat, Hawk reached for her and pulled her across his lap. Cradling her gently, he dropped his mouth to hers in a soft, searching kiss that rubbed his warm lips against hers, sensual but questioning. She sensed that if she struggled, he would set her free. By the same token, if she did not, he would assume she was still willing to let the emotion that was between them have its way.

Irony wanted to run, but not as much as she wanted to stay. She knew she should extricate herself from his arms, firmly push him away — instead, she murmured his name and allowed her arms to wrap around him.

The kiss became less gentle, less uncertain and

more bold. She felt Hawk's heart beating rapidly against hers as he gathered her closer, lowering them both to the sand.

She was drowning—not in the chilly waters of the Lake of the Woods that washed up around them, but in the heated caress of his mouth. His kiss was burning, a demanding flame that drew her. With a sigh of surrender, Irony tightened her arms around his neck and opened her mouth to his. Seeking to elude the coldness beneath her, she strained closer to him, to the granite-like body that covered her, seducing her with its strength and energy.

Hawk moved his head and shaped his mouth to hers with new purpose, deepening the scorching crush of his lips, the arrogant exploration of his tongue. As spurred by desire as she, he was lost to the rational thinking upon which he prided himself. Last night Irony had seemed somehow vulnerable—tonight she was more certain of herself, more mature. Or was it just him? Did he only want to think that? He didn't know. . . .

He wedged one hand between their bodies, searching for the softness he needed so desperately to touch. As he stroked her, Irony gasped, stunned by the powerful thrill that stabbed at her. No man had ever touched her so intimately. Through the wet cotton shirt she wore, her chilled flesh thrust against his chest, her nipples pebbled and aching.

Hawk drew back, the sound she made echoing in his ears. "I didn't mean to hurt you, sweetheart . . ."

"No," she whispered. "No, you didn't hurt me." She drew deep, shattering breaths of air. "Hawk . . ." She didn't know if she was going to ask him to stop, or beg him to go on.

"My God, I need you so much," he groaned.

His words shocked her, somehow awakening her to their circumstances. They were lying half in and half out of the water, their clothing soaked, their bodies ravaged by heart-shaking need. She wanted this, wanted him to make love to her — wanted him to claim what she had never offered another man. But she couldn't do it. God help her, she couldn't do it!

Irony forced herself to remember that, by being part Ojibway, Raphael Hawkes was a symbol of all she feared and despised. Her whole life had been affected by her father's devotion to Indians — hadn't she always burned with resentment because of it? She would not follow his example by falling victim to Hawk's sensuality and her own unsatisfied longings.

"No!" she suddenly shouted. "No, Hawk — we've got to stop!"

With a strength she didn't know she possessed, she pushed away from the bewildered man. She struggled to her feet, then turned to run on wobbling legs. Even so, she knew she wasn't running from him, but from herself.

"Irony, wait!" Hawk was right behind her again, reaching out to grasp her arms and pull her back into his embrace.

"Get your hands off that woman or I'll kill you!"

The furious command issued in an unfamiliar male voice brought both of them back to the world they had momentarily forgotten existed. They turned to see a sandy haired man, legs wide in a belligerent stance, not more than a dozen feet away. The late afternoon sunshine glittered brilliantly on the barrel of the gun he held and on the metal star pinned to his vest.

"Who the hell are you?" asked Hawk.

"Nathan!" cried Irony. "Nathan Ferguson!"

Chapter Ten

The Pine Island camp . . .

"You son of a bitch," Nathan sneered. "I ought to shoot you where you stand."

"You wouldn't mind telling me why before you pull the trigger, would you?" Hawk asked, his tone deceptively calm.

"I think you know why."

"At this moment, I'd say there's a great deal I don't know. For instance, I know you're the man from the train . . . but I *don't* know what you are to Irony."

"I'm her fiancé, Nathan Ferguson. Sheriff's deputy from Thief River Falls, Minnesota."

"Her fiancé?" Hawk cast a look at Irony, who stood halfway between the two of them, her eyes wide and stricken. "Well, well, well. I presume you're the one who's been following us for the last few days, but I can't help wondering why it is she never mentioned you."

"Look, I'm not in the mood to stand here and make idle conversation. Not after the scene I just witnessed."

"I think you got the wrong idea, Ferguson."

"I don't see how I could have. I know exactly what you've put this little girl through—and how you must have threatened her to keep her from making herself known to me on the train." Nathan moved closer to Irony, one hand reaching out to grasp her shoulder. He murmured something that Hawk couldn't hear, and Irony bobbed her head up and down in answer. Nathan's jaw knotted. "You say you're fine, Irony, but it sure as hell didn't look like it a few minutes ago."

And, as if the memory of the scene he had interrupted filled him with renewed anger, he lifted the gun again and aimed it straight at Hawk.

"I'm getting damned tired of having guns pointed at me," Hawk growled. "Irony, if you care anything for this man—and I assume you do—you'd better do some fast explaining."

Irony wasn't sure which one of them Hawk thought deserved an explanation, but when she heard the sharp click that signified Nathan had readied the gun for firing, she dashed the tears from her eyes and stepped away from his protective touch.

"Nathan, it's all right . . . really! He—he didn't hurt me."

Nathan Ferguson's expression was pitying. "Sweet Irony," he said. "You don't have to be brave anymore." He ignored Hawk's sarcastic snort. "I know the truth."

"And what is the truth?" Hawk asked, crossing his arms over his chest as if settling down to listen with genuine interest. "I'd be relieved to hear it myself. For once."

"I know what you Indians do with women you kidnap—we're not entirely ignorant back in Thief River Falls. Irony was exactly what you were looking for—gentle, trusting, innocent." Nathan clenched his teeth as if fighting for control. "You damnable brute!"

Irony still couldn't bring herself to look at Hawk.

She clasped and unclasped her hands, studying them as intently as if she feared they might fly away.

Nathan went down on his knee, careful to keep the gun handy, and unfastened one of the saddlebags he had dropped into the sand. "I knew what you'd done the minute I saw this." He rose and tossed an object at Hawk's feet, disgust written on his features. "Surely you can't deny knowing anything about that."

Hawk stooped and picked up Irony's torn nightgown. He turned his black eyes on her, not saying a word.

"Then when I got to the canoe shed and received the letter you forced her to write—damn! I knew I was going to hunt you down if it took the rest of my life."

"Letter?" Hawk rolled up the nightgown and threw it at Irony with enough force that she barely had to move her arms to catch it. "Do you know anything about a letter, Irony?"

"Oh, well, let me explain that," she said in a small voice.

"There's no need, dearest," Nathan interjected. "The ladies at the boarding house told me everything I needed to know. Of course, not being acquainted with you, they immediately thought the worst. But I know your aunts and how carefully they raised you—you're a lady through and through. That son of a . . . pardon me, that red-skinned savage forced his attentions on you, didn't he?"

"No, Nathan," she exclaimed. "It wasn't like that. Honestly! And he's not a savage. His name is Hawk . . . er, Raphael Hawkes, and he's my guide, that's all. Believe me, he's really very much a gentleman." She seized Nathan's arm and gave him her most earnest look. "He—he even quotes poetry."

"Are you saying . . . he seduced you?"

"No! I'm saying that nothing has happened to me."

177

"You've been alone with . . . with him all this time and you expect me to believe nothing has happened? What about the scene I witnessed a moment ago? You were trying to escape from him, weren't you?"

Irony briefly considered the advisability of telling Nathan the truth, but something warned her he wouldn't want to hear it. "Well, yes, in a manner of speaking." She drew a deep breath, still not daring to look Hawk's way. "It . . . we . . . well, you see . . ."

"What Irony is trying to say is that I kissed her," Hawk spoke up. "She, however, wasn't interested. I guess I misread the signs."

Apparently Irony's words and Hawk's somber confession appeased Nathan enough that he decided to be charitable. "Well, that could easily happen, I suppose. What with you being . . . being a . . ."

"Savage?" Hawk interjected brusquely. "Yes, we savages do have the damnedest time with social amenities."

"Hawk . . ." Irony finally braved looking at him, but the expression on his face caused her inexplicable pain.

"I'll leave you two to talk," Hawk said, starting off.

"Hey, Indian," exclaimed Nathan, "don't walk off while I'm holding a gun on you."

Hawk paused. "Go ahead and shoot if you're so inclined. It'd be the fastest way to bring Goodman and his men running."

"What?"

"I'll explain, Nathan," Irony promised. "But first, let me . . ."

With a loud groan, Nathan doubled over, clutching his stomach.

"Oh, my God!" Irony cried. "What's wrong?"

Straightening a bit, Nathan hastily surveyed the

brushy center of the island, his face scarlet with embarrassment. "It's—it's those wild strawberries I ate this morning." He groaned a second time, and Irony could swear she heard Hawk chuckle.

"Do you mean to say . . . you've . . ."

"Got the greenhorn trots," Hawk crudely supplied.

"Diarrhea," Nathan gasped, looking frantic. He doubled over again.

"For God's sake, put your gun away and go to the bushes," Hawk snapped. "Don't worry, your *fiancée* will still be a virgin when you return."

With a scornful look at both Irony and the deputy, Hawk strode away toward camp.

"I'm sorry, Irony, but I've got to . . ."

"Go ahead, Nathan, I'll be fine. I'll wait for you in camp."

Without further delay, the deputy shoved his gun back into its holster and loped toward the sheltering woods. When he disappeared among the trees, Irony started after Hawk, the telltale nightgown still clutched in her hand.

She found him near their hidden camp, leaning against a slender birch tree, staring out at the calmer water off the south side of the island.

"I'm sorry, Hawk," she said. "I should have . . ."

"Why didn't you tell me you were engaged to be married?"

"I'm not—not actually." She sighed, knowing he probably wasn't going to believe her. "My aunts think I should marry Nathan, that's all. And . . ."

"And what?"

"I guess he does, too."

"What about you?"

She shook her head. "I don't want to marry anyone. That's why I ran away from him at the Thief River depot."

"So you ran away and he's been following you ever

since?" Hawk bent his head to look down at her, and she had never seen him look so severe.

"Yes."

"Then you knew all along who was trailing us?"

She nodded. "I probably should have told you."

"But honesty isn't one of your strong points, is it?"

"I was afraid you'd hurt him."

Hawk straightened. "Let me tell you something. If I was ever going to hurt your brave young deputy, it would have been just now, when he laid his hand on you." He turned and began walking away.

"Hawk, wait—please!" Irony reached out and touched his arm and he stilled immediately. He stood immobile, his face lifted, his eyes looking upward toward the treetops. "I . . ." Her voice trailed away to a whisper. "He's not my fiancé—he doesn't mean anything to me . . . not in that way."

He whirled to face her. "Then why did you act so damned relieved to see him?"

"I—I don't know. I was frightened . . . and suddenly there he was, looking so safe and familiar."

"Poor little girl," he mocked harshly. "All alone with the lusting savage."

"Don't be angry . . ."

"Don't be angry?" he all but shouted. "Why the hell not?"

"It's not my fault I was scared . . ."

"No, it's not your fault. You had every right to be terrified. After all, you're one of those well-informed citizens of Thief River who knows what Indians do to the women they kidnap."

Irony's green eyes filled with remorse as he repeated Nathan's unkind and unthinking words. "No," she protested, "I'm not! I don't know!"

A coldly amused smile flitted across his face. "Then maybe I'd better show you precisely what it is you've been rescued from."

180

He seized her shoulders in a steely grasp and, twisting, shoved her against the trunk of the birch tree.

"Hawk," she gasped. "Don't . . ."

His lips took hers in a punishing kiss, clearly meant to insult—he wanted to incite her to the same enraged hurt he was feeling. He relentlessly ravaged her mouth, using his body to hold hers against the unyielding barrier of the tree. He ignored her struggles, for once taking pleasure in unleashing the wildness that dwelled within him. For those few moments, the veneer of civility and sophistication he had acquired over the years was stripped away, and he was left with powerfully primitive urges that he made no effort to control.

Panting with lust and anger, he raised his head and stared into her eyes. Irony turned her face away, but his hard fingers gripped her chin and forced her to look back at him.

"Is this the kind of thing you're afraid of?" he asked, his voice a harsh rasp. "That I'll forget my manners and treat you like a real woman . . . and not some prissy little spinster? That I'll dare to put my hands on you without your permission—or your aunts' tolerant blessings?"

"Hawk, I can ex—"

"Shut up, Irony," he breathed. "Don't open your mouth to lie to me again. Don't open your mouth at all unless you intend to kiss me the way you've been wanting to since the beginning."

Again, he bent his head to hers. Though she clamped her lips shut, he overrode her mute protestations. His tongue teased the corners of her mouth and pried insistently at the tight seam her lips made. The groan that issued from her throat was a mixture of fright, anger and reluctant passion.

Hawk's hands slid down her arms to her waist,

where they slipped between her body and the smooth trunk of the birch, pulling her to him. Irony felt the heat of his palms through the dampness of her shirt as he spread his hands across her back. He soothed and massaged her chilled flesh, and the spine she would have kept ramrod straight seemed to melt, molding against him as she sought his fiery warmth.

She knew it was useless, she couldn't hold out against him, or against the blazing desire he aroused within her. Something about this man compelled her to simply forget propriety and let matters take their natural course. She had always realized there was far more to love and passion than she had ever known— indeed, had ever dreamed of. And some undeniable something had whispered to her from the start that Hawk was the man she wanted to teach her about all of those things. Despite her fear and resentment for those of his race, despite her aspirations to be a lady and, like her dear aunts, immune to any possible indiscretion, she wanted to fall to the sand right here and now and discover every unknown aspect of passion.

Oh, but it wasn't mere curiosity, she finally admitted. No, Hawk had become increasingly dear to her. Their days and nights together had forced her to look beyond the facade, to the man hidden deep inside. And when that inner man made a rare appearance, as he had on the beach before Nathan's untimely arrival, she was at his mercy. She had come to care far too much for the beautiful and lonely soul he sometimes revealed.

Irony could feel the pain within him and knew instinctively she had been the cause of it. She wasn't certain in what way she had hurt him, she only knew she wanted to do whatever it took to assuage that hurt. Fear was replaced with compassion, yet even compassion was tempered by her swiftly blossoming ardor.

Her mouth softened, her lips parted against his and, with a sigh, she abandoned the struggle. The crumpled nightgown fell to the ground as she unclenched her hands and raised them to his shoulders. Of their own volition, her fingers stroked along the taut flesh, coming to rest at the back of his neck, enmeshed in the unbound black hair that brushed over them. She stood on tiptoe, pressing herself upward against his chest, immediately fired by the sweet abrasion of her breasts as she moved into closer contact with him. With a sharp sound of pleasure, she rubbed against him and let her tongue meet his in tentative exploration. She could feel the reaction that jolted him throughout the entire length of his body, and she grew bolder, letting her accelerating emotions express themselves in the innocently erotic kiss she was bestowing upon him.

Hawk pulled back. "You're enjoying yourself a little too much, aren't you, Irony?" His words were like a splash of cold water. "Aren't you afraid anymore? Afraid I'll do something like this . . . ?" He slid his hands downward to clasp her buttocks, lifting her against him with uncompromising strength. The evidence of his powerful arousal both shocked and thrilled Irony, and she clung to him, uncertain that she could stand alone. He ground his hips into hers, and she buried her face against the side of his neck to keep from crying out with the unexpected need he was creating within her.

Hawk released her, letting her slide down the length of his body. "Or what if I do something like this?" His hands rose to the front of her shirt, covering her breasts and causing the blood to thunder so loudly in her ears that she barely heard his words. His lean fingers unbuttoned the first and second buttons, but then, as if in a frenzy of impatience, he gripped the lapels of the shirt and ripped it open, causing the last four buttons to fly loose, scattering in the sand at their feet.

Irony's cry of protest faded to a whimper of pure pleasure as his hands stroked the bare flesh above the top of her chemise, and when he untied the ribbon and opened her bodice to kiss the rounded sides of her breasts, she bit her lip and leaned her head back against the tree behind her.

She shuddered as his mouth closed over one nipple, the sensual tugging of his lips against the wet cotton chemise sending spasms of nearly painful delight all the way to her toes.

"Oh, Hawk," she breathed, the words drawn out of her by a force stronger than her own will. In another second, she knew she would be begging him to lay her down in the drifted sand and show her the rest of it, everything. It made not one whit of difference that Nathan Ferguson might stumble upon them at any time. The stodgy moral upbringing she had been given by her aunts was the farthest thing from her mind. She wanted Raphael Hawkes to make love to her more than she had ever wanted anything . . .

"Oh, Hawk," he repeated softly, mocking her. "So, suddenly the savage appeals to you, does he? You like this, don't you? You'd be perfectly agreeable if I threw you down right now and finished what has been so effectively begun."

As if unable to stop himself, he dropped a swift, hot kiss on her slightly parted lips and admired the specks of russet in her stunned emerald eyes. "Shall I tear away the rest of your clothes? Is that what you expect of me?" His hands dropped to her waist, and she could feel the heat of his fingers against her stomach as they gripped the waistband of her trousers.

"Tell the truth for once, Irony," he snarled. "It's not me you're afraid of—it's yourself. You've been scared to death that if I touched you like this, you couldn't say no. Wouldn't want to say no."

Silently, she shook her head. She wasn't denying what he said so much as she was denying the possibility he was not going to make love to her.

"So you're going to persist in lying?" He removed his hands from her. "I suppose it really won't matter anymore—now that you've got your fiancé to protect you from my advances."

"I don't need protection from you," she whispered raggedly.

"No, probably not," he agreed. "Because I don't intend to ever lay a hand on you again. If you want to roll around in the sand, do it with your deputy."

He backed away a few steps. "I'm going to move his canoe back into the trees with ours. Tell him for me."

"What . . . what do you want me to do?"

"Just keep off this beach and out of Goodman's sight." He started walking away. "And, more importantly, stay out of mine."

When he had gone, Irony, refusing to cry, fell weakly to her hands and knees and started searching for the buttons he had torn from her shirt.

When Nathan finally returned from his sojourn in the bushes, he found a calmly composed Irony. Dressed in a slightly wrinkled, but pretty cotton gown, her hair neatly combed into a knot at the nape of her neck, she was sitting on a boulder sewing on the ripped nightgown.

"God, you look like you should be in your aunts' parlor in Thief River," he said, dropping onto the grass at her feet. Shyly, he touched her knee through the layers of gown and petticoat. "It's nice to see you looking like your old self, Irony. I didn't know what to think when I first saw you."

"Those clothes belong to the neighbor boy back home," she said faintly. Clearing her throat, she went on in a firmer tone. "They're more suitable for traveling in the wilderness than a dress."

"I suppose so. Still, you sure look pretty now."

From across the clearing came the sudden, loud rattling of pans as Hawk made preparations for supper. He continued to slice side meat into a skillet without looking up, even though he was aware of their strained silence.

"Trust a woman to have a needle and thread wherever she goes, huh?" Nathan teased, ignoring the other man.

Irony gave him a bland smile. "It's something I learned from my Aunt Alyce. She taught me to be prepared for any contingency." Irony thought of the shirt she had just tucked away in her carpetbag, each of the buttons restored to its proper place. "Everything of value that I know, I learned from my aunts," she added with a touch of defiance.

"That's because they love you so much," Nathan commented. "And they only want the best for you." He didn't say "Like me", but the unspoken words seemed to float on the air between them. "What on earth possessed you to run away from me, Irony—dearest? Didn't you know how anxious and upset I'd be? How terrified your aunts would have been had I told them the truth?"

Irony sighed in relief. "So you didn't tell them? I've worried about that."

"I didn't take the time," he stated. "I didn't even wait for the next train. I hired a horse and started after you." He grimaced, and for an instant, Irony

186

wondered if his stomach complaint had returned. "As it turned out, I'd have been better off to take the train. Just when I was about to catch up with you, my horse went lame. I had a devil of a time finding someplace to buy another one."

"I'm sorry I caused you so much trouble," Irony murmured.

"I found you, and that's all that matters." He patted her knee again. "And from now on, I'll be here to take care of you."

Unexpectedly, Hawk towered over them. Nathan glanced up, startled, and even Irony couldn't prevent herself from shrinking away the tiniest bit. The scowl on Hawk's face made him look unutterably ferocious. He shoved a steaming mug under Nathan's nose.

"Here," he ordered. "Drink this. It'll help cure that problem of yours."

Nathan took the mug, sniffed its strange aroma, and asked, "What is it?"

"Tea made from the root of the spotted cranebill. Lucky for you, I found some growing along the edge of the marsh."

Nathan winced. "Yes, lucky for me."

"Perhaps it will help," Irony suggested.

With a shrug, the deputy took a cautious sip of the hot liquid, then strangled and spat it out. "Aarrgh! Are you trying to poison me?"

"I'd drink it, if I were you," Hawk said. "It's sure as hell hard to court a woman properly when you have to keep running to the bushes."

Nathan strangled again, though more from rage, Irony suspected, than from the medicinal tea. She was certain she detected a gleam of satisfied amusement in Hawk's eyes, but at least he didn't laugh outright. Instead, he gave her a cool look and said, "I left the potatoes boiling, and you'll need to turn that meat soon. I'll be back later."

"Don't you want any supper?"

"I'm not hungry."

With that terse statement, Hawk disappeared into the gathering gloom. Nathan stared after him for a long moment before saying, "I see he's dressed more like an Indian . . ."

Naturally, that had been the first thing Irony had noticed when she'd stepped out of her tent after changing her own clothes. Though Hawk wore the familiar breech clout, she was grateful that this time he was also wearing a pair of fringed leather leggings.

"I wonder why," Nathan mused.

Irony ignored the urge to snap at him. "I expect he's feeling very much like an Indian right now," she said quietly.

She sensed that Hawk realized why she had turned away from him, and that now he chose to retreat into the very heritage that was to blame for their estrangement. She should be relieved that he had, but the scorching passion he had aroused in her while venting his anger had left her feeling lost and alone . . . and wanting so many things that were forever out of her reach.

On the windward side of the island, the water was as rough and gale-tossed as before. Hawk decided it suited his mood.

He stood at the edge of the surf and gazed out over the darkening lake, ignoring the soft, silvery mist that was settling in for the night. A tip-tilted crescent moon rode high in the sky, nearly obscured by the haze.

Hawk thought of the scene he had left and cursed bitterly.

For a supposedly educated man, he'd done some pretty stupid things since meeting up with Irony McBride. Stupid things like forgetting his place in society, forgetting his ancestry. Idiotic things like ignoring the fact that, no matter how much he'd tried to better himself, he was still a product of the wilderness. And no matter how much she'd tried to step down from the pedestal Ferguson and her aunts had placed her on, Irony was still a product of her staid, middle-class upbringing.

Goddamn it to hell, why did I ever think there could be anything between us? He started pacing back and forth along the empty beach, striding impatiently with all the unleashed energy of a wild cougar.

How had he allowed himself to be seduced by the long, companionable days on the trail? When had he stopped thinking of her as an annoying hindrance and started thinking of her as a desirable woman?

He slowed his pacing. No, if he was honest with himself, he'd admit that he'd been intrigued by her from the first moment she had whisked into the headmaster's office back at Sweetwater demanding a man. Even now the memory was enough to lift his carved mouth in a half-smile. She'd been like a fascinating little whirlwind, one he'd reckoned he'd enjoy standing back and watching. But somewhere along the way, he'd been drawn right into the heart of the storm, and he seemed utterly helpless to do anything about it.

He supposed he'd been living on false hope since that day in the forest when, thinking him asleep, she'd experimented with kissing him. Hers had been genuine interest, he'd swear, a real liking for him as a man, not simply as a novelty. Throughout his life, he'd been subject to another, less altruistic form of attention from females. It never failed to amaze him how many white women in the Sweetwater community had made themselves available to him—but it had always been done in secret, of course. Part of a thrilling experimentation with the darker side of life, he supposed. He'd taken what one or two had offered, ignored the majority, and suffered as few qualms as the women themselves. But it had never been that way with Irony . . . or so he'd thought.

He knew she was drawn to him not because he was part Ojibway, but in spite of it. She professed to hate Indians, and after hearing the story of her childhood, he had believed her. It had been evident that she was attracted to him, that she wanted to kiss and touch him, and have him respond by doing the same things to her. But somehow she had bewitched him into disregarding the fact that she, too, was only experimenting.

Obviously, he had taken matters too far when he assumed she felt as much for him as he did her. How pointedly that had been brought home to him when she ran from his arms to the safer presence of Nathan Ferguson. Lord, he'd never forget the devastating jealousy that had swept through him as he watched the young deputy comfort her. The worst of it was, Nathan Ferguson had a right to put his hands on Irony, to soothe and caress her. He did not. Never had. And, damn it all, he should have realized that long ago.

He'd regarded her as an innocent—but he was one also. Despite the years of learning lessons the hard way, he'd made a fool of himself again. He'd been grasping for something that was worlds out of his reach. When was he going to figure it out?

Again, he stared out over the water. The wind was calming now, but whether it intended to lay or was gathering energy for a real gale, he wasn't sure. From all the signs, he thought it wise to expect the worst. It wasn't unusual for the wind to roar over the Big Traverse with all the mighty force that nature could put behind it—and when it did, it brought with it the icy chill of the Far North, even in the heart of summer.

That would suit Hawk fine. He'd had enough warmth and sunshine in his life lately—no sense getting used to it.

He continued walking down the beach, calmer now. Maybe it was just as well Ferguson had shown up when he did. This way, things wouldn't have to go any farther. And no doubt the other man's presence would help Hawk remember he was merely a hired guide.

In his own way, he had come close to loving Irony McBride. Or so it seemed to him, judging by what little he knew of that emotion. Thank God, this had happened before he'd had a chance to profess his undying passion to her. Had they spent one more day alone in the wilderness, who knew what ridiculous declarations he might have made? One more day . . .

He stopped and stood looking down, disturbed by the heaviness that had settled within his chest. Just then, the surf rolled in and gently deposited a gift at his feet. He bent and picked it up.

Lying on the palm of his hand was the heron feather that Irony had been wearing in her hair earlier. It must have fallen onto the beach when they were struggling . . .

A good thing, that. Nathan Ferguson hadn't been any too pleased to find his sweetheart in boy's clothing. What would he have thought had he seen Irony's unmindful imitation of a native custom?

Hawk's fingers closed over the feather as images of Irony flashed through his mind. Irony bathing in the river, the look of surprise on her face when she'd fired the gun in the stable—the sweet seductiveness of her in the torn nightgown, her brave dignity. He recalled Irony lying in the bottom of the canoe as they'd glided past Goodman's camp, her green eyes alight with mischief and a hint of apprehension. And the most compelling image of all: Irony in his arms on the beach, her face flushed with passion, her heart beating in time with his own.

That was the Irony he would remember each time he looked at the feather . . . *his* Irony. The one who would stay behind in the wilderness long after the real Irony and her husband-to-be had gone home to Thief River Falls.

MORE PASSION AND ADVENTURE AWAIT... YOUR TRIP TO A BIG ADVENTUROUS WORLD BEGINS WHEN YOU ACCEPT YOUR FIRST 4 NOVELS ABSOLUTELY *FREE* (AN $18.00 VALUE)

Accept your Free gift and start to experience more of the passion and adventure you like in a historical romance novel. Each Zebra novel is filled with proud men, spirited women and tempestuous love that you'll remember long after you turn the last page.

Zebra Historical Romances are the finest novels of their kind. They are written by authors who really know how to weave tales of romance and adventure in the historical settings you love. You'll feel like you've actually gone back in time with the thrilling stories that each Zebra novel offers.

GET YOUR FREE GIFT WITH THE START OF YOUR HOME SUBSCRIPTION

Our readers tell us that these books sell out very fast in book stores and often they miss the newest titles. So Zebra has made arrangements for you to receive the four newest novels published each month.

You'll be guaranteed that you'll never miss a title, and home delivery is so convenient. And to show you just how easy it is to get Zebra Historical Romances, we'll send you your first 4 books absolutely FREE! Our gift to you just for trying our home subscription service.

BIG SAVINGS AND FREE HOME DELIVERY

Each month, you'll receive the four newest titles as soon as they are published. You'll probably receive them even before the bookstores do. What's more, you may preview these exciting novels free for 10 days. If you like them as much as we think you will, just pay the low preferred subscriber's price of just $3.75 each. *You'll save $3.00 each month off the publisher's price.* AND, your savings are even greater because there are never any shipping, handling or other hidden charges—FREE Home Delivery. Of course you can return any shipment within 10 days for full credit, no questions asked. There is no minimum number of books you must buy.

4 FREE BOOKS

TO GET YOUR 4 FREE BOOKS WORTH $18.00 — MAIL IN THE FREE BOOK CERTIFICATE T O D A Y

Fill in the Free Book Certificate below, and we'll send your FREE BOOKS to you as soon as we receive it.

If the certificate is missing below, write to: Zebra Home Subscription Service, Inc., P.O. Box 5214, 120 Brighton Road, Clifton, New Jersey 07015-5214.

FREE BOOK CERTIFICATE

4 FREE BOOKS

ZEBRA HOME SUBSCRIPTION SERVICE, INC.

YES! Please start my subscription to Zebra Historical Romances and send me my first 4 books absolutely FREE. I understand that each month I may preview four new Zebra Historical Romances free for 10 days. If I'm not satisfied with them, I may return the four books within 10 days and owe nothing. Otherwise, I will pay the low preferred subscriber's price of just $3.75 each; a total of $15.00, *a savings off the publisher's price of $3.00.* I may return any shipment and I may cancel this subscription at any time. There is no obligation to buy any shipment and there are no shipping, handling or other hidden charges. Regardless of what I decide, the four free books are mine to keep.

NAME

ADDRESS _____ APT _____

CITY _____ STATE ____ ZIP _____

TELEPHONE ( )

SIGNATURE _____
(if under 18, parent or guardian must sign)

Terms, offer and prices subject to change without notice. Subscription subject to acceptance by Zebra Books. Zebra Books reserves the right to reject any order or cancel any subscription. 079102

GET
FOUR
FREE
BOOKS
(AN $18.00 VALUE)

Chapter Eleven

In the rain

The night was an uneasy one. The three of them sat around the campfire, each reluctant to be the first to seek his bed. Irony did not want to leave Hawk and Nathan alone; Nathan didn't want to leave Hawk and Irony alone. And even though Hawk had sworn to remember he was only a guide, he was less than pleased with the thought of Irony and Nathan together, unchaperoned.

The awkward silence stretched on until nearly midnight, when Hawk finally arose and with a pointed look at Nathan, dragged the overturned canoe next to Irony's tent and tossed his bedroll beneath it.

Glad that someone had made the initial move, Irony sprang to her feet and bade Nathan a hasty goodnight. Even so, he insisted on escorting her to the shelter and, had Hawk not been lingering nearby, she knew he would have kissed her. At that moment, she was so out of sorts with all of them, herself included, that she was grateful Hawk's watchfulness kept the deputy from expressing his affections.

Nathan had to be satisfied with pressing Irony's hands and gazing soulfully into her eyes, and when

Hawk coughed loudly, he frowned and turned away, making up his own bed not more than five feet from her tent.

The next morning, they awoke to gray skies and a cold wind blowing straight out of the north. The bay was churning, the water reflecting the somber tones of the sky overhead.

"Doesn't look like we'll be going anywhere today," Hawk commented.

"Surely it can't be that bad?" observed Nathan, gesturing toward the water. "Once we get across that first stretch, we'd be in the islands. They'd provide adequate shelter."

"They would," Hawk agreed, "if you lived to get that far." He rounded on the other man. "Good God, there are waves ten feet high out there. Your canoe would be swamped within minutes."

Nathan drew himself up, although he was still a good head shorter than Hawk. "I'll have you know that I'm not totally inexperienced, Hawkes. It's my belief that we could navigate the open water by angling toward the south curve of the mainland and get into those islands without too much difficulty."

"Then you go ahead and attempt it," Hawk said. "But Irony stays here."

"Wait just a minute," Nathan began. "From now on, I'll be in charge. If I say she goes, she goes."

"Nathan, Hawk," Irony scolded. "Must you argue over me? I'd like to think I can make my own decisions."

"No," the men shouted in unison.

"No?" she echoed, her tone of voice ominous.

"It won't hurt us to stay here where we're safe and relatively dry," Hawk said.

"But why lose a day of our time?" queried Nathan. "If we push on now, it'll make things easier later on."

"How so?" asked Hawk. "Goodman won't be

going anywhere in this weather."

"How do you know that?"

"He's too damned smart to risk it."

"Are you implying that I'm not?" Nathan bristled.

"I'm not implying anything," Hawk stated quietly. "I'm saying it outright."

Irony quickly stepped between the two men. "Stop it," she ordered. "Arguing will get us nowhere."

"Then the argument is ended," Hawk told her. "Ferguson can do whatever he wants. You and I are staying here to wait out the storm."

He walked away, leaving Nathan to glare after him. "The arrogance of that bas . . . er, that savage."

"Stop calling him a savage," snapped Irony. "If we're going to be stuck on this island, the least we can do is be civil. You're not acting any better than he is, you know."

Nathan looked hurt. "I'm only thinking of you, Irony. I know how anxious you are to apprehend Goodman."

"But if Hawk says it's too dangerous to go on, then I believe him." Irony walked away, leaving him with a surprised look on his face.

Because the forested center of the island broke its impact, the wind didn't strike their camp with full force, but it was still damp and chilly. The three of them huddled in front of Irony's tent and the blankets Hawk had tied up to provide shelter. While Nathan brought Irony up to date on the latest events in Thief River, Hawk peeled potatoes and wild onions and cut up moose meat for a stew.

As the mixture steamed and bubbled over the open fire, Hawk stirred it absentmindedly, listening to their talk. It seemed to him that after hearing all the news of her aunts, Irony lost interest in Nathan's narrative. He, on the other hand, seemed determined to remind her of each and every wonderful thing about their home town. Hawk's mouth lifted in a sardonic smile. Whether Ferguson would admit it or not, he was aware that Irony had taken to the wilderness like a camel to the desert — and he was worried.

Irony herself was experiencing a quandary of emotion. She hadn't recognized how much she had enjoyed being alone with Hawk until Nathan had appeared. Still, she felt guilty that the other man had made the arduous trip from Thief River because he was concerned with her well-being. Even though that had been the aunts' doing, it was her misfortune that respecting their wishes had become a habit.

But, oh, how she'd loved those days of freedom! And with Hawk, she had been free. He'd given her plenty of orders, but all for her own good . . . and none that really hampered her newly emancipated state. Every command Hawk had issued had been for the sole purpose of keeping her safe, not to dominate her. Nathan, however, was too possessive, too innately sure he knew what was best for her, and she found it oppressive in the extreme. She hadn't counted on such restrictions before she got back home.

The rain began just after they had finished eating. It moved across the lake in a huge, gray curtain, draping itself over them with little warning and no mercy. With an exclamation of dismay, Irony scuttled into her tent and Nathan joined her there. Hawk quickly shoved a log onto the fire, hoping to keep it at least smoldering throughout the storm, stowed their belongings beneath the overturned canoe, and, book in hand, ducked into the tent himself.

"Hey, it's too crowded in here for three people," objected Nathan.

"Surely you don't think we'd force you out into the

rain, do you, Ferguson?" Hawk's voice held an insolent amusement and it was all Irony could do to keep from smiling herself.

"I take it you have no plans to leave?" Nathan said stiffly.

"You take it right. It may be crowded here, but it's dry—although we're going to have to lie down or we'll have water pouring in here, too."

"What do you mean?"

"The canvas," Hawk explained. "Wherever we touch it, the rain is going to come through. Our heads are nearly brushing the top, so we'll have to lie down."

With that, he shifted his long body and stretched out on one side of the tent. Irony, having no desire to experience a deluge of water down the back of her neck, did likewise.

"You're making that up," Nathan accused. And like a child, he had to see for himself. Gingerly, he touched the side of the tent near his shoulder, and in a moment, drops of water formed on the inside. Irony cast him a faintly disgusted look and rested her head on her arms.

"It looks like you could have purchased something sturdier," Nathan grumbled ungraciously, flopping down on his stomach. He winced as his still-tender abdominal muscles came into contact with the hard ground.

Trying to ignore his restless fidgeting, Irony stared out into the downpour. It fell so heavily that it obscured the distant shore, shutting them into a small world of sound and smell: the silvery hum of the rain as it sluiced down from the heavens, the relentless rush of the wind, the musty odor of wet canvas, the fragrance of the pines. In only seconds, she became aware of other sensations—the hard feel of Hawk's hip against hers, the clean, warm scent of him, the sound of his slow, steady breathing.

"Irony," said Nathan, "change places with me."

"What?" She was startled out of her introspection by his petulant tone.

"Move over here and let me get into the middle."

"Why? I'm perfectly comfortable."

Nathan gave her a severe look, then, his voice edged with something akin to exasperation, he muttered, "It isn't proper for you to be . . . well, next to . . ."

"Why would it be any more proper for her to be next to you?" Hawk drawled.

"We're engaged to be married, for one thing."

"Nathan, please," Irony said. "We are not engaged . . . not officially. And I wish you would quit treating me as though . . . as though I couldn't take care of myself. There is nothing improper about this situation."

"That's right," Hawk agreed. "Besides, she's better off in the middle where we can both keep an eye on her."

At Irony's disgusted sigh, he chuckled and turned onto his back, opening his book.

Irony lay quietly for a while, listening to the drum of the rain on the canvas overhead. To her dismay, her thoughts insisted on going back to the scene on the beach that Nathan had interrupted. She felt an increasing sense of shame — not because she had nearly given in to the desire that overpowered her, but because she had let her childish resentments rule her actions. She knew she had angered Hawk, but that wasn't unusual in their dealings with each other. It was knowing she had also hurt him that she most regretted. Had he sensed that her ultimate rejection of him stemmed from the fact he was part Indian? Had he realized all the ghosts and goblins of her childhood had risen up to haunt her, and that he was paying the price? And yet — what else could she have done? She was still thankful she had regained her wits in time to prevent one of the worst mistakes she could possibly have made.

Her brain weary from such burdensome thoughts, Irony turned to Hawk and said, "Would you read aloud to us, please? I'd truly like to hear more about Hiawatha."

Occasionally, he had read passages from the Longfellow epic to her, and Irony found herself increasingly interested in the tale. The cadence of the words was soothing, the story itself was a fascinating combination of realism and the supernatural — and the hero was becoming, in her mind, all mixed up with Hawk.

"Want to hear about picture-writing?" he was asking.

She gave an affirming nod, wondering at the wicked gleam in his soft black eyes.

> "Such as these the shapes they painted,"
> On the birch-bark and the deer-skin;
> Songs of war and songs of hunting,
> Songs of medicine and of magic,
> All were written in these figures,
> For each figure had its meaning,
> Each its separate song recorded.
>   Nor forgotten was the Love-Song,
> The most subtle of all medicines,
> The most potent spell of magic,
> Dangerous more than war or hunting!
> Thus the Love-Song was recorded,
> Symbol and interpretation.
>   First a human figure standing,
> Painted in the brightest scarlet;
> 'Tis the lover, the musician,
> And the meaning is, 'My painting
> Makes me powerful over others.' "

Nathan's arm stiffened against Irony's shoulder,

and she knew he disapproved of Hawk's choice of reading material. Still, she had seen so much picture writing on the objects her father had sent her that she wanted to hear more.

> "Then the same red figure seated
> In the shelter of a wigwam,
> And the meaning of the symbol,
> 'I will come and sit beside you
> In the mystery of my passion!' "

Nathan twitched at the word *passion*, and Irony forced back a laugh. There was, she had to admit, a certain faintly lurid quality to the passage, and no doubt, that accounted for Hawk's choosing it. Hawk continued:

> "Then two figures, man and woman,
> Standing hand in hand together
> With their hands so clasped together
> That they seem in one united.
> And the words thus represented
> Are, 'I see your heart within you,
> And your cheeks are red with blushes!'
> Next the maiden on an island,
> In the center of an island;
> And the song this shape suggested
> Was, 'Though you were at a distance,
> Were upon some far-off island,
> Such the spell I cast upon you,
> Such the magic power of passion,
> I could straightway draw you to me!"

"Are you about finished?" Nathan groused. "I'd like to have a nap."

"Shh," Irony said. "I want to hear this."

Hawk kept reading, a suspicious tinge of amusement in his voice.

"Then the figure of the maiden,
Sleeping, and the lover near her,
Whispering to her in her slumbers,
Saying, 'Though you were far from me
In the land of Sleep and Silence,
Still the voice of love would reach you!'
   And the last of all the figures
Was a heart within a circle,
Drawn within a magic circle;
And the image had this meaning:
'Naked lies your heart before me,
To your naked heart I whisper!' "

Hawk's soft, deep voice faded, echoing in Irony's ears. She knew that Nathan was affronted to the point of choking, but she didn't care. The poetry was beautiful, and somehow she knew Hawk had chosen that particular passage for a reason. She guessed that he wished to impart a message to her, and perhaps to Nathan as well. But what that message actually meant, she didn't dare consider.

Early in the evening, the rain ceased falling, though the damp wind kept the three of them huddling around the newly-blazing campfire. Hawk retrieved the kettle of stew from underneath the canoe and set it over the flames to heat for their supper.

They ate in silence and once the plates and forks had been cleaned and stowed away, Hawk brought out the map he had taken from Reverend Goodman's room back at Sweetwater.

"What's that?" queried Nathan, dropping down beside Hawk, a mug of coffee in his hand.

"A map marking the properties Goodman hopes to

sell. Something about it puzzles me."

Nathan took the map and studied it intently. Shrugging, he handed it back. "It means nothing to me."

"No, it wouldn't to someone who didn't know Lake of the Woods," Hawk said. "But . . . if this large body of land represents the Big Island, then some of these pieces of ground have to be in the area where I grew up. Irony, tell me about your father again."

She frowned. "I've told you everything there is to tell."

"How long had he owned these properties before his death?" asked Hawk.

Irony exchanged a look with Nathan. "For years, as far as I know."

"Then there's no chance he could have purchased the land from someone else, just prior to his death?"

"No, I don't think so. Those deeds were in the attic when I was a little girl."

"What year did your father die?"

"What difference does it make?" spoke up Nathan.

"What year, Irony?"

"I was twelve—it must have been about 1888."

Hawk turned back to the map, and when he raised his eyes again, there was an odd expression in them. "You've seen this map—are you certain these X's mark your father's property?"

"As certain as I can be," she replied, "for someone who has never seen the lake. But there used to be a big map of it hanging on the wall in my aunts' library, and these seem to match the ones my father had marked on it. Aunt Tiny used to write him letters every six months or so, and she always said she wanted to know exactly where her letters were going." Irony leaned closer to Hawk to gaze at the map he held. "Besides, I remember this huge bay and this cluster of islands here—Father called them the Three

Sisters. And these two big islands were just below his land . . . at least, it seems that way to me."

"I don't understand how he came to be in possession of this property," muttered Hawk.

"Are you insinuating there was something underhanded or unlawful about the acquisition?" challenged Nathan.

"No."

"All for the best, I assure you. My family has known the McBrides for years, and I feel entirely justified in stating that Samuel Zackett McBride was not the sort of man to be involved in anything shady."

Hawk glanced up, his face going still. "Samuel . . . Zackett McBride?" he repeated.

"My father," Irony said. "Is something wrong?"

"No, nothing." Hawk folded the map and stuck it into the pocket of his flannel shirt. "I'm going to make up my bed before it gets any darker," he said. "The way that sky looks, we can expect more rain in the night, and I want to make sure I'll stay dry."

He strode away into the shadows, his mind working feverishly.

Zackett . . . *Zack*. Hawk had never known his last name, had never thought to ask. Zack had simply been a somewhat eccentric man who often wintered with Hawk's tribe. He was a leather-skinned, bewhiskered backwoodsman . . . whose emerald green eyes had so enchanted the black-eyed Ojibways.

Hawk stood staring into the encroaching darkness. He didn't know how or why Irony had been led to believe her father was dead, but unless he was sorely mistaken, when she got to the McBride property, she was going to find that he was very much alive indeed.

A wry smile twisted his mouth. It might be wisest for him to have possession of the gun when she did come face to face with Zack McBride. Hawk had a feeling Irony was going to redefine the word *furious*.

The night was dark and cloudy, so Nathan lit the lantern he'd brought with him and hung it on a low branch to illuminate the camp site. With an embarrassed expression, he excused himself to make one last trip to the bushes before turning in for the night. As soon as he was gone, Irony went in search of Hawk.

She found him just at the edge of the wavering lantern light, crouched by the overturned canoe, unfolding a wool blanket.

"Hawk?" She spoke tentatively, aware that their casual relationship had changed. "What's wrong? I . . . you looked so troubled."

He turned to survey her, his mind weighing the advisability of admitting his suspicions regarding her father. Would it be better for her to be prepared, or to wander into the situation without any forewarning? He tossed the blanket aside and stood up. He'd tell her, he decided. He'd want to know if it was him.

But then, he hadn't actually seen Zack for more than five years. It was possible something could have happened to him in the interim, so might it not be cruel to announce that he was alive and well . . . and then find out it wasn't so after all?

Hawk sighed. If only she wasn't gazing up at him with such an open, trusting look. It made it difficult to lie to her, but it made the truth completely out of the question, also. He didn't know what the hell to do!

"Where's Nathan?" he stalled.

"Oh . . . he went to the bushes, I believe."

"Is he still bothered by . . . by his problem?"

"No, I guess the cranebill tea must have cured that."

204

"Good."

"Hawk, why won't you answer my question?"

"I'm not troubled, Irony. I don't know why you would think I was."

Feeling suddenly shy, Irony put her hand on his forearm. "Because I know you pretty well after all this time," she pointed out.

"Perhaps."

"Irony, what's going on?" Nathan's voice preceded him as he crossed the area lighted by the lantern and stepped into the half-light with them. "Is something wrong?"

"No, of course not," she said, struggling to keep the irritation out of her voice. She was beginning to hate the fact that she and Hawk never had a moment's privacy anymore. Of course, too much privacy had almost gotten her into an extremely compromising position, but she missed the opportunity for a little simple conversation.

"Was Hawkes bothering you again?" Nathan's hand drifted toward the gun he wore, his distrustful eyes on Hawk's emotionless face.

"Nathan, for heaven's sake!" This time she made no effort to disguise her exasperation. "There's no need for you to be so rude. As I've told you countless times, Hawk is always a gentleman."

Nathan's responding snort was barely audible. "I've been thinking. If he's such a gentleman, maybe you can explain why he's luring you farther and farther into the woods without cause."

"We have cause—we're after Goodman."

Hawk's eyes narrowed at Irony's words, and she sensed that he disliked having her defend him . . . but that he found Nathan's question too insignificant to consider.

"If that's true, why not take the man now and be done with it?" Nathan asked, triumph lighting his pale brown eyes. "Goodman is in a camp only a couple of miles from here — and you're between him and the main body of Lake of the Woods. Why not accost him before he has a chance to disappear in the islands?"

Irony looked at Hawk. "Well, if you must know, Hawk is after someone other than Goodman. We think the man who murdered one of the teachers at the Sweetwater school is joining him sooner or later. That's who Hawk wants."

"Are you or are you not paying for this expedition?" snapped Nathan. "You don't need to agree to Hawkes' wishes or concerns."

"Yes, but wouldn't it make more sense to capture both Goodman and the murderer if we have the chance?"

"And get yourself killed in the process?"

"That wouldn't happen."

"I don't know how you can be certain of that."

"Because I trust Hawk to take care of me . . . of us."

"Honestly," Nathan burst out, "you seem to have completely lost your wits. As your fiancé . . . and as the man your aunts chose to safeguard you, I insist we end this farce right now. I don't know what game you're playing, Hawkes, but I'm calling a halt. In the morning, Irony and I are going back to Rainy River. I'll take Goodman into custody and we'll start back to Minnesota. You can do as you please."

Hawk nodded. "Very well, Ferguson."

Before Irony could make a further protest, Hawk dropped to his knees and slid his body underneath the canoe. Angry, she turned on Nathan.

"We'll discuss this in the morning, Nathan," she said, "but I do not intend to go anywhere without Hawk. Do you understand?"

"Oh, yes," he ground out through clenched teeth. "I think I'm beginning to understand very well indeed."

"I won't even bother asking what you mean by that remark," she informed him, entering her tent. "Goodnight."

"Irony . . ."

She flung the tent flap shut with a snap and left Nathan to seek his own bed.

Irony awoke early and lay listening to the silence created by the total absence of wind. Though it had rained steadily throughout the night, she could feel the warmth of sunshine coming through the tent walls and knew the inclement weather was over.

She dressed quickly, putting on the boys' clothes that Nathan thought so disreputable. They'd be moving on today, and she had no plans to wear the cumbersome cotton gown.

When she emerged from the tent, she saw Hawk bent over the fire, cooking breakfast. The canoe had been righted and reloaded, in preparation for departure. Nathan was just beginning to stir in his bedroll, urged awake by the tantalizing smell of frying bacon.

Irony was drawn to the water, but because Hawk had always cautioned her to stay away from the beach that would be in Goodman's line of sight, she skirted the trees and started toward the windward side of the island. She had actually enjoyed the last two days on Pine Island and wanted to take one last look around.

Hawk watched her go, glad that she would have another day or two of carefree innocence. Once they reached the inner islands . . .

"Hawkes, I want to talk to you."

Hawk turned to see Nathan standing over him, hands on his hips.

"What about?"

"Irony."

"Well?"

"Look, you have to realize how unseemly . . . hell, how *dangerous* it is for her to find you attractive."

Hawk's black brows lifted, but before he could speak, Nathan hurried on.

"Don't bother to deny there's something going on between the two of you. I've got eyes." He ran a hand through his sandy hair, a pained expression on his face. "At first I was so worried about her that I missed the obvious. But after you both managed to convince me that you . . . that you hadn't violated her, well . . . I began to notice things."

"Such as?"

"She hardly takes her eyes off you," Nathan exclaimed. "And she's always finding reasons to touch you—like in the tent yesterday, and last night when I interrupted your private conversation."

"Ferguson, there's something I should tell you . . ."

"No, there's something I should tell you. I know Irony, and I know her aunts. For God's sake, man, I can't let this thing go any further. It would ruin Irony's life if she allowed herself to . . . to care for you. She has endangered her reputation enough by this whole escapade, as it is." He shifted his feet, one hand falling to the butt of his pistol as if he foresaw that Hawk would be angered by his next words. "We can rectify all that if we are married as soon as we return to Thief River Falls. People will forget soon enough. But, damnation, Hawkes, think of the scandal if word gets back to town that Irony was defiled by . . . by an Indian. No, worse than that, by a half-breed."

Hawk made a sudden move, rising to his feet, and Nathan leaped away, drawing the gun.

"Put the gun away, Ferguson," he said wearily. "I'm not going to take offense. Although I'd like to kill you for your insinuations, I won't. Irony is too im-

208

thing?" she asked, her tone biting. "I am damned sick and tired of being a lady." She held up a restraining hand. "And don't ask me not to swear, because I intend to do so whenever the mood comes upon me."

He seemed decidedly uncomfortable. "Is there anything I can say to soothe your anger?"

"This anger will never be soothed," she declared. "Not if I live to be as old as Methuselah."

"All right then, what can I say to improve your disposition?"

"That we're going after Hawk . . . and Goodman."

"Irony, I can't do that. I promised Hawkes I would take you back home."

"Perhaps you should have consulted with me first," she said, "because I refuse to go. I'm traveling on to my father's property."

"Be reasonable," Nathan entreated.

"To hell with reason!" Irony felt some small satisfaction with Nathan's gasp of shock.

"What on earth has happened to your good nature?" he queried.

"Maybe this is the real me, Nathan. Perhaps this is the way I would be if we were married." She seized her carpetbag and tossed it into his canoe. "I'd reconsider my proposal of marriage if I were you."

"You're just upset — you'll get over it."

"I wish you would stop saying that. As far as I'm concerned, I may never get over the anger I feel toward Hawk. Or you. You let him go."

Nathan dropped his eyes and began fidgeting with the straps on his saddlebags.

"Nathan," she said sharply. "Why do you look so guilty? Could it be that you had more to do with Hawk's departure than you've told me?"

As though reluctant to do so, he finally met her eyes. "I . . . I might have suggested that it would be

for the best if . . . if he removed himself from your
. . . from your life."

"What?" Her voice seemed to echo in her own
ears.

"Now, Irony, it was for your own good, believe
me. You have a reputation to consider, after all."

"Damn you!" she blurted out. "Damn you and
damn Hawk! Damn all men!"

"Calm down . . ."

"The only thing that is going to calm me down is
apprehending Goodman. Now get this canoe in the
water and let's be on our way."

Nathan tossed his saddlebags into the canoe, and
began sliding it over the sand toward the water.
"We're not going after Goodman," he said stubbornly.
"We're going home."

At the water's edge, Irony leaped into the canoe
and seized the paddle. "I'm going to follow Goodman—you can do what you like . . . but it's a long
swim back to Minnesota." She jabbed at the lake
bottom, pushing the craft into deeper water.

Nathan swore under his breath, but finally waded
into the lake and eased himself over the side of the
canoe. "We don't have a map, Irony. We'd be lost in
no time."

"I have a map in my head," she replied, still
clutching the paddle. "And you have a compass,
don't you?"

"Well . . . yes."

"And since you know which direction Hawk
headed, we'll simply do the same. We may overtake
him if we hurry. If not, we'll just have to keep going
until we see something that looks familiar."

"I don't know how anything could look familiar—
we've never seen this lake before."

"I've seen the map. And Father's property is somewhere northeast of the Big Island. We'll find it."

Nathan heaved a loud, resigned sigh and reached

214

for the paddle. "I hope you know what you're doing, Irony. If anything happens to you, your aunts will have my head."

Irony rode in aggrieved silence for several hours. Her wrathful tirade had been childish, but it had shown her the satisfaction to be had in speaking one's mind, without regard for social niceties. However, once she had spoken her mind, she found herself with no desire to say anything more.

Crossing the main portion of open water had not been as simple as she'd anticipated. Even with only a light wind, the lake was filled with choppy waves that occasionally tossed the canoe about as if it was made of matchsticks. At times, it was all she could do to clutch the sides of the canoe and hope that the grim, tight-lipped Nathan could keep it under control. When at last they glided into the first of the islands which provided a windbreak, she breathed easier, but even then, Nathan did not lose his tense look.

Irony realized he was probably irritated with himself for giving in to her, and in her mind, it was significant that he had. She knew with an inexplicable surety that if, heaven forbid, they ever married, it would always be like this. She'd stubbornly insist on her own way, and he would be just weak enough to allow it, even though he would make his vexation known. Over the years, she'd become a bullying, opinionated shrew, and he'd become a fussy, dissatisfied martyr.

A smile curled her lips as she recalled the way Hawk had treated her from the beginning. Weakness was a character trait he did not possess, and neither she nor anyone else could bully the man. Life with him would a struggle for compromise, perhaps, but it would never be dull or predictable.

The smile faded. Life with him? What was she thinking?

They came from worlds so far apart that they had almost no common ground at all. His heritage, her upbringing . . . society in general . . . all of it combined to make any thought of an enduring alliance out of the question. Even if she had discovered a wealth of tenderness within herself for him, she knew she could never reveal that tenderness to him. He could not return her feelings or he would never have walked away and left her, without so much as a word of farewell.

The coil of anger inside her tightened. She would probably never see Raphael Hawkes again, so what did it matter?

By midday, they were well inside a veritable maze of islands, though Irony had yet to see anything that looked even remotely like the Three Sisters or any of the other unusual landmarks she remembered from her aunts' map. They stopped long enough to have something to eat, then pushed on. By late afternoon, there was more than a hint of worry in Nathan's eyes, and even Irony was beginning to accept the fact that traveling on Lake of the Woods without a guide was very possibly a mistake.

"Are you certain we're headed in the right direction?" she finally asked, her nervous gaze sweeping over an unending series of piney islands.

"According to the compass, we're going east northeast at this moment," Nathan replied. "That's the right way, isn't it?"

"It's the right way," she answered, "but I don't see how we can be going that direction. The sun is over there—shouldn't that be the west?"

Nathan looked perplexed. "What the . . . ?" Carefully, he studied the compass again. He gave it a shake, then turned it in another direction, before moving it back into position. "It still says this is northeast. I don't understand . . ."

Irony squinted up at the rapidly dropping sun. "That may not be due west, but it has to be some sort of westerly direction. And that means we're actually headed . . . southwest again. Nathan, we're going the wrong way!"

"I don't see how that's possible."

"Neither do I, but it's true. That compass must be broken."

He gave the faulty instrument one last glance. "It worked all the way out here. I can't imagine why it should be incorrect now."

"How could we have gotten turned completely around?" Irony fretted. "We don't even know how many hours we've been traveling in the wrong direction."

"You should have kept your eye on the sun all along," he groused, using the paddle to turn the canoe. "I can't do everything, Irony."

"No, you certainly can't," she snapped. Then, feeling ashamed, she brushed a hand across her forehead and said, "I'm sorry. I shouldn't be blaming you."

"And I shouldn't have said what I did." Nathan cast a worried glance at the sky. "But it's getting late and, unless I'm mistaken, those thunderheads in the north indicate another storm on the way."

"We'll just go as far as we can before sunset, then make camp and try to get settled in before the rain. Everything will be fine, Nathan."

However, by the time another two hours had passed, both of them had to admit that everything was not fine. A sharp wind had come up, blowing a fine mist of rain before it, and night was moving in with unexpected swiftness.

"Keep your eyes open for a suitable camp site,"

Nathan said, his voice tense. They were passing through a series of islands whose rocky bluffs rose high above them. Camping on any of them would have necessitated a steep climb to the top, something that would have been nearly impossible for anyone burdened with gear.

Irony hunched her shoulders inside the jacket she wore and wished she had a hat to help ward off the dampness. Tired and hungry, the anticipation of a dry tent and a roaring fire was all that sustained her. Unwillingly, her mind turned to Hawk and she wondered where he was—whether he was sitting comfortably before his own campfire, and whether he spared a thought for her.

"There!" she suddenly shouted, pointing. "Over there!"

Not far ahead was an island with a curving granite shelf along one side, and, though guarded by several jagged boulders, it provided a flat place to land the canoe.

Nathan grinned and began paddling with renewed vigor. "That looks like a good spot," he called cheerfully. "We'll get the tent up and cook a hot meal—"

There was a loud, rending crash, and the headlong rush of the canoe was halted abruptly. Irony cried out as she pitched forward onto the bottom of the boat.

"My God!" Nathan yelled, as the paddle was wrenched from his hand and sent flying. "We've hit something!"

The air was filled with the brittle sound of tearing birchbark, followed by the soft rushing of water. Irony stared in disbelief as the cold liquid swirled around her hands and seeped through the heavy material of her trousers and jacket.

"We're sinking," she gasped, scrambling to her knees. "Nathan! The canoe is sinking!"

Nathan got to his feet, reaching for her, but the

water had poured in so rapidly that the canoe lurched to one side, throwing him off balance. He uttered a hoarse cry as he was thrown into the lake, his feet entangled in the canvas packs. Irony made a grab for her carpetbag, but it slid easily into the water, sinking immediately into the green depths.

The canoe made a slow, rolling turn, and Irony went with it, helpless to stop her own descent into the lake. Instinctively, she opened her mouth to scream, but the water was already closing over her head, and she swallowed bitter, mossy-tasting liquid.

Irony struggled, fighting for release from the chilling water. With maddening slowness, her heartbeat thundering in her ears and her lungs bursting with the need for air, she propelled herself upward toward the faint glimmer of light overhead. When her head finally broke through the surface, she was seized by a paroxysm of coughing that left her weak and disoriented. It was all she could do to keep herself afloat as she searched frantically for Nathan.

She cried out in pain as her knee grazed a boulder hidden beneath the water—most likely, she realized, the boulder the canoe had struck. Clinging to the rock, she could just manage to keep her head above water as she stared into the deepening gloom. The canoe had completely disappeared, leaving little evidence that it had ever existed. A tin cup bobbed on the lake's surface and, as Irony watched, the lantern slowly sank from sight, a trail of bubbles marking its path. A deep and deathly silence settled over the scene.

Nathan was nowhere in sight.

Irony swallowed a sob. "Nathan," she screamed. "Nathan!" Her voice faded to a whisper. "Oh, God, Nathan, *where are you?*"

Hawk cursed the rain, then forgot it. His mind

was fixed on one thing—Irony McBride. Indeed, he had thought of nothing else since leaving Pine Island. He knew he was a fool, but then, in his estimation, every man was a fool about something. Of course, it would be his damnable luck to discover his obsession involved a lively, green-eyed gamine whose intrusion into his life had tested his endurance beyond all belief.

He knew Nathan Ferguson had been right. Putting distance between himself and Irony was the wisest, most sensible thing he could have done. He'd fully intended to make good his promise to find the reverend and see that he was returned to Minnesota for prosecution. And he'd felt confident that Ferguson could get Irony back to Thief River without further incident. So why had he turned back?

Grimly, he kept his eyes on the shadowed lake ahead. For some reason he didn't understand, he had a need to see that Irony was no longer on Pine Island where he had left her. He needed proof that Ferguson had persuaded her to go home, and he wouldn't be satisfied until he saw the deserted campsite. Only then, when he was sure she was safely gone from Lake of the Woods, could he face the finality of an existence without her.

The long, haunting cry of a loon echoed in the distance and Hawk felt a chill touch his spine. How human the bird's call had sounded. He remembered a story the elders had often told the children of the tribe—a story that claimed the loons were the ghosts of drowned maidens.

The bird's cry came again, thin and quavering, eerie in the half-darkness. And suddenly, with a certainty he didn't understand, Hawk knew Irony was in trouble. In trouble and needing him.

He had no sense of how far away she was, nor any idea how he would find her. He only knew his premonition of danger was so strong that he had no choice but to listen to it and pray that the strange faculty within himself that had warned of Irony's peril would also guide him to her.

Irony had never been so cold in her life. And though the knowledge that at least she was alive had sustained her for a time, even that was beginning not to matter very much. It took a great deal of exhausting effort, but she turned her head, feeling gritty sand beneath her cheek. Nathan lay not more than three feet away, his eyes closed, his face a pale oval in the darkness. Only his harsh and shallow breathing convinced her he wasn't dead.

Irony's throat tightened at the memory of her panic as she had clung to that rock, searching the water for any sign of Nathan. When his groping hand had struck her leg, she had uttered a cry of mindless terror before realizing it was him. It had taken every last ounce of strength she had, but she had grasped his coat and pulled him upward. She had tugged and strained and cursed — and finally managed to get his face above the water. Positioning him against the boulder, she had thumped him on the back, exhorting him to breathe, frantically whispering every prayer her aunts had ever taught her. She'd nearly strangled on tears of joy when he'd started coughing and retching . . . and breathing.

Arms around each other, they had clung to the rock for some time before Nathan had regained enough stamina to attempt the swim to shore. Irony couldn't swim and her legs were numb from the coldness of the water, but Nathan assured her that if she would relax against him, he could get both of them to the island.

"Just don't fight me," he'd muttered, his lips blue with cold.

Wearily, Irony had nodded. She didn't have the

energy to fight him. Indeed, had he let her slide beneath the surface of the lake, she wasn't sure she would care enough to struggle to save herself. She was too cold, too tired. The lifeless sensation that had started in her legs was now working its way throughout her body, and with it came a definite disinterest in whether she lived or died.

Thoughts of Hawk had flooded her mind with startling clarity, and with those thoughts came a resurgence of the anger she had felt at his desertion. She knew she would have to stay alive if she intended to exact revenge for his cruel action. Bolstered by her renewed anger, she had released her grip on the rock and, though it had taken more courage than anything she'd ever done, she had put herself into Nathan's hands. She had to trust him, there was no other choice.

Nathan's feet had struck the sandy lake bottom about a dozen feet from the island and from that point, they had waded, staggering weakly to the edge of the beach. There they had collapsed, to rest and gather strength for the next part of the ordeal — finding some sort of shelter from the rain that pelted them with increasing fury.

Irony's eyelids fluttered shut again. Just a few minutes more rest and she would drag herself into the grass, away from the restless surf.

Again, her thoughts turned to Hawk and she wondered where he was, what he was doing . . .

Hawk ignored the panic clawing at his throat. Something told him he was close to Irony, and at this point, he couldn't allow carelessness or fear to cause an error in judgment.

He realized he had been chanting her name over and over, in the slow, measured cadence of an Ojibway entreaty to the spirits of the earth and sky.

Until then, even he hadn't known how scared he was that something had happened to Irony. Rather than dwell on that thought, he started uttering her name more loudly, and in a few seconds, shouted it with enough force to send it echoing through the darkness. He shouted again, then listened intently.

The night was filled with a myriad of sound—the wind soughing through the tall pines, the noisy rush of rain, the muted calls of forest birds. Once, far away in the distance, he heard the shrill howl of a timber wolf, startling in its unearthly beauty, and he wondered whether Irony heard it, too, and whether it had frightened her.

The bloodcurdling howl of a wolf echoed in her ears, but Irony was too exhausted to be afraid. From somewhere nearer, an owl's hooting call drifted on the night wind, a soft, soothing *whoo-whooo*. Irony smiled to herself—she loved owls. One had inhabited the old oak tree outside her bedroom window in Thief River.

The timbre of the call seemed to change, to distort into the sound of her own name.

"Irony! Irony . . ."

Nathan raised his head from the sand and seemed to listen intently.

It's only an owl, Irony tried to say, but the words refused to leave her mind and be spoken aloud.

Nathan sat up, bracing himself on trembling arms. He tilted his head as the sound came again.

"Irony! Irony McBride!"

"Here!" shouted Nathan, his voice weak. "We're here!"

Irony stirred, thinking she needed to go to Nathan. His mind must be wandering, confused by the ordeal he had suffered.

223

Nathan cried out again and his voice seemed to roar in her ears.

"We're over here!"

"Irony!" came the echo.

Curls of fog from the lake drifted toward her, muffling all but the sounds closest to her — the slap of the surf, the hum of a mosquito. The strange rasping crunch of some object against the sand. The clatter of wood on wood.

A man's figure appeared in the fog, and Irony watched with bemusement as he strode toward her. Even as he knelt in the sand and lifted her into his arms, she felt no fear.

"Hawk," she murmured, nestling her head against a broad, warm chest. "What took you so long?"

Hawk was shocked by the marble coldness of Irony's skin, but he could do little more than wrap her in a blanket from his bedroll and leave her beneath the protection of his overturned canoe while he concentrated on getting a fire started. He had to search the underbrush for enough dry wood to use as kindling, adding larger pieces only after it had begun to blaze.

Pulling the knife from his boot, he began cutting pine boughs to cover the wet ground beneath the canoe. While he worked, he fired questions at Nathan, who hunkered over the fire, doggedly feeding it more of the wood Hawk had gathered.

"What happened? Where's your canoe?"

"We . . . we hit a boulder. It smashed the boat to pieces."

"And your belongings?"

"At the bottom of the lake." Nathan heaved a shaky sigh. "It was all we could do to save ourselves."

"You've no food or dry clothing?"

"Nothing."

Hawk finished arranging the boughs in the make-shift leanto. "Crawl in there and get those wet clothes off," he instructed Nathan. "I'll find something you can put on."

Entering the shelter behind Nathan, he rummaged through his leather satchel and tossed the other man a dry shirt and pair of denim pants.

"I've got to get these wet things off Irony, also," Hawk said, more to himself than to Nathan. "She's already badly chilled."

Nathan paused, his cold, damp shirt half off. "You're going to undress her?" he asked.

"Naturally." Hawk turned to look at him. "You don't think I'm going to let social restriction stand in the way of keeping her from being sick, do you?"

"I . . . um, it's only that . . . well, you're a stranger. Maybe Irony would prefer that I do it."

"No. You take care of yourself," Hawk advised, "and leave Irony to me. She's so cold, she won't care who helps her."

"But I care," Nathan protested. "I'm her fiancé. I'll do it."

Hawk's fierce expression held no compromise. "I'm doing this. You worry about yourself. And turn your back — I won't have you staring at her while she's . . . defenseless."

"Don't you think I'm going to see her sooner or later?" Nathan flared.

"God damn it," Hawk roared, fighting the helpless feeling the other man's words gave him. "Turn your back or I'll toss you into the lake again — and leave you there."

Apparently the savage anger lying just beneath the surface of Hawk's civility convinced Nathan for, without further argument, he turned away and began stripping off his wet clothing.

Hawk turned to Irony, forgetting Nathan in his worry over the paleness of her face. The sweeping curve of her eyelashes lay against her colorless cheeks like smears of india ink.

Gently, he unwrapped the blanket and started unbuttoning the boy's shirt she wore. Beneath it, her chemise was soaked and clinging to her icy skin, and with a clenched jaw, he quickly removed it. He tugged off her boots and slipped the too-large trousers down over her hips and legs. Then, using a corner of the blanket, he dried her, rubbing briskly to restore the flow of blood to her nearly frozen limbs. Although he was aware of the delicacy of her body beneath his hands, he spared no time for thoughts other than those concerned with the need to make her warm and safe.

The abrupt silence from behind told him that the other man had finished dressing and, sensing how Irony would dislike having Nathan see her nakedness, Hawk draped the blanket over her once again. He searched through his satchel for another dry shirt and, his body shielding her from view, he dressed Irony in it, buttoning it all the way to the hem, which brushed her slender thighs.

Irony had not stirred throughout the course of his ministrations, nor did she rouse from her exhausted sleep when he lay down on the pine boughs beside her, drawing her into his arms. She merely sighed wearily and nestled against him.

"What the hell do you think you're doing?" Nathan queried, but his tone was resigned, as though he already suspected his objection would have little bearing on Hawk's actions.

"Trying to get some warmth back into her body."

"Don't you think that I should . . . I mean . . ." Nathan broke off, with an ineffectual shrug.

"I can manage," Hawk stated firmly. "You'd better get some rest yourself. Take the other blanket from my bedroll."

Without further comment, Nathan rolled into the

blanket and lay staring into the darkness. Just beyond the canoe's shelter, the camp fire flared in the wind and rain, but burned bravely on.

"What were you doing here?" Hawk asked after several moments of silence. "I thought you were taking Irony home."

"She wouldn't go."

Hawk's chuckle was barely audible. "I'm not surprised. Maybe that's why I came back to look for you." He turned his face so his cheek rested against Irony's hair. "It's a damned good thing you heard me shouting. The sound of your voice was all that led me to you."

"What about Goodman? Did you lose him?"

"I didn't lose him — I simply quit following him and turned back. He'll be out there in the islands when we want to find him."

"I hope you're right. Irony will be furious with both of us if we've let him slip through our hands."

"Right now I'd give a great deal to see her that angry," Hawk said. "A great deal indeed . . ."

Irony awakened, aware only that the warmth that had been wrapped around her was gone. She shivered and snuggled deeper into the softness beneath her. Gradually she recognized the pungent aroma of fresh pine, the scratch of wool against her legs, and the golden sheen of sunlight. It was morning . . . but the sun shining down on her face contained none of the soul-warming heat she had experienced during the night.

She wanted to move, but her body was filled with such sharp pain that she weakly decided to stay as she was. Gradually, she opened her eyes and found that she was lying at the edge of a pine grove, more than a dozen feet from the lake — a lake that shimmered like blue diamonds in the brilliant sunshine.

She squinted against the glare of the sun on water and saw the silhouette of a man, a man she knew instinctively was Hawk.

Irony's lips curved in a faint smile as she realized that Hawk was naked. He stood with his back to her, poised as though he was going to dive into the water. Irony felt no shame in the curiosity that consumed her. She let her eyes wander along the ridge of his wide shoulders to linger on the strange tatoo, then drift downward along the deep indentation of his spine, to the well-defined muscles that radiated outward. She knew she should avert her eyes from the sight of his firmly honed buttocks and thighs, but the splendid strength and tautness of his body captured and held her attention. Hawk was beautiful—why had she felt such shame and embarrassment the night Reverend Goodman had bound them together? What could be shameful about such pure, masculine perfection?

She watched as he flexed his shoulders, then raised sinewy arms above his head. With no loss of composure, Irony sensed that the warmth she had felt during the night had come from those very arms wrapped tightly around her. And the basic honesty of her nature made her admit that she could ask for little more of life than to have those same arms shielding her from the cold for the rest of time.

Hawk disappeared from her sight so quickly that she thought he must have dived into the water. And yet, a velvety darkness settled down upon her, and she discerned that her eyes had fallen shut again. It seemed too much of an effort to reopen them. The desire to sleep stole over her, and Irony willingly let it come. Hawk would stay close by . . . and that was all that mattered.

Hawk surfaced and swam toward the island, rising

from the clear water and wading the last six feet. In his hands he carried the broken lantern and Nathan's compass.

"No sense in going down again," he said, tossing the lantern aside and dropping the compass onto the sand beside Nathan's knee. "I doubt there's anything of value left to be found."

Hawk had dived again and again, retrieving Irony's sodden carpetbag and Nathan's saddlebags. One of the sacks of provisions seemed to have disappeared completely, but the other had broken open on the lake bottom, and from it, Hawk had brought up a kettle, two mugs, a handful of forks and spoons and a few potatoes.

"This damned compass doesn't work," Nathan commented, picking it up. "That's how we came to be so lost in the first place."

Hawk grinned. "Compasses often fail to work on Lake of the Woods," he said. "There's too much magnetic ore in the rocks—pulls the needle off course."

"Oh. I didn't know that." Nathan glanced up at the man standing over him, so natural in his nakedness, his wet hair streaming to his shoulders. "I guess there's a great deal I don't know about the wilderness."

"You did a fine job, Ferguson," Hawk said. "Especially considering the fact that you had to deal with Irony as well as the elements."

"But she's so sick . . ."

"She's alive, thanks to you."

"I didn't do anything . . ."

"You had enough presence of mind to drag her to the island and to shout for help."

"Actually, she saved my life," Nathan said, shaking his head. "If she hadn't pulled me out of the water . . ." He shuddered.

"It's over," Hawk reminded him. "Forget it now.

We've got to concentrate on getting Irony well. I'm going to whittle a spear from a green limb and catch some fish to boil for broth. We've got to get some nourishment into her." He reached for his levis. "And I imagine you could do with a meal yourself."

Nathan smiled back. "I'll admit, I'm weak as a kitten."

"Start those potatoes roasting while I fish, why don't you?"

When Irony roused up a second time, hours later, the sun was low in the sky. The clothes Hawk had spread to dry over a thicket of currant bushes looked like pale ghosts lurking in the shadows, but they seemed harmless in comparison to the fever she felt raging through her body.

There was a painful roaring in her head and her throat felt as though it was swelled nearly shut. Vaguely she recalled Hawk spooning warm broth into her mouth, tenderly wiping her face with a cool, damp cloth, his anxiety over her clearly evident. She wanted to speak to him, reassure him that she was all right—but she couldn't force the words past the obstruction in her throat.

Slowly, she turned her head, searching for him. Hawk sat in front of the camp fire, next to Nathan. They were engaged in serious conversation, but something about the set of their shoulders told her it was an amiable discussion. She was glad to know that Hawk and Nathan were no longer enemies, and that whatever else this latest dilemma had caused, it had somehow brought about the end of their rivalry.

Her mind eased, Irony allowed herself to drift away into oblivion again.

Chapter Thirteen

Chief White Crane's village . . .

When Irony was younger, Aunt Alyce had read aloud to her from a book of Norse legends. Even as a child, she had been fascinated by the brutal strength of the fierce warriors and their odd, superstitious religion. She still recalled the nightmare she had had after hearing about the death of a Viking chieftain. So vivid was the scene where his men had placed his body in a longboat, his shield and spear resting upon his chest, and set the flaming ship adrift on the North Sea that Irony had dreamed of it, to awaken screaming.

Now she was entrapped within that dream again — only this time, she was the one burning and her screams stubbornly remained silent. The wooden staves of the boat beneath her back were relentlessly rocked by the motion of the water, and she could feel the flames leaping up around her, curling along her arms and legs, devouring her entire body. Why didn't someone save her? Couldn't they see she wasn't dead — that she didn't want to be burned alive? Where was Hawk? Oh, God, where was Hawk?

From her pallet on the floor of the canoe, Irony moaned, thrashing her head from side to side, muttering incoherently. Watching her, Hawk's jaw clenched tightly and finally, he thrust the paddle at Nathan.

"You'll have to take over," he said. "I can't stand seeing her like this . . ."

Quietly, Nathan took the paddle and carefully traded places with Hawk. Once the Indian was in the front of the canoe, he knelt and scooped Irony into his arms, blanket and all. He settled himself, back against the prow of the boat, Irony resting against his chest.

"Shh," he soothed, brushing the damp hair from her brow. "I'm here now, sweetheart — you're going to be fine."

Over her head, his eyes met Nathan's. For once, Hawk realized he saw no animosity there, no jealousy. Nathan appeared to be as worried as he was.

"Paddle as quickly as you can, Nathan," he said softly. "We've got to get her to the village . . . and pray there will be someone there who knows what to do for her."

"I brewed tea from sumac bark," Hawk said, "but it didn't help. I've tried birchbark and currant juice — nothing seems to work." Wearily, he rubbed his eyes. "I don't know what else to do, Snow."

The slender Indian woman regarded him somberly. "How did a white woman come to be with you?" she asked. "And why did you bring her to me?"

"It's a long story," he replied. "I'll tell you later. The reason I brought her to you is that you know more of healing than most medicine men."

"It is important to you, then, that the white woman recovers?"

Hawk returned her probing look without flinching. "More important than anything."

Snow sighed and turned away. "I will do what I can."

"Thank you," Hawk murmured and, with a last

look at Irony, strode from the lodge.

He hated feeling so helpless. He had exhausted his rudimentary knowledge of medicine and still Irony was no better. She alternated between bone-shaking chills and burning fever. She had only awakened once or twice, and then her eyes had been clouded and confused, and Hawk was never certain that she'd recognized him or Nathan.

Irony's illness was terrifying to him. She was ordinarily so full of life and energy, that the sight of her weak and defenseless shook him right to the heart. He blamed himself for leaving her, for assuming their separation was the most prudent action to take.

How many times over the past few days had he vowed never to repeat that foolishness? No matter what, he would never voluntarily leave Irony again. Not unless she herself told him to go, and could make him believe she meant it. And, he promised himself, she would have one hell of a hard time convincing him of that! Not after the way she had called his name and clung to him in her delirium. He couldn't forget that she had turned to him, not Nathan. He wouldn't let her forget it, either.

Irony angled her face away from the pungent cloud of mist that seemed to hover over her. The odor was acrid, making her cough and filling her eyes with tears. She couldn't seem to escape the sharp, penetrating aroma . . .

At least the ground beneath her was steady, and she was swathed in something soft and comforting. Mercifully, someone had rescued her from the longboat — she wasn't drifting away to certain, fiery death anymore. Restlessly, she moved her hand, and immediately felt it enveloped in a hard, warm grip. Hawk. She knew without doubt that it was Hawk. And that he was the one who had saved her.

Hawk always saved her, and she had no doubt whatsoever that he would do so again. At the thought, her parched lips curved into a faint, contented smile.

Watching the smile transform Irony's colorless face, Hawk glanced up to find Falling-Snow-on-Water studying him.

"She's getting better, isn't she?" he asked.

The Indian woman nodded gravely. "I believe it is so. Perhaps it was burning the herbs, or the vervain tea, or the medicine man's incantations." She inclined her head and laid a hand on Hawk's broad shoulder. "Or perhaps it was the prayers you said day and night."

Hawk fought the tide of crimson he knew was creeping upward along his neck. "How . . . how did you know?" he finally asked.

Snow smiled gently. "You and I have known each other for a very long time, Hawk. I can look directly into your heart and see what is there. You were so afraid for the pretty white eyes that you were willing to try anything."

He shrugged, making no further effort to conceal his vague embarrassment. "I took no chances," he confessed. "I prayed to the white God, but I offered gifts to Manitou, as well."

Snow's round, dark eyes narrowed slightly. "You love her, don't you?"

"Snow . . ."

"It is not a surprise to me that you do not love me anymore," she said softly. "You have not loved me for a long time."

"But not because of Irony," he declared. "I've only known her a few weeks."

"I know."

"I'm sorry that things have changed, Snow."

"When our families talked of marriage between us, they did not know what the years would bring." Snow removed her hand from his shoulder and crossed to the cooking fire. Kneeling, she filled a small clay bowl with broth from a steaming kettle. "Your mother did not know you would go away to a mission school and learn to live in the civilized world. And my parents could not know that, even with an education, I would prefer to stay here with our people, too content to think of a life beyond this lake and these forests."

Snow settled herself at Irony's bedside and with Hawk supporting her patient's head, began spooning the liquid into her mouth. "We are two different people now."

Hawk nodded. "I always thought we would marry, Snow. I . . . I would have been content with you as my wife. But something . . . some inner voice I can't explain . . . kept me from coming to you. And now that I have met Irony McBride, everything is different."

"Yes."

"I didn't ask for this to happen."

"I understand that. I wanted to hate your Irony," she admitted with a wry smile. "I wanted to, but I couldn't. Even through her illness, I can see she is very special."

"Irony is the most unique woman I have ever known."

Snow concentrated on dipping the spoon into the broth and carefully transferring it to Irony's lips. "You deserve someone special, Hawk."

Their eyes met and held. "So do you, Falling-Snow-on-Water. I am only sorry it could not have been me. We would have dealt well together . . . and life would have been peaceful." A smile softened his strong features. "A life with Irony may not be possible at all — and even if it was, peacefulness would play no part in it."

Snow laughed. "Then why is it you do not look distressed to say such a thing?"

Hawk's expression was sheepish. "I have grown to

enjoy the . . . the sheer unpredictability of this woman. She is different from all others."

"Like your mother, perhaps?"

"Yes, very much like my mother."

Snow set aside the half-empty bowl of broth and leaned toward him, her eyes serious. "Tell me about your Irony, Hawk. Tell me what makes her so unusual."

He laid Irony back against the mound of furs and took her hand again. Even now, when she seemed so much better, he could not bear to release his hold on her, lest she still find a means of slipping away.

"The first time I saw her, I was standing in the headmaster's office at Sweetwater school and Irony came hurtling through the door, saying 'I need a man. . . .' "

"A man?" Snow put one hand to her lips in astonishment. "Oh, Hawk, she didn't say that!"

"Oh, but she did," he insisted. "And she was carrying a rusty old revolver she'd found in her aunts' attic. Why, she held the gun on me and demanded that I . . ."

Lulled by the rich droning of Hawk's voice, Irony drifted into the deepest sleep she had experienced since becoming ill. The fire crackled and sang, and outside, the Northern twilight grew rosy, then paled and faded into night.

Irony yawned and stretched. For the first time in days, her muscles didn't protest and her head was clear. She opened her eyes and saw Hawk's face above her.

"I'm hungry," she said. "Why am I so hungry?"

"Because you haven't eaten solid food for the best part of a week."

"A week? What . . . what happened to me?"

"You took a chill when your canoe capsized," Hawk

236

answered. "You remember the accident, don't you?"

"Yes," she said slowly. "I do remember . . . What about Nathan? Is he well?"

"He's fine."

Irony glanced down at her pale hands lying on the blanket. She lifted one arm and studied the lace-edged sleeve of her nightgown. "Where did this come from?" she asked. "My things were lost in the lake."

"I recovered your carpetbag . . . and your belongings have been laundered."

"What about my letters—my proof of ownership?" Irony whispered, aware that her small store of energy was rapidly failing.

"The oilskin protected them. They're a bit water stained, but still legible. They're safe."

"What of Goodman?"

"No one here has seen him," Hawk answered. "But I've sent runners into the other villages to warn of his scheme. And Nathan is out scouting around, too. We should have word of his whereabouts any day now."

"Nathan's gone? Then that's why he hasn't come to see me."

"He was going insane with worry about you," Hawk confessed. "It was a relief for him to have something to do besides wait out your illness."

He wasn't yet ready to tell Irony that he had actually sent Nathan out to find the man known as Zack, the man he strongly suspected was her father. There would be time to deal with that dilemma later.

"Where are we, Hawk?" Irony's gaze swept the domed interior of the wigwam, lingering on the bulrush mats and the cooking utensils lined neatly against one wall. "Are we in an . . . Indian house?"

"A wigwam," Hawk corrected her, with a smile. "It belongs to a friend of mine."

"Oh." Her eyes took in the open fireplace in the center of the room. A cooking pot hung from a tripod.

"Do you suppose there is something to eat in that pot?"

"It's stew. I'll get some for you."

Irony watched as Hawk took up a bowl and ladled the hot mixture of meat and vegetables into it. He seemed as at ease with domestic chores as he was with wilderness survival. An idle thought floated into her mind, taunting her with the notion that, had Hawk not deserted them on Pine Island, the accident would never have occurred. She would never have gotten sick, and Goodman's capture would not have been in doubt.

She had recovered enough to feel a renewal of the anger that her illness had forced into retreat, but she reminded herself that Hawk had cared for her and that she did not want to repay his kindnesses with shrewish accusations.

As he returned to her side, she could see the dark smudges beneath his eyes, the slightly haggard look of his face. Guiltily, she knew he must be tired.

"Thank you for everything you've done, Hawk," she said softly.

He accepted her gratitude with silence, but there was a pleased expression in his eyes. He lifted a spoonful of stew to her mouth.

"You don't have to feed me," Irony protested, but her hand shook as she took the spoon.

"Either Snow or myself has fed you for the past week," he pointed out.

"But I am better now." Irony managed a few shaky bites, but her hand gave out more quickly than her appetite.

"Here, I'll finish," Hawk offered.

Irony leaned back against the pile of furs, willing to relinquish her independence for a while longer. "Thank you."

She had just finished the last bite when the hide covering the doorway of the wigwam was pushed aside and someone entered. Irony's hand clutched Hawk's, her nails digging in sharply, as she observed the tall, slender Indian woman who stood there.

"Irony," Hawk said, "this is Falling-Snow-on-Water. She has taken care of you." In a lower voice, he added, "Don't be afraid."

The two women studied each other for a long moment, and then Snow knelt down near Irony's bed. "I am pleased that you are feeling better, Irony. You have been very ill."

Irony's green eyes widened in surprise. "You speak English," she exclaimed. "I . . . I didn't expect that."

Snow inclined her head. "A man who lived among us for many years taught me. Taught all of us, actually. But those of us who were children learned more quickly than did the adults."

Irony wanted to question her more about the man she had mentioned, but her stamina had waned and she found herself struggling to stay alert. She would ask about him later, for she needed to know if many such men had left their homes to live among the Indians. Perhaps Snow had even known her father. Odd to think that a stranger might know more of him than she did.

Apparently, her sleepiness was evident to the others, for Snow rose to her feet and said, "Why don't you rest now, Irony? Later I will help you bathe, if you like."

Irony nodded with pleasure and snuggled deeper into her bedding. Through lowered lashes, she watched as Snow walked with Hawk to the door of the wigwam.

So that is Hawk's friend, she thought, not entirely happy with the revelation. Falling-Snow-on-Water was lovely, young and slender, her oval face and fine features framed by waist-length hair that looked like ebony silk. Men weren't friends with women who looked like that — were they?

* * *

Two days later, well enough to start feeling bored with her convalescence, Irony announced her intention of getting dressed. Snow didn't argue, nor did she make any comment when Irony found her legs were nearly too weak to support her. Instead, the Indian woman brought Irony the things she requested: her freshly washed chemise and petticoat, and the printed cotton gown.

In the time she had been with Snow, Irony had forgotten her initial reticence. The other woman was not at all what she had expected an Indian to be. She was as civilized as Irony herself, and in truth, more proficient in the womanly arts.

Snow cooked and sewed with a calm efficiency that soothed Irony's mind. The tiny tin cones she had sewn along the yoke of her buckskin dress tinkled softly as she moved about, providing a faint music that was so restful it lulled Irony until she dozed the days away.

When Irony was wakeful, Snow told her stories of the other members of the tribe — stories about her friends Singing Grass and Morning Storm, about Gray Wolf, the eldest of the grandfathers, and Kineu and Addik, the Chief's mischievous twin sons. Irony had seen none of these people, but already felt that she was beginning to know them through Snow's lively tales.

Snow never seemed to tire of caring for Irony. She brewed herbal teas and made delicious soups and stews. Every day she baked the flat bread made of pounded corn that Irony had grown to love. It seemed to please Snow to do things for her guest, and she had shyly confided to Irony that she would miss her company when she was fully recovered. Irony thought that she might miss Snow, also.

There was only one thing that disturbed Irony about the pretty young Indian — and that was her obvious closeness to Hawk. She seemed to know him so well that she could anticipate his every want or need. On the days when he would sit reading to Irony from his copy of *Hiawatha,* Snow would bring him a cup of sweet currant juice before he himself realized he was growing thirsty. His sitting mat was always unrolled before he appeared, his tall frame dwarfing the inside of the wigwam, and if he happened to arrive near meal time, there was always extra food for him.

Irony didn't want to feel envy for Snow, but she couldn't avoid it. Something base and ignoble stirred inside her every time she saw Hawk and Snow exchange smiles, or Hawk lay a friendly hand on Snow's shoulder or bring her water or firewood. She hated herself for her jealousy, but she could not vanquish it. Still, amazingly enough, it did not make her like Snow less. It only made her more aware of what she felt for Hawk—what she had felt all along, but what she had so vehemently denied until now.

She had just finished dressing when Hawk announced his presence and stepped into the wigwam. At the sight of Irony in a dress, her hair brushed and tied back with a beaded thong provided by Snow, his handsome face broke into a broad smile.

"Feeling better?" he asked.

"Yes, and bored with lying in bed." Irony took a teetery step toward him. "I've got to regain my strength."

"No need in hurrying matters too quickly," he said. "There'll be time for strengthening your legs later. Right now, a rest in the sunshine should be sufficient."

Without waiting for her approval, Hawk scooped her into his arms and strode out of the wigwam, instructing Snow to follow with some blankets.

Irony blinked furiously when they stepped out into the bright light of day. Gradually, as her eyes grew accustomed to the sunshine, she saw that they were standing in the midst of an Indian village. Her arm crept around Hawk's neck in unconscious alarm as she surveyed the rows of domed huts, scrawny, barking dogs and half-naked children—and the group of bronzed-skinned people who had halted their activities to stare at her. Since awakening in Snow's wigwam, she had known her whereabouts . . . but the reality of the situation had not stricken her before now.

Hawk could feel the tension in Irony's body as he held her close against him. He began to walk forward, talking as he went. "Everything will be fine, Irony. They're just curious about you." He nodded solemnly at a cluster of old women, who flashed toothless smiles at him, then broke into a gabble of shrill chatter. "When Nathan and I brought you here, you were swathed in blankets from head to toe. They don't see many white women here—so naturally, they want a look at you."

"What are they saying?" she whispered, glancing over his shoulder at the women.

"They're fascinated by your hair," he replied, his voice tinged with amusement. "It's the same color as theirs, but so curly that they think it must be possessed by a naughty spirit."

Irony had to laugh, too. "There have been times when I would have agreed with that theory."

Suddenly she felt her apprehension begin to ease. She had wondered about the Lake of the Woods Indians all her life. If anyone could understand their inquisitiveness about her, it should be Irony. The truth was, they didn't seem nearly as hostile as she herself had been when she first left Thief River Falls.

"Would you like to sit here in the sun?" Hawk was asking, lowering her to the blankets Snow had arranged on the ground. "You can rest your back against this boulder."

"Will you stay with me?" she asked, noticing the tide of children sweeping toward her.

Hawk dropped down beside her. "I'll stay," he said. "But there's nothing to fear."

The children gathered around, too shy to speak even though they were staring steadily at her. Becoming unnerved, Irony looked at Hawk, her spine stiffening at the grin on his face.

"I'm not afraid of them," she muttered. "I just don't know what to say that they would understand."

"Say anything," he suggested.

"H-hello. My name is Irony McBride."

The children broke into wide smiles, but said nothing. Irony cast an I-told-you-so look at Hawk and his shoulders shook with suppressed laughter.

She fastened her gaze on one of the smaller children, a little girl with a dirty face and straggling braids. "What's your name?" she asked.

The child clapped a hand to her mouth and turned to her companions, all of whom were whispering and giggling.

"I told you they wouldn't understand me," Irony stated, disappointed that she had been right.

"They understand you," Snow informed her. "They just aren't sure they should talk to you." She said a few words to the children in the harsh Ojibway tongue. The circle of youngsters pressed closer.

The little girl with the dirty face fixed round black eyes on Irony and suddenly, taking a step forward, put out a dusty forefinger and touched Irony's cheek.

"Why you have spots?" she asked, blushing at her own daring.

Irony blinked, then blinked again. "Spots?"

"Freckles," Hawk explained. "These past weeks in the sunshine have brought out the freckles across your nose."

"A lady doesn't have freckles," she wailed, wishing for a mirror.

"A lady might not," he said evenly, "but you do." He leaned closer. "And may I say they are very enchant-

243

ing?"

Irony's hand went to her cheek as she lowered her gaze in embarrassment. "Spots?" she whispered faintly.

"You look like fawn," the little girl said, her teeth gleaming whitely in her brown face. "You pretty."

"Well. So are you. Won't you tell me your name?"

"Rising Mist."

"Such a lovely name! Who are your friends?"

As the child rattled off a mixture of English and Indian names, her constraint was forgotten and soon the children were seated around Hawk and Irony, jabbering as though they had all known each other for years. Irony could only catch occasional words, but she enjoyed the rapid, high-pitched voices and the merry laughter.

Soon a group of women whom Irony suspected were the mothers of the children, began to edge nearer. They did not speak, but observed Irony with grave concern, as if afraid she might be a bad influence on their noisy offspring.

"Why don't they say anything?" she whispered.

"They haven't decided what to make of you yet," Hawk answered, his eyes filled with warm, teasing glints. "They are envious of your dress, your fine complexion, your curly hair. They're worried that you might be here to cast a spell on their men and steal them away."

"Oh, heaven forbid!" she snapped, tossing a furtive glance toward the knot of men watching them from fifty yards away. "There isn't a man in the group that I'd have on a silver platter."

"Not a single one?" he queried.

"No," she affirmed, although her eyes were clearly saying, *Only you.*

"I'm pleased to hear that," he said, then broke into an expansive speech in Ojibway. The women smiled and nodded, looking at Irony with sudden friendli-

244

ness. Several of them spoke in halting English, while those who used the Indian dialect tried to communicate their meaning with vigorous hand gestures.

"What did you say to make them so friendly?" Irony asked.

Hawk reached out to tuck an errant strand of hair behind her ear. "I told them that you were very shy, so I hoped they would make you feel welcome in their village."

"You ver' lucky to be Hawk's woman," one of them said with a bold wink. "He ver' much man."

Irony turned scarlet. "You . . . you told them . . . that I . . . ? That we . . . ?"

His smile wasn't the least bit conciliatory. "It broke their silence, didn't it?"

"Oh, Hawk, how could you?"

The unexpected appearance of a thin, spotted dog and her pups created a most welcome diversion at that instant, and Irony turned away, exclaiming, "Look! Aren't they darling?"

Four fat, shiny puppies trailed the mother, but behind them came a smaller, thinner puppy, limping badly.

"Hawk, what's wrong with him?" Irony cried.

"He broke leg," interjected the friendliest of the Indian women. "Now ver' good for stewpot."

"No!" Irony shouted, making an attempt to get to her feet.

Hawk caught her arm and held her back. "She's only joking," he said. "Good Lord, Irony, surely you don't believe these people would actually eat him?"

"How should I know what to believe?" she flared.

"Ver' funny joke," the woman insisted.

"Not so funny to me," Irony retorted. She appealed to Snow. "Get that puppy for me, will you? I want to make certain he stays safe."

"I'll get him," Hawk declared, rising in one swift motion. He scooped the puppy up, pausing to alleviate its fear by scratching its ears. The dog was black and white spotted, with a comical face.

"He looks like he's wearing a mask," Irony exclaimed, holding out her hands for the animal. "Oh, Hawk, isn't he precious?"

"I've seen more beautiful dogs in my time," he said, but he smiled nevertheless.

"He is your dog now, Iron-nee?" asked Rising Mist. "You keep?"

"Can I?" Irony raised questioning eyes to Hawk and Snow. "Will anyone care?"

"He limps, Irony," Snow reminded her. "His leg will never get better."

"I don't mind." Perfectly content beneath Irony's stroking hand, the puppy had settled into her lap and was licking her wrist. "He's the one I want . . . really!"

"Then it is settled," Hawk said. "If there is ever anything you want, Irony, you have only to ask."

Irony gazed up into his beautiful face, and his look of burning intensity made her wonder at the meaning behind his rather enigmatic words.

In the days that followed, Irony's strength returned rapidly. Each morning she went for a walk, leaning on Hawk's arm and followed by a procession of dogs, children and whispering, giggling women. Her new puppy, whom she had named Rogue, trotted at her side until he tired, and then she and Hawk took turns carrying him.

She had just set out on one such walk when a sudden hubbub of noise caught her attention, and she glanced up to see a small group of men approaching her. Hawk only had time to warn her that the man in the lead was Chief White Crane before he and his entourage came to a halt directly in front of them.

The chief held up one hand in greeting, and Irony

smiled nervously, not at all certain of the protocol involved. Unfortunately, Aunt Tiny, who had taught her the correct etiquette for meeting queens, had never had occasion to instruct her on what was proper behavior when encountering an Indian chief.

"Good to meet you, Iron-nee," boomed White Crane.

"I'm pleased to meet you as well," she murmured, following his lead.

"You have been much sick."

"Yes, but I'm better now."

Chief White Crane nodded solemnly. "Is good."

Irony observed the man standing before her, impressed by his stature and inherent dignity. He was dressed in fringed buckskins beautifully decorated with colorful quillwork, and from his braided hair hung two eagle feathers, the mark of a chief. His face was the color of red sandstone, and though it was stern and lined, Irony thought she could detect glints of humor within his deep-set black eyes. The man seemed fatherly rather than savage or bloodthirsty—he was not at all what she had expected.

"White Crane and his people wish to honor you," the Indian said. "We build wigwam where you stay. You live here until many moons have come and gone."

Irony shot a quick look at Hawk. "My own wigwam?" she queried.

"They want to make you feel welcome here," Hawk explained. "They will build you a lodge where you are free to remain as long as you please."

"I . . . I'm honored," Irony said, feeling confused by such generosity. "But I have done nothing to deserve this."

"You are brave woman," the chief announced. "It is enough."

When White Crane and his council had made their departure, Irony turned to Hawk. "Why should they do so much for me?" she asked. "I'm a stranger."

"Perhaps it's as White Crane said—they want to honor your courage."

"Maybe so." Irony bent down to scratch Rogue's head. "You know, I'm almost beginning to wish my father could be here to . . . to see how well things are going for me in the wilderness."

Hawk swallowed deeply. If his suspicions proved to be true, Irony was closer to having that wish become reality than he liked to think. The prospect made him hellishly uncomfortable.

To hide his unease, he diverted her attention by pointing out the children's latest antics, and after a few minutes they continued their stroll.

Chapter Fourteen

In the Indian village . . .

The members of Chief White Crane's tribe built Irony's wigwam at one end of the village, in a grove of pine that screened it from the other lodges. Hawk explained that they did so because the white eyes they had known had always expected a certain amount of privacy, and it was assumed Irony would feel the same way.

In all honesty, she wasn't sorry that she would be secluded from the others. She was pleased with the thought of her own quarters, with an isolated stretch of beach for bathing. Even if Goodman was apprehended quickly, she would have had the chance to enjoy this extension of her adventure. Her eyes sparkled with mirth as she envisioned what Aunt Tiny and Aunt Alyce would have said about her temporary home.

It came as something of a surprise to Irony that the construction of the wigwam was shared equally by the men and women of the village. She had always believed such domestic chores were left to the females. The men cut and peeled ironwood saplings, which they then set into the ground in an oval pattern, measuring nearly fifteen by twenty feet. As they pulled the tops of the saplings into arches, the frame was bound together by the women, using strong fibers of green linden. The lodge was then covered with wide strips of bark, secured by weighted cords, and a deer hide was hung over the doorway.

Irony was amazed that her wigwam was to be furnished with items generously offered by the villagers. Bowls and pots were stacked along one wall, and two rolled-up bearskin sleeping mats were placed along another. One woman shyly presented her with a fringed buckskin dress, while two others urged newly made moccasins upon her. Several young boys brought firewood, and the children laughingly argued over who got to carry her pail of water. When they had completed their work, the Indians stood back and grinned at Irony, clearly awaiting her approval.

"I can't thank you enough," she said, feeling humbled by their unexpected magnanimity. "Everything is wonderful!"

Hawk repeated her words in Ojibway and they smiled and nodded, then began drifting away toward their own homes.

"I'm overwhelmed by their generosity," Irony told Hawk when they were alone.

"They simply wish to make you welcome," he said. "Would not the civilized people of Thief River Falls do the same for me, were I to visit their community?"

She tried to ignore the satirical tone of his voice, but her current, oddly disturbing mood wouldn't allow it. "I'm afraid that if you showed up in my hometown, you'd most likely be treated with suspicion and mistrust . . . at least, until people got to know you."

Hawk regarded her with puzzled amusement. "Your illness has stolen your fire, Irony," he finally commented.

"Do you think so?" she jibed with mock anger. "Defame me again and I will show you fire!"

With low, rumbling laughter, Hawk suddenly

reached out and pulled her into his arms. "Ah, Irony, I've missed you."

Her smile died as she gazed up into his dark eyes. "You've done so much for me, Hawk . . . and I'm grateful."

"Shh," he said softly. "If I have helped you in any way, it has given me great pleasure."

"Snow says you saved my life."

"No more than Nathan saved your life. No more than you saved his."

Irony dropped her eyes, letting them linger on the pulse at the base of Hawk's throat. "Why did you leave me, Hawk?" she asked in a low voice. "Why didn't you even say goodbye?"

"At the time, I thought it was for the best." His hold on her tightened. "But I was wrong."

Irony forced her eyes higher. "Wh-what do you mean?"

"Don't act so surprised," he chided. "I've been known to admit to making errors before."

"It's not something I've seen," she whispered, a tentative smile tugging at the corners of her mouth.

He drew back, his hands sliding up her arms to grasp her shoulders. "Irony," he said seriously, "I made a mistake by allowing social convention to dictate my behavior. I believed I should put some distance between us because I . . . I thought there was too much feeling there. I knew I was beginning to care too much for you, and I . . . hoped that you felt the same way about me, even though it seemed wrong to encourage such feelings. But as soon as I had been away from you two hours, I realized it wasn't the *feelings* that were wrong. The wrong lies with a society that makes it a crime for two people to . . . love each other simply because they are of different heritages. Why should one blood or one skin color be considered superior to another?"

"Hawk . . ."

"Let me say this, Irony, please. I know what you were raised to believe, and I've certainly dealt with bias in my life—sometimes from my own people. But the time we've spent together has taught me that some things are more important than convention."

"Hawk, I—"

"I made a decision, Irony, and I want you to know about it. I may be part Indian, I may be—"

"Hawk, listen," Irony insisted, putting her fingers across his lips. "Those things don't matter. I don't care any more."

His eyes widened. "You don't . . . ?"

"Care," she repeated. She removed her fingers from his lips, but let them linger along the strong line of his chin and jaw. "I have learned some valuable lessons these past weeks—and one of them is that life is to be enjoyed, savored. I've loved being in the wilderness." She stood on tiptoe and brought her face close to his. "And I've loved being with you."

Irony's mouth drifted softly over his, and she could feel the start of surprise that jolted him. She caressed the side of his neck with her hand, nestling her body more closely against his and deepening the kiss. Her lips patiently coaxed a response from him, and soon, his arms went around her, his hands stroking her back in slow, distracted circles.

"I've made a decision, too," she whispered, letting her kisses define the line of his cheek. "I don't know what will happen when I return to Thief River, but for now—while I'm here—I want to be with you."

There was no mistaking her meaning, just as there was no mistaking Hawk's reaction to it. With a low, wrenching groan, he wrapped his arms about her like bands of iron and, finding her mouth with his, lifted her off the ground, holding her prisoner as he kissed her with an almost violent passion. Irony's arms went around his neck and she returned his kiss with fervor, delighting in the unbridled desire that had sprung to life between them. For once, she had no difficulty in thrusting aside troublesome thoughts of her lady aunts or the disapproval of her friends and neighbors back home. At that moment, reality was the tall, beautiful man holding her as though he would never let her go, plundering her senses with kisses that seared and burned their way into her very soul.

"Hawk," she murmured, "don't you think we should go into the lodge?"

"Mmmm?"

"Inside," she repeated with a smile. "Come inside with me."

Hawk released her so abruptly that she stumbled and had to clutch his shirt to keep from falling. He steadied her, then backed away.

"What's wrong?" she asked.

"There are . . . things we've got to consider," he muttered, obviously struggling to get control of his emotions.

"Right this minute?" Irony questioned in disbelief.

She half expected Hawk to laugh because she was making no effort to conceal her frustration, but he didn't seem to notice. In fact, he was so preoccupied that she wasn't certain he'd even heard her.

"There are risks we shouldn't take." He shook his head. "I'm . . . sorry, Irony, but we can't do this." He turned and nearly fled down the path toward the village.

Irony stared after him. *He'd actually refused her!* That was the only way to describe his action. Raphael Hawkes, a wilderness guide who'd demonstrated nerves of steel more than once, had just run from her sensual invitation as though all the hounds of hell were snapping at his heels.

Irony tossed the leather ball across the floor of the wigwam and Rogue bounded after it, hampered not at all by his lameness. Eagerly, he brought the ball back to her and, absentmindedly, she patted his head and threw the ball again. His pleased, yapping bark caught her attention for a moment, and she realized that the puppy had grown rounder and healthier since she had taken on the responsibility of caring for him.

She remembered Hawk examining the dog's injured leg with gentle fingers that first day. Rogue had merely licked at Hawk's hands in joyful friendliness, reassuring them that the weakened leg caused him no pain. He had learned to compensate for the bad limb by swinging his compact little body to one side for balance when he ran, and as he grew stronger, he was able to keep up with the other dogs in the village. But he didn't play with the other animals very much now that Irony had come into his life. He stayed close by her side, exhibiting a fierce loyalty. If anyone approached her, Rogue greeted them with a growled warning, not relaxing his guard until Irony assured him it was all right. Hawk was the only person the dog accepted without question.

Hawk. Thinking of him, Irony felt a renewal of the embarrassment his rejection had caused her. Had she been too forward, too unladylike? Even though Hawk had taunted her about her desire to emulate her aunts, had he been repulsed by her boldness?

Irony sighed and scratched Rogue's head. It was something of a shock to think that he'd desired her . . . but rather than make love to her, he'd retreated with unflattering haste. Why? She couldn't help but recall those times on the trail when he'd kissed her, touched her with such burning intensity that they had only barely avoided the inevitable. What had happened? Why had Hawk changed his mind about her?

Irony moved across the tepee toward a small, metal mirror hanging on one wall. The chief's wife had given it to her, and Hawk had explained that it had been purchased on the reservation before the Indians had left to return to their homes in the islands. A valuable gift, it had shown the woman's high regard for Irony.

She took down the mirror and looked into it with dread. Perhaps she hadn't realized how much she'd changed since Hawk had first seen her at the Sweetwater school. She flinched at the initial sight of her sun-gilded complexion, the tan freckles marching stalwartly across her nose. But then she turned her face and observed it more critically.

Actually, despite what society decreed, she thought she looked healthier now than before. Avoiding the sun and using lemon water had always faded her freckles and kept her skin lily white, but to her surprise, she found she preferred the glowing, golden cast the sunshine had given her face. The soft apricot blush that hazed her cheeks was attractive, even if she did say so herself. She leaned closer, making a detailed survey of eyes and mouth. Her eyes were still the same aggravating shade of green, and her mouth looked no different than usual.

Her hair was another matter, however. Even at home, where she'd had a steady supply of pomades and hair pins, it had been difficult enough to keep under control. Here in the wilderness, the wind and sun and water had wreaked havoc on it. Unless she confined it in braids, it was completely undisciplined. It cascaded down her back in unruly masses, wisping about her face and spilling over her shoulders in torrents of black curls. Fortunately, Hawk had recovered her brush when he'd brought her carpetbag up from the lake bottom, but even daily brushing didn't quite tame it. Striving for objectivity, Irony decided that it did have a certain wanton look about it — no doubt offensive to a man who was used to women who dressed their hair with bear grease before restraining it into neat plaits. She had just gathered her hair into both hands and pulled it back to the nape of her neck when a new thought occurred to her.

Hawk had said there were risks they dared not take. Risks? What had he meant? Could he . . . could he possibly have been referring to the altogether too likely hazard of a child? Irony blushed at the flustering thought, but she felt a twinge of self-reproach because it was a very real danger she herself had not considered. Suddenly, her heart felt much lighter. Of course — Hawk had worried that the result of their intimacy might alter the entire course of her life. She couldn't very well return to Thief River with a babe in arms. The scandal would put her aunts into their respective graves.

But Irony was smiling. Hawk hadn't rejected her, after all.

She heard Rogue's warning growl, and knew someone was approaching the wigwam. She dashed to the doorway and flung aside the deer hide, words of greeting crowding her lips.

"Hawk, I'm . . . oh! Snow, it's you. I . . . hush, Rogue." She gave Snow a somewhat forlorn smile. "Please, won't you come in?"

Snow chuckled and entered the lodge. "It seems you were expecting someone else," she said. "I won't stay long. I wanted to bring you some of my corn soup for your dinner."

"I really wasn't expecting anyone. I just thought Hawk might . . ." She broke off, sniffing the contents of the kettle Snow carried. "This smells delicious! How thoughtful of you to bring it to me."

"I wanted to do something to mark your first night in your new lodge," Snow said, hanging the kettle over

256

the small cooking fire. She then seated herself on a bulrush mat. "Perhaps Hawk will share your supper."

Irony dropped down on the opposite side of the fire. "I doubt it." She smoothed the skirt of her cotton gown. "He was here earlier and . . ." She raised troubled eyes to the young woman she had come to think of as a friend. "Snow, could I ask you for some . . . well, rather personal advice?"

"I suppose so."

"I . . . well, I'd hoped Hawk would stay here with me tonight . . . um, do you understand what I mean?"

"I do."

"Is that terribly disgraceful of me?"

"Not at all. Hawk is the sort of man any woman would want as her mate."

Irony considered Snow for a long moment. "Have you . . . um, have you ever thought of him in that way?"

Snow smiled gravely. "At one time. But as it turned out, he did not have the same thoughts."

Irony looked so stunned that Snow hurried on. "You see, our mothers once wanted us to wed — and we always thought we would. But then, Hawk went away to Sweetwater and . . . we simply grew apart."

"You were to marry?"

Snow nodded. "And in all honesty, I would have been content to do so had Hawk not changed his mind."

"Why did he change his mind?"

"I don't think even Hawk knows that. It just happened. I had suspected it for a long while, and then, when he brought you here, I knew for certain."

"Me?" Irony queried in a low voice.

"Hawk cares a great deal for you," Snow stated. "It is impossible not to see that he wants you, Irony —"

"He does?"

"Yes, of course."

"But he . . . practically ran from me."

Snow covered her mouth to stifle a dainty laugh. "Poor man, he is probably confused. I'm sure he wants to share your sleeping mat, but no doubt he fears the consequences."

"A child?"

"Yes. Think of it, Irony—if there should be a child, what would you do?"

Irony frowned, but her chin lifted noticeably. "I'd manage."

"Perhaps, but Hawk must be concerned for you. He knows such a thing would ruin your life."

"Shouldn't that be for me to decide?"

"Hawk would also worry about the child," Snow said gently. "Knowing him, he would not believe you'd ever marry him, and he would not wish to father a child for which he cannot be responsible."

"Oh."

"Don't look so sad, my friend. There are other choices."

Irony took in the rosy blush that flooded Snow's face. "What other choices?"

"You did not see a multitude of children in this camp, did you?"

"N-no, not really. There are only a dozen or so . . ."

"There is a reason for that," Snow informed her. "We are a poor people, we cannot afford for each family to have many children. So the women of the tribe prevent childbirth."

"How is that possible?"

"Some regularly chew a certain root that is found in the forest, others drink tea made from tansy or similar herbs. It is a simple method, but it has worked well for the Ojibway." Snow leaned forward to tap Irony on the arm. "It will work for you as well."

Now Irony found herself blushing, but she couldn't resist a question. "Don't you find yourself somewhat . . . well, shocked that I would be considering something like this?"

"No, I am not shocked. I am happy for you . . . and for Hawk. He has been alone for a long time, Irony, and I am pleased that at last he has found you. We cannot know what the next days or months will bring, but you have now, tonight—I think you are too wise to waste it."

"Yes, I am," Irony said with sudden decision. "Thank you, Snow."

The other woman rose to her feet with a swift, graceful movement. "I will bring you the herbs, Irony . . . but there is something you must do to repay me."

"What is that?"

"Could you . . . well, could you tell me something about your friend, Nathan Ferguson?" Snow colored again, dropping her eyes in a timid manner. "He is a . . . most handsome man, is he not?"

Irony smiled broadly. "Indeed he is. I didn't know you were interested, Snow—please, sit down and I'll tell you everything I know about him. Where shall we start?"

Snow dropped gracefully to the bulrush mat and studied her slender hands.

"First, I should like to know . . . does Nathan have a wife?"

The moon had risen high in the summery sky before Hawk came to her lodge. When he had not appeared by the time Irony had eaten her supper and fed Rogue, she had given up on him. For the time being, he had his reasons for staying away . . . and there was nothing she could do about it . . . yet.

When the hour grew late, she poured water into a

basin and bathed, putting on her nightgown. Looking down at the row of tiny stitches, she recalled the night she and Hawk had spent at Ma Flannagan's boarding house. In light of her present thoughts, she could almost laugh. What an innocent she had been then!

Irony was sitting on her sleeping mat, staring dreamily into the fire when she finally heard footsteps coming down the sandy path beyond her door. Rogue raised his head and listened, but did not bark, and she knew it was Hawk.

He said her name softly, then slipped inside the wigwam, letting the deer hide fall shut behind him. Irony swiveled about to look up at him.

"I didn't think you would come," she whispered.

Hawk moved swiftly to kneel beside her. "I wasn't going to," he replied, "but God help me — I couldn't stay away." He put his hands on her shoulders. "You should tell me to go, Irony."

"But I'm asking you to stay."

He rested his forehead against hers for a long moment. "Ah, love, are you sure?"

"Yes, I am."

"Then . . . we have something to discuss."

Irony smiled. "Tansy tea?"

She was enchanted by Hawk's vivid blush.

"Something like that," he finally said.

"I realized what must be bothering you," Irony said, "and so I spoke to Snow about it. She gave me some valuable advice."

He shook his head. "And you'd consider it?"

"Hawk, I'm not the same girl who set out from Thief River Falls. Believe it or not, even I can mature. Please don't think I haven't mulled this entire situation over in my mind a million times." She rested a hand against the side of his face and smiled tenderly. "I thought about this . . . about being with you . . . all the time I was sick. I lay there watching you

260

do everything you could to take care of me . . . and I knew that, as soon as I was recovered, I wanted this to happen."

"I won't take your charity," he said stiffly.

Irony laughed softly. "I assure you, my decision to . . . do this had nothing to do with charity. The truth is, every time I saw you and Snow together, I realized how much better suited to each other the two of you are. She's the one you should be with."

"You were jealous?"

"Yes." Her chin rose. "I can't be proud of it, especially after all Snow has done for me. But, Hawk, no matter what happens next, I wanted this time with you. Tomorrow or next week, I may have to go back home and though it won't be Nathan, I may eventually marry someone. And no doubt, you, too, will marry. I want us to have something to remember in the years ahead."

"And you'll have no regrets?"

"I can't say that," she murmured. "But I can say that I'd prefer to have regrets over something I've dared to do . . . rather than something I didn't have the courage for. I don't want to spend the rest of my life wondering how it would have been to make love to you."

Hawk slipped his arms around her as his mouth sought hers, and her contented sigh of surrender caught at his heart.

"Irony," he whispered against her mouth. "Sweet, sweet Irony . . ."

Her fingers moved to the buttons of his shirt, and he shifted from his kneeling position to sit beside her. When the shirt was hanging open, Irony pushed it aside and as Hawk shrugged it off, smoothed her hands over his steely chest. His flesh had the feel of granite, but it was warm and pulsing with life. She rested her cheek against him, savoring the texture and scent that was his alone. At a time when other men she knew had discovered highly perfumed shaving lotions and hair oils, Hawk had the delectable aroma of sun-warmed fields, of leather and pine and plain, homemade soap. She rubbed her face against him, kissing his collarbone and delighting in his immediate response.

He bent his head and captured her lips with his, holding her snugly against him. There was no need for his kiss to persuade or cajole; Irony was more than willing to meet him halfway. As his mouth slanted over hers, softly at first, then with increasing ardor, she alternately cursed and blessed her naiveté. Had she possessed more experience, she might have known better ways to please Hawk, better ways to express what she was feeling. On the other hand, she sensed that he was glad to be the first man she had ever been with. He certainly didn't seem put off by the slight awkwardness brought on by the sudden shyness she couldn't quite overcome.

Hawk's mouth danced over hers, pressing, then brushing teasingly. His tongue softly explored the curvature of her lips, erotically tracing the bow, then dipping into the corners. Irony drifted in a haze of drugged passion, eagerly allowing him to lead her into this new, astounding adventure. She had never given much thought to this most intimate relationship between a man and woman — not, that is, until her association with Raphael Hawkes had forced her to. Even then, she'd had no idea of the emotions that could be stirred, or of the sensual pleasures to be discovered. As Hawk's lips trailed tiny, hot kisses down her neck and into the opened collar of her nightgown, she couldn't imagine ever doing this with any other man.

Hawk . . . it had always been Hawk . . . and, she feared, it was very likely to remain that way for the rest of her life. And if she couldn't have him, she'd want no one else.

Only Hawk . . .

"Irony," he murmured, his voice breaking on a husky note. "You don't know how I've dreamed of this—how I've wanted you."

"I've wanted you, too," she admitted. "I'm only just beginning to realize how much."

They moved into each other's arms again, but this time they were content to merely hold each other, as if in quiet enjoyment of the fragile new expression of feelings between them. Eventually Hawk drew back to look into her face, smiling a slow, vaguely self-mocking smile.

"You know, when I was a boy back at the mission school, I discovered a love of poetry . . . and amazingly enough, everything important in my life seemed to remind me of one poem or another." He laughed softly at himself, but his eyes were dark and serious. "But there was one poem I've always loved—even though there was nothing in my life that gave it significance."

"What kind of poem?" Irony asked.

"An Ojibway love poem," he replied. "A poem that has haunted me lately—each time I look at you . . ."

She touched his mouth with her fingertips. "Say it for me, please."

Hawk kissed her fingers, then lowered her hand to press against his chest, where she could feel the hammering of his heart.

"Awake! flower of the forest, sky-treading bird
    of the prairie.
Awake! awake! wonderful fawn-eyed one."

His own hand moved to the tiny buttons down the front of her nightgown and, one by one, he unfastened them.

"When you look upon me I am satisfied;
as   flowers that drink dew.
The breath of your mouth is the fragrance of
flowers
    in the morning."

He slowly pushed the white cotton gown backward,
off her shoulders. As he did so, he leaned close to
gently kiss her, letting his mouth move over hers with
sensual deliberation.

"Your breath is their fragrance at evening in the
    moon-of-fading-leaf."

Hawk drew the nightgown downward, and Irony
lifted her arms free, letting the garment fall to her
waist.
The lodge was lighted only by the flickering fire,
and as he watched her, Hawk's eyes gleamed in the
shadowy dimness. His gaze moved from her face to
her neck and shoulders, then lingered upon the sweet
perfection of her small, beautiful breasts. The
reflection of the flames within his eyes heated her
skin and burned away the last of the doubt inside
her.

"Do not the red streams of my veins run toward
    you,"
"As forest-streams to the sun in the moon
    of bright nights?"

His fingers trailed slowly over her skin, gently rubbing the roughened aureole, the pebbled nipple. Irony
gasped in surprised pleasure as he lowered his mouth
to kiss the places his fingers had just touched.
Hawk raised his eyes to hers again.

"When you are beside me, my heart sings;
  a branch it is, dancing,
When you frown upon me, beloved, my
  heart grows dark—
A shining river the shadows of clouds darken,
Then with your smile comes the sun and
  makes to look like gold
Furrows the cold wind drew in the water's face.
Myself! behold me! blood of my beating heart."

He cupped her face with his big hands, tilting it upward.

"Earth smiles—the waters smile—even the
  sky-of-clouds smiles—but I,
I lose the way of smiling when you are not near,
Awake! awake! my beloved."

"Oh, Hawk," she breathed. "That was lovely . . ."
His mouth on hers, Hawk leisurely pressed her
down onto the sleeping mat, following her with his
own body. With slow, stroking motions, his hand caressed her, straying over silken shoulders to tease her
breasts, then slide along a delicate ribcage. His fingers splayed across her flat stomach filled Irony with a
glowing warmth that pervaded every part of her heart
and mind. When his arm went about her, pulling her
hips into intimate contact with his fully aroused body,
she found herself lost to a bewildering wealth of sensations.

She had thought she could be content to lie within
his embrace forever, but the knowledge of what she
was, even in her innocence, doing to him sent her
mind spinning. The sweet torment of his hands upon
her drove her toward a sort of frantic desperation she
had never known and didn't understand. Her body

arched into his, and her hands clutched at his shoulders in supplication. She was silently, yet eloquently begging for . . . she didn't know what. She just knew that Hawk was the only one who could give her the fulfillment she was seeking.

Hawk pulled away from her long enough to divest himself of his Levis, and Irony kicked free of her tangled gown. The sight of Hawk's nakedness was both frightening and arousing. The brief glimpses she'd had of him in the rooming house had not prepared her for his sheer masculine beauty, for the splendid perfection of his physique. She wanted time to observe him, to accustom her eyes to the sight of him, but her admiring gaze seemed to ignite new fires within him and, gripped by an unendurable excitement, Hawk pressed her back onto the fur sleeping mat once again. He rose over her, and though her green eyes expressed her sudden trepidation, Irony raised her arms and drew him down to her.

"I know it will hurt the first time," Irony whispered, "so I am just going to think of all the other times to come . . ."

"Oh, love—you have a brave heart. Braver than many of the fiercest warriors I have known."

Hawk, battling his own fear for her, moved swiftly and with no further hesitation. He burrowed his hands into the masses of her wildly curling hair, lifting her face for his kiss and mingling her gasp of pain with his own hoarse cry. He lay very still until the kiss ended and he felt the initial stirring of her body beneath his.

"I promise you that it will not be this way next time," he said into her ear. "Next time you will gasp with pleasure, not pain—I promise."

"A promise I will hold you to," she said, her words almost a sob.

He made several tentatively moves, and when Irony

relaxed and followed his motions, he began a slow, strong thrusting.

"Oh!" Shyly, she hid her face against his shoulder. "Hawk . . . it might have hurt at first, but this . . . oh, this feels wonderful!"

Her uninhibited joy only served to incite his passion, and in a matter of seconds, he was hurled beyond the point of reason and sanity. His body increased the pace, the clamoring of his senses drowning out his caution. Irony's low, moaning cries of elation sang in his ears and touched him with a piercing thrill.

"Blood of my beating heart," he murmured, his lips grazing her temple, his hands kneading her back and shoulders with savage tenderness.

"Oh, Hawk!" she exclaimed, and in that instant, both were lost to an overwhelming surge of ecstasy that washed over them like the storm-tossed waves that pounded the beach on Pine Island. Irony felt that she was drowning in pleasure, and all she could do was cling, shuddering, to Hawk, his name a fervent litany on her lips.

He was just as shaken by the intensity of their combined emotions, and for long moments afterward, drifted in a state as magical and visionary as that he had achieved in the mystical Place of Dreams when he was sixteen years old.

True sanity did not return to Hawk until sometime deep in the night when he awakened to hear the soft call of a nearby owl. He glanced down at the woman asleep in his arms, and an abiding contentment settled around his heart.

He reached out to smooth a fire-gilded strand of hair from her cheek. Only one thing marred his otherwise perfect happiness—the thought of Irony's reaction to the arrival of Zackett McBride in the village. There could be little doubt that the man was her father. Thus it became necessary for him to warn her in advance, to soften the pain the news was certain to inflict. She had been hurt by Zack's prolonged absence and subsequent death. How was she going to accept the fact that, for whatever reasons, that death had been faked and he had been alive and well for the past eight years?

Hawk drew her closer within the circle of his arm, and Irony stretched languidly, draping an arm across his chest. He'd find a way to tell her—he had to. Somehow he would soothe her anguish. He didn't want to hurt her because he loved her; it was that same love that made him realize there was no way he could avoid bringing her this pain. All he could do was stand beside her. And that was exactly his intention, for as long as she allowed it. For the rest of his life, if possible.

Chapter Fifteen

Chief White Crane's camp . . .

Irony awakened with a smile on her face. So this was how it felt to be unladylike!

"What are you smiling about?" Hawk asked, his own smile showing a flash of even, white teeth.

"You should know," she said, lowering her lashes in sudden shyness.

Hawk pulled her close and kissed her bare shoulder. "Yes, I do know. Last night surpassed even my most vivid expectations."

Irony forgot her timidity in her surprise. She gazed at him with wide, unbelieving eyes, causing Hawk to chuckle and hug her even closer.

"Don't look as though you don't believe me," he scolded. "It's true. I've never known anyone like you, Irony."

"Surely you've known women more . . . worldly. Certainly more beautiful and . . ."

"Hush," he said, brushing kisses along her neck until he eventually arrived at her mouth. "You're the only one that matters—that ever mattered."

The kiss stopped her protest for long moments, and then Hawk was alternately dropping sweet, nibbling kisses on her lips and whispering heated endearments in her ear.

"You're beautiful, Irony . . . the most beautiful
. . . most seductive . . . the most wonderful woman
imaginable."

She laughed and tried to roll away from him.
"Hawk," she laughed, "stop it! It's bright daylight
outside . . . and anyone could . . . come down that
path . . . !"

As though to reinforce her statement, a shout and
the barking of several dogs rang out from somewhere in the village. Rogue growled sleepily, then
settled back into his nest of furs near the fire.

Hawk frowned. He'd been going to argue that
lovemaking needn't be reserved for the night, but
now he decided against it. Irony had already taken a
gigantic step, and he didn't want to rush her too
much. It was only natural that she would worry
about someone seeing him emerge from her lodge.
She and her aunts had spent twenty years safeguard-
ing her reputation, and he couldn't expect her to
break the habits of a lifetime just in the course of
one long, sweet night.

"It sounds as if the village is awakening," he said,
stealing a last kiss, "so I'll go."

"Will . . . will you come back tonight?" she asked
hesitantly, knowing the question probably sealed her
fate as a wanton woman.

Hawk grinned. "You couldn't keep me away."

He tossed aside the bed covering and reached for
his clothes. "I think I'll go down to the lake for a
bath," he said, a mischievous glint in his eye. "Care
to join me?"

"No, thank you! The lake must be freezing at this
time of morning." Irony shivered. "I'm going to heat
some water for my bath."

"City woman," he teased.

"Savage," she retorted, the word sounding more

like an endearment than an insult.

"Irony," he said, suddenly growing serious, "there's something I need to talk to you about. Will you sit outside with me after I've finished bathing? We could share breakfast in the sunshine."

"That would be nice." Her gaze was steady. "I'll . . . I'll have some herbal tea while I'm waiting."

Wearing only his Levis, he paused at the doorway to peer outside. Seeing no one, he threw her a hasty kiss and slipped past the deer hide, heading to the lake down a pathway that wound around behind the wigwam.

Irony put water on to heat, then rolled up the sleeping mat. She smoothed a hand over the thick pelts, thinking of the night she had spent with Hawk. Nothing could ever have prepared her for the wonder of it all—nothing she had ever heard or imagined.

After a cup of tea and a sponge bath, Irony decided to try on the lovely buckskin dress the Indian women had made for her. It fit well enough, and it was soft and comfortable, but she felt so foreign in it that she wished for a larger mirror in order to see her entire reflection. She had just finished braiding her hair into two long plaits when she heard her name shouted.

Thinking it might be Hawk, she stepped out of the lodge. Nathan was running down the path toward her, followed closely by three or four other men. When she saw him, Irony smiled and went to greet him.

"Nathan, you're back!" she cried, seizing his hands.

"And you are fully recovered, they tell me," he said. "Look at you, Irony—dressed like an Indian maiden, living in a lodge of your own.

271

Your father will hardly recognize you."

Irony's smile faltered. "My . . . my father?"

"Yes, I've brought him." He turned to the men behind him. "Come say hello to your daughter, Zack."

Irony's hands went to her mouth as if to stifle a scream of denial. Her eyes grew huge, reflecting the green of the forest around them. "Nathan, what are you talking about? My father has been dead for eight years."

"No—no, he hasn't," Nathan insisted, with a puzzled smile. "Didn't Hawk tell you?"

"Hawk knew?" she murmured, her attention captured by the man in buckskins who had walked forward to stand beside Nathan.

"Hello, Irony," he said. "I . . . do you remember me?"

Of course she remembered him! He walked with a slight stoop now, and his handsome face was lined and sun-darkened. There were gray strands in his dark hair—his hands were gnarled. But his wonderful, keen eyes were just as she remembered, and so was his voice. It had the same deep, soothing quality of the voice she had spent most of her life waiting to hear.

"You don't understand," she said coldly, turning away. "My father is dead. He died a long time ago."

Zack McBride hurried after her, laying a hand on her shoulder. "Irony, I can explain . . . if you'll only give me the chance."

Eyes blazing, she spun about to face him. "Give you a chance? You once had any number of chances to talk to me . . . and apparently, you weren't interested then. Well, now it's me who can't spare the time."

"I want you to know why I told everyone I was dead."

"It doesn't matter," she stated flatly. "I've already grieved over you. And as far as I'm concerned, you can stay dead. Things will be much simpler that way."

"But . . ."

Conscious of the curious eyes of the Indian men who waited nearby, Irony turned and started back to her tepee. But she hadn't taken more than two steps when Hawk appeared on the trail before her. He had just come from his bath in the lake. He was wearing only his Levis, with his flannel shirt flung about his neck like a towel. His chest glistened with droplets of water, and his black hair was wet, carelessly finger-combed back from his face. His smile died slowly as he saw the scene before him.

"My God, Irony!" His fists clenched and unclenched in his anxiety. "Zack—she doesn't know . . ."

"She knows now," Nathan interjected. "Hell, man, I thought you were going to tell her."

"I was . . . I intended to tell her this morning."

"Why the delay?" Nathan queried. "I left to find Zack last week."

Hawk's face was grim. "I realize that . . ." He shifted his stance, obviously upset with himself. "She was so sick at first, and then . . . when she started getting better, I thought she had enough to deal with. I couldn't just spring that kind of news on her—I wanted to wait for the right moment . . ." His glance at Irony was imploring. "I was hoping to break it to you as easily as possible."

"How long have you known?" she asked.

"I've suspected it for quite some time. I didn't know for certain until Nathan called your father Samuel Zackett McBride. Zackett. Zack was the name of the man I had once known."

"And why didn't you tell me then?" she queried, her eyes scorching into his.

"I wanted to be sure before I said anything. Even if he was the same man, he could have died since I'd last seen him. Until I knew the situation, I didn't want to say anything. Irony, listen, it was . . ."

"Yes, I know," she snapped. "It was for my own good!"

"It was! No one intended to lie to you." Hawk lowered his voice. "And I never meant to hurt you."

"It would seem I've been lied to most of my life." Irony let her disdainful gaze fall on her father. "As for being hurt, I got over that years ago . . . back when I was a child who kept waiting for a daddy who never came home. Back when I wondered what was so terribly wrong with me that my own father didn't want me!"

"Aw, God, Irony," Zack moaned. "You've got to let me talk to you."

"There isn't a single thing you could say right now that could make any difference."

Irony half-ran to her newly-constructed lodge, biting her lip to keep back the angry, burning tears that threatened. The sight of Rogue, peering at her from the hide-covered door, his comical face filled with eager friendliness, was a consolation she sorely needed.

"Well, now what?" Nathan fumed, looking from one man to the other.

"I'll talk to her," Hawk declared, running a hand through his damp hair.

"It won't do any good." Zack's flat statement sounded bleak. "She meant it — she doesn't want anything to do with me. And I can't say as I blame her much."

"She's just upset," Hawk insisted. "Good God, Zack—you don't know what all she has gone through to get here and protect your interests. She cares about you, that's obvious . . ."

"Cared, maybe." Zack stuck both hands into his back pockets and stared down at the ground. "Hell, she thought I was dead. She got over caring about me when she was still a child."

"You should have warned her, Hawk," Nathan put in. "You swore to me you would."

"God damn it!" Hawk half-shouted. "I meant to, I told you that. I simply hadn't gotten around to it yet."

"Exactly what had you gotten around to?" Nathan challenged.

"Yes," Zack said. "I might ask the same thing."

Hawk glared at them in astonishment. Before he could frame a reply, Zack continued.

"I haven't seen you in years, Hawk. You grew up to be a mighty fine specimen of a man. And somehow, it didn't seem quite right—you comin' up that path behind my daughter's tepee, looking a little too much at home to suit me."

"I took a bath in the lake," Hawk said.

"Why did you have to take it in Irony's part of the lake?" Nathan questioned.

"Stay out of this, Ferguson," Hawk flared.

"I'll ask it then," interrupted Zack, "Why did you happen to choose Irony's part of the lake for your bath?"

"Oh, for God's sake," muttered Hawk. "Why don't you ask her?"

"Because she won't talk to me."

"Well, neither will I. At least, not on this subject. If you want information, you'll have to get it from her."

Zack scratched his slightly stubbled chin. "That'd be like trying to snatch a chicken out of a wolverine's mouth," he said. "When I walked up and saw her in that buckskin dress, her hair all braided, I thought there might be a chance that she'd listen to me. But no, she's every bit as ladylike and indignant as my two sisters. I'll be damned if she doesn't put me in mind of Valentine when she was that age—full of piss and vinegar and lemon furniture polish!"

"She'll calm down," Nathan stated. "Sooner or later, she'll listen to you."

"To Hawk, maybe. But not to me."

"This whole mess is my fault," Hawk admitted. "I should have told her right away."

"Agreed," Nathan said succinctly.

Hawk glowered at him. "I'll give her a chance to adjust to the shock of seeing Zack alive, then I'll talk to her."

"It might help if you could tell her why I decided to let everyone think I was dead," Zack said. "If she could understand that . . . ! Why don't I explain it to you?"

Hawk shook his head. "I'll talk to her," he promised. "But you'll have to make your own damned explanations."

With that, he strode away down the sandy path toward the Indian village.

After retreating to her lodge, Irony had seen no one but Snow all day. The other woman had brought her a kettle of stew and some corn cakes, saying that Chief White Crane had asked her to provide food for their honored guest. Irony had little appetite, but she had been grateful for Snow's generosity. And grateful that, despite her worried glances, Snow had made no comment on Zack McBride's ar-

276

rival in camp, or Irony's stubborn unwillingness to hear him out.

The afternoon dragged by. Irony stripped off the buckskin dress and flung it into a corner, putting on, instead, her plain cotton gown, faded from wear and repeated washing. Then she and Rogue lay on the sleeping mat, Irony dredging up every wrong she felt her father had ever done her, Rogue snoring peacefully.

By evening, she had stoked her anger into such a blaze that she felt she would burst into flames. She left her wigwam and spent an hour pacing up and down the deserted beach. Finally exhausted, she sat down on a boulder and stared out across the island-dotted lake. The sight of tall sentinel pines against the sunset sky and the shrill, lonely cries of the loons calmed her, but as her wrath drained away, she was left with a feeling of sadness.

Her father was here, within reach. What wouldn't Irony, the child, have given for this opportunity? It was painful to imagine the stories she'd have demanded, the questions she'd have asked. Irony could weep for the lonely little girl she had been.

But now, she decided as she rose and retraced her steps to the isolated tepee, she much preferred soul-cleansing anger. She would cloak herself so heavily in righteous indignation that her father could never hurt her again.

Hawk was waiting for her when she stepped into her lodge.

Squatted in the center of the room, he was slowly feeding small logs into the fire. The flames flared, lighting the recesses of the bark structure.

"What are you doing here?" Irony hissed, amazed at the amount of ire she still felt against Hawk. Last night they had lain together in this very spot, and now she felt as if she could claw his eyes out.

"We're going to talk about this . . ."

"The hell we are," she spat.

To his credit, he didn't blink an eye or admonish her for her profanity. Of course, she reminded herself, unlike Nathan, Hawk had reason to know she wasn't entirely a lady.

"I said," he repeated calmly, "we are going to discuss your father."

"There's nothing to discuss. Now, get out of here."

"I'm staying until you listen to what I have to say."

"I'll scream so loud that everyone in the village will come to my aid."

Hawk was on his feet and gripping her arm before she could make a move. He gave her a small shake. "Scream and you'll be sorry," he growled.

Irony tried to twist away from him, but his hold was like an iron manacle.

"Let me go, Hawk," she said coolly.

"Are you willing to listen?"

"Not until I'm stone-cold dead!"

"Don't tempt me."

She raised suddenly fearful eyes to his. Hawk cursed and released her. "I'm sorry—I didn't mean that. You know I wouldn't hurt you. It's just that you make me so damned mad."

"I make you mad?" she gasped, backing away. "You're the one who lied . . ."

"I didn't lie."

"You should have told me, warned me about . . . about my father." With the back of her hand, she swiped at the tears that had gathered in the outer corners of her eyes. "How could you do that to me, Hawk?"

He heaved a frustrated sigh. "I don't really know how or why I let things get so confused. But Irony, I was going to tell you. That's what I wanted to tell you at breakfast this morning."

"You left it a bit late, didn't you?" Her tone was uncompromisingly bitter.

"Hell, yes!" he shouted. "If I had it to do over again, I'd tell you the first second you opened your eyes." He advanced on her. "Maybe when Snow was spoon feeding you soup! Or maybe that first day you got out of bed. Should I have told you on our little stroll through the camp? Yes, that was the time — then you could have adjusted to finding yourself in an Indian village at the same time you digested the fact that your father was alive and well. It was an inexcusable oversight, Irony . . . forgive me."

"Don't be sarcastic," she retorted. "And don't make it seem as though you had no choice!"

"The way I saw it, I didn't."

"Not even last night?" she bit out. "Couldn't you have told me then? Or were you afraid I wouldn't . . ." She swallowed deeply. "Couldn't bring myself to . . . sleep with you?"

"The one had nothing to do with the other, Irony," he said, his voice lowering. "I had other things on my mind last night . . ."

Her laugh was harsh. "Oh, yes, you certainly did!"

He came closer, stopping directly in front of her. "You know what I mean." He grabbed for her, but she darted out of reach.

"Irony, come back here. I'm not going to let you distort the memory of what happened between us last night with this . . . silly feud."

"Silly?" she shrieked. "How dare you call it silly? I assure you, I do not consider it silly in the least."

"Don't tell me you've forgotten so soon what it was like to be a woman for a change . . . instead of a childish brat!"

279

"Ohh!" she stormed, seizing a clay pot from the stack of cooking utensils along the wall. "Childish?" She hurled the pot at him and, had he not ducked to one side, it would have crashed against his temple.

"That does it!" he yelled. "There's only one way to reason with you!"

"Don't you dare touch me," she screamed, running from his sudden advance. "Hawk, I mean it . . ."

Irony dashed for the door, but he was faster, catching her in his arms and whirling her about to face him. She kicked out, catching him in the shin.

"Christ," he moaned, "I'd forgotten about your habit of doing that!"

She grasped a handful of his hair and gave it a hard yank, and when his hands flew upward in self-protection, she butted her head into his chest and made her escape. Rogue, thinking the whole thing a hilarious game, began to bark and snap at Hawk's pants leg.

Irony braced herself against the far wall, breathing hard, as Hawk knelt beside the dog and soothed it with quiet words. At the sight of his large, yet gentle hand stroking the dog's back with strong, capable motions, visions of the night before crowded hard and fast into Irony's mind. He had touched her like that, had soothed and stroked and fondled until she had been mindless with pleasure. As remembered bliss awakened inside her, it became more and more difficult to hang onto her anger. Had Hawk been intent on hurting or betraying her, he could never have been so tender, so loving during their night together. Perhaps she had been wrong to blame him so vehemently.

With a final pat on the dog's head, Hawk rose from his kneeling position in one swift, smooth move, looking not unlike a cougar who, having decided the chase was over, was moving in for the kill. Irony's new-found clemency fled in the face of his obvious determination. His features were set, hardened into an almost frightening mask of primitive resolution.

She scrambled away, tossing kettles, clothes and sleeping mats into Hawk's path as she went. As he relentlessly pursued her around the interior of the wigwam, his mouth curved into a harsh smile, and she realized he was actually enjoying himself.

"Stop smirking at me," she demanded, suddenly finding it somewhat difficult to keep her own mouth disciplined in straight lines.

"You might as well give up, Irony," he advised. "You can't elude me forever . . ."

"That's what you think!" She darted toward the door, but Hawk flung his body forward, seizing her around the hips and dragging her down with him to the floor. He twisted, pinning her beneath him.

"That's what I know," he panted, his smile disintegrating into a grin.

"Get off me," she ground out through clenched teeth. "I want you out . . ."

"Of my clothes?" he asked blandly. "Certainly."

He released her shoulders and sat up, unbuttoning his shirt.

"Hawk! What do you think you're doing?"

"I'm getting ready to communicate with you in the way we seem to manage best."

He shrugged out of his shirt and, kicking off the moccasins he wore, began undoing the metal fasteners on his Levis.

Irony was incredulous. "I can't believe you! Do you actually think I would . . . would allow you to . . . to . . . ?"

He stood and stepped out of his trousers, his grin more wolfish than before. "I do."

"Well, you're sadly mistaken," she vowed. "I wouldn't let you touch me for all the . . ." Her words trailed away as she stared, transfixed, by his glorious nudity. It wasn't until he dropped on one knee beside her that she regained her senses and began scooting away from him.

One big hand closed about her calf, halting her backward movement. "Come here, Irony," he commanded softly, and pulled her easily toward him.

She slapped at his hand, struggling against his effortless strength. "What do you think you're doing?"

"I thought I'd already explained that, sweetheart. I'm going to make love to you—it's the best way I know of to dissolve some of this tension between us."

"Love?" she sneered, still fighting him. "Love has nothing to do with it! You're just proving you're strong enough to get your own way."

"You'll be getting your way, too, Irony." As he pulled her toward him, her skirts bunched up around her hips. He let his hand drift upward, from her calf to her bare thigh. She shuddered beneath the marauding warmth of his touch.

"You have a great deal of confidence in your abilities," she spat.

"Nothing in your manner last night gave me reason to doubt them," he replied evenly. He tugged her closer.

"What? No poetry?" she jeered.

"Is that what won you over?"

"It certainly wasn't your gentlemanly wooing," she declared, as his hands went about her waist to lift her onto his lap.

"Hell, no," he agreed, bending his head to look directly into her eyes. "If you had wanted a gentleman, you'd have taken Nathan when you had the chance."

His mouth closed over hers with enough force to discourage further conversation. At first, Irony remained wooden, unsure of how she felt about his arrogant assault. But as his mouth softened, erotically coaxing hers into a reluctant response, his hands began to massage the tense muscles of her back and eventually, she gave up resistance and relaxed against him.

No matter how much he had angered her, Hawk was still the haven she sought during the storm. He had sheltered her as no one else in her life ever had—and she found herself distressed at the thought of losing that.

He felt her go limp in his arms, but had no real sense of triumph until she pressed closer to him and raised her arms to encircle his neck. Her mouth reacted to his, her lips parting in an undeniable eagerness, and Hawk's heart began to pound with the sheer joy of having found again the thrilling unity they had experienced before.

"Oh, Irony," he whispered against her mouth. "If only I could tell you how much I regret my part in what has happened . . ."

"Shhh," she returned. "Let's not talk about it now. Just don't let me forget how angry I am with you!"

His hands shook as he undid the small buttons down the front of her gown, and when he spread the material wide to free her shoulders and breasts, his breath grew harsh. He reached for the sleeping mat and lifted her onto it, deftly removing her dress and petticoats. Clad only in a white chemise, she lay quietly beneath his burning gaze, her breasts rising and falling with the exhilarated pace of her breathing.

When he bent to kiss her breast through the thin fabric, she cried out and pulled him down to her. Without thought, without speech, without poetry other than that created by the splendid union of their bodies, they hurled themselves toward a deep and peaceful oblivion. All rage, all pain and sadness was forgotten — lost in the maelstrom of explosive pleasure that swiftly overtook them.

Hawk moaned out in joyous agony, and Irony sobbed against his chest, weak in the aftermath of such sweeping ecstasy. They lay silently for long moments, until their breathing had slowed to normal and their hearts beat together in a less frantic harmony.

"Still angry?" Hawk queried softly.

She rubbed her face along the hard muscles of his shoulder. "A little — what about you?"

"I'm not angry with you, at least."

"Then, who?"

"Myself. This whole mess was my fault."

"Not really." She fell silent again.

Rogue roused himself from his place by the fire and trotted over to lay down beside them. Irony put out a hand to fondle his ears.

"Why did my father have to come back?" she whispered. "Why did he have to do this to me?"

"Everything will be all right," Hawk softly assured her. "The worst is over now. And I'm sure you'll find a way to resolve this dilemma."

Irony sighed heavily. "I could simply turn over the verification papers to . . . to my father and go on back to Thief River."

"Yes, you could do that," Hawk agreed. "Or you could stay here, make your peace with Zack, and see your adventure through to the end."

She regarded him with contemplative green eyes, but said nothing more.

Hawk slipped away just before dawn, but not more than two hours later, Snow came to tell her the latest news.

"That man—Goodman? He made camp on an island near Swimming Bear's village last night. The chief sent one of his braves to warn Hawk."

"What will happen now?" Irony asked, curious despite herself.

"Hawk and Nathan and your . . . and Zack are preparing to leave. They are going to Muskrat Portage to confront Goodman and his men. Hawk asked me to tell you that they will need the papers you have."

"Very well," Irony said. "I'll take them right away."

Hawk watched as Irony approached the rickety dock where several men were loading two small canoes with supplies for the short journey. She was dressed in her boys' clothing, and Hawk thought she had never looked so beautiful. Beside him, Zack straightened, emitting a low whistle from between his teeth.

"Jesus Lord, is that my daughter?" he muttered.

"Better let me handle her, Zack," Hawk warned.

"Gladly."

Irony ignored her father, coming to stand directly in front of Hawk. When her eyes met his, they were filled with such a damn-you-to-the-devil defiance that he couldn't contain the huge grin that spread over his face.

"Did you bring the letters?" he asked innocently.

Irony patted the pocket of her oversized jacket. "I've got them right here," she said. "But I'm going with you."

Zack choked and turned away, coughing.

"It could get rough, if Goodman decides to be contrary about this whole thing."

"I don't care. I'm going."

"Now, Irony, have you given this any real thought?" intervened Nathan.

"Of course I have. Snow is keeping Rogue for me and I have everything I'll need here in this canvas sack. I'm ready to leave any time."

"I don't know," Hawk stalled, rubbing his chin thoughtfully.

"Hawk, I'm going," she insisted. "I started this — and I want to see it through to the finish."

"Well then, I guess there's not much I can say, is there?"

"No. Now, which canoe do you want me in?"

"You'll ride in that one over there," he said. "It's mine." She nodded and, with a brief smile, turned to settle herself into the waiting canoe. Hawk watched her, his eyes warm with approval.

Behind him he heard Zack McBride mumble, "You sure as hell handled her, boy. Yep, you sure as hell did."

Chapter Sixteen

At Muskrat Portage . . .

The journey to Swimming Bear's camp took them through the inevitable avenue of islands, but for once the windswept forests and rugged granite cliffs failed to hold Irony's attention. Her decision to join Hawk and the others had been sudden, and not at all as well thought out as she'd led Nathan to believe. Now the doubts had begun to set in. In truth, she wondered what she was doing, why she hadn't just handed over the papers and started making plans to travel back to Minnesota.

She glanced down at her sun-browned hands with their short, uneven nails. Lord, Aunt Tiny would have a fit when she saw them! Well-groomed hands were the mark of a lady—how many times had she heard that axiom repeated? Somehow, going home seemed a drearier thought than ever.

She wondered about Nathan. She had seen him studying her with a peculiarly resigned look in his eye. Had he finally given up on the idea of marriage? Uncomfortably, she wondered if he was aware of the situation between her and Hawk. If so, would he mention it to her aunts . . . or to anyone else in Thief River? Irony sighed. The notion of keeping her reputation intact was becoming more unlikely every day.

She wished for a moment alone with Nathan so that she might determine his current attitude. She wouldn't ask him not to say anything about her . . . she still had too much pride for that. But if she could judge his mood, she'd be better prepared for what to expect. Unfortunately, Nathan was in the other canoe, and she couldn't even see him without turning to look back. That she would not do because she didn't want her father to think she was looking at him, or concerned for his welfare. She'd have to bide her time.

As the morning sun grew hotter, both Hawk and the Indian in the front of the canoe shed their shirts. Irony stared at the tattoo on the back of the man's shoulder with a faint prickling of alarm. He was one of the Nighthawks, obviously, but surely, had Hawk even the merest suspicion the man had anything to do with Bessie Sparks' murder, he would not have accepted his presence so calmly.

Irony couldn't help but notice that, although the Indian was clearly close to Hawk's age, he was thinner, less imposing—and also much less civilized in appearance. His hair hung down his back in two long braids, glistening with bear grease and ornamented with feathers and beads. His skin was darker than Hawk's and when she caught a glimpse of his profile, she could see that his features were harsher, carved in rugged, austere lines.

Muskrat Portage was less than a half day's distance from Caribou Island, where Chief White Crane's camp was located. By early afternoon, they had landed the canoes at a small, heavily timbered island.

"We'll make camp here," Hawk announced, helping Irony from the canoe. "While the rest of us wait, Eagle, you and Red Wolf can search out Goodman's whereabouts."

The Indian nodded. Eagle was the one who'd been in front of her in the canoe. The other man was taller and broader, and though not as handsome as Hawk in her estimation, a fine specimen of manhood. Both men seemed quiet, strong and capable. And it was obvious Hawk trusted them implicitly.

"By the way, Irony, these are my friends Eagle and Red Wolf. They each wear the tattoo of the Nighthawks. And, incidentally, they accompanied Nathan to find . . . Zack."

Irony greeted them with interest, though she flashed Hawk a meaningful look which made him grin. "Unlike me, Eagle and Red Wolf chose to marry and remain with the tribe. Neither of them has been away from the Lake since mission school days."

So, there could be no possibility that they had been involved with Goodman and his murderous schemes. But if that were so, only one Nighthawk was left unaccounted for—thus, Hawk now knew the identity of the friend who had, for whatever reasons, chosen to live outside the law. She glanced at him again, but he was careful to keep his face devoid of emotion, so she could not tell what he was feeling or thinking.

Camp was set up and after a quick meal, the Indians took one of the canoes and started on their scouting mission. Nathan declared his intention of catching some fish for supper and, with a sidelong glance at Irony, Zack McBride offered to help. It amused Irony that her father felt as ill at ease around her as she did him, but it also filled her with a quiet melancholy. It shouldn't be that way—but, under the circumstances, what else could either of them expect?

"I . . . I think I'll go for a walk," she said suddenly, heading straight into the pine grove that covered the heart of the island.

Zack watched her go, a baleful expression on his face. Hawk read the look and laid a hand on the older man's shoulder.

"She'll come around, Zack. It's just going to take a little time."

"Hell, it's going to take a consarned miracle, and you know it."

The view from the crest of the island was beautiful. In the last weeks, Irony had seen so much water and so many islands and fir trees that she had imagined herself inured to the beauty of the wilderness. Still, there was something so heart-stirring about the scene before her. The same wind that tugged at her hair and flattened her clothes to her body whipped the water into froth as it splashed and shimmered against the rock-edged bits of land that graced the surface of the lake as far as she could see. The greens and blues of the forest and water were glazed by golden sunshine.

Irony drew a deep breath. She loved it here! There was something about this country, something so elemental and strengthening. Its vastness offered space and freedom and, somehow, comfort. Its winds were soothing, its forests protective.

But there was harshness and danger, too. What land that had been formed by a cataclysmic upheaval of earth and water wouldn't be ruthless, even cruel at times? Somehow, that inherent cruelty offered a challenge to men like Hawk and her father.

And, God help her, she was beginning to understand that challenge. It would be a constant struggle to see if the man conquered the land, or the land vanquished him. It would never be an easy life, but it would be exciting and rewarding.

More rewarding than tea parties and charity luncheons and the occasional dress ball, Irony thought, wryly, her eyes following a flock of sea gulls as they skimmed the wind-roughened surface of the lake. *More exciting than counting the silver or doing the mending.*

What was wrong with her? What had happened to her since she'd packed her carpetbag and left her aunts' home? There had been times lately when she wasn't sure she knew herself at all anymore. What on earth would it be like when, at the end of her adventure, she went home and tried to fit back into the staid, predictable routine? Lord, she hated to even think of it . . .

"Pretty view, isn't it?"

The quiet voice came from behind her, and Irony turned to see Hawk standing a few feet away. He had come up so silently that she hadn't heard him at all.

"Yes. I was wondering if a person could ever get tired of it."

"Not if he loves the North enough to live here," Hawk replied. "Each season brings a different sort of beauty."

She looked closely into his face. "You've missed it, haven't you?"

"It would seem so. And even I had not guessed how much." He came forward to stand beside her, his eyes roving over the blue hills in the hazy distance. "Minnesota is lovely and forested too—but Lake of the Woods is so vast and so unique that there isn't another place like it on earth."

"Are you . . . thinking of staying here?" she asked.

He shrugged. "Sometimes I think of it. But I have obligations at the school, also."

Irony frowned up into the sunlight. So, Hawk was torn, too. He had duties and responsibilities that awaited, and yet, the lure of the lake country was making itself felt. Hawk had been born and raised here—how much stronger the ties must be.

"Wouldn't it be wonderful if we always knew immediately what we should do with our lives?" Irony murmured.

"Most of us know what we *should* do," Hawk said. "The difficulty lies in finding the courage to do what we *want* to do."

"Yes, I believe you must be right." Irony studied him. "You're a brave man, Hawk—do you know what you want to do?"

"I didn't always. I do now."

"Oh? And what is it?"

He dropped a hand onto each of her shoulders and turned her around to face him. His hands moved slowly, caressingly, down her arms to her elbows, and he pulled her close against his lean frame as he bent his head to hers.

"I want to start by kissing you . . ."

"You've never needed courage for that before."

"Oh, I don't know, love," he whispered, as his lips moved warmly upon hers. "You've held a gun on me, kicked me, pulled my hair, and thrown clay pots at my head. I think most men would agree it takes a great deal of valor to brave all that."

Irony chuckled. "How could it be worth it?"

"I swear to God, I don't understand that, myself." His lips brushed kisses over her cheeks and eyelids, drifting softly downward to settle on her mouth once more. "But, somehow it is . . ."

His hands left her elbows and located her waist, beneath the flapping jacket she wore. As his long fingers closed over her ribs and back, he could feel the tremulous sigh that escaped her as she leaned into him. Her mouth was no longer timid beneath his—she met his kiss with a fire of her own that caused his senses to reel. He hadn't meant to start anything this . . . serious. They didn't have the privacy for a prolonged encounter. But she was so tempting, how could he be expected to wait until they were alone again in her tepee or his?

His hands slid upward to capture her breasts, and his breathing took on a ragged edge. Irony continued to storm his emotional defenses by letting her sweet-tasting mouth nudge his lips apart, her tongue sensual in its hesitancy as it touched the boldly formed upper rim of his lip and then retreated.

Hawk groaned, unable to force himself to set her away. But all his instincts were urging him to either stop the teasing frustration or bring it to fruition there and then. He felt the cushiony grass beneath his moccasined feet and was flooded with the desire to lay her down among the pine needles and wild strawberries and satisfy them both. He knew their passion would take on an added dimension if they indulged it there, on the edge of the bluff in plain sight of all the glories of nature. Unhappily, it might also be within sight of Nathan or Zack, should they wander down the trail.

"Irony," he managed to rasp. "We can't do this . . ."

"Isn't that the same thing I said to you last night?" she replied softly. "And you turned out to be rather difficult to convince."

"I know, but that was altogether different." Despite himself, his fingers went to the buttons down the

293

front of her shirt. "Here anyone could happen upon us. Nathan or . . ."

As if to prove his point, there was a noisy crashing of underbrush and the decidedly human sound of tuneless whistling.

"Listen," Irony gasped. "Someone's coming!"

She flung herself from Hawk's arms, turning away to hastily re-button her shirt. Hawk dropped his hands to his sides, looking and feeling as awkward as an inexperienced boy. In a matter of seconds, Zackett McBride stepped into the clearing at the crest of the hill and stood eyeing them with something less than approval.

"What the devil's going on, Hawk?" he demanded. "I told Nathan you'd been gone too long."

"Nothing is going on, Zack."

"It doesn't look like nothing . . ."

"I don't think I care for what you're implying," Hawk said, feeling guilt stain his cheeks a dark red. "Irony and I were admiring the view."

"I'll just bet you were," Zack sneered. "Look, you're a man grown and Irony . . . well, she's young and citified, and doesn't know what to expect from the likes of you. I'd appreciate it if you'd . . ."

Irony whirled on him. "How dare you?" she blazed. "How could you possibly have the nerve to neglect me my entire life . . . and then suddenly start trying to act like . . . like a father!"

"I am your father, young lady."

"You've never let that bother you before," she snapped. "Just don't start now!"

She refused to look him in the eye, but brushed past him and retraced her steps to the camp, anger and furious indignation keeping her back straight and her shoulders square.

* * *

Supper was a quiet affair—fried fish served up with silence and stiff-necked pride. Although Nathan cast occasional glances at Irony and her father, he seemed content to stay out of the matter. Hawk, on the other hand, had watched the two of them avoid speaking or looking at each other long enough. The situation wasn't going to improve, he decided, without help from someone.

"Might as well be me," he muttered, shifting his tall frame until he was seated next to Irony at the campfire, directly across the flames from Zack McBride.

Irony glanced up at him in mild surprise. Since her father had challenged him, Hawk had been careful to keep his distance. It was not, she knew, because he was afraid of the older man—it was merely a token of the respect he felt for him.

"What did you say?" she queried.

"I said," Hawk stated, "that it's time we resolved this foolishness one way or another."

"What foolishness?" Irony asked warily. Across the fire, Zack looked at them over the rim of his tin mug, his bushy gray eyebrows quirking upward.

"This foolishness between you and Zack."

"Uh . . . think I'll turn in now," Nathan said, scrambling to his feet and tossing the last of his coffee into the fire. He quickly ambled away, making a somewhat lame excuse about being tired.

"Hawk, I think you'd better just forget this," Zack warned.

"So do I," Irony put in. "It isn't any of your business anyway."

"It is," Hawk said. "When something could have a bearing on whether one of us gets hurt or killed, it sure as hell is my business."

"What are you talking about?" Irony asked.

"Tomorrow or the next day, we're going to meet up with Josiah Goodman. You better than anyone should realize that we don't know what to expect from him. He's armed . . . so are his men." Hawk leaned forward to look into her eyes. "Our safety may depend on how well we work together. Can I trust you to back your father up if the need arises?"

Irony's chin rose noticeably. "When could I ever trust him?"

"That's not what I asked," Hawk said sternly.

"I told you it was no use," interjected Zack.

"I think it's time you two got your complaints out in the open. It wouldn't hurt either of you to know what the other is thinking."

"I don't care what he's thinking," Irony cried. "And he's never cared what I thought!"

"That's not true," Zack began.

"Yes, it is," declared Irony. "Hawk, you can't expect me to sit here and listen to him—I won't!"

She started to get to her feet, but Hawk's fingers closed about her arm in a grip of steel, holding her in place.

"Sit still," he commanded. "Now, Zack, tell her your story."

"She doesn't want to . . ."

"Tell her, for God's sake! I'm through watching the two of you circle around each other like wildcats looking for a fight."

"What is it I'm supposed to say?" asked Zack, clanking his tin cup down onto one of the rocks that formed the fire ring.

"Why don't you start by telling me why you lied about being dead?" Irony ground out.

Zack shrugged. "I thought it was for—"

"I feel I should warn you, Zack," Hawk inter-

296

rupted. "Irony doesn't like to be told things are for her own good. I believe that's a phrase you'll need to avoid if we're going to make any headway here."

Irony cast him a scorching look and attempted to jerk her arm free. Hawk's hold only tightened, and he dragged her closer to him, so that her thigh pressed against his hip. He made no secret of the fact that he didn't intend to release her any time soon.

"Sorry," Zack mumbled. "But it's the God's truth." Looking miserable, he picked up a stick and poked absently at the fire, sending a shower of sparks into the night air. "Maybe I should start at the beginning, Irony—back when your mother and I were first married."

Irony's chin tilted to an even more impossible level, but she didn't speak. In spite of the words she wanted to fling at him, she found herself waiting, listening for the explanation that she had needed to hear for so long.

"I . . . well, I loved your ma—as much as any man can love a woman, I expect. I never thought she'd agree to come out here with me—she was raised in the city like your aunts. All she'd ever known was society dinners and charity teas, and that snooty female school she went to." He jabbed at the embers again, his voice taking on a more distant sound. "But she wanted to see the wilderness, she said, wanted to learn about nature and the elements—and how the red man stood against them. Those were her exact words, Irony . . . I can still see her, sittin' in the front of the canoe, the wind whipping her hair around her head, her eyes glowing with excitement."

"My mother loved the wilderness?" Irony heard herself ask. She had not intended to show one iota

297

of interest in his narrative, but she had to know. Could her own fascination for the forests and lakes come not just from her father, but from her mother as well?

"That she did. When we found out you were on the way — well, I had one hell of a time convincing her to go back home. I thought she'd be safest where she could be attended by real doctors, and where my sisters could take care of her. Finally, Alyce and Tiny with their letters and me with my nagging wore her down, and she agreed to go back."

There was a long silence, broken only by the soft popping sounds of the fire and the lazy slap of water along the beach. Irony wasn't certain if she actually heard the deep, painful breath her father drew, or if she only imagined it.

"I was wrong," he half-whispered. "God help me, I was wrong. I should never have sent her away. She might have been better off in a crude tepee with an Indian midwife to aid her."

Zack tossed the stick into the flames and watched in silence as the fire devoured it. "I was so god-damned happy when I got off that train in Thief River," he said. "I knew I'd have a son or daughter, knew I'd be getting Emily back again. I'd built us a cabin on one of the islands . . . I couldn't wait to bring her home."

For the first time, Irony felt an urge to say something, but she could think of nothing that would soothe the years-old hurt that was still evident in her father's voice. She could imagine the young man he had been, smiling and eager. No doubt he'd nearly run all the way from the depot to her aunts' house — only to be given the tragic news that his beloved wife had died in childbirth.

It occurred to Irony that her father had not had a

chance to say goodbye to her mother, that he hadn't even seen her one last time. He had been met with the cold reality of mourning wreaths at the windows and a newly erected headstone in the city cemetery. For once, looking at the matter from his viewpoint, she was filled with an insight she'd never had before. How did one accept a death if one never saw the deceased, never attended a funeral or experienced the normal outpourings of grief? Irony looked down at her clasped hands and discovered that, at some point, Hawk had released her arm and was now sitting quietly by her side.

She knew without it being said that the house in Thief River had been a haunted place for Zackett McBride. Had he seen Emily's ghost in every room? Had he relived the early days of their marriage, the happy time they shared with Valentine and Alyce before making their trek to the lake country? No wonder he hadn't been able to bring himself to love his daughter—however innocently, she had been the cause of his wife's death.

"I simply didn't know what to make of you, Irony," Zack said slowly. "You were a tiny scrap of a thing, bawling your head off—smellin' of fancy powder and wearing dainty little dresses your aunts had made. Tiny and Alyce fussed over you, argued over who was going to do what for you." His laughter was low, unhappy. "I was just in the way." He glanced up at the starry sky. "In the way and hurtin' so bad I didn't know how I was goin' to keep on living. I know it's no excuse, but I couldn't take care of you, Irony. If I'd have said I was taking you back to the wilderness with me . . . to some Indian nursemaid . . . your aunts would've raised a commotion that would've been heard all the way to Duluth!"

It was true and she knew it. Should have always known it.

"But what about later?" she asked quietly. "When I was older."

She felt his gaze on her, intensified by the golden heat of the fire between them. "I came back when you were two years old, but matters were even worse by then. You took one look at me and ran screaming to your aunts. They told me it was natural, that my beard and long hair and buckskins scared you." Zack reached for the coffeepot and refilled the tin mug. "But I knew then you didn't belong out here with me. That it would be better for you if I left you in your aunts' care."

"Did you ever know that I wanted to come here to live with you?" Irony asked.

"No . . . and I don't suppose you ever knew that I wanted you to," he replied. "There's no way you could have known that I wrote dozens of letters to my sisters, telling them I was coming for you. Of course, I always lost my nerve and tore them up. I'd look around me and . . . somehow, I could never justify taking you away from all the advantages the city had to offer."

"I needed a father," she said stiffly. "I didn't need pretty clothes and toys and school as much as I needed you."

"I . . . I'm sorry," he said simply. "I didn't know you felt like that."

"Whenever you sent a gift, I wished you had come instead." Irony frowned. "Do you know, I pretended to be sick every time my class had any social event that included fathers."

He nodded. "Valentine told me once," he said. "And that was when I decided to come and get you. I'd even made up my mind that if you didn't like it

300

here, I'd move back to Thief River—maybe that's what I should've done in the beginning."

"You say you decided to come for me . . . why didn't you?"

"I did."

"But . . ."

"It was your twelfth birthday," he went on. "I arrived at the house in the middle of the afternoon. I wanted to surprise you, so I slipped inside the front door. I could hear Tiny and Alyce chattering in the kitchen, but there were other voices, as well . . . and I knew you must be having a party." He paused long enough to take a sip of coffee, and Irony realized she was holding her breath, waiting for him to continue.

"Well, I sure didn't want to embarrass you by having all your friends see me before I got cleaned up, so I just peeked into the parlor and . . . my God, Irony—you were all grown up! I couldn't believe my eyes. There you were, sittin' on the sofa sipping tea with your friends, lookin' like a miniature of your aunts."

"I remember the party," Irony said slowly, "but I never knew you were there."

"I saw you in that lace dress, your hair up and tied with green ribbons . . . and I was shocked at how much like your momma you looked. You were a lady, Irony—a beautiful, educated young lady. What did I have to offer you?"

Love, she wanted to say. *Love and caring and the knowledge that you sometimes remembered I was alive! That I meant something important to you.* Aloud, she said, "What happened?"

"I just stood there, wondering what the hell to do. Then one of the girls started bragging about her father, about how rich he was and how he was going

301

to build the biggest house Thief River had ever seen. And do you know what you said?"

Irony thought for a moment, then shook her head. "I don't remember."

"You said that for a man to be rich wasn't as important as what he did with his money. You told them that your daddy was rich, but he spent his money helping the Indians, seeing that they had books and clothes and enough food to eat. God, Irony, you made me sound so fine and noble . . . and in that moment, I knew how selfish I had been." He drained his cup and sat looking into it. "I decided then and there to get out of your life. If I was dead, you'd be forced to forget me once and for all. You'd have that shining image of me in your mind, and I'd never show up and destroy it for you."

"So you faked your death?"

"I did. I left town without seeing anyone, came back to the lake and had one of the braves write your aunts a letter saying I'd died of an illness." He looked up and, surprisingly, gave her a crooked smile. "I wanted to let on that I'd died in some heroic way, but even I couldn't be that dishonest."

"I've blamed the Indians for so much over the years," she said distractedly. "For your leaving—for your neglect. Even for your death."

"I reckon this will all take some gettin' used to," Zack commented. "But Irony, I never meant to . . . to lie or to hurt you. It just seemed I never could do anything else. I'm sorry."

"So am I."

"I'd like it if you—well, if you could ever find a way to forget and forgive."

Irony was silent for so long that Hawk nudged her leg with his knee. She had forgotten he was there.

"I don't think I can ever forget everything that

happened," she said, "but at least I understand it better. And with some consideration of the matter, forgiveness might not be impossible."

The speech was mildly promising at best, but neither man seemed inclined to question it. Irony sighed and got to her feet.

"I'm going to bed now."

"Maybe we can talk again tomorrow . . . or sometime?" Zack ventured.

"Yes, that would be fine." Irony started away, then turned for one last query. "There is one more thing I'd like to ask."

"What's that?"

"Did my aunts know? That you were really alive, I mean?"

"No," Zack answered. "I couldn't make them party to my falsehood. They never lied to you, Irony."

"Good," she murmured. "That I couldn't have accepted. Aunt Tiny and Aunt Alyce provided the only stability I ever had in my childhood. Thank goodness I don't have to worry that the last eight years with them have been a sham."

When she had gone, Zack released a long, shaky sigh. "Hardest thing I've ever had to do," he growled. "Damn your eyes, Hawk—and thank you from the bottom of my heart."

"That little chat was past due, Zack."

"You're right about that. How do you think she took it? Think she's ever goin' to get over hating me?"

"She doesn't hate you," Hawk informed him with a wide smile.

"How'd you know?"

"She didn't kick you one time—or flatten a skillet on your head or throw anything at you." He chuckled. "You've got one hell of a daughter there, Zack-

303

ett."

"Yes—I'm just beginning to figure that out."

Red Wolf and Eagle slipped back into camp in the early morning hours. From the warmth of her bedroll, Irony listened to them talking to Hawk.

"Goodman's there," Red Wolf said, his civilized way of speaking surprising Irony once again. "But he's having a problem with his buyer, John Randolph. We overheard him telling Goodman he wanted to work out a compensation for Swimming Bear's people. He doesn't want to buy all their land out from under them, he said."

"I'll wager it riles Goodman that he tied up with a man of scruples," Hawk declared, a smile in his voice.

"Goodman says he'll give Randolph until noon tomorrow to make up his mind, but he doesn't have time to call for a tribal meeting."

"Of course not," Hawk said. "He doesn't dare let any of Swimming Bear's people see him—they'd know he wasn't McBride."

"So it looks as if he'll have to make his move quickly."

"Did you see Lynx?" asked Hawk.

"He was with the preacher," Eagle replied softly. "He didn't see us, but we got a good look at him."

"So—he's the one," Hawk said, all humor gone from his tone. "I'd hoped it was all a mistake."

"No mistake," Red Wolf assured him. "Lynx is there, following every step Goodman makes."

"Well, tomorrow when we show up at their camp," Hawk stated, "we'll have a talk with our old friend and see for sure which way the wind blows."

Chapter Seventeen

Near Swimming Bear's camp . . .

The Reverend Josiah Goodman was the first person Irony saw as she followed Hawk up the sandy path. He was sitting on a blanket, his broad back turned to them, his hands gesturing elaborately as he expounded on one subject or another. Randolph sat on one side of Goodman, and to the left was a striking young Indian man she had never seen before. The Indians she knew as Running Dog, Broken Knife and Three-Fingers were standing off to one side, their heads together in conversation.

Hawk stopped suddenly, crouching behind a currant thicket, and she crashed softly into him. She could feel the tension in the muscles of his back.

"Is that your friend?" she whispered.

Hawk nodded, reaching around to take her hand and draw her down beside him. "I want you to stay close by me," he said, directly into her ear. "If something goes wrong, I want to be able to take care of you."

She opened her mouth, but he laid a warning finger across her lips. "Shh, just this once—don't argue."

He was gazing at her with such a half-serious, half-teasing expression that she had to smile her acquiescence. Hawk looked very much as if he wanted to kiss her, but he merely squeezed her hand and turned back

305

to the scene before them. After a few seconds, he gestured to the men behind them and crept closer. Close enough that she could now hear what was being said.

"Look, Randolph, it doesn't make any sense for you to worry about these ignorant savages. The government owns most of this land up here anyway — they'll provide for the Indians."

"I tell you, I want to meet with some of the local chiefs," Randolph insisted. "You act as though you don't want me to have any communication with them. Why is that, McBride?"

It came as a jolt to Irony to hear the reverend referred to by her father's name, but she realized that, in order to sell the land, Goodman would have had to pose as Zackett McBride.

"You're imagining things, Randolph," Goodman sneered. He reached for his ever-present leather satchel and unfastened it. "Now, I have the deeds right here — shall I sign them over to you or not?"

"I would advise you not to sign them over," Zack said loudly from his position at the edge of the clearing, "as you are not the rightful owner of this property."

Hawk gave a signal and, releasing Irony's hand, hurried forward to the place where the men sat. Red Wolf and Eagle dashed ahead, brandishing their guns to keep Goodman's companions at bay.

The preacher's head snapped up, his hand instinctively reaching for the gun at his side. Nathan cocked the pistols he held, effectively stilling Goodman's motion.

In that instant, Hawk knelt behind the Indian called Lynx, pressing the blade of his hunting knife against the man's bronzed throat.

"It has been a long time, Lynx," he said quietly.

Despite the blade at his throat, the Indian turned his head and met Hawk's gaze unflinchingly. For the briefest moment, Irony could swear she saw a flicker of pleasure within the ebony depths of the man's eyes, but if so, it was quickly gone and his expression became cold and hard. He said nothing.

Randolph, on the other hand, finally found his voice. He leaped to his feet, shouting, "Who in hell are you? What's going on here?"

"No need to worry, friend," interjected Irony's father, "we're here to save you a headache or two. I'm Zackett McBride, the actual owner of this property. This man is a deputy sheriff from Thief River Falls, Minnesota . . . and this here is Mr. Raphael Hawkes."

John Randolph looked puzzled. "I don't understand what's happening. I thought he was McBride." He gestured toward the glowering Goodman.

"He's a thief and a charlatan," Zack explained. "A so-called preacher who makes a living stealing from old ladies and fools . . . oh, your pardon, sir."

"No, it seems I deserve the title of fool," Randolph declared. "If what you say is true, I've been completely duped."

"My daughter Irony has a letter of introduction from the sheriff of Thief River, as well as affidavits from our bank. And I'll be happy to show you that my signature matches the one on the deeds better than this man's does."

When Irony stepped forth, Goodman emitted a furious hiss, reminding her of a fat, disgruntled house cat. "You!" he snarled. "Will I never see the last of you?"

"Once we get you back to stand trial in Minnesota," Irony said, "you won't ever have to see me again."

"Stand trial?" Randolph echoed. "Then the law is after him?"

"It sure is," Nathan said. "This man is wanted for fraud and embezzlement, as well as several counts of bigamy. And there are some authorities who will be mighty interested in hearing his version of what happened to a certain Miss Bessie Sparks."

At the mention of the schoolteacher's name, Lynx seemed to stiffen, and Irony felt her stomach turn over. So — Hawk's friend actually had been involved in her death.

"Who's she?" Randolph was asking.

"A teacher at the Sweetwater Indian Mission," Nathan replied. "One of these two killed her.. Cut her throat."

Randolph paled visibly. "Good God, what kind of fiends are you?" he cried.

Goodman shrugged. "It's going to take proof to convict me of any crime."

"Proof?" Irony choked. "What do you call these?" She bent to pick up the property deeds that had been scattered over the ground. "And what about my aunt's jewelry that you carry in that case? And the money you stole from her? I should think that would be evidence enough."

"If the truth of the matter is known," Goodman drawled indolently, "a Minnesota deputy really has no jurisdiction here."

"If the truth is known," Nathan stated, "this Minnesota deputy really doesn't give a damn. I'll tell the judge I apprehended you on the other side of the border, and it'll be your word against mine."

"And I'll back him up on that," Hawk put in.

"Me, too," added Irony.

"And I should think it would go without saying," Zack declared, "that I will be more than enthusiastic to appear as a witness against you."

"The devil take you all," Goodman snapped.

"Tell me," Randolph said, "just how did you happen to contact me about this property? You never knew my sister at all, did you?"

"Oh, but I did," Goodman replied. "Only, she knew me as Josiah Goodman . . . back when we were engaged."

Randolph's face grew red. "You! You're the one who cheated Lillian out of her husband's pension? Why, you thieving, black-hearted scoundrel!"

Randolph threw himself at Goodman, pummeling him with beefy fists. Nathan shouted, waving his gun and trying to separate the two men with his free hand. Irony clutched the leather satchel and stepped back out of the way, while Zackett rushed forward into the fray. He grabbed Randolph's arms and whirled him aside. Just as he straightened to face Goodman, the wily preacher flailed out with a fist that connected with McBride's midsection, tossing him backward.

"Damn you!" cried Irony. "How dare you strike my father!" With that, she swung the satchel she held, smashing it against Goodman's face with enough force to drop him onto his rump. He sat there whining, one hand to the nose that was now bleeding profusely.

Randolph took a threatening step toward Goodman, but McBride — after a puzzled glance at Irony — got to his feet and laid a hand on his shoulder. "I think he's had enough for now, friend."

"How are you . . . Father?" Irony asked tentatively, as if testing the sound of the word on her tongue. "Are you injured?"

"No . . . I'm fine." The two exchanged a look that seemed to acknowledge they had finally begun to resolve the differences between them.

"I'm glad," she murmured, a shy smile breaking over her face.

"You pack quite a wallop, young lady," Randolph observed admiringly.

"Well, it's just that this horrid man has done so much to my family — I know I acted in a most unladylike manner, but to tell the truth, I enjoyed it."

"Sometimes there are things more important than being a lady," Hawk offered.

Irony met his eyes and thought they were filled with

warm approval. To see that expression turned on her, she realized that she would gladly bash Goodman a few dozen more times. Appalling! She had turned into a primitive once and for all!

"Let's get these men back to our camp," Nathan said gruffly. "We need to decide the best way to transport them to Minnesota."

"I believe I can simplify the matter as far as these three are concerned," said Red Wolf. "Since you know they were only Goodman's followers and probably not involved in the murder, why not let Eagle and me take them to Swimming Bear's camp? They will be tried by tribal law—and given the punishment they deserve."

"What do you think, Hawk?" Zack asked.

"Sounds good to me. Tribal law is harsh, but just." He glanced at Lynx. "I wish I could do the same for you, my friend, but unfortunately, your crimes are too serious for that."

Again, the darkly handsome young man said nothing. Hawk shrugged and roughly hauled the man to his feet.

"Get the rope and tie 'em up," Nathan instructed Eagle.

A short time later, after Hawk had extinguished the camp fire and tossed the thieves' belongings into the canoes, they were ready to leave the island. Eagle and Red Wolf had tied their three prisoners together and were taking the largest of Goodman's canoes to the nearby Indian camp.

Goodman, his hands bound behind him, was in the front of Zackett's canoe, looking like a pouting child. His gingery hair was uncombed, falling forward over his broad forehead; his mesmerizing eyes had lost their commanding glow. He sat with his shoulders slumped, looking in no way like the charismatic man who had wooed and won so many lonely, gullible women.

"God, I can't believe I was so stupid," Randolph growled as he stepped into another canoe. "Right out of the blue, that man wrote me a letter, telling me he'd known my late brother-in-law and understood I was interested in buying property in the lake country. And I believed it!"

"Perhaps it will make your sister feel better when you go home and confess you were duped by Goodman, too," Irony pointed out, a glint of mischief in her green eyes.

Randolph looked affronted, then sheepish. Finally he smiled, saying, "Yes, I suppose I'll have to make that admission, won't I?"

He and Irony shared a canoe, while Hawk and Nathan paddled the third one, Lynx sitting between them, his hands tied, his head lifted proudly. Unlike Goodman, he had not given in to defeat. Irony suspected that he was a man who never would.

They spent the night at their former camp, not wanting to be on the lake after dark. Though the Indian sat stoically, staring straight ahead into the night, Goodman chafed at his bonds, complaining and whining at every turn. His face hurt, he grumbled, and his nose was most likely broken.

Finally, Nathan waved his gun under the preacher's battered nose and demanded silence. Goodman stretched out on his makeshift bed, groaning, but saying nothing further.

Hawk, Irony and Zackett lingered at the camp fire. Zack had drunk two cups of strong, hot coffee before gathering his courage to say, "Thanks for helping me out in that little skirmish this afternoon, Irony." His grin flashed in the semi-dark. "I'm just glad you were on my side."

"I have to confess something," Irony said in a small voice. "I . . . I was actually pleased by the incident.

311

Oh, not that you got into a fight, Father, but that there was some excitement involved in Goodman's capture." She sighed and gave both men a rueful smile. "I'd followed him for so many miles, and imagined that moment for so long that—well, frankly, it was somewhat of an anticlimax. I guess I'd expected more . . ."

"We did take 'em kind of easy, didn't we?" remarked Zack with a grin.

"But that struggle, however brief, added a touch of danger and excitement," Irony noted. "It will give me something to talk about at the Thief River tea parties for years to come."

"You sound sad about that," Zack said. "But you don't have to stay there, you know. I promised Nathan I'd go with him to take Goodman and the Indian to Thief River, and I planned a little visit with my sisters. After that, I'm coming back here. You can, too, if you want."

"I'd like that—but think of the aunts! They'd be heartbroken if I left them. Besides, what would I do out here?"

"Same things you'd do in the city," Sack stated. "Get married, have a bunch of youngsters—do charity work. These Indians need your help every bit as much as anyone back home. Unfortunates there have the Ladies Auxiliary and the churches; the Indians don't have anyone, except the likes of me."

Irony's attention had fastened on the first part of her father's statement, and she barely heard the rest. Get married? Why on earth would he say that? She wanted badly to ask him exactly whom he thought she should marry, but Hawk was sitting beside her, and she didn't dare. The thought was intriguing, and very disturbing. Would her father approve a marriage between her and a half-breed Indian?

She sneaked a look at Hawk, and her heart sagged in her chest. He seemed oblivious to their conversation, whittling on a piece of driftwood with his knife and tossing the shavings into the fire. Apparently, the notion of marriage had never occurred to him!

Irony turned away. It didn't matter—she couldn't stay anyway. Her aunts needed her, depended on her. She knew they fully expected her to fill their declining years with children and family activities. She couldn't disappoint them . . .

Hawk was alert to every nuance of Irony's mood. He'd nearly choked when he'd heard Zackett McBride suggest a wilderness marriage as though he would sanction and defend her right to make that decision. What was Zack's game? And what was Irony's reaction to the advice? He couldn't tell.

At first, he felt her surprise, then her thoughtful consideration of the matter. But then, he'd sensed her glance in his direction and from that point on, he hadn't known what she was thinking. He needed to learn if she would ever contemplate such a thing as marriage to him, because if she would, he would not let her go. On the other hand, if he attempted to coerce her into it, might not he be sorry later, when she discovered she'd made a mistake and wanted to be released from her vows? No, if Irony was going to stay in the wilderness, it had to be her decision entirely.

Hawk smiled to himself. In the past two days, he'd seen her undergo some drastic changes. He'd pretty much sat back and kept his mouth shut, letting her work things out for herself. She'd come around as far as her father was concerned, hadn't she? Now he simply had to trust her to come to the right conclusion about Lake of the Woods, about him, and about any future life they might have together.

Summer had reached its zenith and now, imperceptibly, had begun to wane. The morning sun was met with

313

thicker mists rising off the water, haunting the islands and marshes until the warmth of mid-morning drove it away. By contrast, the still heat of the long afternoons seemed to enervate the birds and what small animals were to be seen. And the twilights were slow to come, slow to disappear. Banners of rose and gold lingered in the treetops for hours, it seemed, until the ebony sheen of night overpowered them. And then, as often as not, the Northern Lights made a spectacular showing.

Irony had lain awake in her bedroll, staring up into the sky through the feathered branches of the pines. She had been fascinated by the display of lights, ranging in color from palest sea-green to deep, rich emerald. She wondered if there was no end to the spectacle of the North.

Somehow, she had sensed Hawk's wakefulness, also. She had a feeling that matters other than the beauties of nature were on his mind. And being honest with herself, she admitted she, too, was beginning to entertain disturbing thoughts. Thoughts of trying to rearrange her life so that she might remain in the wilderness. What would Hawk say if he knew? Would he encourage or discourage her? She wished she knew.

In the morning, she had awakened and turned to find him not more than four feet away, gazing at her with an expression that seemed to declare every tender emotion she had dared to dream he'd feel for her.

"I miss you, Irony," he whispered, a roguish smile tilting the corners of his mouth.

She knew what he meant, and she had missed him, too. Their time alone together had been all too fleeting. Now, as his black gaze moved down to loiter on her mouth, she was filled with a welter of feelings — a warm stirring of awareness of his sheer physical beauty, the desire to touch him, to share more of the heady kisses they had not had the chance to indulge in for far too long. He was close enough to reach out to her, yet he

314

couldn't—not with Nathan and her father so near.

Irony hoped it might be different once they were back at Caribou Island. And then she realized that Nathan and Zack would want to leave for Minnesota immediately with their prisoners. The thought that she might not have even one more night alone with Hawk closed around her heart like a cold fist, and she swallowed back her panic. Perhaps she could persuade him to travel with them—it would be the only way for them to stay together longer.

Her mind was made up. She might have to return to Thief River Falls and the life she had once known, but she wasn't going until she had the chance to spend one more night in Hawk's arms. Or until she had told him how much she loved him.

The brigade set out as soon as its members had shared a hasty breakfast and broken camp. Again, Hawk and Nathan guarded Lynx, and the reverend was placed in a canoe with Zackett. His face bruised and stiff, his shoulders permanently bowed, Goodman no longer presented much of a threat. When he complained that the rope had rubbed his wrists raw, Zack suggested they untie him.

"A sorry weak-knees like him won't cause much trouble," he said when Nathan objected. "If he moves too fast, I'll just knock him in the head with my paddle. He might end up drowned instead of goin' back for trial."

Goodman shot him a pained look, but refrained from making the fractious comments that obviously trembled on his tongue, and finally, Nathan cut the rope, freeing his hands.

Irony settled back into the prow of Randolph's canoe and watched the passing scenery as if it was the last time she would see it.

The lake was tranquil, the water cool and deep.

Irony was lulled by its serenity, intrigued by the way the water appeared so blue in the distance, shading to deep green nearer the canoe. If she looked directly over the side of the craft, she could see down for several feet, as far as the gold bands of sunlight pierced the depths. Occasionally, she caught the silver flash of a fish, and once they came upon an entire family of soft-shelled turtles sunning themselves on a dead log. One by one, they slid into the water and disappeared.

Pale yellow water lilies bloomed in every secluded inlet or bay, and Irony amused herself by trying to pick one of the blossoms. Their stems were so long and resilient that it was impossible to pull up the flowers. She soon found that a firm grip on the plant would drag her out of the canoe before it garnered her one of the lilies.

She had just given up the quest when, with a gentle bumping of his canoe against Randolph's, Hawk handed her a blossom he had cut free with his hunting knife. As she took it, their fingers brushed and would have clung, had not the waves pushed the two canoes apart again. She smiled her thanks and put her nose to the water lily. There was very little scent, but she didn't care—the coolness of its petals soothed the heated rush of blood to her face. The look in Hawk's eyes was just as intent as it had been earlier that morning. The promise held within them was just as potent, just as shattering to her poise as it had been then.

Irony's mind registered yet another truth. Hawk was so utterly different from any man she had ever known, but in some strange, indefinable way, he had come to symbolize everything she thought a man should be. He was strong, he was tender; he was a gentleman . . . with a slightly savage streak that would never be tamed. The hunting knife he had held at a villain's throat, he now used to cut flowers. To her, he would always be a warrior poet—and the poetry he quoted would forever be laced with sensual fire. Beside Raphael Hawkes, all other men faded into a quiet sort of anonymity.

Well, she thought with sudden insight, *all men but my father. He, of course, is in a classification all his own.*

It amused her that she had already found much to admire in Zackett McBride. If nothing else came of this unlikely trek through the wilderness, she had finally found the father she had always wanted. Now, knowing he was speculating over the incident with the flower, Irony gave Zack an innocent smile and turned back to her study of the islands slipping past.

Smoke spiraling above the timber was the first indication that they were nearly back to Chief White Crane's camp. A group of children playing on the beach saw the brigade of canoes coming and ran to tell their elders. By the time they had made their way into the sheltered bay, a group of people stood awaiting them.

"There's Snow," Irony cried. "And, look! Rogue is happy to see us!"

The puppy was bounding up and down the water's edge, barking furiously. As soon as Randolph had maneuvered the canoe up onto the beach, the dog flung himself into Irony's arms, nearly toppling her backward. Laughing, she seized Goodman's satchel and climbed over the gunwale.

Glancing up, she saw that the chief and his usual entourage had come to greet them. She started forward to tell him of their successful capture of Lynx and Goodman, when a familiar voice rang out.

"Irony! Oh, Irony, dearest!"

"Oh, my God!" she murmured under her breath. Aunt Valentine? No, it couldn't be!

In disbelief, Irony stared at the short, stout woman careening down the pathway toward her. It was, indeed, Aunt Tiny . . . and right behind her came Aunt

Alyce, progressing at her own, more ladylike pace.

Irony was stunned. Not only were her aunts here on Caribou Island, they were dressed in the most unusual clothes she had ever seen them wear. Both had on chambray shirts tucked into blue denim garments that looked like some sort of trouser-skirts.

"Aunt Tiny?" she faltered, and in that instant, sheer hell broke loose.

Goodman had just staggered from the canoe, drawing Tiny's attention. First, her mouth twisted in distaste—but almost immediately, it dropped open in shock. She screamed a piercingly shrill scream that seemed to echo through the trees.

"Zackett! It can't be—you're dead!" With those words, she clapped a hand to her chest and fainted, falling to the sand with a thud. Alyce uttered an anguished cry and fell to her knees beside her sister, calling for assistance.

Distracted by the commotion, Zack started toward his sisters, momentarily forgetting his prisoner. With a renewal of his old strength, Goodman moved with surprising speed and agility. He knocked the gun from Zack's hand, scooping it up into his own with one swift movement. For a second, everyone stood frozen, uncertain what to do.

"Hold it right there, Goodman," Nathan yelled, cocking his own pistol. Before he could train it on Goodman, the preacher sprinted across the sand and seized Alyce by the arm, jerking her to her feet. He placed his gun at her temple, and she closed her eyes in fright.

"If anyone so much as moves a muscle," Goodman announced, "I'll kill this woman."

Hawk heaved a disgusted sigh, followed by a short, explicit swear word. "What do you want us to do?" he asked wearily.

"Throw your guns into the lake—now."

There seemed to be no other choice. The fanatic

318

gleam in the preacher's eyes told them his threat to kill Aunt Alyce was not idle. At that point, he had little to lose, and they all knew it. Obediently, they did as he commanded.

"Now what?" growled Zack.

"Get up there on the beach . . . all of you."

Slowly, the knot of men moved toward the place where the others stood, looking on helplessly.

"You there," Goodman said to Irony. "Toss the satchel into that canoe."

"But . . ." It infuriated Irony that he was, after all, escaping from them. But there was nothing she or anyone else could do that wouldn't put Alyce into very real danger. She dropped the leather case into the canoe.

"Now get up there with the rest of them," ordered Goodman.

"What are you planning to do?" Hawk asked calmly.

"I'm taking Miss Alyce here as my hostage — if anyone comes after me, they'll find her floating in the lake with a couple of bullets in her head."

"And if we don't follow you?" questioned Zack. "Will my sister be safe?"

"She'll be safe. All I want is a twelve hour head start." Goodman started backing toward the canoe, half-dragging the terrified Alyce with him. "Give me that and in the morning, you'll find her unharmed on one of the islands."

"How in the hell are we to know which one?" Hawk demanded.

Goodman gave Alyce a shove and she fell into the canoe, curling into a ball in one end. He stepped in and, with a nasty smile, made his reply. "You'll just have to search until you find her," he said. "I might leave a signal fire if I'm satisfied that no one follows me."

"We're not goin' to follow you, you bastard — but you'd better be damned sure you don't hurt her!"

Irony didn't recognize the speaker — he was a

bearded man in buckskins who had pushed his way to the front of the crowd. She suspected he must be the guide responsible for bringing Valentine and Alyce all the way out to Caribou Island.

"If anything happens to her, I'll cut your goddamned gizzard out and feed it to you piece by piece!"

Goodman merely laughed, enjoying his moment of power. He no longer resembled the bowed, beaten man he had been earlier in the day. He used the paddle to push the canoe away from shore and, laying the gun on the bottom of the boat within easy reach, began paddling. Alyce made no move except to gaze back at those gathered on the beach with bright, unblinking eyes.

"She's terrified out of her mind," Zack said, with a low curse.

Irony shook her head. "No, Father, I don't think so. She may have been afraid at first, but now I have the feeling that Aunt Alyce is looking upon this as something of an adventure."

"Adventure, my ass," snarled the guide. "That little lady had better not come to any harm."

Irony had another feeling. One that stirred a small amount of hope within her. The Reverend Josiah Goodman had made a lot of enemies in his time, but somehow, she had the feeling he had just made an enemy of a man who would stop at nothing to see him brought to justice.

Out on the lake, the canoe grew smaller and smaller . . . and eventually disappeared into the distance, leaving those on shore to stare at each other in frustrated bewilderment.

Chapter Eighteen

On Caribou Island . . .

"Where am I?" mumbled Aunt Valentine. "Am I dreaming?"

"Aunt Tiny," said Irony, bending over the fallen woman. "Are you hurt? Can you sit up?"

The plump, silver-haired woman brushed away the helping hands. "I'm fine—just tell me, did I or did I not see my brother Samuel Zackett?"

"You saw me, all right," Zack said, coming forward. "I'm not dead after all, Valentine."

"So it would seem," she said crisply. "Well, don't stand there like a nitwit, help me to my feet!"

Zack and Irony each took an arm and pulled Valentine into a standing position. Irony solicitously brushed at the back of Tiny's chambray shirt, fending off an urge to ask her aunt where in the world she had gotten the extraordinary clothing she was wearing.

"I assume there's an explanation for your miraculous reappearance?" Tiny fixed him with a fierce scowl.

"Yes, of course. But it's rather complicated, and . . . well, something more important has come up."

"And what might that be?"

"It's Aunt Alyce," Irony said carefully. "Reverend Goodman has taken her as a hostage."

"What!" Valentine's hand fluttered to her heart once

again and she tottered backward. The big, bearded woodsman caught and steadied her.

"She'll be safe enough as long as none of us follow him for twelve hours," Zack explained.

"Safe? With that evil-hearted swindler?" cried Aunt Tiny. "How could you possibly have allowed him to take her?"

"We didn't have a whole lot of choice in the matter, ma'am," spoke up Nathan. "Goodman grabbed your brother's gun and threatened to shoot Miss Alyce."

"Damn it, this is all my fault," declared Zack. "If I hadn't been so anxious to feel remorse over that worthless bas—"

"Never mind that," snapped Valentine. "What are we going to do about rescuing our sister?"

"I think we'll have to honor Goodman's wishes, Aunt Valentine," Hawk interjected. When Tiny's bright gaze fell upon him, he favored her with a winsome smile and inclined his head politely. "I do apologize for being so familiar with you, but Irony has spoken of her aunts so often that I feel I know you. By the way, I'm Raphael Hawkes. I accompanied your niece here from the Sweetwater mission."

Tiny returned his smile, offering him a dainty hand. "It's a pleasure to meet you, Mr. Hawkes, even under such trying conditions."

Irony couldn't help but notice the hint of coquetry in her aunt's manner. She obviously found Hawk an intriguing man, despite his mixed heritage.

"Hawk . . . um, Mr. Hawkes has been a most helpful guide," Irony contributed, her innocuous words drawing her aunt's severe attention.

"I can only be glad that you were fortunate enough to stumble onto someone who was proficient. When the Thief River station master informed us that you had slipped away without poor Nathan, I simply could not understand your willful disregard for your own

322

safety. Nor could I," she added, turning to Nathan, "understand why you did not return to tell Alyce and me the truth. Oh! Poor Alyce, I'd almost forgotten her predicament." She whirled to face Hawk again. "Now, Mr. Hawkes, you say that, in your opinion, we should abide by Goodman's dictate?"

"Yes, I believe that's all we can do at this point."

"And so, what plan of action do you suggest?"

Irony bit her lips to keep from smiling. She couldn't remember Aunt Tiny ever asking anyone else's plan of action.

"We'll give Goodman his twelve hours, then Nathan, Zack and I will go after your sister."

"Ain't no way you're keepin' me from goin' after that son of a bitch," announced the large man standing behind Valentine. "I'd like to cut off his—"

"Nose?" Tiny hastily provided. "Now, Madden, I'm not sure that would do much good."

"I don't believe we've met," Irony said, wanting to know more about this mysterious stranger with whom her aunts seemed so friendly.

"I'm Madden Heywood," the man said, his enormous hand engulfing Irony's. "Your aunts hired me as their guide when they decided to make the trip to Canada."

"Madden has been wonderful," Aunt Tiny stated. "He's so knowledgeable about the forest and all. I simply don't know what Alyce and I would have done without him."

"We'll be glad to have your company, Mad," Hawk said, extending his own hand. "There's no telling where Goodman will abandon Alyce, so it's imperative that we find her as quickly as possible."

"I don't know that fancy word you just spouted, son," Mad drawled, "but I reckon it means we've got to get to Miss McBride before the weather or the wild animals do."

"Yes . . . that's more or less what I meant," Hawk averred, at the same time that Aunt Tiny gasped and whispered, "Wild animals?"

"She'll be fine, Aunt Tiny," Irony assured the older woman.

"Hawk?"

For the first time since stepping out of the canoe, the Indian, Lynx, spoke.

"I want to go after Goodman."

Nathan opened his mouth in protest, but Hawk held up a restraining hand. "Let him talk, Nathan." Hawk turned back to his friend. "Why would you expect us to allow such a thing?"

"I want him."

"So do we."

"Not as much as I do." Lynx's eyes glittered with a fearsome hatred. "I want to be the one to kill him."

Hawk nodded, almost in satisfaction. "I knew there was more to this thing than we knew. Let's go sit down and discuss it."

Chief White Crane graciously offered his lodge for their use, and as they sat talking, several Indian women passed among them, serving bowls of venison and wild rice. Irony noticed that Snow made certain she waited on Nathan, and though he had paid little attention to the other servers, he glanced up when Snow knelt before him and put a steaming bowl into his hands. Seeing her serene smile, he smiled back. It pleased Irony that when Snow rose and gracefully walked away, Nathan's eyes followed her.

Irony was wondering whether or not she should speak to Nathan on her friend's behalf when Hawk said, "Let's hear your story, Lynx. Why were you really with Goodman?"

The young Indian let his obsidian eyes move slowly

over the faces of those seated around him, as if estimating his chances of being believed. Finally he began speaking in a low, harsh voice.

"Two years ago I settled near Koochiching Falls. I was to marry a maiden who lived and worked at the mission there. Only a few days before our wedding, someone broke into my woman's room and attacked her, beating her so badly that she nearly died of her injuries." He paused a long moment, and the silence in the lodge grew nearly deafening.

"Goodman?" Hawk asked softly.

"Yes."

"But why?" Nathan queried. "What had she done to him?"

"She had refused his advances," Lynx answered calmly, although his eyes glowed with almost frightening intensity. "He was engaged to one of the school-mistresses at the mission . . . but that didn't seem to quell his ardor for other women. Especially young and beautiful ones."

Lynx stared down at the untouched bowl of rice in front of him. "Waubagone could not speak for many days—so she could not tell me who had hurt her. But I found this in her room . . ." He opened the beaded pouch he wore on a thong around his neck, taking out a small golden cross on a delicate chain. "Though I didn't recognize it, I showed it to one of the teachers who told me it belonged to Goodman. I wanted to kill him, of course, but the white man's law has stripped us of the right to defend our honor in the old way. I had no choice but to wait until we were away from civilization."

"And so you threw in with the weasely little bastard," commented Madden Heywood. "Not much else you could do, considerin'."

"Goodman followed his intended wife to the Sweetwater mission where she was taking on a new assignment," Lynx went on. "She never suspected a thing . . . until I went to her in secret and told her what had happened. She'd begun to have serious doubts about Goodman, she told me, because of his all-too-apparent obsession with money. Her husband had died some years earlier, leaving her very comfortable. When the reverend kept insisting she turn her money over to him so that he could invest it, she got suspicious. So, when I went to her with my story, she was ready to help me in any way she could."

"That woman . . . she was Bessie Sparks, wasn't she?" Irony asked.

"She was."

"The woman Goodman murdered?" John Randolph questioned. "Good God! When I think of my sister involved with that criminal . . . !"

"What happened that day?" Hawk inquired.

"Bessie Sparks and Goodman got into an argument when the rest of his men showed up at the school and she found out he was planning to leave. She accused him of his crimes, among them attacking and beating Waubagone. He flew into a rage and seized a knife . . ."

"Why did witnesses find you standing over the body holding the bloodied knife?" Hawk's gaze was direct, and Lynx met it unflinchingly.

"Goodman just stood there looking down at her. I took the knife and pushed him aside . . . that's when I saw what he had done. That she was dead."

"How horrible," murmured Aunt Tiny.

"It was my fault," Lynx stated. "I should have known something like that could happen."

"You couldn't know that Mrs. Sparks would lash out at him in such a way," Irony pointed out. "You can't blame yourself for that."

"I should never have involved her in the first place. No, it was my fault . . . and suddenly, I had two wrongs to

326

avenge. I decided to follow Goodman into the wilderness and when we were far removed from the law . . ." His strong jaw clenched and he raised his head defiantly. "At night when my anger kept me from sleeping, I would plan every detail of his torture. I was going to kill him, but only after he begged me to do it."

"Only thing you could do," agreed Heywood.

"When Goodman fled from Sweetwater, I told him I had business to attend to, but that I would join him on Rainy River. While he contacted Randolph, I went back to Koochiching to see Waubagone."

"And had your young woman recovered?" asked Valentine.

"Her physical injuries had nearly healed," Lynx replied. "But her spirit was broken—her mind clouded. I do not think Waubagone will ever be herself again." His glance clashed with Hawk's once more. "And that is the reason I ask you to release me so that I may hunt Goodman down."

"When the twelve hours have ended," Hawk said, "you are free to go."

"Wait a minute," objected Nathan. "We have only this man's word that he's not a murderer."

"I believe him," Hawk said. "Lynx is a man of honor. From the moment I knew he was the one with Reverend Goodman, I had difficulty convincing myself he was guilty of the same crimes Goodman had committed."

"Because you were childhood friends?" Nathan queried. "Look, Hawk, people do change."

"He's my blood brother—I trust him."

"But . . ."

"I give you my word that if Lynx betrays our trust, I myself will stand in for him. You can arrest me, put me on trial."

"You must think I'm a real greenhorn," Nathan scoffed in disgust.

"I'd say, sonny, that for a lawman, you got a lot to learn about judgin' a fella's worth," said Heywood. "Lynx here ain't a liar, and Hawk ain't a coward. And I'd wager my own sweet ass on that."

"Oh, hell, do whatever you want," Nathan grumbled. "Goodman's the one I really want—and right now, it may take all of us to find him again."

"We'll find him," Lynx vowed. "On the graves of my ancestors, I swear it."

"This is your very own wigwam?" Aunt Tiny said, looking around the interior of the small lodge.

Irony nodded, aware of the bark walls and the packed earth floor. "The chief had it built for me . . . as a sort of honor."

"How nice. I never realized Indians could be so civil." Tiny unrolled a woven mat and dropped onto it, sitting cross-legged. "Do you suppose we might have a cup of tea? There's a tin of China blend in my things there."

Irony filled the kettle from a pail of water, then hung it over the small cooking fire. She set out two clay drinking bowls, carved horn spoons and a birch-bark basket of maple sugar. Tea time in the north woods was a far cry from the correct social ritual with which she had grown up. She remembered the starched cloths, the fragile Haviland cups and sugar cubes in crystal dishes. Would Aunt Tiny find her surroundings impossibly crude here in Chief White Crane's village?

"We brought a few of your more serviceable dresses with us," Valentine said, eyeing Irony's clothes. "We thought you might be in need of them." She cleared her throat delicately. "And that was before we realized you'd had to resort to dressing like a beggar child."

Irony smiled faintly. "I . . . well, I found these

328

things to be most comfortable for a strenuous journey. But I'm afraid they're rather the worse for wear."

Surprisingly, Aunt Tiny merely chuckled. "Perhaps you noticed the new divided skirts your Aunt Alyce and I sewed up for our trip. They're modeled after those bicycling skirts they wear in Minneapolis."

"They certainly look . . . durable." Irony spooned tea leaves into the boiling water. "I can't help but wonder why you and Aunt Alyce decided to make such a journey."

"We were concerned about you, my dear. For all we knew, you were alone in the wilderness."

"Didn't you receive my telegraph message?" Irony asked.

"Oh my, no. It must have arrived after we'd already left home."

"Well, I'm sorry I worried you. I was always perfectly fine." She replaced the lid on the tin she held. "Of course, I didn't think you'd find out that I had . . . gotten separated from Nathan."

Apparently, Tiny was going to disregard Irony's small white lie, for she smiled blandly and said, "Isn't it fortunate that you met up with such a nice young man as Raphael? I understand he's a schoolteacher."

"Yes, at Sweetwater."

"Hardly the type of man one would expect to be an accomplished wilderness guide. How did you acquire his services?"

Irony blinked three times in rapid succession. "Oh . . . well, Auntie, that's a long story. I'm sure you'd be bored to tears. Why don't you tell me something about your own guide instead? How on earth did you and Alyce come to hire Madden Heywood?"

Tiny accepted the bowl of tea Irony offered. "When we decided that it was up to us to see to your safety, we went to Fletcher Carstairs at the mercantile. We thought he might know of someone who could guide

329

us—you know, someone who had stopped in to purchase supplies or something."

"And he knew Mr. Heywood?"

"There was a notice up on the wall." Aunt Tiny sipped her tea in ladylike fashion, but her blue eyes were twinkling furiously. "It seems Madden was between jobs . . . and interested in hiring on as a guide. For a substantial fee, of course." She smoothed her skirt with one hand and smiled in amused recollection.

"You should have seen his face when Alyce and I arrived at the boarding house where he was staying and announced we wanted to hire him! Well, he tried his best to discourage our making the trip, but we McBride women can be determined." Her laughter trilled gaily. "We soon wore him down . . . and here we are."

Her laughter faded abruptly. "Of course, it was a more satisfactory situation before Alyce was kidnapped. If I didn't have so much faith in Madden and your Hawk—and of course, that wonderfully melancholy Lynx—well, I just don't know what I'd be feeling right now. As it is, I have every confidence they'll bring her back safe and sound." She stifled a yawn. "Although I'll probably be unable to sleep a wink tonight worrying about my poor sister."

Irony nodded her head absently. She was amazed by her aunt's casual reference to Raphael Hawkes as *her* Hawk. That was the way she had secretly begun to think of him . . . but she hadn't known it would be quite so obvious to anyone else.

Aunt Tiny had fallen into an exhausted sleep by the time darkness fell. Leaving her snoring peacefully, Irony slipped outside and followed the path down to the lake. She needed a moment alone.

Since returning to Caribou Island, things had been happening too fast, and a sudden sense of urgency had begun to nag at her. She was worried about Aunt Alyce, and confused about her own reaction to the thought of going back to civilization.

Irony stood at the brink of the water, looking upward into the night sky. It shimmered with a million pinpoints of light that were faintly reflected on the surface of the lake. From deep in the forest came the long, clarion call of some animal and Irony shivered and wrapped her arms around herself. The cry was so eerie, so . . . sad, somehow. She thought of her aunt and wondered if she was alone and frightened.

She heard the footfalls on the path behind her, but knew it was Hawk without bothering to turn. She had sensed that he would come looking for her. She was enveloped by a calming warmth as he stepped close to her, putting his arms around her and drawing her back against his chest. His heated breath stirred the tendrils of hair that curled along her neck.

"I thought I might find you here," he murmured, his lips teasing her nape.

"It's so beautiful out tonight," she whispered. "Just look at those stars."

She regretted her words when his mouth abandoned her neck and he raised his head dutifully. But she leaned closer into him, turning her own face to lightly kiss his jaw. Out of the corner of her eye, she saw a trail of light overhead.

"What was that?"

"A flaming star," Hawk replied. "Or at least that's what the Indians call them."

"I've seen them before. My aunts taught me to make wishes on them," Irony told him.

"My people used to believe that when a man saw a dying star, it foretold his own death."

Irony caught her breath. "How awful!"

331

His chuckle echoed pleasantly in her ear. "That's what my mother said. She told me there was another legend that she liked much better."

Irony rubbed her head against his shoulder. "Tell it to me."

"She said that flaming stars were the souls of the dying—and that earth people only saw their glory for an instant, the time it took for them to set off on their journey across the heavens into the next life time." Hawk kissed the top of her head and rested his chin upon it. "It seems to us that those stars burn out quickly, but according to the legend, they blaze on through the endless skies . . . for other eyes to see in other lifetimes."

"That's a nice legend," Irony said quietly. "Do you think we live more than once?"

"Men have debated it since the beginning of time . . . and some very great people have believed in the theory."

She turned in his arms. "What about you? Do you believe we will live again?"

His black eyes glowed with mirth. "I believe it is possible. But just in case we do not, it is my plan to make the best use of the lifetime I have now."

She smiled back. "That answer is so typical of you, Hawk. Your philosophy is very much the result of two cultures, did you know that?"

He shook his head and rocked her gently in his arms.

"You have a way of taking whatever suits you best and weaving it into your life," Irony continued. "You are a remarkable combination of sophistication and innocence."

"And is that acceptable to you?"

"Very."

She raised her mouth to his, clinging to him as his arms went about her, lifting her against his body. The kiss was long and sweet, leaving them entirely too aware of their isolation from the rest of the Indian village. Their teasing mood vanished, to be replaced by something stronger and more elemental. Desire sparked between them, starting a slow, mesmerizing fire.

"These past days have sorely tested my gentlemanly behavior," Hawk breathed, his eyes roving from her lips to the pulse in the hollow of her throat, then to the rise and fall of her breasts. "I have wanted you so, Irony, that I didn't know how I could keep my hands away from you one more minute."

"I was counting the hours until we were back here at the village," she softly confessed. "I had planned your seduction so cleverly . . ."

He hugged her, his laughter low and happy. "Oh, Irony, sweetheart — you had no need to *plan* a seduction. You seduce me every minute of every day, with each move you make — with every beautiful expression on your face."

"I love you, Hawk," she said against his lips.

"And I love you — in this lifetime and whatever others there may be. Someday, when your aunts are both safe and Goodman is in custody, I want to attempt to tell you how very much I do love you." He brushed light kisses across her eyelids. "But for now, I'll be content with the knowledge that at least I've had the chance to say it. In words," he added wickedly, "and other ways . . ."

"I cannot allow myself to think of that," Irony said, with equal mischief, "or I will forget that my dear old auntie is peacefully sleeping just a few yards away."

"When this is all over, Irony, we'll find the time to be together, to talk about . . . all the things we have to talk about. I promise."

"Yes, I —"

"Irony? Are you out here?"

A glimmer of white moved near the rounded shape of the wigwam and Irony realized that Aunt Tiny, clad in her voluminous nightgown, was coming in search of her.

"It's my aunt," she murmured. "I've got to go . . ."

Hawk seized a hasty kiss. "Sleep well, love. I'll see you tomorrow."

Irony moved quickly along the path to the tepee. "I was only taking a walk, Aunt Valentine. Be careful that you don't fall in the darkness."

"Oh my, but it's lovely out here, isn't it?" Tiny asked, looking up at the sky as Irony gently, but firmly guided her back into the lodge.

From his position in the shadow of a spruce, Hawk clearly heard Valentine's final comment, "Oh . . . goodnight, Raphael."

He grinned to himself as he strode past the wigwam toward the village.

Dawn was just breaking across the sky when the canoes set out in search of Alyce McBride. After a brief argument with Hawk and her father, Irony had managed to convince them to take her along. She shared a canoe with Hawk; Zackett and John Randolph were in a second one, and Heywood and Nathan in a third. Lynx had been given a canoe of his own.

Each canoe was headed in a slightly different direction, spreading out to cover a radius of several miles to the north and west of Caribou Island. Lynx had advised that Goodman would most likely be traveling toward Kenora at the north end of the lake.

"Keep an eye out for Goodman, in the event he's still in the area," Hawk said. "And look for signal fires or markers. If you find Alyce, fire two shots into the air at intervals of ten minutes until the rest of us get there."

The first hour passed quickly, but after that, it slowed to a crawl. Throats were raw from shouting and eyes strained from peering into the shaded interiors of the islands. As the canoes drew farther apart, it became more and more feasible that signals could be missed, islands bypassed altogether.

The sudden, jarring sound of shots startled Irony, then filled her with hope.

"Someone has found her," she cried. "Thank heaven!"

Hawk turned the prow of the canoe into the direction from which the shots had come, and in a short time, they heard a second firing. The bright blue plaid of her father's shirt was a welcoming beacon to Irony, and she breathed a sigh of relief as she saw her aunt, alive and well, gesturing excitedly as she talked. Lynx was just offshore in his canoe, and as Hawk and Irony approached, he waved a hand and started off in the way Alyce had indicated.

Irony was out of the canoe as soon as it touched the sandy beach. "Aunt Alyce! Are you all right?" Irony threw her arms around the older woman and hugged her tightly. "We've brought you food . . . and some warmer clothing."

"I'm just fine, child," Alyce assured her. "Other than a number of bruises on my arms and a disgustingly ravenous appetite, I'm none the worse for my night in the wilds."

"I told Father you were thinking of this as an adventure," Irony exclaimed.

"Well, you must admit, nothing this thrilling would ever have happened to me in Thief River Falls."

"Thrilling?" queried Hawk, a puzzled expression on his face. Irony had led him to believe her aunts were staid and proper. He was rapidly being disabused of that idea!

"Oh my, yes. Once that wretched little toad of a

man made it clear that he'd keep his word about not killing me, I truly enjoyed my stay on this island. Last evening I saw a family of minks playing in the water . . . and the loons called and called until it grew dark. And the sky was incredibly beautiful! Zackett, I declare, I've begun to understand your fascination with this country."

"Alyce, my girl!" As the third canoe nosed its way onto the sand, Madden Heywood leaped ashore and cleared the ground in long, running strides. He threw his massive arms around Alyce and, swinging her off her feet, whirled her about in dizzying circles. All she could do was clutch his shoulders, laughing delightedly.

"I survived my night on the island, Madden," she finally managed to say. "But I can't be certain I'll survive your exuberance."

Her calmly spoken words seemed to bring him to his senses, and he lowered her to her feet, his face a deep scarlet as he awkwardly backed away a step or two. "Sorry—I was jist so glad to see you."

"Yes, and I'm glad to see you, too."

"You sure that cussed preacher's gone?" Heywood asked.

"He left sometime in the night," Alyce replied. "Maybe a couple of hours before dawn."

"Which way did he go, or could you tell?"

"From the sounds I could hear, I believe he went off to the northwest. Lynx has already started following him."

"I think we should get back to Caribou," Hawk said. "Your sister is very worried about you."

Alyce's green eyes glowed with secretive glee. "A good idea—but first, there's something I want to show you."

She retreated to the edge of the beach and, kneeling, pushed aside a small pile of speckled stones. With her hands, she brushed away a layer of sand.

"My God!" cried Zack. "Where'd that come from?"

The rest of them gathered around to stare at her cache of money and jewelry. Alyce sat back on her heels, smiling proudly.

"I sneaked them out of Goodman's satchel." Her smile grew somewhat dimmer. "Last evening he took perverse pleasure in enjoying a meal from the supplies that were in the canoe we took. I didn't mind him eating in front of me, but I truly envied him that hot coffee. And I simply couldn't resist the opportunity for some small revenge. Every time that blessed coffee took him off to the bushes, I stole something else from his case and hid it here." She brushed the sand from her slim hands with an air of satisfaction. "I could barely keep from laughing aloud when he placed the satchel beside his bedroll with such a proprietary manner. Had he but known, my sister's jewels and money had been replaced by a handful of rocks."

"Oh, Aunt Alyce, you've saved the day," declared Irony, lifting Valentine's amethyst necklace from the hole in the sand. "Aunt Tiny is going to be ecstatic!"

"You can bet Goodman won't be," Zack commented. "Damn, but he'll be confounded when he discovers those rocks. Wish I could be there to see it."

"Why don't we get the ladies back to camp and take out after Lynx?" asked Heywood. "We jist might be in time for the party."

"Good idea," put in Nathan. "I believe I'll join you."

As they moved toward the waiting canoes, Heywood paused thoughtfully, then with determination, turned back to scoop Alyce up into his arms and carry her to his craft. She uttered a small cry, but her face was flushed with pleasure and she made no effort to dissuade him.

"I jist decided what the hell," boomed Heywood. "I'm right glad to see you, woman, and I don't give a

337

moose squitter who knows it!"

Irony gave Hawk a sidelong glance as she climbed into their canoe. His mouth was firmly curved into a smile, but a sweep of thick black lashes masked the devilish expression in his eyes.

"What's a moose squitter?" Irony whispered, her voice edged with laughter.

"Well . . . it's a bit difficult to explain, but I will say that I wouldn't want to step in it." He took up the paddle and gave her a wry grin. "And I thought *poetry* was romantic."

Chapter Nineteen

The Place of Dreams . . .

Irony could almost be glad that Goodman had not yet been apprehended, for it meant the delay of the journey back to Thief River Falls. Only Madden Heywood had followed Lynx on the search for the escaped preacher. After much debate, it had been decided that the others should stay on at the Indian camp in the event Goodman discovered Alyce's trickery and returned, bent on revenge.

It was also agreed that, if neither Madden or Lynx returned with Goodman, or at least the tale of what had happened to him, Irony and her aunts would leave for civilization before the onset of the rainy season in September. So she had until then.

The days of late summer passed lazily—yet with an increasing air of urgency. Irony wasn't sure if the sense of immediacy came from the nip of approaching autumn in the air, or her feelings concerning Hawk. Since Alyce's safe return to the camp, there had been no chance for Irony to be alone with him.

Both aunts now shared her tepee, while Nathan, Zack and John Randolph had moved in with Hawk. They saw each other frequently, but always in the company of others. For several days, they had contented themselves with meaningful glances, casual touches, and longing smiles. But it was becoming increasingly frustrating that that was all they were allowed. Irony knew what sort of ungratified longings seethed within herself, so when Hawk turned his burning ebony gaze upon her, she realized exactly what he was thinking. It was enough to make her knees grow weak and her heart start to pound. Finding a way to be with him soon took precedence over everything else in her daily existence.

The afternoon was the hottest one they'd had for weeks — probably due to the thunder storm building up in the north. Hawk stared at the thunderheads without really seeing them. His mind was, as usual, firmly fixed on thoughts of Irony and he had reached the end of his endurance. One more day of being close enough to touch her, but not daring to, was going to send him over the edge of sanity. He couldn't stand another night of tossing and turning, finding himself at the mercy of long, sensually stirring dreams. The ache for her that lodged within him had grown into an untamed beast, and he knew he couldn't hold it at bay much longer.

Now, this afternoon, he was going to abduct the little green-eyed temptress and — he smiled at the very notion — have his wicked way with her. If her father discovered them and put a bullet through Hawk's heart, he'd die knowing it had been worth it.

As Hawk stormed up the path toward Irony's tepee, he was hailed by her aunts. They were sitting in front of Snow's lodge, watching as she showed them how to scrape hides in preparation for picture writing. From their puzzled glances, Hawk realized that he must be scowling. He forced a more pleasant expression and even managed a smile.

"If you're on your way to see Irony, she isn't in her tepee," Aunt Tiny announced gaily. "She's off in the woods somewhere, gathering blueberries for supper tonight."

Aunt Alyce smiled benignly as she took the sharp,

340

curved implement Snow handed her. "Of course, she did say that if you . . . happened by, to tell you she'd be somewhere near the aspen grove."

Hawk's smile took on more genuine warmth. "Perhaps I should try to find her. Uh . . . she probably needs help with those berries."

Alyce and Tiny exchanged amused looks.

"Oh, I'm certain of it," Tiny murmured.

"And you may tell her for us," Alyce added, "that she needn't hurry right back. Sister and I will be learning the fine art of scraping hides for most of the afternoon."

Hawk nodded solemnly, keeping his eyes downcast so that the ladies wouldn't catch sight of the happiness dancing within them. He walked sedately down the path until he was out of sight of the wigwam, and then he broke into a run.

When he arrived at the aspen grove, he didn't see Irony, and so continued on to the end of the narrow, winding trail. He found her there, seated on a fallen log watching Rogue chase the leaves that drifted lazily down from the aspen trees overhead.

Hawk had grown so used to her being attired in either the bedraggled boy's clothing or the faded cotton dress that he was unprepared for the picture Irony made. She was wearing a summery white gown, printed with dainty green sprigs. The ruffle that fluttered around her shoulders was repeated in a wider ruffle at the hem. Her black hair had been piled atop her head and tied with green ribbons that streamed out gently in the breeze.

As when anything greatly moved him, Hawk's mind was flooded with poetry — images and phrases diligently learned when he was a boy and not forgotten in the years since. Standing in the shadows of the trees, he began to recite in a voice that was rich and deeply mellow:

341

"From the Desert I come to thee
　On a stallion shod with fire;
And the winds are left behind
　In the speed of my desire.
Under thy window I stand,
　And the midnight hears my cry:
I love thee, I love but thee,
　With a love that shall not die.
　　Till the sun grows cold,
　　And the stars are old,
　　And the leaves of the Judgment Book
　　　Unfold!"

Irony stood and walked into his arms.

"I thought you'd never get here," she sighed against his lips. "I've been waiting such a long time."

He made no reply, but, gathering her closer to him, let his mouth fall upon hers, moving with all the imperious urgency that had been building within him for days. Hungrily, he kissed her, growling with pleasure as she met and returned his passion with equal desperation. Hawk's fingers tightened at her waist as he sampled her kiss, taking what she offered and giving it back with growing ardor.

Irony's arms slipped around his neck and she stood on tiptoe to better fit her body to his. Her fingers entwined in the hair that fell over his collar in back, as if glorying in the heavy, silken feel of it. He shuddered at the brush of her hands against his neck, and she slid them slowly along the hard planes of his shoulders, into the opening of his buckskin shirt.

"My God, how I've missed you touching me," he murmured, releasing her long enough to loosen the front lacing of his shirt and strip it off over his head. He seized her hands and placed them on his bare chest, flattening her palms against his tautly muscled body and moving them in slow, sensual circles.

Irony's fingertips tingled with the sensation caused by the friction of his skin against hers. Warmth flowed upward, along her arms and into her own chest, filling her with a suffusion of delightful emotions. She spread her hands wide and bent to kiss his flesh between each of her fingers.

The feel of her soft, heated lips against his skin whipped his desire into near-frenzy. The days of abstinence had taken their toll, and Hawk knew he could hold himself back no longer. With shaking fingers that longed to rip away the soft, cotton fabric of her gown, he began an assault on the long line of buttons that marched down the valley between her breasts.

Sensing his growing impatience, Irony placed a kiss upon the hard curve of his mouth and, gently brushing his hands aside, unfastened the buttons herself.

Hawk pushed the dress off her shoulders, and with a twist of her body, Irony relegated the folds of material to the ground at her feet. She untied her petticoats and let them slide away as well.

Hawk smiled grimly at the sight of her in thin chemise and pantalettes and, had it not been for the passionate excitement that flared in his dark, dark eyes, Irony might have thought he disapproved. But there was nothing of disapproval in the way his hands closed over her shoulders, pulling her to him — there was no reproach in the way his mouth sought hers in a long, sweetly enthralling kiss, nor in the manner he dragged his lips slowly down the length of her neck, over the hollow of her throat to the ivory swell of her breasts.

With somewhat less care than she had taken with her gown, Hawk tore at the fastening of her undergarments, removing them with an almost uncontrolled haste. The impelling urge to see her standing naked before him, her exquisite body bathed in the dappled

343

sunlight, overrode what common sense remained to him.

Irony's hands were just as frantically employed with the removal of his clothing, and when the last garment had been shed, she took his hand and led him a few steps into the forest. When he saw the bed she had fashioned of pine boughs and covered with her cloak, he turned to her with an expression of wonder in his eyes. She had been waiting for him—had cared enough to prepare a place where they might be alone to indulge their need for each other. It seemed impossible to him that this small, fragile girl, born and reared so delicately, could return his passion with such fervor and fire—that she could surrender herself so willingly to his superior strength and, in so doing, conquer him more completely than anything or anyone had ever managed to do. He was totally enslaved by Irony McBride, but yielding to his imprisonment with an eagerness that still shocked and amazed him.

Irony lowered herself to the outspread cloak, pulling him down with her. He stretched out, rolling her gently in his arms until his body half-covered hers. As his mouth descended in yet another fiery, stirring caress she became aware of the harsh feel of wool beneath her back, and the smooth, hard warmth of him pressed against her. A languorous autumn-scented wind touched them, bringing with it the pungency of pine, the tang of the lake.

One pale gold aspen leaf drifted downward from overhead and settled on Irony's breast. Hawk brushed it away with his face, and as he turned his head, his mouth caught one rose-hued nipple, sending a jolt of pleasure racing through Irony. Murmuring his name, she slipped her arms around him to stroke his back, to trail her nails down his spine.

Hawk's mouth was hot and harsh, goading her into a fevered response, and when she cried out, her unfet-

344

tered excitement drove him to the brink.

"I can't wait any longer, Irony," he gasped, raising his body over hers.

"Neither can I," she confirmed with a whisper, pulling him down to her. "I have wanted this so much . . ."

Their bodies found each other with unerring instinct. Hawk wrapped her in his sinewy arms, and Irony buried her face against his neck, reveling in the warm, masculine scent of him, the taste of his tanned skin against her lips.

"Later," he breathed, "I want to love you slowly . . . and more thoroughly than you've ever been loved." He dragged in a deep draught of air, struggling to control the tremors that were beginning to wrack his body. "But for now . . . oh, God, Irony, for now . . . it has simply been too long since we were together . . ."

"I know, I know," she consoled, clinging to him as she felt him being swept away by merciless waves of sensation. Irony thrilled at the realization of his helplessness. He was lost in a shattering ecstasy, overwhelmed by sweet, searing emotion. Then, as his hands splayed possessively over her back and his mouth took hers in a wanton kiss, Irony herself felt as though she, too, was being hurled through space. For countless seconds, she burned with an intensely glorious agony that finally burst into magnificent fire. Like showers of sparks, she soared into the sky, then fell softly, gently back to earth. Clutching Hawk's broad shoulders, Irony snuggled more deeply into his embrace and sighed with exhausted contentment.

Grrrr.

Hawk's mellow chuckle broke her tranquillity, and Irony lazily opened her eyes to see the black and white puppy standing near them, holding Hawk's fringed shirt in his teeth and shaking it ferociously.

"He wants to play," Hawk said with a smile.

"I'm too tired," she murmured, her shy expression veiled by a sweep of thick black lashes. "You go play with him."

Hawk nuzzled her ear. "I'd rather play . . . hey!"

He sat up abruptly as Rogue came closer, shook the garment at him, then dashed away. The dog ran right to the edge of the lake where he dropped the shirt into the water, then stood looking at Hawk, his eyes bright with challenge, his tongue lolling from his mouth.

"Bring that back," Hawk shouted, leaping to his feet. "You're getting my shirt all wet."

As he started toward the dog, Rogue snatched up the shirt again and plunged into the water, dragging it with him. To Irony's delight, the splendidly naked man splashed into the lake after him. Rogue dropped the shirt and swam away, hampered not at all by his lameness. Hawk grabbed the garment and wrung the excess water from it before tossing it onto the grassy bank. He turned to survey Irony.

"Come on in," he invited.

"No! The water must be freezing."

"The day's cloudy," Hawk reminded her. "So the water feels quite warm. Come on, I dare you!"

He dived into the lapping waves, allowing her to admire the sleek beauty of his wet body. When he surfaced, he swam in pursuit of Rogue, who splashed into shallower water, yapping noisily.

Happily, Irony watched the man and the animal cavort. Never could a scene like this have taken place within the confines of Thief River Falls, she realized. But here it seemed so natural . . . and so appealing. Life in the wilderness could be filled with such simple pleasures—and she could no longer deny that her heart was entreating her to consider what she would be giving up if she left Hawk behind and went back to what was once the only home she had ever known.

"Come here, Irony," Hawk called, and this time, when he held out his hand, she went to him.

Unashamed of her nudity, she marched into the water beneath his appraising eyes. As he had promised, the lake was warm, inviting her to play. Just as Hawk reached for her, she flashed him a saucy smile and slapped the surface of the lake, splashing him. She plunged into deeper water, struggling to keep her footing on the slippery rocks that covered the lake bottom. Relentlessly, Hawk came after her.

"You little witch," he exclaimed, a crooked grin lifting one corner of his mouth. "Come back here and take your punishment like a man!"

"But I'm not a man," she tossed over her shoulder.

"No . . . no, you're certainly not." He pursued her a few more steps before coming to a halt. "Have you forgotten that you don't know how to swim?"

"I can—"

Irony gasped and shrieked as the lake bottom sloped sharply downward. She lost her footing and would have slipped beneath the surface had not Hawk surged forward to clasp her about the waist. He pulled her close to him, and in her relief at being saved from a thorough dunking, she wrapped her arms and legs around him.

"Mmmm." He lifted her higher against him and let his mouth settle firmly over hers. The coolness of her lips quickly warmed beneath the bold heat of his. When he drew back to look into her eyes, his own were filled with a dangerously determined glint. "Let's go back to shore," he murmured, nipping softly at the curve of her neck and shoulder.

When he scooped her into his arms, Irony made no protest. She rested her head against his damp chest, her face softened by a pleased smile. He began wading toward the shore, where Rogue waited for them, his tail wagging furiously.

A low, ominous roll of thunder sounded as the wind gusted to life, swirling dry leaves about them.

"Perhaps we should go back to the tepee," Irony suggested, as Hawk, keeping an arm around her waist, let her feet touch the ground. "It's going to storm . . . and my aunts told me they'd be away the rest of the afternoon."

Hawk stooped to retrieve her chemise. "That's a good idea . . . although it seems such a pity to dress again."

Irony pulled the chemise over her head and reached for the rest of her undergarments. "It doesn't have to be for long," she promised.

Hawk grinned as he stepped into his discarded Levis and slid his feet into leather moccasins. But, grimacing at his wet shirt, he decided to forego its dubious protection.

When Irony had once again donned the green-sprigged gown, Hawk closed the distance between them and began to button it for her. As he reached the last button on the high collar, he stroked his thumb across the fullness of her lower lip.

"Irony," he said seriously, his eyes searching hers. "There's something I want you to do for me."

"What is it?" she queried.

He shook his head slightly, his gaze drawn to the first distant flash of lightning. "I realize I should be more patient. I should wait until . . . well, until I know that you love me enough to grant my request."

"I do love you," she said quietly.

Hawk gripped her arms and stared fiercely into her eyes. "But do you love me enough?"

"Enough to what?" she asked, smiling with barely controlled impatience.

"To stay here with me." He bent his head and

brushed a light kiss over her mouth. "Irony, don't leave me . . . please don't ever leave me."

Irony lifted a hand and closed it over his. "Hawk, I—"

Rogue's sudden, sharp bark rent the air, and the animal flung himself against Hawk's leg.

A canoe eased its way out of the heavy shadows along the shoreline. As it moved into the light, Hawk and Irony could see every detail of the man sitting upright within it. The Reverend Josiah Goodman, a smug smile on his face, had laid the paddle across his knees and was pointing a gun at them with obvious intent.

"And so we meet again," he said, a trace of weariness in his voice. "May I say that I've enjoyed watching your little play time?"

A deeply crimson blush crept up Irony's throat and into her face, but she raised her head proudly and refused to be daunted by the man's words. Hawk took her hand and squeezed it reassuringly.

"For God's sake, Goodman," he snarled, "what have you come back here for?"

Goodman's smile died abruptly. "As you know, we have some unfinished business."

"Surely any business you had with us is over and done."

"Far from it, my friend."

"What do you want?" asked Irony, even though she knew without being told.

"The money and jewelry your bitch of an aunt stole from me." The canoe nudged the shore and Goodman stepped out into ankle-deep water. Pulling the canoe up onto the beach behind him, he walked toward them. "We've led each other a merry chase for some time and, while it lasted, it was rather interesting. However, my energy and patience are running out now, and I want to conclude our dealings and be gone."

"I don't see how we can help you, Goodman. Neither Irony nor I have the money . . ."

Goodman waved the gun wildly, a fierce scowl contorting his features. "Don't lie to me!"

"He's not lying," Irony insisted.

"He may not have the money now," Goodman sneered, "but by all that's holy, he'd better have it within the next fifteen minutes."

"I couldn't get my hands on it that fast," Hawk protested.

"You'd better," Goodman advised, "if you want to keep your pretty playmate alive."

The preacher leveled the gun at Irony. "Come here," he commanded.

Irony glanced at Hawk and, a grim expression in his eyes, he nodded. "It seems we have small choice in the matter . . . at the moment."

As Irony approached Goodman, he reached out and clamped a hand on her wrist, yanking her to his side. Rogue burst into a frenzy of barking and would have sprung at the man had not Hawk seized him.

"Silence that animal or I'll kill him," Goodman said.

"Hush, Rogue." Hawk murmured soothing words into the dog's ear, gently muzzling him with one hand. Irony held her breath for she knew that if Goodman gave away his presence by firing one shot, he very well could decide to shoot each of them. The truth of the matter was, at this point, he really had very little to lose.

"Now, Indian, you go get that money," Goodman said. "Do whatever you have to do to get it, but don't tell anyone that I'm here. If you do, or if you fail to return within fifteen minutes, Miss Irony is going to die a rather painful death. And the same thing will happen should anyone try to follow me from this island."

"Irony?" Hawk's troubled gaze moved over her.

"I'll be fine," she said stoutly.

"Then I'll be back as soon as possible."

"Take the dog with you and shut him up some-where," Goodman ordered.

With Rogue in his arms, Hawk turned to start down the trail.

"Oh, one other thing," Goodman called after him. "It would be foolish to attempt to arm yourself."

When Hawk had disappeared, Goodman gave Irony a shove. "Get into the canoe—we'll wait there."

Overhead, the roiling clouds blackened, backlit by jagged streaks of lightning. Irony huddled in the canoe, the booming thunder no louder than the beating of her frightened heart.

Hawk was back in less than ten minutes. It was a simple matter to retrieve the loot Goodman wanted. The money had been placed into a canvas sack, and the jewelry had been packed into Aunt Tiny's carpet-bag. Thus, finding Irony's lodge empty, it hadn't taken Hawk long to gather the items.

Giving Rogue a final pat on the head, he left him inside the wigwam, carefully securing the deer hide over the doorway. He stood in the pathway a few seconds considering the wisdom of trying to secrete a knife on his person, but he knew it wouldn't be worth the risk. Without a shirt or boots, there was no secure hiding place, and it would only take Goodman an instant to find it. The man had been driven to desperate circumstances and with his back against the wall, there was just too much danger to Irony. If they were to extricate themselves from this situation, they would have to depend on their own resourcefulness.

And, Hawk mused as he stalked back toward the spot where Goodman held Irony, *a hell of a lot of good luck wouldn't hurt either.*

"You're taking us with you?" Irony questioned, her green eyes wide with apprehension.

"What did you think?" Goodman said. "That I'd turn you loose to alert the entire village to my presence? No, my dear, I've been delayed too many times already. I intend to make my departure once and for all — and I need a bit of insurance."

"What do you intend to do with us?" she asked.

"Let's just save it as a little surprise, shall we?"

Goodman chuckled to himself as he settled back into the canoe and indicated with a sweep of the gun he held that Hawk should commence paddling.

Irony strained her eyes for any sight of another living being as the distance between them and Caribou Island increased. Only lazy spirals of smoke above the treetops indicated the presence of other people. Although she couldn't ask outright, she had to assume Hawk had not found a way to warn the others of their danger at the hands of the deranged preacher. Goodman would take them out into the lake and shoot them . . . and there seemed to be nothing she could do to prevent it.

The look in Hawk's eyes told her that he hadn't given up — that he was biding his time until he could make a move without endangering her. Irony could only hope that, when the time came, she could be helpful. They had gone through far too much to be defeated by Goodman now.

A sudden flash of lightning illuminated Goodman's face, making his features look harsh and evil. His days on the run had given him a more gaunt appearance and desperation lingered in his expression.

They had traveled about thirty minutes when Goodman pointed into the near-distance. "There," he shouted above the rumble of thunder, "that's where I want to go."

Turning her head, Irony saw an island, its small, natural harbor guarded by a crudely carved wooden totem—a figure that was the combination of a fierce war eagle and a black bear.

"What is this place?" she asked in a half-whisper.

"The Place of Dreams," Hawk replied.

"This is where you came to seek your vision?"

He nodded in affirmation. "This is sacred ground, Goodman. Why are we stopping here?"

"It amuses me to do so," the man snapped, taking several loops of rope from the bottom of the canoe and winding them over his shoulder. "Now hurry up and get us ashore."

As they beached the canoe and set foot on the island, Irony could sense Hawk's growing determination to put an end to Goodman's dominance over them. She noticed the slight squaring of his shoulders, the nearly imperceptible clenching of his fists. She steeled herself for the moment, knowing that if she could not be of assistance to him, she would need to get safely out of the way. Their very lives depended on Hawk's ability to overcome the preacher, and she did not intend to hamper him.

A narrow trail wound along the beach and into a thick grove of trees before meandering into a small clearing. With an impatient jerk of the gun, Goodman indicated that he wanted them to follow it. As they emerged into the clearing, Hawk paused and Irony knew he had decided to make his move.

He never got the chance. Even as he was turning, Goodman swung the gun upward, striking Hawk's temple a cracking blow. Irony winced at the sickening thud of metal against flesh and bone, biting back a scream of terror as she watched Hawk crumple to the ground.

She dropped to her knees beside Hawk, but Goodman ordered her to stand up. "Help me drag him to that tree over there," he growled.

"I won't . . ."

Goodman pressed the barrel of the gun against her cheek. "Don't be stupid, Irony—I no longer have the inclination to humor you."

Numb with fear, she bent and grasped one of Hawk's arms, while Goodman took the other. Twice they had to stop and gather their strength, but Hawk showed no sign of regaining consciousness. Had it not been for the occasional groan that issued from his lips, Irony would have thought him dead. The very thought was enough to make her heart trip over itself as it heaved within her chest.

"Tie him to the tree," Goodman instructed, tossing down the rope he carried. "And don't try to be a heroine, Irony. You and your damned aunts have caused me enough trouble."

Forcing Hawk into a slumped position against the trunk of a tall white pine, Goodman watched as Irony began wrapping coils of the rope around his body.

"Tighter," he said. "And use that small length of rope there to tie his hands."

"Why are you doing this?" Irony asked. "You've got what you came after—we can't stop you now."

"I have the money and Valentine's jewels, but my dear, that isn't all I came for."

Irony tied the final knot and turned to face him. "What else do you want?"

"To see you and this meddling half breed die," Goodman said calmly.

Another streak of lightning slashed across the purplish-black sky, reflected eerily in the man's maddened eyes.

"But there's no reason to kill us now," she argued.

"Hawk is unconscious . . . and I certainly can't stop you. No one else even knows you came back. You could be miles from here before . . ."

"Shut up!" he yelled. "Get against that tree."

"No . . . I won't let you kill him!" she cried, throwing herself against Hawk's inert body.

"That's fine," Goodman stated. "Die face to face, if you like. It makes no difference to me."

He began winding the rope around her, and when she would have struggled, he tapped the gun against her temple. Instantly, she went still. If she angered him enough to render her senseless, too, there'd be no way she could save either of them.

By the time he'd finished, her bonds were so tight she could barely breathe. With sinking spirits, she realized that managing to untie herself would be impossible. The small, desperate moan that escaped her was drowned in the cymbal crash of thunder, and she was grateful. She didn't want Goodman to know how mercilessly terror was clawing at her.

"And now, dear child, I must be off." Goodman stood back to study them for a long moment, his face twisted into a maniacal smile. "If only you hadn't interfered . . ."

Abruptly, he whirled and strode away down the trail. Irony held her breath until he was out of sight, and then, relieved, she sagged against Hawk. Goodman hadn't shot them! She could hardly believe it — he'd said he intended to kill them, but apparently he was simply going to leave them to die of exposure. She rested her head on Hawk's chest, listening to the steady beat of his heart. He hadn't shot them — they still had a chance!

It was only gradually that she became aware of the smell of smoke on the wind.

"Hawk," she whispered frantically. "Oh, my God, Hawk! He's set the island afire!"

Irony struggled against the bonds that held them, sobbing and cursing in her panic. "Hawk . . . wake up! Wake up . . ."

Plumes of gray smoke emerged from the clump of bushes at the head of the trail, but when she turned her head, Irony could see that Goodman had set similar fires on all sides of them. Fed by the dry undergrowth and leaves, and whipped into a fury by the wind, the fire would sweep over the island in no time, consuming everything in its wake.

Hawk moaned, turning his head and gasping for breath.

"Hawk, oh, please wake up," she cried urgently. "We've got to get loose."

"Irony?" he mumbled, straining against the ropes that cut into his shoulders and arms. His eyes came open slowly as her fingers clutched at him.

"Goodman tied us to this tree, Hawk—then set the island on fire. We're going to burn to death if we can't get free!"

"I . . . I can't move," he groaned. "Jesus, I can't move."

"You've got to! We're going to die!"

They could hear the crackle of flames now, the singing rush of the fire as it devoured the smaller pine trees in its path. A curtain of heat rolled toward them.

To Irony's terrified eyes, the clash of thunder and lightning overhead and the insidious on-rush of the fire all around them created an evilly fascinating replica of Hell. She squeezed her eyes shut against the scorching smoke and rested her cheek along Hawk's throat. "What are we going to do?" she whispered.

"Irony," he said grimly, his lips moving against her hair, "I hope your lady aunts taught you how to pray . . ."

A shower of sparks burst overhead and, as the full horror of their situation struck them, Hawk and Irony

356

struggled against their bonds.

"It's no use," sobbed Irony. "We're going to burn to death!"

"Don't give up hope," Hawk murmured, his lips against her temple. "As long as we're alive, there's still hope."

But she had never heard such desolation in his voice, and she realized that Hawk did, indeed, think they were going to die.

She raised her tear-streaked face to his. "I love you, Hawk," she said softly.

His smile was like a soothing balm. "And I love you." His mouth was sweet and gentle as it touched hers. "More than life . . . more than any mere existence in this flawed world." His next kiss was firmer, but with nothing of farewell in it. Irony pressed against him, filled with gratitude and renewed courage.

"If . . . if we do have to die," she said, "at least we'll be together . . . and I won't be so afraid." She rested her forehead on his chin. "But, oh, Hawk! I don't want us to . . . to lose everything just when we've found it!"

"Shh, sweetheart," he whispered. "I know."

The roar of the fire grew louder, and they could feel the wall of heat moving nearer. Irony shuddered uncontrollably.

"Talk to me, Hawk—talk to me so I won't lose my nerve."

Feeling the deep, labored breath he drew, she strained closer to him, trying to provide what meager solace she could.

"Remember the day on Rainy River when you found the blue heron feather floating in the water and put it in your hair?" he asked.

She nodded. "But I lost it later."

"And I found it . . . on the beach where Nathan

357

discovered us."

Irony laughed softly. "I remember that night."

"I've kept the feather all this time, Irony. It's in my shirt pocket right now."

She rubbed her cheek against the pocket. "Why?"

"It was a symbol to me—a symbol of the qualities I loved you for. Qualities you have in common with my mother, the only other important woman in my life . . ."

Irony gasped as a line of flame snaked toward the hem of her skirt. "Hawk!"

"Irony," he said sternly, "look at me. Concentrate on my face, on what I'm saying . . ."

As she raised her eyes to look up at him, a broad figure at the edge of the flames caught her attention. "Oh, my God," she gasped. "It's Goodman!"

The man stood at one side of the clearing watching them, not moving until greedy fingers of fire began reaching out to touch him. Then, with a clearly audible laugh, he turned to go.

Suddenly, there was a shout and two other figures mysteriously emerged from the smoke just in front of him.

"Lynx!" cried out Goodman, his laughter gone. "Where did you come from?"

Lynx's smile was cold. "Hawk turned me loose to hunt you down, Goodman. Heywood and I have been following you for days."

"Why should you want to hunt me down?"

"Remember the Indian girl named Waubagone?" Lynx asked. "She's the reason."

Goodman grew very still. "I don't know what you're talking about."

"I think you do." Lynx took a step toward him. "You should have known you'd have to pay for what you did to my woman."

"*Your* woman?" Goodman's eyes narrowed. "You

were waiting for the chance to kill me all along, weren't you?"

"That's right. It's too bad I didn't have the opportunity before you murdered Bessie Sparks. But now it seems the gods have delivered you right into my hands."

A massive rumble of thunder shook the earth, and the first fitful drops of rain started to fall. Within seconds, the heavens opened to pour forth a chilling deluge.

"And I'm here because o' what you did to Miss Tiny and Miss Alyce . . . and a dozen other women like 'em," drawled Madden Heywood. "Good thing we saw ya double back. It sure woulda been a pity if you'd gotten away without receivin' the justice ya deserve."

"Justice?" shrilled Goodman. "The two of you know nothing of justice!"

"You've taught us your kind of justice," said Lynx. "Will that not be good enough for you?"

"No!"

Ignoring the rain that flattened his ginger-colored hair to his head and ran into his eyes, Goodman clawed at the gun hanging on his hip, bringing it up and firing in one motion. With a muffled groan, Heywood clutched at his shoulder and staggered forward, falling to his knees. Goodman turned and fled, leaving Lynx to see to his friend.

"I'm jist winged," Heywood grunted. "Go after him."

Hawk and Irony watched in breathless silence as Lynx rose and followed Goodman, disappearing into the thick fog of rain and smoke that hung over the island. After a few minutes, Heywood hauled himself to his feet and came toward them.

"Damn good thing that rain's puttin' out the fire," he muttered. "We coulda all burned to death."

Pulling a knife from the sheath at his side, he cut the ropes that bound them. "Help yer friend, Hawk. I

359

ain't able . . ."

Hawk had already started sprinting in the direction Lynx and Goodman had gone and, after making certain Heywood was all right, Irony followed. As she stopped to catch her breath at the end of the path, she saw that Hawk had stopped, his eyes trained on Goodman and Lynx ahead.

The preacher had raised his gun. "Don't come any closer, either of you—or I'll shoot!"

Lynx continued walking toward him. "I'm not afraid, Goodman. You're the one who should be preparing his soul for death." Lynx moved with the all the grace and stealth of his namesake. "You're the one who should be trembling at the thought of meeting his Maker."

"Silence!" Goodman all but screamed, waving the gun erratically. "Stay where you are. I'm warning you, I'll shoot!"

"How does it feel to face someone who is not afraid of you?" taunted Lynx. "I'm no woman . . . no defenseless girl."

"I never hurt your woman, Lynx," Goodman suddenly declared.

"Do you swear it?"

Goodman seemed to summon the last of his bravado. "May God strike me dead if I'm lying!"

Like a reprimand from Heaven, a shaft of lightning streaked out of the bruised clouds above. It struck the tallest of the pines, and the tree erupted in fire. It broke as easily as a matchstick, and with a terrible rending sound, its heavy branches toppled to the ground. Eyes wild with terror, Goodman cowered, screaming out a blasphemy as one of the limbs caught him and carried him down with it.

Irony, too, screamed and threw herself into Hawk's arms. As she trembled in his embrace, she became aware of the strange, stricken silence that had fallen over the island. The rain still fell, but its din had turned into a soft, silvery sound. The only thunder to be heard rumbled faintly in the far distance. Slowly, she raised her head and looked into Hawk's rain-streaked face. Something in his eyes chilled her. She turned and saw Lynx standing near the fallen tree.

"He's alive, Hawk . . . but the tree has crushed him."

Hawk put Irony aside. "Stay here," he murmured, moving to join Lynx.

Irony only recognized a need to remain close to Hawk—without deliberate thought, she followed him. She stopped short at the sight of Goodman's chalk white face staring up at her. Blood trickled from his nose and mouth, and he seemed to be trying to speak. She gasped, then turned away retching as she saw the huge splinter of raw pine that had pierced the man's chest.

"Ahh . . . the pain . . ." Goodman's harsh whisper was barely louder than the rain. "Please . . . kill me . . ."

Lynx raised black, nearly expressionless eyes and Hawk nodded. He reached for Irony and drew her back into his arms, shielding her from the gruesome scene.

"Ya got to, lad," said Madden Heywood, coming up behind them. "It's th' only humane thing to do."

Lynx drew his knife and studied the long blade for a moment. Then, with a deep, steadying breath, he moved forward and knelt beside Goodman.

Hawk's arms tightened around Irony and she burrowed her face into his chest. She was thankful she didn't have to witness Goodman's death, but she knew Lynx's words would remain in her memory for the rest of her life.

"I never meant his death to be an act of mercy," he said, seconds later. "But he trespassed on sacred ground—and I think perhaps Manitou took matters into his own hands."

Lynx glanced down at the bloodied knife he held, then gave it a toss into the lake. Opening the leather pouch hanging around his neck, he drew forth the delicate chain from which dangled the small, shining cross. He lifted his hand and let the chain fall onto Goodman's now lifeless body. "Waubagone is avenged."

"Let's get back to camp," Hawk said quietly. "Heywood's wound needs seeing to . . . and the others will want to know what has happened."

Lynx raised his head proudly. "What will you do with me, Hawk? You have just seen me kill a man. According to white eyes' law, I will have to be punished."

"My friend, you have been punished enough. As far as anyone needs to know, Goodman was killed when lightning struck the tree. The other Nighthawks and I will return to bury him, and it will remain our secret."

"Go on back to yer woman, Lynx," suggested Heywood. "She needs you."

Lynx inclined his head. "I had thought of taking her north to winter at Red River."

"Then go," said Hawk. "And may the protection of the Grandfathers go with you."

The two friends clasped forearms in the Ojibway manner, and Heywood stepped forward to present Lynx with his own hunting knife.

"Take this, Lynx. No man should face the wilderness without a good knife. God go with ya, son."

When Lynx had gone, Hawk walked over the island, making certain the last of the fires was extinguished. Then, wearily, he held out a hand to Irony.

"Let's go home," he said.

"Yes," she repeated with a smile. "Thank God, we can go home."

Chapter Twenty

In the wilderness . . .

A butter yellow sun hung low in the afternoon sky, glinting off the calm waters of Lake of the Woods. Irony had stared at its reflection for so long that she was beginning to get a headache.

Now that Goodman was dead, the McBride property recovered and her estrangement with her father healed, her adventure in the wilderness was coming to an end. It was time to decide once and for all what she was to do.

Oh, she had made her decision to stay with Hawk easily enough. She realized it had been made even before he'd asked her not to leave. But now came the truly difficult part—telling her aunts.

With a feeling of dread, she steeled herself for the confrontation and went to find them. As she entered the village, she saw them sitting outside Snow's lodge.

Snow offered a serenely polite greeting, but Aunt Tiny was bursting with enthusiasm.

"Irony, wait until you see," she called out. "Snow has taught us to make these lovely birchbark baskets."

"How nice . . ."

"I declare, it's more fun than crocheting! And next week we are going to use them to harvest the wild rice."

Irony had to smile. Her aunt, clad in her trouser-skirt, was wearing a man's flannel shirt and had taken only enough time to pin her silver hair atop her head in a rather haphazard fashion. She looked very little like the president of the Ladies' Auxiliary at this moment.

"I'm only going if Madden is well enough to go along," spoke up Aunt Alyce. "I don't think he should be left alone."

Irony opened her mouth to remind Alyce that the Indian village would not be entirely deserted, even for the rice harvest, but something in her aunt's attitude stopped her. She stared in amazement as the tall, willowy woman hovered over the pallet where Madden lay in the sunshine, holding a clay bowl so that he might have a sip of water. Solicitously, Alyce inspected the bandage that covered his chest and shoulder, then tucked the blanket more securely about him. For someone who had always been so decisive in her claimed immunity to men, she seemed inordinately concerned with Madden Heywood's comfort and well-being.

"No sense fussin' over me, woman," Heywood growled, looking pleased. "I ain't a baby."

"Now, Madden, you've done so much for Sister and me that you couldn't possibly object to my returning the favor," said Alyce, rising. When she saw Irony standing nearby and noticed her interest in the scene, she blushed brightly. "What is it, Irony? Is something on your mind?"

"Yes, I'm afraid there is." Irony drew a deep breath—she'd almost forgotten the gravity of her mission. "I need to talk to you and Aunt Tiny."

"Must it be this exact minute?" asked Tiny. "Snow was about to show me how to seal the seams in this basket."

"I will show you later," promised Snow. "Irony looks troubled."

364

"You aren't worried about Raphael, are you?" queried Tiny. "He only went to . . ." She shuddered visibly. ". . . to bury Reverend Goodman. The other men are with him—he can't come to any harm, I'm certain."

"No, this doesn't concern Hawk. Well, in a way it does, but you see . . ." Irony broke off, not knowing how to broach the subject.

"Why don't you go down to the beach where you can speak privately?" suggested Snow. "I will see to Mr. Heywood while you are gone."

"Thank you, Snow," Alyce said. "Come along, Irony—this must be a serious matter to have you so tongue-tied."

Irony followed her aunts the short distance to the sandy beach. She watched as they settled themselves on sun-warmed boulders, but found she could not bring herself to sit calmly. She began to pace back and forth at the edge of the water, pausing occasionally to glance out over the lake.

"What seems to be the trouble?" Aunt Tiny finally asked.

Irony looked down at her clenched hands and forced herself to speak. "There's something I have to tell you, but . . . well, first I want you both to know how much I appreciate everything you've done for me. I realize the sacrifices you've made on my behalf . . . and I'm aware that I haven't always been easy to deal with."

Valentine tipped her head, her blue eyes as bright as a bird's. "What is it you're trying to say, girl?"

Alyce smiled sweetly. "She'll get to it in her own good time, Sister. Be patient."

Irony wet her dry lips. "When I came out here, I really don't know what I expected to find . . . certainly not my father . . . and certainly not a . . . a love for this untamed country."

365

"Nor," said Tiny slyly, "love of any other kind, I'll wager."

Irony shot her a puzzled glance, but the older woman was smoothing her skirts, her eyes downcast, a bemused smile on her lips.

"Uh . . . there's something I have to tell you," she began again.

Alyce chuckled. "You've already said that, dear."

"I have? Oh, yes, of course." Irony brushed back a tendril of silky black hair. "I realize that this will come as something of a shock to you, but . . . well, I've decided not to—"

"Go back to Thief River Falls?" finished Aunt Tiny.

Irony blinked, then blinked again. "Yes! How did you know?" Her expression sobered. "Oh, but that's not all. You see, I want to stay—"

"With Raphael?" spoke up Aunt Alyce.

"I think . . . no, I know that—"

"You're in love with him," concluded Aunt Tiny triumphantly.

Irony dropped onto the nearest boulder, her mouth ajar. "You knew all along?"

"Certainly," said Alyce crisply. "We're a little past middle age, Irony, but we're not in our dotage!"

"Are you . . . are you very disappointed in me?" Irony asked in a small voice.

"Disappointed?" snapped Valentine. "Why on God's green earth would we be disappointed?"

"This isn't exactly the life you expected me to live." Irony gestured at the trees, the water. "It's a far cry from Thief River. I won't ever be president of the Ladies' Auxiliary . . . or church treasurer. I won't be able to go shopping with you or invite you to tea."

"Irony," Tiny said slowly, "surely you don't think . . . ? Why, you do! You think we'd be selfish enough to want to run your life, don't you? You think we want to keep you under our thumbs without regard to your own happiness."

"No, I've always known that you wanted what was best for me. It's just that I hate so much never being able to become the lady you wanted me to be . . ."

"What ridiculous nonsense is this?" exclaimed Alyce. "You're yourself, Irony, and that has given us a very great deal of pleasure. Why, what did you think we expected of you?"

"I think you expected me to learn to walk and talk properly," Irony replied with a wry laugh. "I think you hoped I'd learn to serve tea without sloshing myself or someone else . . . that I'd learn to keep my opinions to myself . . . not to tell falsehoods . . ."

"Do you really believe we think those things are so terribly important?" huffed Aunt Tiny. "Child, I'm ashamed of you."

"It distresses me that you've misinterpreted what we've tried to teach you. How you drink your tea or butter your bread doesn't matter a whit," scolded Alyce. "What really matters in this life is the ability to live it to the fullest, to laugh and cry, and care for other people more than you care for yourself."

"You're that kind of person, Irony," stated Tiny, "and we're so very proud of you. Do you know what kind of old maid stick-in-the-muds we'd have been without you in our lives?"

"But—I thought—"

"What? That'd we want to disown you because you didn't show any signs of wanting to marry Nathan Ferguson and settle down?" scoffed Alyce. "You know, it was something of a blessing in disguise when Josiah Goodman walked into our lives. He unwittingly provided the impetus you needed to discover for yourself what it was you really wanted."

"But I—"

"Ran away from Nathan?" put in Tiny. "Dressed as a boy—ordered people around at gun point? Even shot a man? Traipsed through the wilderness as if it was Boston Common?"

"And don't forget," added the other aunt. "She attacked a man with a skillet, then nearly drowned and died of a fever before settling down to live with the Indians. After, I might add, thoroughly castigating her father for his reprehensible behavior."

"How did you know all that?" Irony asked.

"Raphael told us, naturally," answered Tiny. "He thought we should know."

Irony leaped to her feet, her face burning. "Is there anything he didn't tell you?"

Alyce chuckled. "Not much, dear. And what he didn't say, we guessed."

Irony didn't dare even think about that.

"It took us a mere two seconds to figure out the direction that wind was blowing," Tiny said sagely. "One has only to see you and Raphael together . . ."

"And you're not angry about it?" Irony ventured. "Or disappointed?"

"Angry?" cried Alyce. "Angry that you were smart enough to recognize a man's true worth? Disappointed that you fell in love with one of the finest human beings ever put on this earth?"

"But he's part Indian," protested Irony.

"And he's part poet," Tiny pointed out. "He's a teacher, a warrior — a man, Irony. A man who looks at you as if you were the most important thing in his life."

"My Lord, child," interjected Alyce. "We'd be disappointed if you hadn't had the good sense to fall in love with Raphael!"

"And angry if you gave up a chance for your own happiness because you thought we cared more for . . . for social convention than for you."

"What about what people will say?" Irony asked. "People back home."

"Frankly," said Alyce, "I don't give a . . . a moose squitter what people back home think!"

Irony had to smile, but she wasn't completely finished with doubt. "But . . . what about the two of you? How can I simply walk out of your lives?" Irony chewed her lower lip. "That's how it would be if I go with Hawk."

Alyce and Tiny exchanged self-satisfied smiles. "Oh, not necessarily," murmured Alyce. "You might see more of us than you think."

"You know, Irony," reflected Aunt Tiny, "we really didn't follow you to the lake country because we were upset with you. Or even because we were worried about you." She laughed softly. "We took a good look at ourselves and realized that our lives revolved around inanities—what cookies to serve at a club meeting, how much starch to put into the antimacassars. We envied you, Irony—envied you the marvelous adventure you were having!"

"And one day we simply decided to set out on an adventure of our own." Alyce's hazel green eyes shone with remembered pleasure. "When we met and hired Madden, I knew we were really going to do it. I was so excited, I couldn't sleep for days!"

"Even after all of Zackett's letters, we never knew what the wilderness was actually like," commented Tiny. "We weren't prepared for the beauty, the sense of freedom. Irony, this journey has been the highlight of our dull, staid lives."

"It has?"

"And you needn't think that we will ever just tamely return to Thief River," declared Alyce. "Now that we've found our brother . . . and Madden Heywood, why, I have a feeling we'll be spending most of our summers here.

"And we've already decided it might be best for us to monitor the situation that appears to be developing between Nathan and Snow. We've grown quite fond of the girl, and we plan to make certain that young man's intentions are honorable."

"Then, when we're back in Minnesota during the winter months," said Tiny, "you and Raphael and your children can come to visit. He'll tell you—we've already worked out all the details."

Irony frowned. They had worked out the details of her life with Raphael—with Hawk? Would they never learn that she was perfectly capable of making her own decisions? She opened her mouth to protest, but her lips suddenly curved upward into a big smile. One of the lessons she seemed to have learned on this trek into the wilderness was that people only did what they thought was best for her because they loved her, and cared about what happened to her. How could she object to having three such well-meaning guardians?

"I'll be interested in hearing these details," she said blandly.

"Good," said Alyce, "because the men are coming now, and I'm certain you and Raphael have a great deal to talk about."

"Oh, yes, indeed—a very great deal."

By the time the canoes had landed, a small crowd had gathered on the beach. Snow, having left Madden sleeping, had shyly come down to meet Nathan. As they strolled past Irony, Nathan stopped and gave her a friendly grin.

"Hawk tells me he's asked you to stay," he said, absently patting Snow's hand as it rested in the crook of his arm. "I wanted to tell you that I'm happy for you, Irony."

"Thank you, Nathan. I must say, you're a generous man not to resent the way things turned out."

"I have no complaints," he replied, smiling down at Snow. "Oh, by the way, we may run into each other now and then. I . . . . uh, I plan to be spending considerable time up here in the lake country from now on."

A pleased smile played over Irony's face as she watched their departure.

"They make a lovely couple, don't they?" asked Aunt Tiny. "Goodness, it's so romantic!"

"I suspect it might be a good idea for me to check on Madden," Alyce said suddenly. "It looks as if Snow is preoccupied, and I don't like the thought of him being alone." She scurried off down the path, leaving Tiny behind, shaking her head.

"Silly old fool," Tiny muttered. "She waited a long time to find a man, but when she fell, she fell with all the grace of an elephant!"

"Well, Madam," spoke up John Randolph, " 'twould seem everyone has found a partner but you and I. In light of that fact, would you, perhaps, care to stroll along the beach with me before the evening meal?"

Valentine simpered with all the finesse of a born coquette. "Why, I'd be delighted, Mr. Randolph. Besides, I'd love to hear more of your plan to assist my brother in improving the plight of the Lake of the Woods Ojibway."

"Very well."

"Irony?"

Irony turned to find her father coming down the well-worn trail from the village. Rogue loped along at his heels, distracted by every winged insect or falling leaf.

"Yes, Father?"

Zackett McBride drew his bushy eyebrows together in a scowl. "What's this I hear from Alyce about you planning to stay on here?"

"Do you mind?"

"Of course not. That is, if matters are squared away as they should be."

"What matters?"

"Hmmph, you don't think I'd allow you to live

371

with Hawk without benefit of clergy, do you?"

Irony started to bristle, then recalled her earlier self-lecture. All right, maybe she had *four* well-meaning guardians.

"Father," she said carefully, "I understand how you feel, but the truth of it is, Hawk hasn't actually asked me to marry him."

"The damned rascal!"

Irony laid a soothing hand on Zack's arm. "I must also tell you that . . . well, I want to stay with him even if he never intends to marry me."

Zack's eyebrows shot upward. "So—you love him that much?"

"That much and more. I know that I was raised properly and shouldn't even consider such a thing, but Father, I've gone through too much to lose him now because of some long-standing social convention."

Zack threw back his head and laughed. "No, you haven't exactly let convention guide you up to this point, have you?" Lightly, he raised her chin with his curled fist. "I'm not worried, Irony. If Hawk is half as smart as I think he is, he'll get a ring on your finger first chance he gets."

"And would we have your blessing?" she asked quietly.

"You would."

"Thank you, Father. That means so much to me."

Irony stepped forward and put her arms around Zackett. He returned the hug, patting her awkwardly on the back.

"Here comes your young man now, Irony. Go give him the chance to propose."

She smiled happily. "Yes, sir!"

Zackett took a few steps, then paused to look back at her. "Irony," he said with a crooked smile, "thank you for pretending that my opinion mattered a damn to you. I'm obliged."

"Strangely enough," she countered, "it did matter. More than a damn, too."

"One other thing . . ."

"Yes?"

"When you and Hawk have children, name them something plain and simple . . . Sam or Mary or something like that. Don't saddle them with some peculiar name like I did you."

"Father," she stated firmly, "believe it or not, since coming to the wilderness, I have grown quite fond of my name. I should never have liked Louise or Arabella or Martha half so well!" Despite a flare of rose coloring in her cheeks, she hurried on. "And if you are ever faced with imminent grandfatherhood, you can be certain we will be asking for your help in selecting suitable names."

"I . . . ahem, shall be honored to assist." A blush crept across his cheeks.

"Assist in what?" queried Hawk, coming to stand beside her.

"Ah, you'll find out in due time, son," chuckled Zackett. "In due time."

McBride set off in the direction of the village, Rogue at his heels. Hawk turned to Irony, a quizzical expression on his face. "What was that about?"

"Nothing pressing. I'll tell you later."

For a long moment, Irony filled her eyes with the pleasant sight of the man who had grown so dear to her. He was wearing Levis and moccasins, a plaid shirt flung over his shoulder. Her hands fairly burned with the need to stroke the firm flesh that covered the well-defined muscles of his bare chest.

"Come walk with me, Irony."

She glanced up and, for the first time, detected the signs of strain in his face. The job of burying Goodman could not have been an easy one.

"I'd love to," she said softly, taking his hand.

They moved in the opposite direction from the village, past Irony's lodge and onto the smooth sand of the beach.

"Did things go well?" she asked after a few minutes.

"Yes, everything's taken care of. We removed Goodman from the Place of Dreams and buried him on one of the other islands." With a sigh, he sank down to sit cross-legged on the sand. "I decided to tell Nathan what happened and let him see the body. If something came up—if Lynx ever had to stand trial, it might help that an officer of the law could testify to the nature of Goodman's death."

"You did the right thing," I believe. It must have been evident to Nathan that the man was going to die anyway," Irony stated. "A jury would surely take that into consideration."

"Let's hope no one ever questions our word." Hawk gazed out over the water. "And let's hope that Lynx and Waubagone find some kind of peace and happiness together."

Irony stepped up behind him and, tossing aside the shirt draped over his shoulder, began to knead the tightly clenched muscles of his neck and back. Hawk bowed his head and gave himself up to her ministrations.

"There's something we need to discuss," she said presently.

She could feel the slight stiffening of his shoulders. "Yes?"

"Yesterday, before Goodman interrupted us, you asked me a question."

He nodded silently, and the sun glinted off the raven hue of his hair. Irony touched it softly.

"I didn't have the chance to answer you," she said, dropping to her knees and pressing close to his naked back. "That's what I want us to talk about now."

"You know how I feel, Irony."

"Mmm, yes — you feel wonderful," she teased.

She moved away just far enough to place her hands on his shoulders, letting them smoothe gently over the granite ridges. With one finger, she traced the lines of the strange tattoo. When she bent to place her mouth where her finger had touched, Hawk's entire body jerked.

She let her lips move from the Nighthawks' symbol to the nape of his neck, burying her face among the thick strands of hair that held the fresh scent of the wind and forest. She leaned into him, allowing her hands to caress his upper arms, from elbow to shoulder.

With an impatient cry, Hawk twisted about and seized her, pulling her onto his lap. She laughed delightedly, even though there was not a trace of humor in his ebony eyes as they burned into her own.

"For God's sake, woman, will you give me your answer?" he growled.

"Are you going to make believe that my feelings in this matter are of importance?"

"What do you mean?"

"It has come to my attention that you have discussed our future with nearly everyone in White Crane's village — except me."

"I did not," he protested, unable to conceal a guilty flush. "Well, perhaps I mentioned it to Zack once . . ."

"And my Aunts Valentine and Alyce," she added. "Not to mention Nathan . . . and probably Snow."

He closed his eyes. "Damn it, Irony, you're not going to complicate this with another fit of temper, are you?"

She rubbed her cheek against the breadth of his chest. "Only if you tell me you did it for my own good."

"But I . . . oh, hell," he muttered. "I'm tired of

games. Just tell me, are you going to marry me or not?"

"Marry?" she murmured. "That's the first I've heard of that idea."

His eyes flew open in surprise. "What did you think I was asking of you? Surely you couldn't think I'd expect you to stay here on any other terms?"

"It didn't matter," she whispered, pulling his face down for her kiss.

Her mouth moved sweetly over his, urging him to put an end to the conversation. But Hawk was having no part of that. He set her away from him and looked into her eyes.

"Tell me, once and for all, will you marry me?"

"I will."

"That easily?" One corner of his mouth quirked upward. "Without argument? Without poetry? Without questioning where and how we'll live?"

"Yes, that easily. I'll marry you, Hawk . . . and go wherever you go."

"I thought we could live at Sweetwater during the school year—unless you'd like for me to find a teaching position in Thief River Falls."

When her mouth fell open in astonishment, it was his turn to laugh and press a swift kiss to the tip of her freckled nose.

"You'd live in Thief River?" she asked. "But why?"

"I've heard a great deal about that paragon of cities," he replied. "And I've grown very fond of Alyce and Tiny. Perhaps we could even persuade Zack to spend an occasional winter there."

"And in the summers?"

"We'd come back to Lake of the Woods . . . and live as savages."

Irony blushed, then laughed.

"As I have learned, there is much to be said for . . . savages."

Hawk's arms tightened around her and, as his lips covered hers with deliberate intent, he lay back on the sand, taking her with him.

"I love you, Irony," he said against her mouth. "I only wish I could tell you how much."

"Write me a poem, Mr. Hawkes," she lovingly suggested. "Later . . ."

A mischievous autumn breeze stirred the tops of the pines and swooped to ruffle the water along the edge of the lake. It touched Hawk's crumpled shirt, nudging a blue heron's feather from the pocket and lifting it gently. The feather drifted on the wind, hovering above the lovers for a long breath of time before settling gently, like a tender benediction, upon them.

For Irony

A flaming star blazes bright
    against the midnight skies . . .
With a burst of shining glory,
It seems destined but to die.

Yet if we traced that very star
    across the timeless skies . . .
And through the far-flung universe,
Again, we'd see it rise.

The vastness of the heavens
    contains unending skies . . .
And so the deathless star burns on,
To be seen by other eyes.

As constant as the fire-stars
    of all the midnight skies . . .
Is my eternal love for you,
I vow it will not die.

Raphael Hawkes

Calling One's Own
Ojibway

Awake! flower of the forest, sky-treading bird of the
    prairie.
Awake! awake! wonderful fawn-eyed One.
When you look upon me I am satisfied; as flowers that
    drink dew.
The breath of your mouth is the fragrance of flowers in
    the morning,
Your breath is their fragrance at evening in the moon-
    of-fading-leaf.
Do not the red streams of my veins run toward you
As forest-streams to the sun in the moon of bright
    nights?
When you are beside me my heart sings; a branch it is,
    dancing,
Dancing before the Wind Spirit in the moon of straw-
    berries.
When you frown upon me, beloved, my heart grows
    dark—
A shining river the shadows of clouds darken,
Then with your smile comes the sun and makes to look
    like gold
Furrows the cold wind drew in the water's face.
Myself! behold me! blood of my beating heart.
Earth smiles—the waters smile—even the sky-of-clouds
    smiles—but I,
I lose the way of smiling when you are not near,
Awake! awake! my beloved.

Translated by Charles Fenno Hoffman
(1806-1884)

Gesner, George: Editor. *Anthology of American Poetry.*
New York: Avenel Books, 1983.

Serenade
(From *The Spanish Student*)

Stars of the summer night!
   Far in yon azure deeps,
Hide, hide your golden light,
   She sleeps!
My lady sleeps!
   Sleeps!

Moon of the summer night!
   Far down yon western steeps,
Sink, sink in silver light!
   She sleeps!
My lady sleeps!
   Sleeps!

Wind of the summer night!
   Where yonder woodbine creeps,
Fold, fold your pinions light!
   She sleeps!
My lady sleeps!
   Sleeps!

Dreams of the summer night!
   Tell her, her lover keeps
Watch! while in slumber light
   She sleeps!
My lady sleeps!
   Sleeps!

—Longfellow, Henry W. *Voices in the Night: Ballads and Other Poems*. Chicago and New York: Belford Clarke and Co., 1839

The Comedy of Errors
(Excerpt from Act III, Scene ii)

"There's none but witches do inhabit here;
And therefore 'tis high time that I were hence.
She that doth call me husband, even my soul
Doth for a wife abhor; but her fair sister,
Possess'd with such a gentle sovereign grace,
Of such enchanting presence and discourse,
Hath almost made me traitor to myself:
But, lest myself be guilty to self-wrong,
I'll stop mine ears against the mermaid's song."

—Shakespeare, William. *The Complete Works of William Shakespeare*. New York: Avenel Books, 1975

Bedouin Song

From the Desert I come to thee
 On a stallion shod with fire;
And the winds are left behind
 In the speed of my desire.
Under thy window I stand,
 And the midnight hears my cry:
I love thee, I love but thee,
 With a love that shall not die.
  Till the sun grows cold,
  And the stars are old,
  And the leaves of the Judgment Book
   Unfold!

Look from thy window and see
 My passion and my pain;
I lie on the sands below,
 And I faint in thy disdain.
Let the night-winds touch thy brow
 With the heat of my burning sigh,
And melt thee to hear the vow
 Of a love that shall not die
  Till the sun grows cold,
  And the stars are old,
  And the leaves of the Judgment Book
   Unfold!

My steps are nightly driven,
 By the fever in my breast,
To hear from thy lattice breathed
 The word that shall give me rest.
Open the door of thy heart,
 And open thy chamber door,
And my kisses shall teach thy lips
 The love that shall fade no more
  Till the sun grows cold,

And the stars are old,
And the leaves of the Judgment Book
   Unfold!

—Taylor, Bayard. *The Little Book of American Poets (1787–1900)*. Boston, New York and Chicago: Houghton Mifflin Company, 1917

All other verses quoted were from: Longfellow, Henry W. *Song of Hiawatha*. New York: Platt and Munk, 1963.

CAPTURE THE GLOW
OF ZEBRA'S HEARTFIRES

AUTUMN ECSTASY   (3133, $4.25)
by Pamela K. Forrest

Philadelphia beauty Linsey McAdams had eluded her kidnappers but was now at the mercy of the ruggedly handsome frontiersman who owned the remote cabin where she had taken refuge. The two were snowbound until spring, and handsome Luc LeClerc soon fancied the green-eyed temptress would keep him warm through the long winter months. He said he would take her home at winter's end, but she knew that with one embrace, she might never want to leave!

BELOVED SAVAGE   (3134, $4.25)
by Sandra Bishop

Susannah Jacobs would do anything to survive—even submit to the bronze-skinned warrior who held her captive. But the beautiful maiden vowed not to let the handsome Tonnewa capture her heart as well. Soon, though, she found herself longing for the scorching kisses and tender caresses of her raven-haired BELOVED SAVAGE.

CANADIAN KISS   (3135, $4.25)
by Christine Carson

Golden-haired Sara Oliver was sent from London to Vancouver to marry a stranger three times her age—only to have her husband-to-be murdered on their wedding day. Sara vowed to track the murderer down, but he ambushed her and left her for dead. When she awoke, wounded and frightened, she was staring into the eyes of the handsome loner Tom Russel. As the rugged stranger nursed her to health, the flames of passion erupted, and their CANADIAN KISS threatened never to end!

Available wherever paperbacks are sold, or order direct from the Publisher. Send cover price plus 50¢ per copy for mailing and handling to Zebra Books, Dept. 3459, 475 Park Avenue South, New York, N.Y. 10016. Residents of New York, New Jersey and Pennsylvania must include sales tax. DO NOT SEND CASH.